Killtest

'Yes, it's already happening,' he continued. 'In America people are actually being killed for fun, for entertainment. If you thought the gladiatorial business folded up with the fall of Rome, think again. People are being paid huge amounts of money to kill each other, and in the most indescribable ways. Not world heavyweight boxing, but World Heavyweight Killing – that's the new sport!'

'I don't follow,' Kippy said, trying to concentrate. 'What do you mean – sport?'

'I mean what I said. People are paying money, sometimes thousands of dollars, to go into a stadium to see good old-fashioned gladiatorial combat . . . fights to the death.'

Killtest

Graham King

Arrow Books

Arrow Books Ltd
3 Fitzroy Square, London W1P 6JD

An imprint of the Hutchinson Publishing Group

London Melbourne Sydney Auckland
Wellington Johannesburg and agencies
throughout the world

First published 1978

Set in Intertype Plantin

Printed in Great Britain by
The Anchor Press Ltd, Tiptree, Essex

ISBN 0 09 917560 6

OFFICE OF THE DIRECTOR

UNITED STATES DEPARTMENT OF JUSTICE
FEDERAL BUREAU OF INVESTIGATION
WASHINGTON, D.C. 20535

GCF/AR
/UK200307

November 24, 1977

Mr G. P. King
[redacted],
[redacted]re
London, S.W.1
United Kingdom

Dear Mr King:

In reply to your communication received on October 16th, I can confirm that the copies of documents you submitted are genuine, insofar as they match the original documents in our files.

However, I cannot offer any opinion on exhibits numbered 7, 13, 16-21, and 30, also relating to the KILLTEST investigation, as the originals are not in our possession.

Sincerely yours,

G C Faulkner

Gene C. Faulkner
Director
International Records Division

TOWARDS the end of 1977 certain documents came into my temporary possession.

THEY proved what my enquiries over many months could only hint at – that gladiatorial combat to the death, thought to have ceased as an entertainment in Roman times, was very much alive as a clandestine 'sport' in the 1970s.

MOSTLY for reasons of national security – for the astonishing, horrific events described in this book shook the very roots of the intelligence services of half a dozen major nations – few of these documents are ever likely to see the light of day.

FORTUNATELY I had the advantage of interviewing, at considerable length, one of the DI6 (formerly MI6) agents who played a key role in the remarkable investigation which destroyed the malignant organization known as Killtest Inc. and which banished, for the second time in two millennia, the hideous philosophy of 'death at the box office'.

IT IS from his invaluable memoirs that I have attempted to piece together the story of this extraordinary achievement.

FOR obvious reasons the names of the persons involved have been changed.

I

For the past four or five hours, half awake and half dozing, Kippy had watched cloud shadows wander over the flanks of Box Hill, making patterns. There was little else he could do, considering the jangled state of his mind.

A large cloud drifted over, bigger and blacker than the rest, making the distant yew trees look like blobs of spilt ink. Nearer, on the undulating links that ran from the base of the hill right to the hospital grounds, a golfer teed off from the thirteenth.

The cloud passed and the white room lit up like an arc lamp. The vertical bars which enclosed the only window threw harsh stripes across the dazzling coverlet.

Bars?

Despite the pain Kippy strained to look about the room. White. Everything was white: the metal bedside table, the clothes locker, the walls, door . . . even his limp left arm, sun-starved from nine months in Moscow. His right arm throbbed; it was shackled to the iron bed-frame with handcuffs.

He glimpsed a movement through the little observation window set into the door. Then a nurse opened the door and Pringle, wrinkling his nose, walked in.

'Aaha! We've woken up at last, have we?' Pringle had a talent for vicariously sharing the predicaments of others. He parked his behind on the bed and then, noticing Kippy's contorted face, moved it off his leg. 'I must say, old son, the countryside's perfectly delightful around here. And what a stunning day – '

The young man rattled the handcuffs. 'What the hell's this all about?' His voice came back to him muffled and distant.

Pringle industriously explored his pockets and located the key. 'Yes, I'm sorry about this, but the establishment doesn't have a padded cell.' He unlocked the manacles and Kippy massaged his wrist.

'What are you saying? That I was raving?'

'Absolutely demented. All last night. Couldn't hold you down. So we borrowed the cuffs from the local police station.'

'You've got to be joking!' Kippy said, though he knew Pringle never joked.

'It was for your own good, son.' He brightened. 'Anyway, how are you feeling?'

Kippy struggled to a sitting position, and winced. 'Jesus! I ache all over.'

'Come on, now,' Pringle said solicitously. 'A little pain never hurt anybody.'

A nurse came in with a small tray on which was a cup of tea and two aspirins in a little plastic cup. Pringle took the cup and tossed the pills into his mouth, sipping the tea to wash them down.

The nurse lingered. 'And you, Mr Leering? Feel up to some lunch? Doctor says you can. You haven't had anything solid for five days, you know.'

Kippy blinked. 'Five days . . . !' Come to think of it, it could have been fifty, or five hundred. And where was he? The nurse spoke English and Pringle was certainly here – his cigarette ash was already soiling the coverlet – and the landscape framed in the barred window *looked* English enough. . . .

'A boiled egg on some toast, perhaps?' the nurse was saying. 'Or scrambled?'

Kippy remembered when he'd had his tonsils out, aged eight; they'd fed him for a week on raspberry jelly and ice cream, and he'd never forgotten. 'I'd like some raspberry jelly and ice cream,' he told the nurse.

She was about to say something but Pringle dismissed her with a wave of his hand. That was something you could still do in private hospitals.

'What's this about five days?' Kippy asked. 'And what the hell happened?'

Pringle drained his tea and set the cup down on the bedside table, stubbing his cigarette in the saucer. He walked to the window. 'Poor Adamson out there . . . he's played more golf in the last week than he's played all his life. Swears he'll never touch a five iron again.'

'Adamson . . . ? From the old Cyprus unit?'

'Correct. He's on protective surveillance. Just routine, nothing to worry about.'

'That explains Adamson,' Kippy said. 'But what about me? Where are we?'

Pringle left the window and began to square the room. 'Where are we? We're in the Oaks private hospital, that's where.'

Kippy knew about the Oaks, often jokingly called the Doll Repair Shop or Quarantine. It was used from time to time by the Service for clandestine surgery, bullet extractions, overdoses and, more recently and increasingly, as a departmental rest-home.

'And why are we here?' Pringle continued with his customary Churchillian weightiness. 'We're here because you copped an arse-full of Immobilion-B, that's why.'

'Bloody hell!'

'Precisely. You're lucky to be alive.'

In the past few months Immobilion-B had become the darling new weapon in the intelligence arsenal and, ironically, Pringle himself had played an important part in its development. About two years previously the basic compound, Immobilion, had killed a vetinerary surgeon who'd accidentally jabbed himself while injecting a sick colt in Oxfordshire; three days later his heartbroken assistant, who'd been his lover. deliberately killed herself with a massive dose of the same drug. Impressed by its lethal qualities, Pringle had ordered research on the compound and some months later the labs came up with an even more powerful, more versatile derivative. Immobilion-B.

The drug's lethality in small doses could be matched by dozens of other substances, but the means by which it was applied was particularly ingenious, if not grotesque. By the end of 1975 the technical lab had developed a tiny ejector gun, no larger than a cigarette lighter, which contained two chambers: one for the Immobilion-B and the other for liquefied inert gas. By operating a microscopic valve mechanism a measured amount of the drug was ejected into a needle-shaped mould, immediately frozen by the gas into a solid needle, and then fired at high velocity by the compressed gas. Within seconds of entering a body the needle dissolved, disseminating its poison throughout the bloodstream, paralysing the victim almost instantly and – if the maximum dose was used – killing in the space of a minute, leaving no trace whatsoever. The latest ejectors incorporated a device which measured the dosage according to purpose; any human prey could be immobilized for as briefly as ten minutes or up to twenty-four hours. Or for ever.

'It was touch and go,' Pringle continued. 'We know what Immobilion-B does, but we don't know yet how to undo it.'

'So I've been a guinea pig, is that it?' Kippy complained.

'A fortunate one, I'm happy to say, but yes, you have been a martyr to the cause, in a way. We've had you pumped full of anti-serums, saline drip, every damn thing we could think of. But until last night . . . nothing.'

'So what did the trick?'

'We don't know. But suddenly, for no reason, you went berserk. They called me to come down here after you knocked out one of the nurses. She's fine now, apart from a sore jaw. As for you, you'll be under observation for a few more days while we try to sort you out.'

Kippy resisted the urge to close his eyes and drift off to sleep. Pringle's sepulchral voice, like a tape recorder running slow, always had that effect on him, but never more than now. Any conversation with Pringle was to be strenuously avoided; in ten minutes he could make you feel as though you'd wasted a whole day. But a contradiction nagged him. . . .

'So I was winged with an Immobilion-B gun?' he asked his boss.

'No doubt about it.'

'But . . . does this mean the other crowd have got it? I thought – '

Pringle laughed. 'No, nothing like that. It's still two hundred per cent secret. No, you were shot by one of our own men.'

That, of course, was supposed to make it funny, which explained Pringle's smirk. What a jolly, funny game!

Perhaps in a weird way it was, but that wasn't how he'd imagined it when he'd blundered into the civil service jungle. With his redbrick BA he'd promptly been judged by the Whitehall sub-mandarins as unsuitable material for career diplomacy and was shunted through various doors of the Foreign Office before finding a desk as an assistant technical officer with the Personnel Policy Department. At the time this section was fingering likely FO neophytes for below-stairs work in the intelligence services, among them a branchlet of the Arms Control and Disarmament Research Unit. Kippy was offered a six-month crash course in disarmament strategy and then various observational postings which led him to Moscow.

But he hadn't merely been polishing a seat during the past year. While it wasn't exactly a James Bond kind of experience, nor had there ever been any danger of his being dumped in the Don wearing a pair of concrete boots, he'd found himself increasingly involved in inflammable DI6 enterprises. In Moscow he had begun to live three lives: as an embassy clerk, as an undercover Disarmament Research Unit observer, and as an occasional intelligence operative. The 'occasional' had been removed from his status only four months before when the *Analogue* case pushed him out on to some very thin ice. A short story in the sci-fi magazine had described a new British bacteriological weapon in such accurate detail as to defy any argument that it was imaginatively coincidental; the task of uncovering the source of the information fell to the Disarmament Research Unit and Kippy was given the Moscow end of the assignment. Three weeks later he was able to report that the description of the weapon, the result of Soviet espionage and some astute guessing, had been given by the KGB's *Bureau D* – the Russian's counter-espionage Bureau of Disinformation – to an obscure German scientific journal, and then expanded by an alert story writer.

Kippy's was the most modest of beginnings in the craft of spying, but then had come the microwave business, which had brought him into contact with Pringle.

For some months during the early part of 1976 both British and American embassy staff had showed the disquieting signs of anaemia, although this was not uncommon at the end of a Russian winter. But by May the anaemia had assumed the proportions of an epidemic. The circumstances were baffling. Diets were checked and all embassy personnel were urged to swallow vast doses of vitamins and liver extract. Still the anaemia persisted. The female employees were the hardest hit; their fingernails broke, their hair fell out and many reported menstrual periods lasting three weeks. By June seventeen of the British staff were too ill to work and four were in hospital suffering from unidentified blood deficiency and marrow diseases. The US ambassador himself fell ill. At last it was understood that the anaemia was a stealthy attack by the KGB – possibly using microwave beams.

The familiar microwave oven, although it can cook a plastic-wrapped steak in a minute or less without burning the wrapping, only utilizes half a per cent of the potential microwave technology – so what were the Russians up to? Few of the embassy staff fancied slow-grilled kidneys – especially their own – so covert help was requested from London.

Nobody in the Department had the remotest clue about microwave death rays, but someone remembered that Pringle had once held forth at great length on the subject. It had transpired that Pringle had repaired one of the new ovens for his wife and, with his gift for making the insignificant seem overpoweringly complex, had left his afternoon tea audience with the impression he'd taken a fast breeder reactor apart and put it together again. In the event Stan Pringle was promptly despatched to Moscow in the guise of a cement consultant, and Kippy was briefed to assist him. More through simple observation than technical know-how, Pringle soon isolated the cause of the anaemia, noting that the cables connected to many of the embassy employees' television sets were abnormally thick: specially designed coaxial cables capable of carrying high-frequency microwaves to the innards of what appeared to be ordinary television sets. Within the circuitry of the receiver was built a supplementary circuit capable of amplifying the microwaves to an alarming level, able to destroy not only healthy red blood cells but also the marrow which produced them.

Having isolated the cause, Pringle and Kippy then set out to try and trace the origin of the microwaves and the purpose of the caper. It was a delicate business. Diplomatic complaint would certainly be blown up by the Russians into a major incident. Any number of East European agencies might be involved. The only way to resolve the matter was to use the 'we know what you crafty buggers are up to' technique; to pull the plugs and depart with a superior sniff, without even bothering to make an issue of it.

Although they lacked the sophisticated detection equipment necessary for tracking down transmissions, Pringle and his young apprentice managed to narrow the field to half a dozen possible locations, intending to search them at night. The risks were enormous but the capture of hostile microwave beaming equipment would be a devastating coup. But the searches in metropolitan Moscow yielded nothing; most of the suspected transmitters turned out to be small radio broadcast units.

What the searches did precipitate was one of those blunders bound to occur within a clandestine organization whose right hand was frequently at odds with its left. During the fifth and last nocturnal break-in, on the top floor of a language laboratory in central Moscow, the two men discovered a radio transmitter in a locked room. After satisfying themselves it was not the culprit and as they were about to leave, they surprised a man hiding behind some cabinets in an adjoining room. Equally surprised, they fled, but before they had quitted the building Kippy inexplicably passed out. Pringle somehow half-dragged, half-carried the inert agent back to their hotel, pretending to be in charge of a vodka-soaked friend. The embassy doctor diagnosed a deep coma, cause unknown, and ordered Kippy to be flown back immediately to London for tests. It wasn't until two days later, with Kippy still unconscious, that it was discovered he'd been the victim of an Immobilion-B needle discharged by another British agent. This agent had been on surveillance duty in the building, for the language school was suspected of transmitting KGB disinformation, and had fired the needle thinking he'd been flushed out by the Russians.

'It was just one of those things,' Pringle explained calmly. 'I've put in a report and nobody has thrown a tantrum, so I doubt if we'll hear any more about it. The only worry higher up is that we might have blown our covers, and in any case we've been banned from any further work in the East European sector.'

Despite the mist that wafted gauze before his eyes, Kippy looked keenly at Pringle for signs of disappointment. In intelligence terms being denied East Europe, the busiest sector, was like being confined to a wheelchair. In career terms it meant no more mixing it with the big boys, and unless another espionage front suddenly emerged, no more assignments with military or political significance. To put it bluntly, full stop – unless you counted a succession of trivial time-wasting routine investigations with paper up to your tits. Yet Pringle was still smiling.

'So we're all laughing,' Kippy said sourly, closing his eyes. The fact that his own career had ended before it had begun had just registered.

'We live to fight another day, if that's what you mean,' Pringle said with a laugh.

'With biros and paper clips at ten paces.'

'Not a bit of it, old boy!' He'd noticed the disillusioned tone in the younger man's voice. 'We've got ourselves a new assignment!'

Kippy dragged his eyes open to see Pringle walk quickly to the door and snap the latch. A thin, continuous bleep indicated he'd switched on his pocket-size white noise generator.

'Yes, we start officially on Monday. You, me, Sam Humbert and a couple of others. I've been asked to head it up . . . the Anti Crypto-Sadism Unit.'

'The Anti – what?'

'Completely new. Something really out of the box. I've had very little time to do any background on it yet, but it's big, Kipling, about as big as they come!'

'What sector?' Kippy asked.

'Forget that nonsense. It's international – as international as organized crime itself. Funded by the Government, the Americans and – wait for it – North Korea!' He waited for Kippy to give a shout of joy, but realizing he could do little more than mumble, continued.

'Look, I'll just think aloud, fair enough? Who isn't concerned about all the violence and violent crime? That's the fear that haunts Britain today, and not only Britain. Most countries which call themselves civilized suffer from it. Violence and vandalism. Mugging. Teenage thuggery. Old people scared witless by gangs of little pricks. Rape is commonplace.

'Well, the Government's really worried. Right now it's chewing over a report based on national surveys taken last year. Violence and vandalism emerge as the two biggest problems the country has, according to the thousands of people interviewed, way ahead of inflation, unemployment, racial problems, housing, tax, strikes and nationalization. People are screaming for tougher sentences, even the return of the death penalty.

'And that's the real problem for the Government. Unless there's a colossal shift in judicial policy, the sentences handed out for violence can't be much tougher. Remember last year – the Brendan Dowd Provo trial? – the five of them were hit with fifty-five charges and they got sixteen life sentences between them, a total of 627 years. But did that stop them? It's still going on . . . another two bombs yesterday, three killed. So appointing hanging judges isn't the answer.

'The Home Office is biting its nails. It's getting worse. And all the indications spell out the fact that violence is becoming a way of life. The real worry is that the public will grow indifferent to it . . . "so long as I'm not bashed and robbed, why should I care about the other fellow?" . . . and that'll be the beginning of the end.'

Kippy's interest stirred. 'So what are we then . . . this team?

Eliot Ness and the Untouchables? The Superman Club? If you're Batman, can I be Robin?'

'No – I'm merely giving you the background.' Pringle brushed back the lock of straight, steel-grey hair which constantly fell over his eyes. 'As I said, the biggest danger is that violence – and sadism, depravity, brutality – will become a way of life, like shopping at the supermarket. But what I should have said is that it's *already* happening.'

In his characteristic way Pringle let this sink in, and sucked on his ponderous upper lip.

'Yes, it's already happening,' he continued. 'In America people are actually being killed for fun, for entertainment. If you thought the gladiatorial business folded up with the fall of Rome, think again. People are being paid huge amounts of money to try to kill each other, and in the most indescribable ways. Not world heavyweight boxing, but World Heavyweight Killing – that's the new sport!'

The shadows of the window bars threw horizontal stripes across Pringle's suit, making him look like a comic convict.

'I don't follow,' Kippy said, trying to concentrate. 'What do you mean – sport?'

'I mean what I said. People are paying money, sometimes thousands of dollars, to go into a stadium to see good, old-fashioned gladiatorial combat . . . fights to the death. Not your healthy duel or sword-fight, though – this stuff is really perverse, sickening. Part of the fun, apparently, is to invent ingenious ways for men to kill one another. You wouldn't believe it! And women, too! It's distilled sadism, with every patron a paying peeping tom. They watch it live and also on closed circuit TV. Take it from me, it's sick! Who wants to watch a couple of boxers beat the hell out of each other with soft gloves when you can watch a man push a stick of gelignite up a woman's whatsit and detonate it –'

'But this is Britain,' Kippy protested. 'You're talking about America. Why can't they shovel the shit out of their own nest?'

'It's happening in America, yes,' Pringle explained, realizing he'd jumped ahead of himself. 'But it's an international threat. It's spread to Canada and Mexico and South America and

God knows where else. As far as we know it's not here yet, but it probably won't be long. And we're not dealing with a bunch of tin-pot gangsters, either, or a clutch of Forty-Second Street porn merchants. From the evidence gathered so far it's a multi-million-dollar world-wide syndicate, run by powerful and ruthless men and even protected by a private army.'

'But why us? Why Britain? We used to be the world's peace-keeper, but all that was a century ago, for Christ's sake! We haven't got the teeth to bite into a jam sponge nowadays.'

Pringle smiled, with a touch of latent pride, and mused aloud as he paced slowly around the white room, his thumbs in his red braces.

'It's a funny country, this, Kipling. We may be a bit low on battleships, the economic arse may be out of our trousers, but we've got something on this island few other countries have, and that's a deep-rooted sense of human rightness. We've exported it all over the world, but this is where it's manufactured – here. Right here! Respect for human dignity. Scratch any Englishman deep enough and you'll find a humanitarian, a man with a basic sense of what's right and what's wrong. As individuals we ignore and scorn this quality, but don't let that fool you. It's there, in the fabric of British life, traditional, an institution, like the Mother of Parliaments, the original cradle of human rights. Who created it? The British! And it comes to the surface when it's needed most, when the going it toughest – take the last war! While the rest of the world gave this pimple of a country hardly any chance of surviving, every Englishman never wavered from a hundred per cent, and knew it right to his marrow! I –'

Kippy could not help smiling now. This was Pringle in full, jingoistic flight; all he needed was a bigger paunch and a Union Jack waistcoat and he'd be John Bull.

Pringle noticed the smile, and floated gently back to earth. 'There are, of course, other reasons,' he said, more soberly.

'For us being involved in something that has nothing to do with us?'

'Precisely. This business is something the CIA would normally handle, but there's a problem. Not resolved as yet, but it seems there's a bad apple in the barrel, top layer, too. Consequently the Americans want to bypass the CIA; otherwise there'd be a cover-up and the investigation would get nowhere. And although it's not in the brief, they're obviously hoping the bad apple will drop out in the course of events.'

'I can remember,' Kippy reflected, 'having hammered into me that assignments with mixed motives score a notoriously high failure rate.'

'That's the theory, true.' Pringle played with his cigarette packet for thinking space. 'But trip wires are built into every good operation. The important thing is that the Americans think it's worth a million to them . . . they're funding fifty per cent of the project. With that sort of money we can include a few traps for our own people – some of our operatives haven't been properly cased for years. We've never had the budget.'

'But what's this about North Korea?' Kippy asked. 'Are you trying to tell me the Americans and Kim Il Sung are now getting into bed together? I don't believe it!'

'I agree that's a hard one,' Pringle admitted. 'But, as usual, things aren't what they seem. Take your mind back to that Panmunjom incident last year, you know, when two American truce officers were hacked to death by the North Koreans when they tried to prune a tree in the joint security zone. Remember? There were the usual fireworks: the Americans despatched a task force to the border, President Park of South Korea screamed rape; but what happened was as improbable as the Second Coming – Kim actually apologized for the incident. Apologized! And it turns out that once they'd made contact, the Americans liked him better as a person than Park, who'd just jailed half the Opposition for complaining about rigged elections. Of course, getting the Americans' ear was a coup for Kim, and he'll stoop to anything to embarrass Park. Among a hundred other things he's convinced Park and his cronies are up to their eyeballs in shady deals, including the financing of commercial sadism. He offered to go halves in an exposure operation and for the reasons I've stated the Americans have passed it on to us.'

'Two million pounds!' Kippy breathed.

'Dollars,' Pringle corrected.

'How do we know it isn't some kind of political trap?'

'We don't. We hardly ever do. But if there is a trap in this assignment, the boys in Analysis haven't picked it yet.'

'You'll excuse me,' Kippy said with a pause, 'if I tell you the input isn't being processed with complete comprehension? In fact I wonder if I'm properly out of that coma – '

'Well, perhaps I haven't explained it very well,' Pringle acknowledged, lighting a cigarette. 'But as soon as you're well there's a whacking great report on the whole business waiting for you. Try to get down to reading it over next weekend so we can start operations on Monday. In fact the Unit's got a man in the field already.'

'What's this outfit called again?' Kippy asked.

'The Anti Crypto-Sadism Unit.'

'I see . . .'

Actually, he didn't. Perhaps with a few more Service years under his belt he'd have been better fitted to cope with the surreal character of Pringle's project. But then even during his brief contact with the workings of MI6 and MI5 it hardly compared with some of the cracked notions he'd heard about. It was the blend of naïve amateurism, cool professionalism and unexpected brilliance which threw him, an amalgam deeply embedded in British life. And perhaps it was that 'well played, old chap!' outlook which explained the Department's philosophical attitude to failure; it was *how* you played that mattered, not whether you won or lost. Kippy looked at Pringle, who was to be his boss and mentor in the forthcoming operation; his life, he realized with dismay, would be in Pringle's hands, and the thought didn't exactly fill him with confidence.

Pringle had certainly had his full ration of failures. Officially a field officer, he was attached to Section Four, often referred to as the 'Department of Blue Skies' because of the *ad hoc* nature of its assignments. One assignment, for instance, had been training turkey vultures to locate dead bodies in difficult terrain; Pringle's big moment came when ten of the birds were released during the search for the missing peer Lord

Lucan in the south of England in 1975, but they all flew away and were never seen again.

A year after this he landed the blame for an extraordinary diplomatic clanger. It wasn't his fault entirely, only Pringle had been the last to duck when the shit hit the Foreign Office fan. Two of his men were seconded to Special Branch to join a contingent of mercenaries bound for the Angola War in 1976. The idea was to infiltrate among the ninety-four British recruits both to keep track of their activities and to report on the revolutionary war. As an office concept it sounded fine but what happened was that one of the men died of a heart attack and the other was accidentally shot in the groin by one of his companions. But that wasn't the real embarrassment. When the mercenary exercise was roundly condemned in the Commons the Government was accused of complicity as it had authorized, unknowingly of course, two agents to accompany the routed and discredited dogs of war.

It would be wrong, though, to blame these kind of failures for the fact that throughout his career Pringle had achieved a status no higher than a desk-bound drudge. And, given that it was impossible for Pringle not to be aware of the *real* reasons, it was remarkable that he harboured no bitterness. At any rate it didn't show. Pringle simply hadn't attended the right schools. His original ambition, doubtless nurtured by his parents, was to join one of the fashionable Guards regiments, but not having been to Eton, Harrow or Winchester only the less elegant rifle and light infantry regiments had been open to him. His ex-army father found a chink for him in the Foreign Office, then – this was pre-war – firmly controlled by the diplomatic clique who did most of their recruiting in White's or Boodle's. As a result Pringle vegetated in the chink like a tuft of moss, ignored and mocked, while future spies like Guy Burgess, Old Etonian, undergraduate communist, passionate and arrogant homosexual, anti-American, alcoholic, racist, abysmally indiscreet, Hitler Youth sympathizer, effortlessly eased themselves into the Foreign Office and the intelligence units with no awkward questions asked. And 'Third Man' Philby . . . along with many other staffers, Pringle never overcame his deep suspicions about the man after Burgess and Maclean fled to Moscow in 1951. He'd been one of a dozen signatories to a petition complaining about Philby's reinstatement in 1955, which was subsequently pigeon-holed; and during the eight years before the spy's exposure in 1963 none of the dozen had shared a single promotion between them. Nor were they ever forgiven. With a couple of the others Pringle hung on, hoping the rotten Establishment pillars holding up much of the departmental structure would crumble, but they never did. Now, he had given up hoping, having realized that no individual could ever take on the Old Boy network and survive; instead he plodded on without rancour towards his retirement pension. He lived quietly and comfortably in a big mock-Tudor house on the outskirts of Esher with his young wife Shirley, an attractive blonde in her early forties with heavy legs and large behind who showed up once a year at the staff Christmas party. Somehow it seemed impossible that, considering Pringle's general unattractiveness, Shirley wasn't playing around. Indeed, the thought occurred constantly to Pringle, who would telephone her at intervals throughout each working day, rationalizing unanswered calls by assuming she must be at the hairdresser's, or the butcher's, or at golf or tennis. Only one thing obsessed him more, and that was his tireless search through every spy novel by Graham Greene, le Carré, Fleming, Wheatley and Muggeridge – all Secret Service members in their time and Pringle's distant colleagues at one time or another – for any suggestion of a caricature of himself. Perhaps there was, but he failed to recognize it.

Like everybody who came in contact with Pringle, Kippy felt genuinely sorry for the man, even fond of him. Mentally, he was no slouch. He was addicted to mathematical puzzles and was a skilled chess player. He was fluent in Swahili. He tackled problems with supreme objectivity; their size and difficulty never daunted him. He was the eternal enthusiast. But . . . whom did the Department turn to when it wanted a body to head up a team to probe this sadist thing . . . a gang of crooks conducting human cockfights on the other side of the world? It was hardly in the national interest, not even in the wildest flight of fancy. It mattered so little the

Foreign Office probably knew nothing about it, despite the force of Pringle's rhetoric. A file had landed on someone's desk; it had been passed along, and it grew and grew, and who did they throw the assignment to? To 'Turkey' Pringle, who might well lay another egg.

Well, perhaps it would all fizzle out, as such projects often did if you dithered long enough; even two million dollars could be made to evaporate by the dull warmth of inactivity. Kippy found himself gazing out of the barred window, to the rolling green Surrey countryside. It was sunny, now. Adamson was still there on the thirteenth, practising drives . . . now why was it considered necessary to provide him with a £4500 a year guard?

He turned slightly, to see Pringle unlocking the door to let a nurse in. His grey suit hung from his frame like an old elephant skin.

'Will you be staying for lunch, Mr Talbot?' the nurse asked Pringle. He glanced at the tray she was carrying and shook his head.

'I'm afraid there's no ice cream,' she said to Kippy. 'And the jelly's off. So I've brought you some caramel custard.'

'There are times,' Kippy mumbled to Pringle when she'd gone, 'when I could willingly kill, just for the sheer pleasure of it.'

Then he released the brakes on his eyes and dismissed Pringle, his turkey vultures, caramel custard, Kim Il Sung and the whole crackpot investigation from his mind.

2

Henschel Oppenheimer emerged from the revolving door of the De Janeiro Building and walked out into the late morning heat of Fifth Avenue. After the alpine air conditioning it was like being hit in the face by a jet of steam, and by the time he'd reached Fiftieth Street his grey-striped seersucker jacket hung from his shoulders like a limp dishcloth. It had to be punishment, he thought, for being in New York in July.

He crossed by Saks and walked down Fiftieth towards Madison, composing his thoughts for the meeting ahead. Gulao had answered most of his questions, but knowledge did not constitute a cure for the most serious penetration into the Organization's security so far. There was a hole in the wire, and the fox in the chicken house had to be dealt with promptly.

It was fortunate the Brazilian was in the Organization's pay. General Castelo Gulao was ostensibly on the staff of the Brazilian Military Attaché in Washington but in reality was the country's deputy security chief. He carried a lot of muscle. A hundred-thousand-dollar cash deal over two years ensured the Organization's freedom to operate unmolested in Brazil; and as there was no threat to Brazil's internal security Gulao doubtless felt his conscience was clear. The Killtest Games in Paranagua had been a resounding success; 800 fans had watched two bloody bouts and also Electrochess, the world's first life-and-death chess game, an event which had 'added fresh lustre to the modern gladiatorial arts'.

At least that's how it had been described in the July issue of the underground sado-mag *Cain*. The star of Electrochess had been the former American master player Barney Outnayher, driven to this desperate move by a rare wasting disease which gave him a life expectancy of two years. With the forty thousand dollars he hoped to win, Outnayher would live out the twilight of his life in grandmaster style.

His opponent in the game was an anonymous player with the pseudonym of Fianchetto; and the fact that he was an unrated player had been considered a reasonable handicap seeing it wasn't his life that was at stake. If Outnayher lost the game, he lost his life.

At the Paranagua Killtest, Outnayher was dressed in a kind of *Alice in Wonderland* outfit as the white king, and moved the other fifteen live white chessmen by calling his moves from the huge chessboard. Fianchetto, his face hidden behind a black king's mask, sat away from the board on a high podium. Each of his eight pieces and eight pawns were Brazilian blacks dressed as chessmen, and each was armed with an electric bullock-stunner of the kind used at abattoirs. If Outnayher was mated he would be touched with a stunner by his captors and killed instantly: the ultimate end-game.

Outnayher developed the classic Ruy Lopez opening on his third move, advancing his king's bishop to Kn-5 and subsequently taking the first pawn of the match with a knight. For half an hour the experienced player clearly had the upper hand, but as the pieces were removed from the giant board painted for the occasion on the stadium floor, nervousness understandably crept in and he began to make errors, losing in successive moves a knight and a rook. During the following half-hour he fought back brilliantly, but the early errors were to cost him the game, and his life. Two hours from the start the courageous old player, alone on the vast board except for a white knight and a bishop, was finally checkmated by Fianchetto's black queen and king. The king, a huge Negro from Recife, delivered the *coup de grâce* by touching the defeated Outnayher on the forehead with his cattle-stunner with a barely discernible blue flash. As he fell, his white cardboard crown rolled to the centre of the floor, drawing the gaze of the 800 spectators away from the huddled body of the dead champion.

Only the Ring – Killtest Inc.'s board of management –

knew the identity of the masked Fianchetto: a senior US consular official from Brasilia named Ernest Gams, who'd pleaded for the opportunity to participate. Oppenheimer had readily agreed; the potential for blackmail was too rich to ignore. The implication of US Government patronage of Killtest Inc. through one of its diplomats was also a bonus which might be used to advantage one day.

Unfortunately a strip of negative film in Oppenheimer's jacket pocket testified to a grave weakness in the stratagem, and that it was intercepted at all was due solely to Gulao's alertness. All the patrons attending the Paranagua Killtest had been automatically screened by Gulao's men, and so had any mail despatched from the hotels at which the fans had been billeted. From one of the packets, mailed to the manager of the Anglo-Australian Alloy Export Co. in London, had fallen a sheaf of fake orders for metal shipments, and taped to the back of one of the sheets was a three-inch strip of exposed 2.5 mm film of the kind issued to British Intelligence agents. Gulao had the film developed and immediately wired Oppenheimer, for the film was a sequence of shots of the chess game and, more importantly, of Gams backstage with his mask off. The graphic evidence unquestionably identified Gams as a Killtest participant. The question was – why? To spark off some diplomatic embarrassment? The Anglo-Australian Alloy Export Co. was an address used by British Intelligence; Oppenheimer had quickly established that fact from CIA files. But what was their interest in discrediting Gams, a non-military career diplomat of no significance whose only passions were pornography and chess? As he walked along Fiftieth Street Oppenheimer was troubled with a vague disquiet. Was this unexplained discovery the first indication that some unknown but irreparable damage had been done?

He waited for the lights and crossed Madison towards Park Avenue and the canopied entrance to the Waldorf Astoria, briefly losing himself in thoughts of iced tea. But only briefly: for the others would demand better guessing than he'd come up with so far.

The Organization's security wasn't his direct responsibility, though. It would be McSwiggan's head on the block, not his. But that was opting out. He was boss and the second biggest shareholder in Killtest Inc. *Everything* was his responsibility if he was to survive to realize his dream. The alternative was dishonour, imprisonment, utter failure – and he'd never failed at anything in his life. The thought drenched him with perspiration. Somehow he had to handle this crisis with the coolness the others expected of him.

In the frigid lobby of the Waldorf he hesitated, then headed for the cloakroom. He was a few minutes early, anyway. Once in the marble washroom he loosened his tie and unbuttoned his shirt, mopping his balding head, neck and chest with a towel. From a small ivory container he shook out several antacid tablets and swallowed them with a glass of water.

He cursed himself for panicking. His entire life had been a series of crises, so why this faltering, this ebbing confidence? Perhaps it was a sign of age. He saw himself in the mural of mirrors: compact without the paunchiness of middle age, bald but not obscenely so, smooth-skinned and tanned. By comparison the few others in the washroom were lily-white, overweight wrecks. Could he be growing old? It was conceivable; so much had happened in his life.

Henschel Oppenheimer was a third-generation Chicago German who graduated from college in 1943 to join the US Air Force, retiring in 1954 as a colonel with the Medal of Honour. Inheriting a considerable sum from the sale of his father's chain of barber shops the ex-colonel spent the money and the following ten years globetrotting, sometimes to his profit and sometimes not. One of his more publicized ventures was an expedition to locate the buried million dollar payroll abandoned by the British Army during its retreat from Greece in 1941. The search was unsuccessful but the publicity brought in a number of offers which kept him adventuring for years. It also brought him to the attention of the CIA, then short of skilled observers in the troubled Middle East, and within three years he was appointed a full-time operative.

From 1965 Oppenheimer's career became submerged in professional obscurity, surfacing only at rare intervals. British

Intelligence files recorded his involvement in the funding of a new Arabian hospital – a political payoff – in 1971, where his biggest problem, it seemed, was to suppress the fact that the first operation to be performed there was the surgical removal of the right hand of a recalcitrant sheik. Then in 1974 he headed an investigation into the Peace Ship Fund, which was behind plans to sail a pirate radio into the Mediterranean for Israeli propaganda purposes. In 1975 he was in Nigeria, mediating on behalf of the American owners of fifty ships stranded in Lagos Harbour and loaded with cement irresponsibly ordered by the previous regime. With a hundred and fifty other ships full of cement also anchored there it might seem that Oppenheimer had been sent to get the Americans to the head of the queue. On the contrary, the bribing was to keep them there for as long as possible, for in their leanest year ever ship-owners were being paid up to £2000 a day compensation by the oil-rich Nigerian government for merely waiting.

But these minor assignments were hardly responsible for Oppenheimer's elevation at the end of 1975 to the post of regional director of the CIA's covert action programming. The ex-Air Force colonel was, in fact, one of the architects of the famous project to recover the sunken Soviet G-class atomic submarine some 750 miles north of Hawaii. On Oppenheimer's recommendation the salvage contract was awarded to the Summa Corporation, one of Howard Hughes's companies, to equip a deep-sea research vessel, the *Glomar Explorer*, to locate and raise the sub for the secrets it might contain.

The carefully drawn plans soon went awry, however. The construction of the salvage ship was plagued with costly delays so that when a portion of the Russian submarine was eventually raised, the little information it yielded was out of date. Worse, the cost of the operation had soared from an estimated 60 million to 140 million dollars, and because of this Oppenheimer faced an internal enquiry set for the end of the year. Professionally he could expect some admonishment but eventual exoneration, but privately it was quite a different matter, for six million dollars of the money had slipped into the CIA man's pocket, and even now the dead billionaire's lawyers and government accountants were puzzling over the massive discrepancy in the accounts.

Consequently Oppenheimer was planning an orderly retreat before the disclosures which would be the inevitable result of the enquiry. The Mafia offer to invest in and run the Killtest Organization had been a gift from the gods. He had accepted it on the spot. In just one year, he calculated he could double, perhaps treble, his six million dollar investment, and then disappear. And no British agent, he swore under his breath, was going to stop him.

The washroom was beginning to fill with the lunchtime crowd as he belched several times with relief. He wiped his head again and, now cooled, adjusted his white shirt and tie. An elegant, assured entrance was everything. The attendant came up and helped him on with his jacket, brushing it with one hand and accepting a dollar with the other.

'You look like a million dollars, boss,' he said.

Georges Mrabet gazed through the thirty-ninth floor windows of the Waldorf Towers into the jumble of skyscrapers which almost hid the distant green lung of Central Park, but noting, with Catholic pride, that although dwarfed, the twin white spires of St Patrick's Cathedral were no less ennobled. Already the midtown area was overhung with clouds of vapour that would, by the afternoon, turn the streets below into oppressive, steamy canyons. Even now, Morningside Heights and Harlem had disappeared in a grey haze.

He turned as the door bleep sounded and waited while the lock combinations buzzed through their cycle. It was Lethnal, fresh from his daily sauna. He walked into the big room, and smiled at Mrabet. The huge, carved committee table separated them.

'You're looking well, Georges,' he said in a Kissinger accent.

'And you, too. You must introduce me to your masseuse.'

Lethnal smiled again and went to the oversize antique walnut bureau bookcase. He opened the big glass doors and the books disappeared; they were only leather-bound spines attached to the glass. Inside was revealed a bar and two refrigerators.

'Can I get you a drink, Georges?'

'Is there some mint tea there? And some ice?'

Lethnal was the Organization's head of finance. Although in his mid-sixties, Lethnal had clearly been a handsome man, and Mrabet begrudged his looks – not without reason, for while he himself was only thirty-eight most people took the two men to be the same age. Age had endowed Lethnal with an aloof charm; he always looked relaxed and immaculate. Of course, hair transplants and the ego-satisfying attentions of Chloe Wilder, his young mistress, doubtless helped, but the man's smug, serene contentment was the source of secret annoyance to Mrabet.

Lethnal came up to the table and set down Mrabet's mint tea on a Grand Marnier coaster.

'I hear there's a nigger in the woodpile,' he said, conversationally.

'So I hear. Paranagua.'

'A pity. In every other respect the Paranagua games were our best yet. I've just finalized the accounts. We netted just over three million.'

Mrabet smiled, but his heart wasn't in it. Although he was head of administration the grand title hardly disguised the fact that he was little more than a servant to the other members of the Ring, with Oppenheimer above him as the policy-maker and chairman, McSwiggan in charge of security and Lethnal in control of the cash. But there was no challenging the situation for as the Organization's bagman Lethnal had every qualification going.

During 1973 the British newspapers had invented a scapegoat for a currency exchange scandal of frightening proportions; £150 million sterling was one figure announced by the press. The headlines dubbed him 'Dr Dollar', an international finance wizard, mastermind of mammoth banking deals and wheeler-dealer extraordinary, who was supposed to operate from secret headquarters in Zürich. He was never actually named, never brought to trial, but Dr Dollar was certainly real. He stood at the end of the table, opposite Mrabet.

Dr Carl Lethnal was the supreme business brain of Killtest Inc., although away from the Waldorf Towers he was a quiet-living, modestly successful Wall Street stockbroker indistinguishable in his Brooks Brothers attire from thousands of others in his profession.

It was no coincidence that by dropping the *n* you could change Lethnal to 'lethal', but only Oppenheimer knew the facts about the brilliant financier's past.

Lethnal was born Franz Luebke in 1911. His father had taken part in the Munich Beer Hall *putsch* in 1923, and although Luebke Snr died before Hitler came to power a decade later, this act of loyalty was his son's passport to greater things in the Nazi party. After graduating as a Doctor of Philosophy at Cambridge he returned to Germany to become a party-backed official at the Krupp works in Essen, liaising with the government on armament production just prior to the outbreak of war in 1939. At thirty, he was appointed head of armament development.

In 1944, when it became obvious that the tide had turned and Germany would be defeated, Luebke escaped to Switzerland, where he'd been accumulating funds for several years, changing his name to Dietrich. In post-war Zürich he operated first as a black marketeer and then as an investment broker, specializing in currency manipulation. By the late 1960s he was a mark millionaire may times over and his career as a clandestine financier only ended with the Bank of England currency smuggling scandal of 1973. Once again he slipped the net and now, as Dr Karl Lethnal, with access to bank accounts totalling over twenty million dollars in Liechtenstein, the Bahamas and in a dozen countries around the world, he was Killtest Inc.'s banker and biggest shareholder.

Lethnal's experience as a global currency trader was essential to the operation, for ticket revenues, betting wagers, fees and payoffs ran into millions with each Killtest event. Transferring several million dollars from one country to another, often in the form of gold bullion, was not a task for the amateur, nor was the 'laundering' of illegal revenue. This was achieved by heavy investments into the most respectable institutions Lethnal could find. The British government would have been appalled to discover that a puppet trust financed by Killtest Inc. had been for two years a partner in a North Sea oil exploration company. When the deal had been completed, Oppenheimer joked: 'It's like creeping into a man's bed in the dark and fucking his wife, with neither of them any the wiser.' Lethnal had merely smiled.

And he was still smiling, with arrogant amusement. Mrabet sipped his mint tea and glanced around the big room with a reawakened glow of importance. The elegant décor was all his. So was the cover concept.

To disguise the true nature of their operation, the syndicate hid behind the cover of another, rather more altruistic organization Mrabet had dreamed up and called the French Connection Committee.

The supposed aim of the committee was to promote the 200th anniversay of France's recognition of American independence and to encourage the celebration of that day, 6 February 1778, when the French had signed a treaty with Benjamin Franklin acknowledging the autonomy of thirteen states.

In Mrabet's view the anniversary celebrations would be in little danger of attracting too much enthusiasm; every American citizen had been thoroughly saturated with the Bicentennial nonsense anyway. Although from time to time he'd keep the pot simmering by holding an exploratory discussion with some state official, or by issuing a formidably dull press release, the cover worked perfectly: the French Connection Committee was politely tolerated as a harmless bunch of public-spirited nuts, and ignored.

Mrabet strolled over to the plaster bust of Franklin, adjusted some folds in the Tricolour flag hanging above it, and proceeded to prowl around the room.

The dominant feature was the gigantic bare black boardroom table which, with its twelve high-backed chairs, occupied a good third of the room; beyond it, through three large windows at the end, was a mid-town vista of Manhattan, broken at intervals by skyscrapers. Around the half-panelled walls hung gilded mirrors and ornately framed reproductions of portraits of famous French and American statesmen. Bookshelves were packed with yards of unread leather-bound volumes; small forests of potted palms sprouted from each corner; several settees were grouped about marble coffee tables, and to make a final cultural point an unplayed, gleaming white grand piano had been positioned in the centre of the room.

'*Vive la France!*' breathed Mrabet.

The door bleep sounded again, each of the six lock combinations as it was turned giving out a different tone. The notes played the opening bar of *La Marseillaise*; if they didn't, an alarm was sounded, alerting six security men posted at the hotel's street entrances on meeting days.

For so pacifist an organization, security devices had been installed to the point of overkill. Oppenheimer had had the place microscopically examined for bugs. All the glass in the windows had been invisibly misted to counteract the latest laser snoop beams which could look into a room from a mile away. The wallpaper concealed metallic fibres woven into it like a printed circuit through which buzzed, twenty-four hours a day, constantly changing magnetic fields. The main entrance was fitted with magnetic field generators which obliterated any sound tape or videotape which passed through it, and an X-ray fogger similarly dealt with photographs and film, exposed or unexposed. The suite, the corridor outside and even the elevators bristled with hidden detectors and alarms. The staff and cleaners were not only screened, but screened every day.

The two new arrivals were Frank McSwiggan and General Ton Dinh Quan; they must have met outside the door because it was a Ring rule never to ride the elevators together. McSwiggan, tanned and good looking despite a face which bore the marks of a violent life, strode straight to the bar, while the dapper Vietnamese composed his slight figure on a green-patterned settee.

'Greetings, my friends,' was all he said.

McSwiggan, perhaps prompted by this remark, turned belatedly and shot a husky, 'Hi!' to Mrabet and Lethnal. McSwiggan ran the security and protection side of Killtest activities, the *armée privée* originally set up by Mrabet who as the rate of killings was stepped up, thankfully relinquished control to the less inhibited Irishman. Jinking half a dozen ice cubes in his tumbler of Scotch, McSwiggan walked over and sat on one end of the long table, placing a dusty shoe on the velvet seat of a chair.

'Jesus! I could do without this Paranagua hassle,' he said, lighting a cigar. 'Fuckin' Limey agent pokin' around in my backyard. I'm goin' to stop him like a Hiroshima watch.'

He drained the Scotch in two vast swallows, crunched several ice cubes with his teeth and marched again for the bar. 'Want a drink anyone? George?'

Mrabet had almost finished his iced tea but had an aversion for any sort of favour from the stocky Irishman.

'No, I'm fine, Frank,' he called out.

Why was it that he always felt put down by his colleagues? Except for Oppenheimer he could find no rapport with any of them. They grated. Like McSwiggan soiling the chair just now. He often had the feeling he was being squeezed out, yet he'd been the first man Oppenheimer had approached after wrapping up the Killtest deal. Night after night he'd helped Oppenheimer draw up plans for the Organization, well before McSwiggan, Lethnal and the General. Yet here they were acting as though they, and they alone, were running the show.

At a minute past noon the bleeps sounded again and Oppenheimer entered the room, a model of composure. He greeted them all genially, with that insinuating voice you could never quite trust, and stood at the end of the long table. On cue, the others sat down at their accustomed places, and the meeting of the Ring commenced.

'Well, gentlemen,' Oppenheimer began. 'You're all aware of the Paranagua hiccup, but I'll bring you up to date. I've just seen Gulao at the Brazilian Consulate and he's positive it's an isolated infiltration.'

He drew out his wallet and from an envelope extracted a tiny strip of film.

'I don't have the enlargements with me but this little item would have blown Gams's identity wide open and backfired on us in any one of a hundred ways. Fortunately we intercepted it by a combination of chance and good management so everything's cool – in fact it's done us a favour by alerting us that we have a security weakness, and a serious one, too.'

'Why should anybody want to do a plumbing job on us?' McSwiggan asked in a cloud of cigar smoke.

'Why? Frank, you tell me! My guess is it's a stray piece of a jigsaw, and the sooner we find some other pieces to find out what it's all about, the healthier we'll feel. A British agent of some category, we know that much. Nothing's come through Central Intelligence wires yet, but I've got them tapped just in case.'

'Don't we have *any* clue to this guy's identity?' Mrabet prompted, glancing obliquely at McSwiggan.

'Negative,' Oppenheimer answered. 'Frank's been through all the screening records of our Paranagua customers, but nothing. I've had the Agency's records division go through all the mug shots, but again, nothing. And obviously I can't approach British Intelligence, even indirectly. Too dangerous.'

He let the others ponder on this before continuing, in case anyone came up with a suggestion.

'All we can do in this situation is take a gamble. With his film lost this agent, whoever he is, will probably want to try again. Now all the Paranagua clients were given ticket options in the usual way for the next Killtest games in Macao – '

'July fifteen,' Mrabet reminded them all.

'Correct. A week from today. A hundred and eighty-four options were taken up and my hunch is that this agent took one of them. And even if he didn't he'll soon get a ticket from his previous contact when he finds out his film never turned up in London.'

'I'm not so goddam sure,' McSwiggan put in. 'A missing item like that could tip him off we're wise to him.'

'As I said, Frank, we're gambling,' Oppenheimer said evenly. 'I wish I could remove the chance element but I can't. In any case if he doesn't surface at Macao he'll very likely show up at the one after. We'll get him in the end. But Macao is our best bet, and I want an all-out security effort there to nail him. Take Ginorini with you. You'll also have Lao

Man and his Triad boys from Hong Kong.' He turned to General Ton Dinh Quan. 'And Dino – why don't you go along, too? We can't have too many on this particular hunt, and it's on your home ground.'

They all looked towards the Vietnamese who, behind his test-pattern sunglasses gave no perceptible indication he'd even heard.

With his dark, impassive face, the diminutive General Ton sat at the Organization's conference table like a badly decayed incisor in a row of white teeth. Ton was one of dozens of trumped-up generals who fled the Vietnam war for America, armed with two suitcases hastily packed with one and a half million dollars in banknotes and gold.

He too was a one-time Oppenheimer aide, one of his 'dirty tricks' agents, and claimed privately that the CIA had protected his extensive bar girl racket in Saigon. And although he refused to confirm or deny it, he was almost certainly involved in the CIA-assisted murder of President Diem; it was even claimed he had a hand in the revenge shooting of President Kennedy three weeks later. Derided by the US military brass in Vietnam as a thoroughly unreliable ally (even the *New York Times* branded him as 'almost universally corrupt'), Ton secured US entry through the influence of Oppenheimer and the curious provision which allows the CIA to bring into the country up to a hundred aliens a year outside the usual immigration procedures with no questions asked.

The deal was, of course, that the contents of General Ton's suitcases would be made available to Oppenheimer, and in addition the Vietnamese leaned on a number of his fellow generals, gathering up half a truckload of illegal loot. This spectacular injection of cash capital enabled the infant Organization to expand its chain of closed circuit outlets to more than eighty by the end of 1976.

Apart from the money and an occasional smile of agreement, General Ton contributed very little to the running of Killtest Inc. On the other hand his network of military and political contacts promised lucrative new frontiers throughout the East when the time was ripe. But for the moment he was content to sit silent, like some miniature Buddha in Army-issue Polaroids, emanating vibrations of security and sanctity.

But was Ton going to Macao or not. Mrabet wondered? Why couldn't he simply say yes out loud instead of smiling? In fact he didn't even smile, but merely displayed a few more millimetres of brown lip.

Then, unexpectedly, General Ton spoke.

'He'll be at Macao. Foolhardy, you know? The British still haven't got used to the fact they're not running the East any more. You Americans might call us gooks, but the British looked through us as though we didn't exist. They always underestimate us Asians. This agent will think the Macao show is run by Chinese – a pushover. He'll be there, and so will I – I'll smell him out!' The Vietnamese then lapsed into his accustomed silence, which was to last for the remainder of the meeting.

'Good, Dino, great!' said Oppenheimer enthusiastically. He turned to McSwiggan. 'Frank, you'll direct operations there, but keep Dino at your hip. He knows the goo– the Oriental psychology.'

Oppenheimer then turned his attention to Mrabet. 'How's the gate for Macao, Georges?'

'Looks promising. A capacity crowd, I'd guess. That's just under 500. The Chinese community responded very well; they'll make up at least half the audience, and we're also running a charter flight from Brazil. We've opened up three closed circuit outlets in Rio and two in São Paulo, so we're off the ground there, too.'

'And Stateside?'

'Hundred and five. We could have had a dozen more but we've run out of chromagen screens.' The screens were a necessary part of the closed circuit set-ups in theatres and halls; they allowed a TV-screen-size image to be blown up to twelve feet square.

Lethnal clucked through his teeth. 'We could double the Paranagua receipts if expenses weren't so savage.'

'Yes,' Oppenheimer recalled. 'What about this junk you've hired, Georges?'

'It's no damn junk – it's a bloody great yacht in the Onassis class with its own swimming pool, the *Santa Coronado*. No worries, it's all fixed, a hundred per cent security-tight and only thirty-five hundred dollars a day – and that includes ferries and patrol boats. We're pirating the satellite facility from Unicom Data. Their signals will be in trouble but by the time they wake up our transmission will be finished.'

'Fine, Georges. And the acts? You're not running short of Dadins, are you?'

'No way, Hensch. Triple bill, including two women in the final bout.' The four other men around the table seemed to lean forward, even General Ton, and Mrabet, for the first time that day, felt the intoxication of importance. He enjoyed the moment and sipped the dregs of his mint tea.

'Yes,' he resumed, 'two women against a man. Real raunchy.'

'Ahh, we've had that before,' McSwiggan cut in.

'Fools rush in!' Mrabet said with a smile. 'There's a catch. I thought it up myself. Each of the gladiators is armed with a whip – they've been training for the past two weeks. And on each of them, right over the heart, will be taped a blister of plastic explosive, primed with a detonator. One crack of a whip in the right place and – WHAM! – the loser won't know anything about it.'

'No danger to the spectators, I trust?' Lethnal asked, thinking about insurance.

'Simak's taken care of that. And I'll be there, personally.'

'Great!' Oppenheimer stood up, cracked his knuckles and barely managed to stifle a belch. 'It's all set, then. But remember, the most important contest of the lot will be to find that agent. If we don't – ' he drew a forefinger across his throat and looked pointedly at McSwiggan, ' – we're *all* dead.'

3

As the Jumbo swung sharply around for its final approach to Kai Tak Airport, McSwiggan drew out his wallet and passport to familiarize himself with his temporary identity. Like always flying tourist-class, this was a strict routine introduced by Oppenheimer, to be carried out five minutes before landing. From the passport a grey face looked blankly out, copied from a snapshot taken three years before. According to the document he was Frank Wilde, forty-two, blue eyes, 5 ft 10 in., a farm machinery salesman from Chicago en route to Sydney with a seven-day vacation stopover in Hong Kong.

McSwiggan closed his eyes and memorized his address, the names of his wife and two daughters, the names of his company colleagues, and details of the business he intended doing in Australia.

He opened the wallet. It contained dollar bills, business cards, a family photo, a folded and refolded letter from his wife, credit cards, an El ticket stub and a couple of receipts in the name of Wilde. His attaché case held farm machinery brochures, order books, a file of company letters, copies of *Newsweek* and *Playboy*. After carefully checking everything he popped a strip of Beechnut gum into his mouth to complete the stereotype. Then the giant jet banked down through a gap in the mountain peaks, thundered over the sardine-can tenements of Kowloon and finally screeched in to land on the long finger of tarmac that stretched a mile out into the harbour.

Hong Kong made McSwiggan uneasy. For one thing the colony had perhaps the most alert police force in the world, neither completely honest nor totally corrupt but definitely bad news for carpetbaggers like him. He'd only been to the place once before, to meet Lao Man, the Triad chief of the region, who was not only well known to the police but actively hob-nobbed with them. But while Lao Man obviously enjoyed the cat and mouse game it was not McSwiggan's style nor, in his view, was it good for the Organization. But from the time the Triad boss had fulfilled his first contract there was no turning back, no removing him. Even Oppenheimer called him the 'Chinese Leech'. It frustrated McSwiggan to know that as far as Killtest Inc.'s security was concerned the whole of East Asia was firmly in Lao Man's grip. To assert any authority at all he was forced to order the Chinese to fly all the way to New York – a security risk in itself – just to give him a few instructions, for only in the Ring's suite in the Waldorf Towers was McSwiggan the real boss. Now, back in Hong Kong, would Lao Man be his enemy or his subordinate? His jaw ached from clenching his teeth as he mulled over this subtle but irritating challenge to his authority. It was a challenge that would have to be met, and he had no intention of losing.

Frank McSwiggan had come up the hard way, and although his tanned, sullen face bore the marks of the journey he was, at forty-two, undeniably handsome. 'More lines on his face than the Enfield marshalling yards,' someone had said once. But startling blue-grey eyes and prolific greying hair drew attention away from the lines and a damaged nose, and he moved his rugged frame with the ease of an athlete.

Despite his accent, McSwiggan had spent only a few months of his life in Ireland, and that in Belfast. He was born of Irish parents in Bootle and was introduced to the rough and tumble life as a Liverpool docker in his late teens. From that start his career progressed steadily towards criminal violence, first as a strong-arm picket for his union, then as a used car dealer, professional boxer and scrap metal merchant with a string of petty convictions on the side. It was in the scrap business that he began to deal in illegal bullion and arms, which led him to Belfast in search of IRA money. He was no Republican sympathizer, though; he was was quite happy to promise anything, grab the money and run. He was in Belfast when the Angola war broke out, and contracted to supply mercenaries at £400 a head; and in the troubled province he found more recruits than he could place. Some of the more desperate of his unplaced recruits insisted on spending their death-wish somewhere, and subsequently McSwiggan found a profitable outlet for it in Killtest Inc.

His dedication soon convinced the Organization that he would serve it better as a partner than as a freelance, and within six months he had graduated from recruiter to security boss and Oppenheimer's most trusted aide. As the outfit's hatchet man McSwiggan's zeal and devotion turned him into a brutal killer without conscience, a man to be feared, a savage guard dog trained to carry out orders but never to be completely trusted.

It was this reputation the Irishman enjoyed most, and he developed the role with relish. Already his athletic gait had assumed a swagger, and when he became angry his face could contort to a ball of crumpled brown wrapping paper. Yet, like many violent men, there was a sentimental side to McSwiggan: Frank, the family man. He'd brought his ex-beauty queen wife and young daughter to America where they lived sumptuously in a ten-room, white-painted mansion just north of Stamford, surrounded by two acres of landscaped garden in which, unknown to admiring neighbours and his wife's PTA friends, was concealed a deadly obstacle course of trip wires, mantraps and alarm systems.

In the airport lounge McSwiggan waited near the arrivals indicator; Lao Man's Pan Am flight had landed fifteen minutes before, just behind his. The first passengers were beginning to emerge from Customs so he sauntered to the Exit and walked out into the paraffin-flavoured murk. A black Austin Princess came up to him and he climbed into the rear after exchanging a Triad sign with the driver. A Chinese seated beside him watched silently through the rear window while the limousine sped to the parking area. Five minutes later another car drove up and Lao Man quickly transferred to the Princess, which then speeded towards the cross-harbour tunnel.

'You had a good flight, I hope?' Lao Man said, smiling. 'I slept all the way.'

Of course he would; a man with no worries. A fortune in gold gleamed momentarily from the smiling mouth, and McSwiggan envied his cynical urbanity. Like Ton Dinh Quan, Lao Man concealed his lethality behind a façade of pure silk.

McSwiggan scowled, and grunted: 'Where the hell are we going?'

Lao Man sank back into the grey upholstery and inserted a cigarette into a stained ivory holder. 'We have two apartments on the Peak, one for you and one for Mr Ginorini. The General will stay at the Ambassador Hotel in Kowloon. Every comfort, and quite safe, of course. I have my own place at Aberdeen, as you know.' Aberdeen was the fashionable beach on the north of the island, and Lao Man's house was reputed to be luxurious beyond belief. 'You understand that it would not be wise to have you staying there, much as I wish I could be your host.'

Not wise, McSwiggan thought: more like putting him in his place.

The car was now in a queue heading for the entrance to the harbour tunnel that would take them to Hong Kong island. The harbour itself was crowded with ferries, junks, lighters and craft of all kinds; a dozen big freighters stood out in deeper water.

Lao Man pointed to a sleek white yacht anchored near the Star Ferry terminal on the island side.

'That's the *Santa Coronado*,' he said. 'It sails tonight for Manila but will anchor for three days about five miles off Macao. All the lighting, television and transmitter equipment has been installed. Mr Simak and Mr Taubes have done a very thorough job.' Simak and Taubes, Mrabet's assistants, were responsible for setting up locations and staging the bouts. 'As you'll appreciate, by holding the Killtest games on a ship we'll have very good security. We're making it very easy for this British agent to get on. But whether he can get off . . . ahh, that's another question.'

'We can always scuttle the boat and drown the lot,' McSwiggan suggested. 'That way we'd be sure to get him.'

Lao Man considered the joke seriously. 'Perhaps a little wasteful, Mr McSwiggan,' he said. 'After all, Killtest customers aren't as plentiful as Chinese.'

The door chime sounded at nine o'clock exactly, and the *amah* padded across the carpeted room to answer it. Outside on the balcony, with a large, chilled Scotch in his hand, McSwiggan could hardly tear himself away from the fascinating tableau below. From the typhoon harbour to the distant lights of Kowloon his gaze took in four million people, and now the swelling hum of all this humanity packed into such a tiny space came up to the Peak on the warm evening breeze. Crowds and masses of people never failed to excite him.

Lao Man and General Ton Dinh Quan entered together, prompting McSwiggan to go to the telephone to call Ginorini's apartment, four floors below. While Tony Ginorini wasn't exactly a member of the Organization he was a *mafioso* 'uncle' whose job it was to keep tabs on a considerable Mafia investment in Killtest Inc.; and only on rare occasions was it considered judicious to exclude him from Organization business.

The white-jacketed manservant poured drinks for the others, and they sat around a low teak table in the centre of the sparsely furnished room. Notwithstanding the low-key lighting, General Ton still wore his sunglasses.

Ginorini came in with a large packet and gave it to McSwiggan.

'Right, let's start.' The security boss opened the packet and extracted several large photographs. One of them, grainy and grey, was a group shot of about a dozen men.

'Now, I'll tell you what we've done,' McSwiggan said to the others. 'On that strip of film we intercepted was a sequence of shots of the chess game at Paranagua, all taken from the same position. In other words, from the same seat in the audience. Now, using the chessboard marking on the floor as a reference we were able to fix the position of the camera pretty accurately – ' He turned the photograph over and read from the back ' – somewhere in Rows F, G and H, and seats 16, 17 and 18. Whoever took the photographs had to be sitting in one of those nine seats, get it? We videotape the entire audience at each show, so what we did was to run the tape through to the point where our camera covered those seats.' He turned the photograph over again and held it up for the others to see. Nine faces in the photograph had crosses under them. 'With this result. One of these nine creeps has to be that bloody agent.'

McSwiggan then spread out the other photographs. They were fuzzy enlargements of the faces from the group shot. 'Here they are. I want you to have these copied tomorrow morning, Lao Man, so we all have a set.'

'What if he's disguised?' Lao Man asked.

'I haven't finished, yet,' McSwiggan said. 'We've done some checking on the people who had the tickets for those seats. They're all clean except one, and we can't trace him. But what really interests me is that his ticket was one of a batch of ten sold in London.' He picked up one of the photographs which showed the woolly image of a man with dark, straight hair which fell over his forehead; he wore a white shirt and dark tie. The men around the table studied the blow-up in turn.

'He's probably our man, then,' Ginorini said.

'Yes, he most likely is.' McSwiggan agreed. 'But just in case, keep an eye peeled for the other eight.' He gathered up the photographs and gave them to Lao Man. 'Now, next question. What happens if we think we sight him?'

Lao Man smiled. 'You can put your mind to rest. There'll be sixteen syndicate men on the *Santa Coronado*, two on each ferry and two on the checkpoint here on the island. We'll take care of him.'

McSwiggan knew he had to feel assured, for the Triad was frighteningly thorough. Individually its members were nothing more than street thugs, but the iron-fisted discipline imposed by the secret society made all the difference. Its origins went back hundreds of years, but its aims had radically changed. Formerly a blood-brotherhood with masonic undertones, pledged to protect moral and spiritual ideals, the Triad movement had in the nineteenth century degenerated to extortion, gangsterism and blackmail. Until recent years, police crack-downs and fierce inter-gang warfare had kept the Triads in check, but now they were established again and powerful, with branches in Britain, America and several European countries.

The fact that Lao Man had emerged, unscathed, as its top chief, was worthy of respectful consideration, and he sat there now, smiling and tranquil, basking in his triumph.

'I saw Taubes this evening,' McSwiggan said, changing the subject. 'Everything's set like a jelly. As far as the yacht and the other facilities are concerned, the whole show's been chartered by a film company, which is always a good cover. There's seating for 480 built around the swimming pool on deck, and the whole shebang is covered by a marquee. The customers will be taken there and back by two hydrofoils; all the charter firm knows is that we're shooting a party scene and they're the extras.'

'We've got a full betting service this time, too.' Ginorini added. 'That should shake down half a million.'

'Right. Plus two bars, free liquor for everyone. It should be the best Killtest yet.'

A sudden thought clouded McSwiggan's face. 'There's just one thing,' he said, looking point blank at Lao Man. 'You've put in for eight contracts on this Macao show. Eight! That's double the usual quota.' A contract was of course the euphemism for murder, a necessary preliminary in the setting up of each Killtest event. There was always some difficulty with a supplier, some nosy individual or a local hoodlum who resented the Organization moving in on his territory.

'What you're forgetting, Mr McSwiggan,' the Triad chief said with a fixed smile, 'is that the price of contracts in Hong Kong is modest, to say the least. The eight contracts are for five thousand dollars apiece – '

'Plus twenty thousand bucks in handouts – ' McSwiggan interrupted.

' – a total of sixty thousand dollars, plus incidentals. That's not so much more than your usual budget, now, is it?'

It wasn't. A single contract in the States was now costing twenty thousand dollars.

'Or look at it another way,' Lao Man persisted. 'As I understand it, the expected gross for Macao is about seven million.

So you're looking at barely one per cent to take care of all the trouble. I'd say you were getting it cheap. Cheap, Mr McSwiggan.'

It wasn't quite as simple as that, as McSwiggan knew well. The contracts and bribes unavoidable with each Killtest operation were only a small part of the picture. Every single patron who attended a Killtest event, whether live or on closed circuit, was a potential risk. The temptation to brag to friends that he had actually witnessed a gladiatorial death made each patron a security threat. To even the balance, it was demonstrated in explicit terms to every customer what would happen if he was careless, with an occasional, well-publicized example to drive home the point that the Organization would not hesitate to eliminate informers.

A dossier was kept on every patron for blackmail purposes. But with the phenomenal success of the Killtest enterprise the security problem had become dangerously bloated, and keeping tabs on over sixty thousand clients on three continents was proving increasingly difficult. Already, McSwiggan had eighty people on the security payroll, not counting the Triads who were paid by Lao Man from his retainer. So far the organization had overcome threats to its security with complete success: by murder, blackmail, memory scrambling or, in the case of one gladiatorial survivor who proved a dangerous psychopath, by drug addiction. When the law did actually become involved, as it had on a dozen or so occasions, the Organization's team of lawyers went into battle like a well-trained commando force. But despite the successes, the knife-edge on which McSwiggan walked was becoming decidedly sharper, and it sharpened until infinity. And he was also under intense pressure from Oppenheimer on the question of security costs.

When setting up Killtest Inc., Oppenheimer had allowed five per cent of the gross against the budget for security and protection. Now, after only six months, the proportion had soared to nine per cent and threatened to climb higher. The Macao show, with its promised gate of seven million dollars – two million more than any previous event – would give McSwiggan some breathing space, but he was uncomfortably aware that the *armée privée* was dangerously close to running out of control. By its very nature, because of the type of people it employed, because the sheer number of potential security risks grew at the rate of thousands each week, his private army was the weakest part of the organization. Nor was any relief in sight; legalization of gladiatorial combat, if it ever came at all, was light years away. McSwiggan knew that his own contest aboard the *Santa Coronado* tomorrow would be no less a mortal engagement than that of any of the Killtest gladiators; that agent, whatever his purpose, had to be caught. McSwiggan's life was on the line, and he suddenly resolved to do something about it.

'This is your territory,' he said to Lao Man, at the same time pulling out his revolver and coolly checking its chambers. 'And what happens tomorrow is your baby and yours alone. I'll be talking to Oppenheimer tonight, telling him I've handed over all responsibility here to you. You've said many times you prefer no interference in this neck of the woods, so I won't interfere. But I'll be watching.'

It was an adroit bit of sidestepping, he thought, and no doubt Lao Man would appreciate the touch of oriental bluff. Now the Chinese couldn't afford to fail; the loss of face would inevitably topple him from the top of the Triad tree.

4

The *Santa Coronado,* heavily ballasted to counteract the effect of 500 people on its top deck, rode low in the mid-summer swell of the South China Sea, five miles from Macao and twenty miles west of the Saigon shipping lane.

Most of the patrons were already on board and the last of them were now climbing the gangplank from one of the two hydrofoils which had served as ferries. Two junks near by were apparently fishing, but in reality they were powerful motorized vessels manned by Lao Man's people on security standby. The spot had been expertly chosen, for no other ship appeared on the horizon; no aircraft droned overhead.

Up on the *Coronado*'s bridge, Frank McSwiggan and General Ton Dinh Quan looked down at the queue of men filing up the gangway, laughing and joking, and carrying their jackets because of the heat. Each one was thoroughly frisked by the guards.

'Like a lot of fuckin' schoolboys goin' to their first strip show,' McSwiggan observed. He looked at the ship's chronometer; it was 11.45. The show was timed to start at 12 noon, which would be 8 p.m. in Los Angeles and 11 p.m. in New York. According to Jay Simak, who kept in touch with Oppenheimer and the others via the scrambler, the Macao event was a sell-out everywhere.

The Irishman walked into the suite of top-deck cabins, packed with video recording and transmission equipment flown from Tokyo. In one of the cabins three Japanese engineers had just locked signals with the selected satellite and were beginning the countdown.

He walked to another cabin and looked in. Mel Taubes, the events director, came over and introduced the chief engineer.

'Everything's apples,' he said to McSwiggan. 'We're just waiting for a reply to our test scramble.'

'It's coming through now,' the engineer called out, glancing briefly at a huge bank of oscilloscopes and dials. 'Looks okay.'

The signals from the *Santa Coronado* were being bounced off the pirated satellite and received at the Organization's new mast in Nevada before re-transmission to nearly 150 decoders scattered over the US, Canada, Mexico and Brazil. There they would be unscrambled into video pictures before audiences in darkened, heavily guarded theatres, halls, poolrooms, boardrooms and even private homes.

Taubes gently guided McSwiggan out into the corridor.

'I've set up your monitors in the next cabin,' he told him confidentially. He led the way to the cabin door, which was opened by a guard. Inside, Ginorini was seated in front of a block of ten TV monitor screens, each numbered according to its source camera.

Taubes steered McSwiggan to a seat behind a small desk on which was mounted a microphone.

'Cameras Eight and Nine are yours,' he explained. 'The cameramen are on headsets and you can talk to them through the mike. They're small, portable radio-remote cameras, so they can go anywhere, point anywhere you want them.' He gestured again to the monitors. 'Camera Ten will be a roving wide-angle over the audience the whole time. If you see anything suspicious on Ten, just tell the remotes over the mike to go in for a closer look – you'll see their pictures up there. A few of Lao Man's boys are hooked up to you as well, so you can instruct them, too.' McSwiggan had to check himself from making congratulatory remarks, for the monitoring system was marvellously comprehensive. But where was Lao Man?

A white-jacketed waiter brought in a large tray of drinks and ice, and left with Taubes.

'Some set-up!' Ginorini remarked, pouring whiskies for them both.

McSwiggan settled back in his chair. Above the monitors, pinned to a display board, were the enlarged photographs, one of them the suspected agent. His photograph was mounted in the centre, with a border of red tape around it. McSwiggan studied it for fully half a minute before giving his attention to the monitors. Several cameras were still undergoing line-up testing, and others were out of focus, waiting for the action to begin.

The picture from Camera Ten showed the patrons returning from the bars and betting ring, being ushered to their seats by half a dozen Chinese girls wearing smocks of transparent silk mesh and nothing else – Triad girlfriends in for some extra loot, no doubt, but a good idea; several customers were already becoming noticeably inflamed. Ginorini leaned over to the mike and asked one of the remotes for a close-up of an usherette, and within seconds there was a navel-to-thigh shot on monitor Eight.

'Jeez!' Ginorini breathed. 'I could use a piece of that sideways nooky tonight!'

Two more cameras focussed on the swimming pool, in the centre of which had been erected a platform, about six foot square and some six feet above the water, connected to the side of the pool by a long plank with a handrail. Spotlights came on and there was some cheering as a man in a red dinner jacket made his way gingerly out to the platform.

The cabin door opened and Taubes returned, followed by Jay Simak, reflecting the monitor images from his shiny Kojak skull. Taubes dimmed the lights. 'One minute to go,' he said. 'And everything's apple pie in the sky.'

Taubes was the youngest member of the Killtest hierarchy, a chain-smoking, twenty-nine-year-old Harvard graduate who'd cut his teeth as a rock impresario in the early 1970s as tour manager for such groups as Going Down On Mother, Cow Burp and Children's Children. In three years he'd climbed the rock management ladder so fast and so spectacularly that he was expected, according to the *Village Voice*, to 'ultimately claim the entrepreneurial crown of rock – management of the Rolling Stones'. Unfortunately this hope went up in smoke when a disastrous fire reduced four articulated lorries – containing a hundred thousand dollars' worth of touring stage equipment – to blackened, twisted metal. None of it was insured; Taubes had used the premium money to settle some pressing debts.

About this time Oppenheimer had instructed Simak to buy the best impresario he could find; after reading of the young man's predicament Simak readily bailed him out. From then on, Mel Taubes was a not unwilling Killtest captive. With huge budgets to spend on these new, daring productions Taubes was realizing his obsessional ambition; the morality and illegality of what he was doing hardly seemed to concern him. Even now, in the harsh, kaleidoscopic light from the flickering monitors, his dark, handsome face was enraptured by the knowledge that what was about to take place was unique in the world of entertainment, his very own creation.

The man in the red dinner jacket on the platform above the pool began to say something, and Taubes turned the sound up.

'Hi there, folks! I'm Buck Lines, and it's my pleasure to welcome you to the Eighth World Series of Killtest Games,' the man announced. Lines's gravelly voice stamped him as a veteran stadium announcer. The audience was now in anonymous darkness, and the man's jacket glowed crimson under the intense glare of the spotlights. 'To those of you new to the gladiatorial arts, what will take place here during the next hour or two may come as a shock – although nothing like the shock in store for half the contestants!'

The remark unloosened a few sniggers and some subdued laughter. 'It's an experiment,' Taubes explained in the monitor cabin. 'I'm trying a warm-up to relax the audience.'

Buck Lines continued. 'What I want to impress on you folks is that this is entertainment with a capital E, real man's entertainment, and the gladiators who'll fight here today are doing so to entertain you, to excite you with raw nerve and courage – good, old-fashioned courage – and to do this they are willingly prepared to offer the highest sacrifice they can make – their lives! Right now they're waiting in the wings, waiting perhaps for death, and I want them to hear your acknowledgement and approval of their sacrifice – come on, now – let's hear it – come on, let's have it . . . LOUDER!'

The clapping and cheering, hesitant at first, rose and swelled to a roar that lasted almost a minute.

McSwiggan glanced up at the colour monitor from Camera Ten. The audience was a mass of insanely clapping hands and shining, look-alike faces, each with a moving black hole which was a shouting cheering mouth. At the back of the top tier of seats one group of men stood stiff and silent. He spoke into the mike and asked one of the remotes for a close-up; and there was Lao Man, surrounded by half a dozen Triad henchmen, absorbed in watching the audience.

The dying applause was the cue for Buck Lines to announce the opening bout. Two men in long silk gowns materialized by the poolside, just within the arc of white light.

'Ladies and gentlemen of the Killtest fraternity,' Lines shouted oratorically, notwithstanding the apparent absence of women, 'it is my great pleasure to present the first contest today, codenamed BOOT, for a purse of forty thousand dollars – '

At that moment a large transparent plastic globe was lowered by a pulley to just above the announcer's head. It was packed with bundles of dollar bills.

' – and here are the contestants!'

It was a bizarre sight. The two gladiators, their silk gowns flapping about them, hobbled with difficulty along the gang-plank to the platform in the middle of the swimming pool. Both men had their left legs heavily encased in plaster to mid-thigh. Buck Lines took their hands and held them aloft.

'On my right – ' he continued, 'Danny Dickson from Arkansas, United States of America. On my left, Angelo DiCicco from New Jersey, United States of America.' A red-jacketed assistant came along the plank and took the gowns from the two men. Except for black body-builder jocks they were naked.

Lines let go their hands and they shadow-sparred to loosen their muscles. 'Each gladiator, as you can see, is handicapped by a boot of heavy lithium cement. Both contestants will engage in hand-to-hand, all-in combat to the death. The first contestant to be knocked off this platform into the water will drown. Gentlemen – the salute!'

With the announcer's prompting, the two men raised their arms in a salute to the purse, dangling tantalizingly above them. Buck Lines held the microphone in front of Dickson, the bigger man, who stumblingly repeated the ancient gladiatorial salute to Caesar: *Ave Imperator, morituri te salutant* – 'Those who are about to die salute you!' It was Oppenheimer's idea – he claimed money was more powerful than Caesar ever was – and the salute had become the standard preamble to all Killtest bouts.

Lines then passed the microphone to DiCicco, a dark, wiry man, who betrayed his nervousness by having to be prompted on the final two Latin words.

The formality over, the announcer then guided the two men into opposite corners and walked back along the plank to the poolside. The plank was then withdrawn and the gladiators were alone on their mortal little island.

A bell clanged and the two men warily approached each other, dragging their plastered legs.

'That plaster weighs over sixty pounds, know that?' Taubes told the others in the monitor cabin. But they were all completely absorbed in the row of pictures coming from the platform above the ship's pool.

For almost a minute the fighters hardly made a move, until suddenly the bigger man lunged forward to deliver a savage karate chop to DiCicco's neck. The small man ducked, and as his attacker tried to regain his balance, brought his knee up into Dickson's face. Blood sprayed over the canvas-covered decking as both men tumbled into a heap, hammering at each other's bodies with furious punches.

Ginorini was jumping about in his seat like a kid at a circus. 'My money's on the little bastard! Take him, Angelo! Take him!'

But Dickson, with his superior size and strength, slowly began to get the upper hand, holding DiCicco down by planting a knee on his chest and raining powerful blows to his head. It looked as though DiCicco was unconscious, but when Dickson attempted to push him to the edge of the platform the small man sank his teeth into an ear. Dickson yelled with pain and recoiled, but anchored by the heavy plaster boot could not move away fast enough and DiCicco sat up and butted him in the testicles.

Simak winced. The violence seemed to be multiplied by the seven monitor screens in the cabin. Two of the cameras were fitted with ultra-closeup lenses, and their pictures of the blood were only for strong stomachs – like Ginorini's; his was now as tense as a tight knot, as he followed every move.

By now Dickson was maddened with the pain and almost helpless, allowing his opponent to seize the advantage and to propel him towards the platform edge. But just as DiCicco was about to heave him into the pool, Dickson slid beneath him so that the small man fell forward, his head and shoulders protruding alarmingly over the edge. Only a miracle could save him now. With a mighty effort, Dickson used his body to lever the unfortunate DiCicco further off the platform so that only the great weight of the lithium plaster prevented him from slipping over. Almost defying gravity DiCicco clawed the air in panic before he managed to swing around and grab Dickson's wrist. For over a minute the deadly contest went on, directional microphones capturing every grunt and cry. The bigger man's face was a shining crimson mask, and from time to time he shook his head violently to clear the blood from his eyes. Inch by inch DiCicco edged his way back on to the platform, but just when it appeared he was safe, Dickson, with his free hand, began to pulverize his opponent's kidneys with continuous heavy punching. In trying to escape the mauling DiCicco made the mistake of moving away towards the edge again, allowing Dickson to wrap an arm around his plastered leg. He lifted the bulky white casing and then with a tremendous heave swung the encased leg over the smaller man's head so that he somersaulted into the water with an engulfing splash.

Taubes stood up at this point and went over to one of the monitors.

'You might be interested to know,' he said to the others in

a lecturing tone, 'that at this spot in the pool the water is exactly six and a half feet deep.'

'So the little bugger will drown?' Ginorini asked, disappointed.

'That's correct. DiCicco is only five foot seven high.'

When the turmoil of the water subsided, two hands broke the surface in a frenzy. Anchored by the lithium boot DiCicco was drowning before 500 hypnotized onlookers. Isolated shouts came from the audience, some in protest, but most spectators watched in stunned silence. The fallen gladiator could be seen in the water, stretching up and struggling for his life, just a few inches above his contorted face. Two minutes went by until, as though waving a final farewell, the exhausted hands sank and floated horizontally just below the surface. DiCicco was drowned.

A separate spotlight swung on to Buck Lines as he reappeared at the poolside. With gestures he motioned to the crowd to keep quiet, and for a further two minutes nobody moved or talked. Only a muted orchestral lament over the PA broke the silence. Then a bell shrilled loudly to signal the end of the bout. The gangplank was extended out to the platform and the announcer walked to the victorious Dickson, who had now managed to stand up. For a victor he looked sadly defeated, and seemed unable to take his eyes off his drowned opponent, only a couple of yards away from him. The plastic globe of money was lowered and Buck Lines unhooked it with one hand, holding Dickson's limp arm aloft with the other.

'The winner, Killtest fans! Danny Dickson from Arkansas! Winner of the forty thousand dollar purse in eleven minutes, thirty-three seconds.' The announcement was greeted with self-conscious, half-hearted applause. For many of the patrons the manner of DiCicco's death had obviously come as a shock. Lines announced an interval of fifteen minutes before the second bout, and retired, with Dickson, from the pool.

'Jesus H. Christ!' McSwiggan breathed. Taubes twisted the dimmers and the lights went up in the room. Simak mopped his head with a paper serviette, and went to the drinks tray.

Only General Ton Dinh Quan was unmoved, inscrutable in his dark glasses. 'Any sign of our British friend?' he asked nobody in particular.

McSwiggan and Ginorini realized that for the past quarter of an hour neither of them had given a thought to the agent who might be on the yacht, and the omission showed guiltily on their faces.

'I was just going to take a look around,' McSwiggan said. 'I'll check with Lao Man to see if his boys have come up with anything.'

The burly Irishman eased himself through the cabin doorway, past the guard, and walked down to the main deck. Chinese and Japanese technicians seemed to be everywhere. Under the big marquee they were moving camera positions, laying down video cables, adjusting equipment. DiCicco's body had already been removed, and the water was being pumped out of the swimming pool in preparation for the next bout. Most of the patrons had left their seats, which rose in steep tiers around the pool, either for the bars or the betting ring. Betting was a new innovation at Killtest events, franchised to bookmakers on a commission basis. And for the first time there was a favourite among the gladiators; over seven hundred thousand dollars had been bet on Huw Gwent, a Welsh-born wrestler who had already survived a previous Killtest bout and by the odds being offered was clearly expected to survive today's test.

McSwiggan nosed about, looking closely into the faces of the patrons, noticing that several Triad men were doing the same. During the interval he covered the length of the ship without result. When the bell sounded to warn the fans to return to their seats he went to the marquee, taking an aisle seat near the back which he'd observed had been vacant during the first bout. From there he surveyed the crowd.

Most of the men were middle-aged, and he was surprised to count a dozen women, wives perhaps. Almost half the audience were Chinese, a tribute to Lao Man's persuasive and influential syndicate; and in one section there was a Brazilian contingent who'd flown in the previous evening. Every single head he could see represented five thousand dollars, but one of them might represent millions – lost. It was crucial to locate that agent, and McSwiggan pondered on possible moves should he elude them by the end of the event. He had, probably, less than an hour.

The announcer ran through the preamble and a bell rang to signal the start of the second bout, codenamed THUNDERBALL. In the swimming pool, now empty and lined with shimmering plastic silver film, two men advanced towards each other. They were completely naked and each was armed with a steel ball, about the size of a large grapefruit, on the end of three feet of stout chain. The purpose of the balls was soon made clear as the stocky Huw Gwent swung viciously at his opponent. The other man parried and the two balls met in mid air with a sickening crack that echoed around the marquee. Contact with a skull would mean instant death.

Now that the audience was engrossed with the action down below, McSwiggan glanced around. One patron to his left, a European, was hiding his head in his hands, and the security boss noted the number of his seat for further investigation. He also took the numbers of the dozen or so vacant seats he spotted.

Both combatants in the empty pool were now taking gigantic swings at each other but their murderous balls, weighing some twenty pounds and requiring such an Olympian effort to swing, were easily avoided. THUNDERBALL had been Simak's idea, and it wasn't proving a very good one.

As the two gladiators pursued one another, McSwiggan rose from his seat and slowly circled around the marquee, walking along the gangways at the top of the tiers. Nobody noticed him, so intent were the spectators on the combat taking place. Triad guards were at the top of each aisle, each watching his designated area with glazed concentration. A mass cry went up and McSwiggan looked down to the spotlit circle. Gwent had stumbled, and the other man, quick to seize the opportunity, swung his lethal ball and chain. In a flash Gwent rolled over several times in a desperate attempt to get out of range, and the ball whizzed past his head with only inches to spare. The momentum of the steel ball swung his attacker around, and for a moment his legs were entangled in the chain, but by the time Gwent struggled to his feet he'd regained his balance.

McSwiggan dragged his eyes away. It was becoming apparent to him that the agent, if indeed he *was* in the audience, was unlikely to draw attention to himself. It was possible, also, that another agent might have been substituted; he might even be Chinese. He spotted Lao Man walking down one of the aisles and quickly followed him, catching him up near one of the marquee entrances.

'Any results from the body searches?' he asked. The Triad leader led him into a near-by cabin, and closed the door.

'Nothing yet,' he said. The guards who'd conducted the searching as the customers had come aboard had been instructed to report anything irregular, and the screening had resulted in fifteen suspects. All had been cleared, except two.

'I'm waiting on a radio-telephone call,' Lao Man said. 'Two identities don't check out so we're contacting the American ticket agents from Hong Kong. Regretfully it may take an hour or two – '

'An hour or two! The bloody event will be over – '

'I'm aware of that, Mr McSwiggan, but I assure you we're doing our very best.'

McSwiggan scowled, handed Lao Man his notes on the vacant seats, and without a word left for the monitor room.

As he entered, a deafening roar went up and surged through the ship. On the monitor bank one of the close-up cameras zoomed into the inert, bleeding body of a naked man lying in the centre of the silver-lined pool, and slowly panned up to the head. It had been smashed in beyond recognition. Several yards away, glistening with perspiration, Gwent sat on his haunches, breathing heavily. The Welshman had just become a Killtest statistic as the first gladiator to survive two bouts.

'Christ! Am I relieved!' Jay Simak shouted gleefully. 'For a while I thought we'd be waiting until Doomsday for a kill!'

Buck Lines had jumped down into the pool to declare the winner and to award the purse of a hundred thousand dollars. Ignoring the bloodied corpse, he jokingly lifted

Gwent's lethal ball, pretending to stagger under its weight. 'Well, folks,' he was saying into the microphone, 'You've just seen Huw Gwent here land a body blow that would've demolished Grand Central Station! What a fighter! What a man! Well, Huw, you might never make it in the pages of *Who's Who*, but let's hope you never appear in *Who's Thru!*' The shocked crowd managed only a few sporadic laughs.

'Someone should slit that bugger's jocular vein,' Ginorini suggested in the monitor cabin, pouring himself another large Scotch.

'Never mind the crap,' McSwiggan cut in. 'What about this fuckin' agent? Time's racin' on and you're all sittin' here, swapping gags.'

'Perhaps he isn't here at all,' Ginorini suggested.

'I *know* he's here,' General Ton Dinh Quạn said quietly. 'I can smell him. Spies have two smells: fear and fresh money – '

'Then why the hell don't you go down there and sniff him out?' McSwiggan interrupted testily. 'Do anything, anything – but don't just sit there massaging your gums and handing out advice I can't use.' He sloshed some Scotch into a tumbler and sat down, fuming and impotent, able to do nothing more than watch the third and final bout.

This much-heralded event had been dreamed up by Mrabet, who'd codenamed it WHIPLASH. Two women were to fight a man, each armed with a five-metre whip, each wearing a lethal package of plastic explosive taped over the heart. One crack on target would be sufficient to explode the primed charge, calculated to kill instantly.

Buck Lines, now wearing a bright blue jacket, went through his pre-match announcement while the restless crowd composed itself. Then suddenly, as though the sound control had suddenly been turned down, there was a strange hush. The two women were making their entrance, slipping out of long lamé gowns before climbing down the ladder into the silver-lined pool.

The appearance of the two female gladiators, Patsy Kemper and the redheaded Rusty Fender, produced an extraordinary effect upon the audience, as later recorded in a pseudonymously written piece published in the August issue of *Cain*:

'A SHIVER ran around the tiers of seats. Kemper was naked, flaunting her nudity with a contemptuous audacity, sure of the power of her flesh over all these men. Her Amazon breasts, the rosy nipples of which stood up as stiff and straight as spears, her broad hips, which undulated voluptuously, her generous thighs, the foamy whiteness of her skin – the effect was like Venus rising from the waves, with no veil but her long blonde hair. When she raised her arms to greet the audience the golden hairs of her armpits glistened in the glare of the lights that ran around the empty pool. There was no applause. The spectators' faces were tense and frozen, their nostrils narrowed, their mouths prickly and parched. A wind seemed to have passed over them, a subtle wind with hidden menace. And then Rusty Fender walked in to share the spotlight, and stood there, legs planted apart, a disturbing female proclaiming all the impulsive madness of her sex, revealing the gates of some unknown world of desire. She smiled, the deadly smile of a man-eater.

A collective whisper arose, swelling like a long, drawn-out sigh. There was some clapping, and binoculars were raised to a hundred eager pairs of eyes. The two women had taken possession of the audience, and now every man was under their combined spell. They emanated a wave of lust as though from bitches on heat, and it drenched everyone. Occasionally they cracked their whips and each crack triggered off flames of desire. Backs arched and tensed as though unseen violin bows had been drawn across them. In the front row one young man was half-lifted from his seat by passion. Others sat still and silent, the blood drawn from their faces; some were apopleptic; still others ogled the women with the admiring attention of horse-dealers judging mares. Towards the rear tiers, in the shadows, eyes gleamed cat-like, phosphorescent, speckled with gold. The atmosphere reeked with hot human scent. The whole audience seemed to sway slightly as if drugged by fatigue and excitement, totally possessed by the promised carnal delights to come. But the two women, with red blisters of deadly explosive taped to their left breasts, under the glare of the lights, in front of this fascinated audience of five hundred men, remained serene, victorious from this demonstration that their sex was sufficiently powerful to destroy the entire assembly.'

LOAZ

Now a single spotlight separated itself from the others and swung towards the side of the pool. Climbing down the ladder, naked except for the explosive blister, a head-hugging mask of red satin and a whip coiled around his waist, was a young man, probably no older than twenty. His sleek, athletic body glistened with the oil that had been rubbed over it. He walked to the centre of the pool to loud cheering, the whip handle swinging at his side like a sword.

A much larger plastic sphere descended into the blaze of the spotlights, and the three gladiators saluted it with rehearsed precision. This time the purse was the biggest ever offered for a Killtest engagement: two hundred thousand dollars

'Killtest fans, meet the Cochineal Kid from Mexico City!' Buck Lines shouted hoarsely. The announcement drew a fresh round of cheering. 'You are about to witness gladiatorial combat unique in the annals of Killtest,' he continued, with a pause before almost every word. 'The rules of WHIPLASH are these. No body contact. No use is to be made of the whip stock. The survivor – or survivors in the case of our lady gladiators – will collect the purse. And it's my happy duty to tell you folks that the management have just agreed that if the two women emerge victorious they will be awarded double the purse – two hundred thousand dollars each. There is no sexism in Killtest!'

Buck Lines had been reading this from a small prompt card. Unnoticed, the Cochineal Kid had untied the whip from his waist and with a single flick it suddenly snaked towards the announcer's hand. There was a sharp crack and the card disintegrated, leaving Lines holding a piece of cardboard the size of a bus ticket. The crowd bayed and stamped its feet while Lines, plainly awed by the proximity of so much explosive and an irresponsible whip-cracker, backed away from the gladiators and raced up the poolside ladder to safety.

The incident transfixed everyone in the monitor room, all thoughts of the spy hunt abandoned.

'I've got ten grand on the Cochineal Kid,' Ginorini said. 'At four to one. He'll tear strips off those scrubbers'

The three combatants took their places; Patsy Kemper and

Rusty Fender at opposite ends of the empty pool, and the Cochineal Kid in the middle. For a minute they limbered up and cracked their whips, and then the bell sounded for the bout to begin.

It was soon obvious that all three were expert whip handlers. The braided coils zipped and snapped like the long tongues of angry serpents. A touch with the knotted end could draw blood and produce crippling pain.

The Cochineal Kid was clearly at a disadvantage; for while one of the women threatened him from the front, her partner, demonstrating skilled teamwork, attacked him from the back. He also had some highly vulnerable exposed genitalia. Not surprisingly the Kid was the first to shed blood; a bright red diagonal weal suddenly appeared across his back, from shoulder to buttock. The knotted end of Kemper's whip had curled over his shoulder but had miraculously missed touching off the explosive by mere inches.

'Shit! That was close!' Simak croaked in the monitor room.

McSwiggan glanced up at Monitor Ten, which showed a wide-angle view of the audience. It was difficult to concentrate and he wished he had the nerve to order all the other monitors to be switched off. The small, crowded room sounded like a shooting range; the whip cracks reverberated from the loudspeakers like rifle shots. What if one of them *was* a gunshot?

The amazing contest was hypnotic in its effect. The spectators all held their breaths, expecting a dreadful explosion at any moment. All three combatants moved with graceful, even reptilian movements, but like goaded vipers there was deadliness in their grace. They danced among the flickering whips, jumping and diving to escape the fierce stings. Then the Cochineal Kid made a strike; his whip wrapped itself like a boa around Rusty Fender's waist. Instantly she spun her body towards the Kid, deliberately encircling herself tight in its coils almost to the stock, rendering him helpless and exposing him to Patsy Kemper. For half a minute it was merciless. Unable to free his whip the Kid huddled to protect his chest from the biting lash, yelling loudly with pain as it picked little pieces of flesh from his back. Finally, with a desperate effort, he ran fast towards one end of the pool, tugging his whip at the same time, and leaving Rusty spinning like a top. Once free, he cornered the two women and advanced towards them, whip curling up from the floor and crackling like lightning. Patsy dropped her stock; she'd been stung on the hand and it was paralysed. The disaster put her partner on the defensive, and while the Kid prevented Patsy from retrieving her whip she was pushed, yard by yard, into a corner. The young Mexican now had the upper hand and almost teased the two women, stinging them again and again. Suddenly Rusty cried out; her right nipple had been cut and a stream of blood coursed down her breast and belly to lose itself between her thighs. Five hundred expelled breaths resonated like reeds in a wind. The Cochineal Kid was now after a kill; even when Rusty turned away from him he expertly flicked the whip-end over her shoulders and even up between her legs, as exquisitely placed as lovers' kisses. There was no escape. It was torture. Even when Patsy Kemper managed to pick up her whip at last to flay their attacker from behind the young man hardly seemed to notice, despite the alarming red welts appearing on his body. For perhaps sixty seconds the flaying went on until Rusty could bear the torment no more and turned, in panic and tears, towards the Kid, a shocking sight with streams of blood running down her torso like a beaded curtain. Then, in a flash and an ear-shattering detonation she was hurled against the side of the pool and fell, after an awful second, on her face. The wound itself wasn't visible but evidence of it certainly was, for the entire corner of the pool was now carpeted in blood and flesh and even bits of bloodied bone.

This was the moment when the Cochineal Kid's remaining opponent had the option to capitulate or continue, and the bell rang to signal two minutes of neutral time. Patsy Kemper was allowed no advice. If she declared now it would be as a loser, and she would win nothing except her expenses. But to continue . . . ? She must be aware by now that she was outclassed. On the other hand the Kid might be weakened from loss of blood, and distracted by pain. But the Kid was also displaying some remarkable resilience and accuracy; proof of it was lying on the pool floor in a bloody heap. The echo of the explosion was still ringing in her ears. She was sickened; it was all so unbelievably horrible. Tiny pieces of her companion were stuck to her stomach and thighs, and she distractedly picked them off with a fingernail while she tried to make up her confused mind.

The audience, however, were far from uncertain as to what Patsy Kemper should do. 'Fight him!' the fans were yelling. 'Kill the Kid!' It swelled to a chant. 'Kill! Kill! Kill the Kid!' Whole sections of the crowd stood up and stamped and clapped, while the ushers and guards, fearful that the exuberance might get out of hand, ran about pushing the men back into their seats.

From the monitor bank it looked nothing less than an uproar. McSwiggan was watching the view of the crowd from Camera Ten.

'Stupid bastards!' he spat out. 'They all want the whip taken to 'em.'

'She won't continue,' observed Jay Simak. 'Rusty was the one with the guts. You can see Patsy's gone to pieces.'

One camera held a medium close-up on the pathetic figure of Patsy Kemper, a sadly disillusioned wreck of the proud Amazon who'd intimidated five hundred men with a single, arrogant flick of her whip only a quarter of an hour ago.

Simak continued to watch the monitors as the seconds ticked by.

'I'm surprised at you, Mel!' he said suddenly to Taubes, who was also viewing the astonishing scene with growing consternation. 'I thought you were serving the customers a better lunch than fuckin' hamburgers!'

The slight on his professionalism stung Taubes and he swivelled around in his chair. 'Hamburgers? What fucking hamburgers?'

Simak pointed to Monitor Ten. One man in the middle of a group of yelling, bawling men was standing there, munching a hamburger wrapped in white paper.

'Well, it's not our grub,' Taubes protested. 'You know damn well what we served for lunch – all Chinese dishes and salads. If some rube wants to bring his own lunch, that's his problem.'

They all watched the man, who stood out starkly from his hysterical fellows, a silent figure in a row of men chanting and urging the female gladiator to make up her mind and fight.

'It's a strange way to eat a hamburger, in any case,' General Ton Dinh Quan observed quietly from the rear of the room. 'He's not chewing.'

'Yeah!' McSwiggan agreed. He leaned over to the microphone on the little desk and flicked it open. 'Eight and Nine, get in on the character standing in the starboard section, middle row, about six rows up. He's eating a hamburger or something.'

The two monitors claimed their complete attention. At first all they saw was a blurred jumble of bodies as the cameramen moved in closer with their shoulder-mounted units, trying not to be spotted. Nine came up with the first close-up, from the aisle. The man had straight black hair and a large moustache. He wore a pink check shirt under a light coloured suit. From time to time he raised the small parcel to his mouth but, inexplicably, drew it away again without taking a bite.

Monitor Eight lit up as its camera zoomed in for an extreme close-up. McSwiggan snapped his fingers. 'That's no hamburger!' he shouted, springing up from his chair and making for the door. 'And that's no American!'

Five minutes later he was back. They'd all witnessed the capture on the monitors, achieved without fuss so that none of the crowd was aware of what had taken place. The interest of the audience was elsewhere, for Patsy Kemper had decided in the end to capitulate, to a massed chorus of booing. The agent had been seized as he left his seat with all the others.

McSwiggan produced a small parcel, and peeled aside the paper wrapping to reveal a cleverly made plastic replica of a hamburger. Between the two halves of plastic roll was a tiny silver camera, the size and shape of a cigarette lighter.

'A Velox-Scanic two-point-five,' he said to the others. 'British Intelligence.'

Lao Man came into the cabin, smiling.

'He's hot, then,' Ginorini said, somewhat alarmed. 'What the hell's he here for? What are we going to do with him?'

'Have no fear, Tony,' McSwiggan replied with a smile. 'I think we can safely leave that to Charlie Chan and his Boy Scouts.'

5

Kippy Leering sank into the Eezy-Lax chair and prised open the resisting green card covers of the thick file, marked COPY FIVE.

Pringle was pushing him a bit. Only yesterday he was still bed-bound at the Oaks, with numb fingers and toes, blood still in his pee, ponging like an opened grave and with a maddening twitch around his eyes – all the result, as they'd complacently told him, of the Immobilion-B still resident in his system. In that condition you'd have thought they'd have provided a limousine at least, right to the door, tucked him into bed and laid on a nurse. Not on your life! Strict Departmental practice won the day, and Pringle's pool driver had dropped him off at Bond Street Underground to ride the one stop to Marble Arch and then to walk the two blocks to his flat, lugging a heavy suitcase. Only it was difficult to be anonymous in the crowd when you were reeling like a drunk and exuding a hideous, powerful odour of crushed ants.

Now he was back in the tiny apartment, and although it was mid-July he felt strangely chilled in the sunless living-room. He hadn't been in the place for six months. He and Rosa had taken a two-year lease on the place; it was to have been their love-nest. Then five weeks afterwards he'd been posted to Moscow. He'd managed to fly back every few weeks or so, either at the Department's expense or on a diplomatic rebate ticket, but the succession of unannounced arrivals and sudden early-morning departures had proved too overwhelming for Rosa. She couldn't cope. It had all ended with an exchange of letters, sad, reasoned, resigned.

He wondered what she was doing now, and whether it would be wise to try and find her. She'd been a temporary interpreter at the FO; she'd left without a trace, but his memory of her was disturbingly tantalizing . . . dark featured, energetic, ample. A divorcee, she was three years older and with her he'd explored his sexuality far more than with any other woman he'd ever known; if she hadn't exactly taught him how to wipe his arse she'd certainly taught him how to wipe it properly. She had style, effervescence, flair . . .

Kippy contemplated the red-papered room. She'd had it done a few days before he got his Moscow notice. 'How percipient!' he'd commented, and they'd celebrated at the Gay Hussar with seven flasks of flavoured vodka. What a mad, intoxicating night that was! How different from their last night together . . . the shaggy rug with its patch of dark grey from an overturned ashtray sharply reminded him of their bitter argument, and a stray bra peeping from beneath the settee, of its sequel . . . she'd tearfully packed and had sat up all night, refusing to go to bed with him, before leaving in the morning.

His toes felt dead again and he struggled to his feet. Keep walking about, the white-coated pundits had said, wriggle your toes every fifteen minutes – to do with the circulation, or gangrene, or something. He wandered across the room. The Kentia palm had died from lack of water but judging from the angry notes pushed under his door the bathroom still leaked into the flat below. Ironic, that. A problem, too, because he couldn't just call *any* plumber in to fix it. The department had done away with fancy locks on the doors and windows of operatives' homes and had instead installed ingenious hiding places, sometimes bugged and booby-trapped. His was a compartment between the bath and the wall. 'Abso-bloody-lutely impossible to locate', the fixer had confidently informed him. Except by your friendly local plumber, that is.

Kippy found himself in the bathroom, confronted by his somewhat pallid image. In two years he'd be thirty, yet already there was grey in his hair. He yanked the light cord and inspected his lean face more closely. The short Moscow haircut and a long neck with prominent adam's apple helped suggest one of those attenuated El Greco portraits, ever so slightly ravaged. Yet he'd been told often enough that he had the face of an overgrown schoolboy; it was the eyes, of course, arrestingly blue and innocently large. And the easy, gangling walk of a tall man, still youthfully supple.

He sniffed, and raised an arm. He was wearing the same shirt he'd worn in Moscow the night they'd flown him out, unlaundered and disgustingly sour. Rosa had always attended to that sort of thing. He opened the bathroom cabinet and applied Rosa's half-used roll-on, and then some of her talc for good measure. Visions flew together like pieces of a jig-saw until he caught sight of the soiled clothing soaking in the bath. He hated laundromats; he never knew how to work the machines, how much washing powder to put in, how to pass the time there. That was a fresh challenge he'd have to face.

With the exception of the bra, deodorant and talc, Rosa had taken all her things but had pointedly left those items they'd regarded as 'theirs' – a chrome and glass coffee table from Harrods, two antique soda siphons, an Augustus John pencil sketch, the Guinness mirror, three blimp-sized Persian cushions and several Japanese prints. She'd returned, obviously to carry away all her books, and now the bookcase looked ridiculously bare, dominated by his leather-bound set of the works of Kipling. He'd been born on the tenth anniversary of the writer's death and the books, along with his Christian name, were a baptismal gift from his father. That was ironic, too; he'd never experienced a desire to read them. It could have been worse, of course; he could have been named Rudyard. Kim Philby, Pringle's *bête noire*, had coincidentally been named after Kipling's most famous character, and Kippy hoped the sum of all the ironies didn't add up to a portent . . .

The record player was his but most of the LPs had been Rosa's. There were only half a dozen survivors. The Herbie Manns were his and he stood there to replay mentally those sessions when they'd made love accompanied by the sexiest flute in the world. He picked up Albinoni's *célèbre Adagio* and placed it on the turntable, turning up the volume to compete with the rumbling traffic six floors below. The warm, solemn melodic line of the music was like slowly stirred honey, and he settled down again in the chair to tackle the pretentiously titled report: '*The Origins, Growth and Commercial Exploitation of Crypto-Sadism and the Killtest Phenomenon – A Memoir and Compilation* by Ludovic Bernard assisted by Samuel Humbert'.

The Introduction followed the usual pages of departmental warnings and disclaimers:

The Following is a compilation of notes and observations gathered from a variety of sources on the phenomenon of gladiatorial combat – humans fighting to the death, either willingly or forced, before an audience, and essentially for entertainment.

Although the psychological motivations that inspire approval of gladiatorial contests is undeniably strong, such impulses have been suppressed for humanitarian, aesthetic or political reasons over the past two thousand years with only occasional exceptions. The human sadistic urge is, however, apparently never totally quiescent, and typically seeks vicarious gratification in such spectator sports as animal-baiting and witch-ducking during the Middle Ages, bare knuckle contests in the nineteenth century, and cinematic violence and body-contact sports in our times.

Recently there has been an upsurge in the popular demand for competitive mortal violence at first hand, and there is evidence that this demand is being covertly gratified on a commercial scale.

The following Memoir attempts to set down the history of gladiatorial contest and to document the disturbing escalation of commercial porno-sadism during the last decade.

Although Sam Humbert was no stranger to him, Kippy had known the other author only fleetingly. Ludovic Bernard was regarded as a brilliant and versatile loner – and painstaking, too, for the Memoir began like the Bible at the beginning, with notes on the primitive foundations of sadistic entertainment. He riffled through the pages and skipped the historical section – Christians and lions, bare-knuckle fights and so forth – until an item on the Sudanese Nuba tribe caught his attention.

The stick and bracelet fighting of the Nuba. The inter-tribal contests of the south-eastern Nuba may be considered fights to the death, for the bouts ended only when one of the contestants was so weak from terminal exhaustion or from loss of blood to carry on. In recent times, however, referees stop the fight if one of the contestants appears in mortal danger. Each of the fighters is armed with a stick, which is soon abandoned, and a bracelet of razor-sharp bronze discs which is used to attack the face and skull of the opponent. Within minutes their bodies are covered in blood, which draws approving shouts from the gathered tribes. These contests have rarely been witnessed by outsiders but a British anthropologist reported the 'sickening thuds of bracelets against skulls' in 1930, and the German photographer Leni Riefenstahl recorded a bout in 1974.

This item was followed by a lengthy dissertation on similar African and Polynesian contests, but the Memoir only came to life for Kippy at the entry on boxing. From that point it completely seized his attention.

Boxing fails to satisfy. The high point of boxing as a 'soft' gladiatorial entertainment was reached on October 1, 1975, when Muhammad Ali beat Joe Frazier in an epic fourteen-round world heavyweight title fight in Manila. Millions of people around the world witnessed, and relished, forty-two minutes of unremitting violence. Hundreds of TV commentators and newspaper boxing writers wrung their vocabularies for every bloody adjective to describe the savagery of the 'Chiller in Manila'.

At its conclusion Ali, the supreme fighter of the age, had accumulated in just twelve months gross earnings of seven million pounds from sixty-three championship rounds. Subsequent fights have earned him purses as high as nine million dollars (for the Norton bout) but at the date of writing no serious contender has appeared to guarantee a contest of the sadistic calibre of the Manila fight. Indeed the search for such a contender has assumed an element of desperation, as when Ali was matched with Japan's pro wrestling champion Antonio Inoki in a six million dollar farce in Tokyo billed as the World Martial Arts Championship:

'A mis-match from the first round, Inoki spent most of the time on his back trying to kick the boxer, while Ali managed to land only two good punches in fifteen rounds – three million dollars per hit. The bout ended in a draw, and there was more fighting to be seen among the angry fans who had paid up to six hundred dollars a seat, when they realised the fight was

nothing more than a rip-off. Ali confirmed this later: "I was just in there to earn six million dollars," he said.'

Such ludicrous attempts aside, no other contest is likely to capture the enthusiasm of the world as the Manila spectacle did, and by the time a suitable challenger does emerge, boxing's biggest draw, now thirty-four, is likely to be in permanent retirement. To many thoughtful promoters, the bell at the end of the fourteenth round in Manila sounded the requiem for the heavyweights, and the question on their lips was: 'Where do we go from here?'

It was an appropriate time to examine the social validity of professional boxing. One British newspaper commented:

'It is impossible not to admire the strength, the skill, the raw courage of the fading ring giants who fashioned the Chiller in Manila. There is a horrible fascination about the spectacle of their reducing one another to a state of frenzied exhaustion over fourteen mean, mauling rounds. But can any thinking person avoid the conclusion that one day boxing will be ranked with gladiatorial combat and duelling as "sports" that civilisation outgrew? Muhammad the Mouth and Smokin' Joe have brought that day nearer.'

Since Manila, heavyweight boxing has clearly been unable to satisfy the morbid requirements of the crowd, and it is no coincidence that many of the theatres and halls which formerly offered close-circuit telecasts of boxing contests have now been converted to show Killtest events.

War as an outlet. War has frequently been considered an outlet for violent impulses in the human male, but in reality this claim is dubious. Modern warfare – as in the Vietnam conflict – is for the individual soldier more often a matter of *avoiding* hurt and injury; of endless waiting, of blindly following orders and counter-orders, of waste, of frustrating bureaucracy, of bewildering technology.

But when there exists an opportunity for close fighting or 'adventurous' warfare, there seems no shortage of mercenaries willing to risk their lives for an ideal of approximately £150 a week. I draw the reader's attention to a quarterly journal, *Soldier of Fortune*, launched in 1974 with a print run of 15 000 copies and currently selling just under a quarter of a million world-wide. The brutalizing editorial is carried into the extensive advertising section, which offers a large range of sophisticated weaponry besides serving as a global recruitment agency. Also offered are

'Mercenary of the Month' posters – pin-ups holding guns, grenades and other armament. The vital statistics printed with the poster are not the girl's, however, but the weapon's: 'Heckler and Goch G3–A3 7.62 NATO assault rifle'. The success of *Soldier of Fortune* has enticed other publishers to launch similar journals and it is currently estimated their combined circulation is above two million.

Erosion of values and morals by the media. The media must be held substantially responsible for the increasingly docile acceptance of vicarious violence in both life and entertainment. A photograph of a suicide in the act of falling from a building will always command the highest price from a newspaper. The AP photograph of General Ngoc Loan in the act of shooting a captive in the head during the Vietnam war was published in almost every daily newspaper in the world, to AP's great profit. The act of killing is news. The media offers very little resistance to the tradition of dwelling unhealthily on the morbid, the ghoulish and the bizarre, although there are isolated protests. With the announcement that, 'in keeping with Channel 40's policy of bringing you the latest in blood and guts and in living colour, you are going to see another first – attempted suicide', thirty year old Miss Chris Chubbuck, hostess of a morning talk show on Florida's WXLT–TV, pulled out a .38 revolver and killed herself, right in front of the cameras.

While newspapers and television have proved only too eager to place their stamp of approval on gratuitous violence in the guise of news, they are cowardly when it comes to extending the frontiers of sadistic gratification. This role, though, has been well filled by underground publications and the movie industry.

The toes again. Numb. And the stylus had been stuck in a groove of the Albinoni for the past five minutes. Kippy sighed and stood up in a wave of dizziness, then lurched over to the player to place a coin on the cartridge. The stylus dug in and found its way out of the groove.

The last bit in the report, he mused, was almost certainly Sam Humbert's contribution, for the Special Operations man hated the newspapers. In the late 1960s his mother in Winchester had been fined for refusing to pay a gas bill she was sure was incorrect. One newspaper ran the story with the headline SPY'S MUM CHARGED; of the seven paragraphs under it, four were fictions about her son, who was overseas at the time. Sam returned too late for the court hearing but soon established that the meter reader had made a mistake. He tried to have the case reopened and to force the newspaper to retract the story, but without success. Three months later his mother died, disillusioned and bitter. Only because of the newspaper's hopelessly inaccurate reporting was Sam able to preserve his cover, but just the same he had to endure a three-year stint behind a desk as a precaution.

Kippy walked into the tiny kitchen to make some coffee. An unwashed cup, its rim lightly stained with lipstick, remained in the sink. He filled the kettle, plugged it in, and opened the larder cupboard. It had always been well stocked, and it was still, only with stuff you hardly ever ate like fondue mix, canned guavas and tinned cocktail sausages. He picked out a cracker from an opened packet. It was flabby, like damp cardboard, and probably tasted like it. He made the coffee in Rosa's old cup, and returned with it to the living room to resume reading, sipping from the unsoiled part of the rim.

The sadism of the underground comics and unfunny funnies. If the younger generation – the under 30s – seem indifferent to the outrageous porno-sadism purveyed in the media today, the reason might be found in the so-called 'underground comics' published widely from the mid 1960s.

The typical features of an underground comic are: a simplistic and anarchistic attitude to all conventional behaviour, good and bad; the brutally extreme treatment of taboo themes; a total absence of any form of censorship on matters of presentation and taste; and a 'holier-than-thou' posture that the freedom with which artists depict violence has the inherent value of any uncensored art form.

By 1973, underground comic sex, which had been sublimated into horror and violence for nearly a decade, sought new depths for its expression, namely blasphemy and sadism.

Thus in a comic entitled *The New Adventures of Jesus* (1969), the artist has the Lord uttering, 'Well, I'll be dipped in shit!' and, 'God, it's hot!' among other blasphemies. In another, *Insect Fear No. 2*, a fight is staged to the death between Oldra of the Interstellar Unit Thranx 7 and One Tit Lucy of the 37th Death Rangers in a slime pit, with an all-female audience yelling, 'Tear her arm off and beat her to death with the bloody stump!' Cannibalism and necrogenic fantasies are commonplace; in *Mom's Homemade Comics* (1971) madmen are shown chopping girls to pieces and pickling them. *Death Rattle No. 1* has a female going down on a man; she bites his penis off, eats it, and proceeds to devour the rest of his body. Although the pages of underground comics are saturated with blood, disembowellings, decapitations and castrations depicted in clinical detail, the erotic connection is ever-present. Quite typical is a sequence showing a surgeon and his nurse copulating across the disembowelled body of a patient on the operating table. (See Exhibits H–M: *Hydrogen Bomb Funnies, Skull, Zap, Zip Comics, Krupp Comic Works* and *Real Pulp Comics.*)

The movies: from porn to sadism. The medium which has exercised most influence on public attitudes and behaviour in respect of sadism is undoubtedly the motion picture.

With the success of several commercial hard-core pornographic movies in the early 1970s – *Deep Throat* grossed 25 million dollars – a great proportion of the world's cinema screens were given over to a tidal wave of movies ranging from the artistically respectable *Last Tango in Paris* to the tasteless, inept 'quickie' made with a slag and a stud and a rented camera for less than the price of a family car. But indigestion soon set in and by 1975 the porno moguls were searching for fresh sensations. Last year a Swedish film director announced his intention to make a blatantly pornographic film about Christ, and at about the same time the actress Elizabeth Taylor turned down a £2.5 million offer to star in a blue movie. Similar offers to act explicit sex scenes were made to other famous stars. The price placed on Robert Redford's genitals was reportedly put at £3 million, and for half a dozen partings of the labia one film producer was prepared to pay £4 million to Julie Andrews. Even the ageing Bette Davis was allegedly offered £1.5 million for a half-hour session with three young studs.

'Snuff' movies arrive and depart. Unsuccessful in its campaign to win over the top stars of the industry, and with box office receipts faltering, the porno camp turned to sadism, bestiality and violence.

The most sensational development in this direction were the so-called 'Snuff' films which, until a few minutes before the end, looked much like ordinary pornographic movies. But at the moment of climax the unsuspecting girls – usually prostitutes lured into the studios for small fees – were murdered and even disembowelled.

'Snuff' films were reputed to be circulating from the time of the trial of mass murderer Charles Manson but the first verified viewing of the genuine product (known to the authors) was made in 1975, in Argentina. With no scarcity of trendy people willing to pay hundreds of dollars for a single viewing and 2500 dollars for an 8 mm print, mass production was soon under way for the American and Latin American markets. Inevitably the Mafia soon cornered the business.

Unfortunately the sanguine expectations of pornophiles received a blow when it was revealed that most of the 'Snuff' movies were fakes, with pig's blood and camera trickery substituted for the real thing. One such movie, distributed by the Monarch Releasing Corp. of New York, actually achieved national exhibition, although at the Regency Theatre in Philadelphia protests by women closed it after one day. By the end of 1976 this particular genre had lost all credibility among sado fans.

Other porno film-makers turned to bestiality, particularly in Denmark. The watershed film in this genre was *Animal Lover* (1973), purporting to be a documentary but essentially an account of the farmyard activities of a plump blonde farmgirl and a dog, a pig and a horse. Although at first arousing intense disgust even among the pornophobes of Times Square, *Animal Lover* was soon eclipsed by other bestial epics, involving both sexes and a menagerie of animals, pigs and donkeys being most favoured.

Exploiting a far more commercial vein, film-makers at all levels found the most profitable cinematic theme was violence, conventional and bizarre. *The Godfather* and *Godfather Part II* between them grossed 102 millian dollars in 1972–4, but this was only a preliminary. *Rollerball* and *Death Race 2000*, also successful, were far more explicitly sadistic, as was the sequel to the latter film, *Death Sport*, billed as 'the ultimate in violent sport set in futureworld times'. The genre still thrives, of course; the recent *Texas Chain Saw Massacre* hit a new peak in the exploitation of violent horror. Serious critics excused these films by claiming they were anti-violent because they presented violence in a 'jokey way'; in truth they were simply very badly made. No subterfuge was used in the movie industry, however, where such films were frankly promoted to exhibitors as 'shamelessly loaded with sex and violence'.

But for people wanting the ultimate in cruel depravity, movies were not the answer. As violent and sadistic as movies might be, they lacked the presence and unpredictability of live action, an aspect which was very quickly exploited by other sections of the entertainment industry.

Violence and sadism – live! A bullfight in Spain, where animals are tortured and slaughtered, excites little interest; should the same spectacle be presented in London's Trafalgar Square or in New York's Central Park, the response would be outrage. On the other hand Spaniards might think battery hens were being cruelly treated, whereas in Britain assembly line farming is accepted without protest by the huge majority. It seems to be a matter of social attitude.

Allowing that each nation has a degree of hypocritical stance as to what is cruel and what is not, the writers note a sharp increase in animal cruelty and its acceptance. During 1976 Sunday bullfights were introduced in Spain for the benefit of families with children; the matadors are midgets and clowns romp among the children and tease the bulls. The young audience can watch up to ten bulls being killed in a single bloody afternoon.

Rather less publicized is the resurgence of illegal dog fighting, particularly in Canada, the US and Mexico, in which two dogs tear, bite and claw at each other in a contest that only ends when one of the animals dies or is so badly mangled it has to be destroyed. This 'sport' is promoted by means of underground magazines – one is called *Pit Dogs* – which publish form, win-loss records and breathless round-by-round descriptions of recent fights: 'Dogs meet hard in the centre of the pit with Lou going for the shoulders and Missy holding him off with ear holds. . . . Lou gets into the shoulder deep and throws Missy and bites hard making Missy cry out, but Missy gets on the nose and busts an artery on Lou's cheek. . . .' Thousands of dollars change hands when a dog dies in the pit. In 1973 the American Dog Owners' Association estimated that 1000 such contests were held each year and from recent enquiries the so-called sport is growing enormously.

Animals vs. *humans*. While animals fighting animals to the death appears to gratify the sadistic whims of some, the prospect of man *vs* animal accommodates a greater range of appetites for violence. This appeal had already been exploited by two Italian documentary-style features, *Savage Man, Savage Beast I* and *II*, both compilations of footage gleaned throughout the world dealing with barbaric activities like the castration of sharks, tribal penis rites, primitive abortion techniques in Africa, mass drowning and mob lynching.

The first recorded live contest between a man and an animal this century was a match between a bare-handed, nineteen stone Vancouver garage attendant and a deliberately enraged bear, staged in a suburb of Portland, Oregon, in March 1976. The fight lasted only seven minutes and the man died in hospital three days later from extensive internal ruptures.

The most publicized event of this kind, however, was the abortive fight to the death between a shark and an Australian skin-diver for a 500 000 dollar purse – although how the shark was to collect if it emerged the victor was not explained. The duel was to have taken place in a 60 ft underwater arena off Samoa in mid 1975 and plans were advanced to have the contest relayed by satellite TV to several hundred closed-circuit cinemas in the US. The promoter, who estimated the event would gross 15 million dollars, told newspapers: 'It's a sick idea, but we've got a society and social system that's obviously sick enough to make rich men out of all of us.' After outraged protests – on behalf of the shark, not the human combatant – from the American Humane Society and the International Society for the Protection of Animals, the project was dropped and the promoter went bankrupt.

Although abandoned, the proposed man *vs* shark contest signalled the emergence of a new era in gladiatorial combat, two millennia after its demise. From that benchmark it was only a short step to the concept of man *vs* man in a fight to the death.

'Sporting' sadism. For interested promoters observing from the sidelines, the advent of what came to be known in Britain as 'Murderball' must have been encouraging.

The very essence of rugby is disciplined violence, and Murderball was, quite simply, a sixty minute free-for-all rugby game with only one rule – to go out and cripple the other team. 'The referee has almost nothing to do,' one player summed up. The first recorded game of this type was played at Watford, near London, in March 1976, between the Mean Machine and the Rest of Hertfordshire, each side fielding 25 men. Although there were no fatalities, eleven men were injured, three seriously. Luton police investigated, but as there were no complaints no action was taken.

Subsequently, about a dozen clandestine no-holds-barred

Murderball contests were staged in various parts of Britain during 1976, most of them grudge matches between rival groups. Two fatalities in Scotland were suspected to result from such games but because of lack of evidence local police took no action.

Kippy found his mind wandering. He had a sour taste in his mouth. and it wasn't from the stale coffee. Outside, the rumble of traffic was quieter; the lull between the going-home traffic and theatre time. He switched on the reading lamp, then rose, walked to the window and opened it. He looked down at the ants below. Violent? Even potentially violent? Impossible – London was such a friendly town. He'd lived thirty years without his body having received a single blow in anger, leaving aside the occasional schoolboy fracas. But perhaps things were changing. Coming back from the hospital in Surrey, Pringle's driver – who was forever taking devious short cuts that always turned out to be longer and slower – had driven the car through some back streets in Brixton. He hadn't bothered to put his finger on it at the time but now, recollecting, there had been disquieting signs: broken windows, boarded-up shopfronts, abandoned cars and a vague atmosphere of surliness. Of course you could say, 'So what!' because Brixton was a black enclave, and after the Notting Hill carnival riot blacks anywhere in Britain had reason enough to be violent. But that was a side issue; colour antagonism did not explain the hellish increase in violent crimes, the upsurge of violent worker groups, crowds running amok at football matches. Or had it always been like this? What about Auschwitz–Birkenhau? The slave trade? And at least crowds didn't gather to watch public executions any more. Perhaps today's mugger is merely yesterday's footpad; today's Broadmoor psychopath yesterday's Jack the Ripper. . . .

Kippy lit a cigarette and returned thoughtfully to his chair. He'd arrived at a section of the report prominently marked RESTRICTED on the customary yellow insert, a procedure which had always puzzled him but was doubtless appreciated by unapproved readers who were saved the trouble of wading through the inconsequential dross.

He turned the yellow page, and read on.

The organisational phase. By mid 1976 all the elements of the commercially viable gladiatorial contest were present, inviting exploitation. The experience of vicarious violence through the medium of the cinema had palled, as had pornography. Sadistic contests between animals proved to have only limited appeal and the lack of suitable contenders had driven heavyweight boxing into relative obscurity. A cheated public was ready and waiting for the real thing.

So were thousands of promoters, distributers and exhibitors, financially hurt either by law enforcement activity or – more commonly – by public satiation. In the US, Mexico and Canada alone, an estimated 2600 theatres equipped with closed-circuit TV apparatus lay idle.

The initial move to organise these outlets into a network was made by the New York based Mafia, which had been involved in the financing and distribution of pornographic films for several years. In a December 1975 investigation by the NY Police Department the Mafia was cited as having direct control of two porno publishing and distribution companies (*Screw*, *Smut*, *Hot Stuff* and *Hooker*, combined circulation 300 000) and with having interests in several national porno film circuits. Profits for 1975 alone were estimated at more than 25 million dollars, a large proportion of which found its way back into legitimate film production.

No strangers to violence, the Mafia soon realised the commercial potential of an organised network of closed circuit outlets for purveying sadism. Its experience with 'Snuff' movies confirmed the vast public appetite for acts and contests of this kind. Acquiring the outlets was a simple matter. By making examples of those exhibitors and theatre owners who resisted, the rest promptly succumbed to traditional Mafia pressures. It was like Prohibition all over again.

By October 1976 the Mafia had a hold of some kind or another on sixty per cent of all the closed circuit theatres in North America; and once these theatres staged an illegal exhibition the owners and staff were subject to blackmail and thus effectively under Mafia control. At the same time other clandestine circuits were drawn into the organisation, including the dog pits, porno theatres and many gun clubs. The net went out internationally, too, resulting in a hook-up with the Triads in South East Asia and dozens of individual entrepreneurs in the Middle East, Africa, South America and Europe. With something like 4000 outlets secured, all that remained was to equip them and to create the product.

The man who played the biggest part in putting this circuit together is reputed to be Antonio Ginorini, one of the Gambino *mafiosi*, then the largest and most powerful of all the Mafia families in the US. Ginorini seems to have realised that the potential of the enterprise he was planning would be beyond the resources even of the Mafia, reputedly one of the biggest 'businesses' in the country. More significantly, the Mafia is still subject to harassment by law enforcement bodies at all levels, and its entry into an entirely new field of organised crime would almost certainly invite an all-out war from the government. Despite its many friends – few politicians in the US can state with truth and certainty that at least some of their funds are not Mafia tainted – Ginorini must have been less than enthusiastic about any move which might upset the existing *entente cordiale*, however tenuous.

Extrapolation by S. Humbert. At the September 1976 national council gathering of the Mafia in Los Angeles, Ginorini proposed that the mob should relinquish direct control and administration of the infant organisation, codenamed *Killtest Inc.*, suggesting instead an independent majority shareholder. Half the profits, he argued, were better than none. But who could take over and run this gigantic undertaking? Who could be trusted to protect the Mafia's investment?

Hearsay has it that Ginorini had already approached a likely partner, a senior official in the CIA, and won support for his appointee. The man had access to sufficient funds, valuable international connections and a proven flair for adventurous management. His key position in the CIA also gave him access to information on matters of national security, sufficient to deflect government and police investigations. He was the ideal chief executive of the proposed enterprise.

Analysis has shortlisted thirty-six top-level CIA personnel who conform to twenty per cent of the suspect model, but in the absence of further input, analytical methods have been discarded for the present.

The founding of Killtest Inc. (NB: The following notes are presented in scenario form in view of the considerable extrapolation involved in relating known facts from sources of variable status. LB & SH)

Killtest Inc. became a fact in October 1976, headed by the Mafia–CIA puppet who shall be referred to as K. K not only inherited working control of a network of closed circuit outlets set up by Ginorini, but also some daunting administrative headaches. The fact that he was able to overcome these in such a short time points to K as a man with stupendous drive, business acumen and imagination, operating from a secure and potent power base.

One of K's first moves was to establish separate divisions within Killtest Inc., each specialising in a particular aspect of the operation and each headed by a forceful individual.

The first of these was an engineering unit which within four months had re-equipped the biggest of the closed-circuit theatres and locations with highly sophisticated video receivers linked by cable to one of three stations capable of receiving satellite signals. Made to order by electronics factories in Japan, Korea and Taiwan, the entire transmission system is filtered through Infinicron digital scramblers so that while the organisation's signals may be intercepted and monitored at any point by government agencies (as indeed they were and still are) all that can be seen is video snow and low-pitched hum. The scrambling system is variable and infinite and is generated by three interlocked computers, ensuring that the signal is not decoded into picture and sound until just before it reaches the 10 ft square rear-projection chromagen screen on which the patrons view the action. Each outlet receives a *different* scrambled signal and the coding changes constantly, at suspected half-second intervals. A surveillance unit of MI–8 in Washington, retained after the war, and other government cryptanalysis bureaux, have been trying to break the code system since April this year without success. Although several defecting employees of Killtest's engineering division (part of which hides behind the cover of a New York firm calling itself the Signal Videotronics Corporation) have been interviewed by the FBI, insufficient information has emerged to be of any real assistance.

The engineering unit is also responsible for the remote telecasting of each gladiatorial bout staged by the organisation, the transport and setting up of the equipment, and pirating satellite time – a completely new phenomenon. Although it is known that three or four Killtest events have been staged, the exact locations have not yet been established.

At this point in the Memoir a pink Addenda slip had been inserted, dated 12/7/77:

Bernard has reported a Series VII (seventh event) Killtest at Paranagua in Brazil, and is currently investigating a report of Series VIII to be staged in the vicinity of Hong Kong.

The addenda was initialled SP. Kippy glanced at his watch; it was 21 July. Perhaps Ludovic Bernard was in Hong Kong now, and would return with enough evidence to bust the thing wide open. It was all so fantastic, like something out of *Dr No!* What on earth were the Americans doing, letting them get away with it like this?

He daydreamed for a while, then read on.

Killtest Inc. – the showbusiness aspect. In addition to the engineering unit an entrepreneurial division also appears to have been established to recruit gladiators, publicise events and stage the contests.

Recruitment is effected by direct contact, word of mouth or, increasingly, by advertisements in selected underground journals. The advertisements are usually for some spurious mail order service and may contain the codeword DADIN hidden in the text. DADIN is the acronym for *Do Anything, Die If Necessary* (see Exhibit 2). The advertisers are usually unsuspecting agents, unaware of the true nature of the advertisements.

It is also believed that Killtest enlisting agents are active wherever there are likely to be suitable recruits; during its investigation of British and Irish mercenary recruitment for the Angola war in 1976 a Foreign Office team established that at least fifteen men who applied through known channels never reached Angola and still have not been accounted for.

Killtest recruiters are also on the lookout for distressed and desperate people. The FBI has a file on such people who have had probe contacts from suspected Killtest agents. Most of those interviewed had placed 'Help' ads in newspapers, of which the following are typical:

'VIETNAM WAR VET NEEDS DOLLARS. Help. Box 18, Blackstone, Va. 22184.'

'UNEMPLOYED VET needs money desperately. Please help. Box 316.'

'PLEASE HELP. $6,850 needed a.s.a.p. Send donations to Wakefield, Box 700, Junction City, Kan. 67905.'

'THREE YEARS BAD LUCK. Four children, incapacitated wife. I know you'll help. All donations blessed. R. deVore, Box 112, Clinton, Mo. 64479.'

As might be expected, many of these advertisements are placed by people whose only distress is a consuming greed, and many would be likely to view a Killtest proposition favourably. It is believed the FBI is now placing similar ads in newspapers across the US in the hope that eventually a Killtest scout will make contact.

Officers of our Bangkok station are currently investigating a line of enquiry which has suggested that a number of DADINS – Killtest gladiator recruits – have been 'stockpiled' at a secret training centre in Thailand in readiness for future contests.

The Killtest box office. The existence of Killtest events is now generally known, as this excerpt from a recent issue of the show business paper *Showbill* testifies:

'KILLPIX NOW IN BOFFO CLASS

After a slow climbout, highly illegal killpix are now scoring boffo coin for courageous exhibs.

Although the product is as nasty as ever, pro presentation and triple billing are pulling customers to an estimated 2000 locations thru US and Canada. One East Coast location is rumoured to peel off 15G a night for closed circuit screenings of "live" killtests and 5G a night for video replays. Sadophobes shell out $200 and more a head for the taped shows.

Underground tradesters forecast a banner year ahead for the killpix circuit which has neatly regenerated the fading porn market to what looks like a gross billion dollar boom.

The law is still the problem but with organization muscle and Mafia pacting backing killpix, distribbery is less nervous about handling the hot product. The fact that two recent prosecutions failed to stick is seen as an encouraging sign that the authorities may be prepared to live and let die.

Most of the early technical hitches have been eliminated and originations have speeded up from six weeks apart to almost two events a month. Sado buffs and other sensation seekers can now drool over three killings a night in some weeks, guiltless in the knowledge that the actual "performers" earn up to 200G – if they live to collect.

But despite current boffo confidence the long-term future of prohib killpix remains in doubt. Not everybody goes along with the killpix interpretation of an Irish poet's line that "the quality of life is often best seen in the process of dying".'

Such after-the-event news items, however, are of little use to people who actually wish to witness a Killtest performance, either live or on videotape. These must be contacted via underground channels used to disseminate Killtest information.

Word of mouth is still probably the chief means of circulating news of showings, locations and playdates; and fear of reprisal from the organisation ensures security; you hear very little loose talk about the contests. Every patron is apparently screened by Killtest's security division and it seems that once a client is on their files it is impossible to get off: an effective guarantee of future patronage. Doubtless blackmail is frequently resorted to. This applies especially to live performances, to which patrons graduate from video screenings. Like membership in some secret societies it is considered a privilege to be invited to pay out £2000 and more to attend a live event.

In recent months some publishers have begun to pirate hearsay information for republication in underground magazines like *Sadie, Cain* and *Gladiator,* which also carry long and clinically detailed descriptions of Killtest bouts. These magazines sell for five dollars but their value to sadistically-inclined readers is limited because much of the information is inaccurate. But they are increasing in number and improving in precision.

Killtest security. Evidence exists that Killtest Inc. has its own security arm and private police force, probably Mafia-backed, which has been active since December last year. A known *mafioso,* Carmine Tabasco, at present being held by the FBI on several charges including contempt, is suspected with having some connection with Killtest Inc.'s strong-arm unit and will be placed under close surveillance when released at the end of this month in a 'homing pigeon' gambit.

Abundantly clear is the fact that the security division is run by cold, brutal killers. At least six and possibly thirty homicides during the first four months of 1977 are thought to be connected with Killtest activity. There have been several arrests but no charges have been brought which bear directly on to suspected Killtest operations; although one interesting coincidence is that two of the alleged killers – one in Atlanta and the other in Las Vegas – were both armed with the latest high velocity L39A1 rifles equipped with the Rank image-intensifier night-sight, the most sophisticated sniper's weapon available today. This lead is being investigated.

The present writers believe that Killtest Inc.'s security force is a formidable private army with representation in many countries, including Britain. One possibly significant finding is a reference to an *armée privée* indicating some French or Canadian connection. And it appears there is more than passing contact with the Triad, which, although headquartered in Hong Kong, has an influential branch in New York. Our view is that the security division consists largely of professional killers recruited from the Mafia and Triad secret societies, and their strength should not be underestimated.

Stapled to the edge of a page at this point in the Memoir was another pink slip of paper headed *Addendum B* (14/7/77). Under this was a short note typed on a large executive machine:

TAPE FROM FBI TODAY NOTES LAO MAN TRIAD CHAPTER 14–K SIGHTED NEW YORK DEPARTING PAN AM 001 FOR HONG KONG PRESUMABLY OVERSEE FORTHCOMING KILLTEST. AS HE KILLTEST SECURITY SUSPECT INTEND TAILING FROM KAI TAK AIRPORT ON ARRIVAL. DORIC.

Doric was one of the code names used by Ludovic Bernard, and he'd obviously sent the message from the old Hong Kong station after a tip-off from the FBI. But at the bottom of the slip someone had handwritten a further note, dated 15 July, sadly recording that Bernard had somehow missed sighting the Triad chief at Kai Tak.

The administration. As previously noted, collective intelligence points to a senior CIA official as the administrative mastermind of Killtest Inc. referred to as 'K'. This has created a profound handicap as far as a multinational investigation is concerned because necessarily the CIA must be by-passed until this official is located and removed. Thus all US enquiry is proceeding through the FBI which is also feeding several CIA stations with fictional information intended for executive consumption. Until the security of Killtest Inc. is sufficiently breached, the FBI intend continuing with their holding operation apart from three other lines of investigation.

In November 1976 the FBI circulated an interim memo to

the effect that a bag-man was active among Vietnamese expatriates, mostly ex-military personnel, collecting for a purpose unknown. Estimates of the take range from five to fifteen million dollars, much of it in bullion. This money is now presumed to have finished up in Killtest coffers and taps have been approved on a number of suspected contributors. At the same time, known links between senior CIA staff and high-ranking Vietnamese Army officers in the US are also being explored.

In May, 1977, a further FBI memo was issued at the conclusion of an investigation into the Muzak Corp. In February a US Air Force Electronic Reconnaissance team detected foreign test transmissions being bounced to satellite receiving stations set up by the Muzak Corp. as part of a long range plan to supply customers with canned music in forty-nine countries. In March similar strength signals were intercepted but scrambled in code of the digital type known to be used by Killtest Inc. Muzak complicity was suspected but the FBI is now satisfied the signals were received unintentionally and the company was the victim of airwave piracy. The FBI now possesses thirty-four of these taped test signals which are currently being studied by several government and military cryptologic bureaux.

Apart from these tenuous leads very little else is known about the administrative machinery of Killtest Inc. or about the individuals who control it. There is speculation about the probability of foreign complicity, namely by South Korea and Chile. Both countries have been infiltrated to saturation level by the CIA which operates with considerable government support there. In South Korea the CIA front is the Institute of Current Affairs in Seoul, and has an abysmally dirty record. The situation in Chile is not so clear but obviously the Pinochet regime owes such a great debt to the CIA for its support in ousting the socialist Allende government that anything is possible. All CIA officers who have been involved with affairs in Vietnam, South Korea and Chile during the past five years are currently the subjects of investigations by the FBI.

The financing of Killtest Inc. (Note by C-22 Economic Intelligence Unit). With so little evidence at hand the views of the unit must be treated as highly speculative. It seems that this illegal organisation is substantially funded from a variety of sources and we would put the possible capital outlay as high as £40 million and the payroll at between 3000 and 4000. In other words we are suggesting that Killtest Inc. operates on a scale comparable with that of a large multinational corporation, although with one important exception: the investors would expect financial returns ten times those reasonably expected by legitimate investors. This leads us to believe that long-term profits must be of the order of £400 million per annum, based on a turnover of £1000 million. If this is in fact the scale of the operation, then we are dealing with an awesome problem.

Problems of law enforcement. To date of writing there have been only four instances of attempted law enforcement actions, all in the US. Three were local police actions while the remaining case was a Federally-backed test raid. The results were negative and only minor charges were laid.

The difficulty in enforcing the law on Killtest activity at consumer level is the absence of evidence. In the case of the FBI raid in Austin, Texas, the theatre manager was able to trip the scrambler mechanism which immediately switches the Killtest programme off and replaces it with a feature film which is transmitted in parallel – an ingenious counter-measure intended for just such occasions. Electronics experts brought in by the FBI were unable to resume the original transmission. None of the 165 patrons in the theatre at the time could be charged, and the closed circuit receiving equipment, which was impounded, had eventually to be returned to the owner.

In one of the other cases (Lansing, Mich.) two police officers, posing as patrons, watched a suspected Killtest show for half an hour and witnessed a 'kill' – two naked men fighting hand to hand on a plank below which was a forest of foot-high needle-sharp spikes. The manager, his assistant and 73 male patrons (all members of a local gun club) were arrested and charged on various counts, but none of the charges were proceeded with because the manager, represented by the Killtest legal team, successfully argued that what he was exhibiting was a fictional simulation and not the telecast of a real event. The equipment was also impounded and examined but beyond establishing that a complex system of combinations was required to operate the receiver – known only to the manager – little was learned. The only success that can be claimed is that four suspected Killtest outlets have been temporarily closed, but it is realised this is not the method to be pursued to permanently stamp out this organisation's activities.

The FBI is well aware that police actions of this kind at grass roots level are attended by grave risk. Already three police officers and one FBI agent have been murdered in circumstances which implicate unidentified Killtest personnel.

Recommendations. As this Memoir only summarises a small proportion of a mass of collected evidence and material studied by the writers, they feel the opportunity should be taken to add certain recommendations, based on *all* the documentation, as to future action.

1. That no contact whatsoever be made with any CIA officer, either in the US or abroad, by any of our own officers associated with this enquiry.
2. It would not surprise the Killtest organisation to find that government agencies are investigating its activities. Therefore various CIA stations should be informed that an enquiry is in progress by this department, but misinformed about its direction and progress.
3. Mr Ludovic Bernard, co-author of this compilation, is to leave immediately on field duty specifically to follow up aspects of the report. It is hoped he will return with sufficient evidence on which to build a base for future investigation and action.

Kippy closed the binder and contemplated its green cover. At the beginning the document displayed the cold distance of most reports of its kind, but by the end it conveyed something vaguely alien, certainly something discomforting, to his gut. Perhaps it was cramp from sitting still for so long, or the numbing effects of the Immobilion-B shot. He rose stiffly, walked to the kitchen, and returned with a vodka and flat tonic, jinking the ice against the glass for company.

He picked up the manila packet which had accompanied the report and shook out the contents on to the coffee table. A dozen photographs slithered across the glass top; each had the red C–17 file stamp on the back. He turned them over, one by one, with a growing sense of shock. The photographs were of Killtest bouts or of the victims. A naked man trussed on a sort of perch in the throes of electric shock. The naked body of a woman, or what looked like a woman, lying in a a pool of her own blood, blown apart by some diabolical explosive device. Most of them were fuzzy blown-ups, probably taken surreptitiously by a member of the audience. A man, still alive, but surely bleeding to death from thousands of cuts caused by close-set lines of razor blades set into the floor on which he'd just wrestled for a fortune and his life – and lost. The corpse of a young woman lying on a wooden bench, her legs sprawled apart as though broken, and, standing behind her looking confused, four naked men. The title told it all: NECROBANG.

Kippy sifted through the rest, deliberately shielding his feelings with indifference and a second vodka. The barbarism was appalling, but he knew from experience that anger was an occupational hazard in his job; it had to be suppressed. It made you lose sleep at night and played hell with your judgement. It pumped out your adrenalin when you needed it least. The obscenities before him were depraved in the extreme, loathsome acts by man against his kind. He picked up the photograph of the dead girl again and looked closely into the face, trying to see into the blurred, anonymous greyness but not to imagine the unspeakable horrors of the last minutes of her life.

The photographs weren't in colour but he could see why someone had dubbed Killtest performances 'Red Theatre'. He studied a mugshot; on the reverse it said 'Valentina Corrosco, Mexican national, prostitute, disembowelled. 6.2.77'. The girl had posed before the event with an uncertain smile, and the eyes were apprehensive. A poor, dumb tart, enticed by a few lousy pesos to entertain thousands with her death at the moment of orgasm. It could have been a moment of joy and creation, but fashionable depravity had decreed otherwise.

Kippy drained his vodka and chewed the ice cube. Then the telephone rang, the grey one. It was Pringle, his voice down to a croaking thirty cycles a second.

'We've just had a signal from Hong Kong,' Pringle said. 'They've just found Ludovic Bernard. Dead.'

6

SunFun Holidays Ltd was one of a dozen small travel agencies dotted along the Haymarket, with nothing in particular to distinguish it from the rest. It had been carefully designed that way.

It was just after nine the next morning that Kippy emerged from Piccadilly Circus Underground and sauntered past the tacky tourist bistros towards Trafalgar Square. The dizziness had gone but his shoes felt as though they had marshmallow soles. He paused by the plate-glass door of SunFun Holidays, then entered, vaguely examining the display of brochures on a rack along one wall. Nobody else was in the place except Joyce and Bruce, behind the mock marble counter. He knew them by sight and they knew about him, but not a flicker of recognition passed between them. That was training for you.

He used the July code.

'Monaco . . . you don't happen to have a brochure on Monaco, by any chance?'

'Monaco . . . yes. Seven-day package or fourteen?'

'I was told there's a twenty-two-day holiday. . . .' Kippy checked his watch; yes, it was the 22nd. What a mad business, pretending to plan a holiday the day after Ludovic's death!

'Yes, I'm sure it can be arranged,' Joyce said brightly; an artificial brightness. She'd heard the news, too.

'Um . . . good. And Oman – do you have the scheduled services to Oman?' Just as well Joe Q. Public wasn't listening. Monaco and Oman . . . !

It was the second half of the code, O for Oman, the seventh month, July. January was India, February was West Samoa, then Italy, Sweden, Hungary, Turkey, Oman, Egypt, Norway,

Tunisia, Ecuador, with Romania for December. The first letters spelled out I WISH TO ENTER. Cute, huh? Pringle's, of course.

Kippy heard the lock bleep and opened the door marked MANAGER, bounding up the steep dark stairs two at a time to halve the likelihood of accident. Pringle met him in silence at the top. Behind him stood Angela Hotchkiss in a black twin-set and skirt, and with a very stiff upper lip. Nobody said a word. Pringle returned to his desk and sat down to resume sipping his tea. A white fleck on the surface betrayed the aspirin in it.

Angela Hotchkiss's presence was a surprise. Although she rarely saw field duty she was probably the most unlikely agent in the service. Perhaps that was her strength. Of indeterminate age in the forties region, she walked as though she had a tubular steel backbone, emphasizing her tallness by a habit of peeping over her spectacles. She spoke as though she had a permanent speck of dust at the back of her throat in a voice a quarter-tone higher than you expected. Her blonde-grey hair was cut unfashionably and unwisely short above a long neck which disappeared either into a severe suit or one of a dozen twin-set combinations; to add that she was aridly flat-chested would be superfluous.

Angela's private life was as secretive as her figure. She lived with her mother somewhere north of Paddington, that much was known. Office speculation was that apparently no man had ever stumbled in her path, or if he had he'd made a quick getaway. 'Unfair!' cried some, generously presuming some succulent sensuality buried deep beneath the corsetry, but Sam Hubert had succinctly, if crudely, crystallized the poor woman's departmental image for all time. 'Screwing Angela,' he'd said in his cups one evening, 'would be like giving up alcohol. It can be done, but why do it?' Nevertheless, to her rescue came a cluster of sobriquets; from Whitehall to St James's she was known variously as Angel Crotchkiss, Angela Hotkiss, Hotlips, Hotpiss, Hotchiecrotchie and even Jellybaby. But never mind; to all the chiefs she was sexually incorruptible, and few would claim to be that.

Kippy went over to the window and peered through the

nylon net. Not a sound from the traffic below came through the triple glazing; the buzz was from Pringle's bugging scanner ticking over under his desk. Across the roadway Sam Humbert was extricating his large frame from a cab.

Angela let out a quiet sob and Kippy turned to see Pringle hurry to her with his handkerchief. He'd forgotten that she and Ludovic Bernard had worked together for years, from the Cold War period almost, specializing in Russian spyship policy.

Sam came in and unbuckled his crumpled fawn trenchcoat. He always wore it, even on warm days like today, and the mileage was beginning to show. He sat down without a word and Kippy walked across the spongy, double-carpeted floor to slump in the seat beside him.

Pringle cleared his throat and unexpectedly found something to clear. After an awkward pause Angela handed his handkerchief back and he spluttered into it.

'Well,' he said, after a bout of hacking. 'You've all heard the unfortunate news.' He opened the folder in front of him and withdrew a folded sheet of primrose paper a yard long, a decode from Telex Central. 'It's bad enough, but the details are worse.' He glanced down at the sheet. 'They found Ludovic yesterday. Spotted by a fishing junk and picked up by the Hong Kong police, two miles off the island at the mouth of the Canton River. The postmortem showed his lungs full of seawater, but with traces of chlorine – '

'Swimming pool – ?' Kippy prompted, before he could check himself.

'Plus seawater,' Sam added. 'Swimming pool near the sea. Or on a boat?'

'Or on a cruise liner?' Pringle put in. 'Who knows? Speculation. Anyway, they picked up another body, also drowned, Caucasian, half a mile from Ludovic, with one left leg missing . . . lopped off surgically.'

'Did he have two?' Sam asked, straight-faced.

Pringle stopped, puzzled. 'Two? Two what?'

'Two left legs.' The black throwaway gag was Sam's way of hiding his true feelings. With half a smile Pringle showed he understood; they'd known each other for a long time. But the joke came as a shock to Kippy.

'The second body,' Pringle continued, 'may or may not have anything to do with Ludovic, but we're going to assume it has. Because I have to tell you that Ludovic was tortured.' He paused for perhaps ten seconds. 'He last reported on the morning of the fifteenth. According to the pathologist's report he died on the nineteenth, so we have to account for four days. The extent of the effects of the torture suggest it had taken place over several days . . .'

'Do we know whether he managed to get a look at the Hong Kong Killtest?' Kippy asked. 'When was it – ?'

'Night of the fifteenth. No, we don't know. There could be something delayed in the pipelines, but unlikely. I got his prelim on the Killtest show at Paranagua, only the barest outline but the most valuable first-hand document produced on this business so far. But beyond that, nothing.'

'They could be on to us, then?' Kippy suggested.

Angela Hotchkiss was horrified. 'No, he'd never talk! Never!' Stout fellow, Angela.

Pringle pricked her balloon. 'Now, now. Who knows?' He held the decode out to her. 'You can read the details of the torture in private, if you like. He must have gone through sheer hell. Frankly, I'd have talked like Capital Radio. Burns, shock, drugs, an arm and three fingers broken, an eye – so who knows? I'm sorry, Angela, but we have to assume the worst . . . that he did.'

Kippy broke a long silence after this; what might have happened to Ludovic Bernard didn't bear thinking about. 'So where do we go from here?'

Pringle folded the telex and closed the folder. 'Formalities first. Lady and gentlemen, those of us now in this room constitute the Anti Crypto-Sadism Unit, Division D.'

Sam scowled. 'The wha-at?'

'Don't blame me,' Pringle shot back defensively. 'It came down from the Assistant Deputy.'

'Ak-soo. . . .' Sam worried over the cheated acronym. 'It doesn't even spell anything.'

'It isn't supposed to. Anyway, we're the bunnies. You've

been dilettanting for a couple of months already, helping Ludovic with that report. I was pulled in a week ago, then Angela, and finally Kippy. They had to get some sort of a team together to spend the money, I suppose, and I very much doubted they really believed in it. But finding Ludovic last night has convinced them that this Killtest thing is an ugly business, and dangerous, too.'

'It's like they only notice you when you croak,' Sam commented.

'Yes, it's a pity it needed a man to die to underline the importance of this investigation,' Pringle went on. 'But there it is. We've lost one of the team and we haven't even started – '

'You're forgetting Ludovic's report, aren't you?' Sam interrupted. 'We put three months into that, and he was still working on it – '

'Yes, yes,' Pringle corrected. 'I'm sorry and I apologize. The report is a tremendous foundation. It was thoughtless of me.'

Sam looked down at his shoes, apparently satisfied. But it was difficult to know what he was thinking, he was so unpredictable. 'Original,' somebody had said once. 'That *rara avis*, an original!' There certainly was much about him that was different. Although six foot four and fifteen stone, Sam had a larynx that seemed stuffed with cottonwool and a slow drawl that earned him the nickname of 'gentle giant'. The voice, loaded with fruity vibrato, had never, in anyone's recollection, ever been heard above a near whisper, even in anger. His body took its cue from the voice, a constant trap for strangers who tended to dismiss Sam as some kind of statue. It was quite the reverse. He'd taken his doctorate of philosophy at Oxford at twenty-five and had packed more in the subsequent decade than most men manage in a lifetime. He began by specializing in statistical method, equations of group theory, computer analysis and crypto-systems – the latter specialty leading him into MI6. But all that was merely Sam's professional deskwork. In the late 1960s he'd taken off for two years to East Asia, learned four languages, immersed himself in Oriental culture, carried out several successful assignments and had returned as one of the section's leading China watchers. He promptly completed an extension course in forensic medicine, wrote a textbook on international law affecting intelligence activities, and earned a black belt in judo. Meanwhile he reviewed books for a literary journal, collected rare icons, sailed his own yacht, edited a book on the poetry of Pound and Yeats, supervised the restoration of a group of Georgian houses in Brighton – and with his left foot cracked the proverbial walnuts. All without apparently moving faster than three miles an hour.

This was not, obviously, your typical counter-intelligence man, and in fact Sam Humbert's only concession to the popular image of a spy was absurdly theatrical: the shabby Aquascutum trenchcoat he wore more often than he ought on account of the shabbier clothes underneath.

Somehow he'd found the time to marry but not the time to sustain and preserve marriage, and two years ago joined the growing band of divorcees in the department. Absence, he discovered, did not make the heart grow fonder. But with his roughcut shock of blond hair, the attractive blend of gentleness and manliness, and a quiet, wry style, Sam was rarely alone, even though he might prefer to be. The current interest was a fashion designer named Sally; she hated yachting, had difficulty reading even *Vogue* and couldn't tell an icon from an ink bottle, but somehow it seemed to be working.

Following his apology with a respectful pause, Pringle continued.

'Our task is an important one on several counts. I think I've already touched on the political implications. The United States doesn't want the international finger pointed at it for originating a cancer which threatens to spread across the world – '

' – like Coca-Cola and Kentucky Fried Chicken,' Sam joked, restoring good relations.

' – but their hands are tied because of the CIA dilemma. So they've turned to us. It's a hell of a responsibility, when you think about it. Then there's North Korea, Kim versus Park, a real can of worms! Toss in the Mafia, the sensitivities of half a dozen countries, the Triad and, at the bottom of the heap, this Killtest set-up – two million dollars is a bargain basement price for getting that lot sorted out!'

'You might add one other ingredient,' Sam said. 'We're also up against a base but basic human instinct. Aggressive violence.'

'That's a matter of belief, Sam,' Pringle argued. 'It's not a case of humans being shits until proved otherwise – at least not as far as I'm concerned. Easily led, perhaps, but not necessarily instigators. It's not us against the whole world, just a few backsliders, deviates.'

Having baited Pringle successfully, Sam was about to continue the discussion when the counter buzzer sounded. They all turned to look at the TV monitor on the wall which showed a fisheye lens view of the SunFun Holiday office below. Pringle flicked it to CU, squinted at the distorted face which peered back, and pressed the lock release under his desk. Five seconds later the door opened and a tall, stooped young man entered the room.

Pringle stood up and extended his hand. 'Welcome to the Anti Crypto-Sadism Unit, Ellis,' he said, a trifle self-consciously.

Kippy also stood up. 'Ak soo!' he said, and bowed. He knew the new member of the team from his early Disarmament Research days: Ellis 'Sox' Haversham – 'Sox' because of his absent-minded habit of frequently wearing odd socks. Haversham was a lanky computer analyst with Megafile who majored in computer 'combing'. This was a technique whereby the mass of information coming into the department was fed into a master computer which was then electronically 'combed' to locate links between seemingly random and unconnected data. To demonstrate the analogy Haversham would often whip out a comb and run it through his hair. The coarse end of the comb would emerge clean but the fine end would produce a snowstorm of dandruff, which listeners would surreptitiously brush off their persons while Sox held the floor for half an hour explaining his quite pointless demonstration. Kippy fervently hoped he wouldn't stage an exhibition today.

Pringle was introducing Haversham to the others.

'Ellis is joining us,' he was saying, 'and in point of fact

you've already begun work on the project, haven't you, Ellis?' Pringle regarded the computer wizard like kids regard doctors.

Haversham parked his angular bum on the edge of Pringle's desk and was away, sprinkling his enthusiastic lecture with jargon.

'Well, yes. I haven't actually done any computer runs yet but I've set up some models and scenarios designed to isolate analogues and incongruities of the type that might interest us.'

Noting Kippy's puzzled face, he explained. 'What I mean is, I've gone through the Killtest report for any factors that might be common to Killtest activities. E.g., block bookings on airlines. The Paranagua Killtest was held on June 24 according to . . .'

He paused, perhaps out of deference to the murdered agent.

'. . . according to Mr Bernard, and checking out airline passenger movements to Rio de Janeiro and São Paulo during the week before I found that bookings were three hundred seats above the average for that time of the year, mostly from American points of departure. There was also an untypically high proportion of block bookings. The same thing happened between July 10 and July 15 on the US to Hong Kong route — four hundred and fifty seats above the average, which of course could be accounted for by the people who went to see the Killtest.'

'Or on the other hand,' Sam Humbert mumbled, 'it could be nothing of the kind.'

Knowing Sam was a computer man himself, Haversham became wary. 'Well, of course, but I hardly thought that needed spelling out.' He turned to the others. 'Naturally you'll find instances of high booking densities on a dozen different routes at any given time. All I'm saying is that here's one way of narrowing the field. The reasons for an upsurge in bookings on a route can be very quickly checked, but when there's no explanation for a sudden and unusual rise in arrivals at a certain point of entry, it immediately comes under suspicion as a Killtest venue. Fair enough?'

There was nodded general approval, so Haversham continued.

'Okay, then. I've arranged with IATA and the main carriers to let us have booking returns every twenty-four hours which I'll feed straight into Megafile's master computer, along with the equivalent bookings for the same days last year and the year before. That way any upsurge will be tripped out for follow-up enquiry. There's a chance – just a chance, I'll admit – that we'll be able to forecast when and where a Killtest event will be held.

'For instance there was a trip-out this morning, just before I came over here. KLM reported heavy bookings next week between the US east coast and Curaçao in the Caribbean, plus a charter from Newark and another from O'Hare in Chicago. I took the liberty of calling our man in Surinam but it turned out to be a diamond buyers' convention.'

Pringle, at least, was beginning to be impressed. 'It all sounds very promising, Ellis. But what about other data – '

'Of course. I've been looking at motiveless homicides. I've noticed that with four of the previous Killtest events, those we have accurate dates for, there were sharp increases in this category of homicides in those areas, usually within a three-week period before the event. I know unexplained murders may have nothing at all to do with Killtest activity but it's highly likely there's some strong-arming going on, so I'm monitoring it.'

'I think we get the point,' Sam Humbert said, with an uncharacteristic note of sourness in his voice. 'I take it you've fed Ludovic into the box . . . ?'

It was an unpleasant, unnecessary remark. Haversham stuttered and went red-faced. Then the bug scanner screamed from under Pringle's desk, warning of electronic interference in the vicinity. After some seconds Kippy rose and went to the window, and looked up.

'A chopper,' he observed. It was the scheduled helicopter service from Heathrow.

They all relaxed, until they remembered Sam's remark. Sensitive to the tension he'd created, Sam shuffled his feet.

'Sorry, Sox. Shit on the liver, that's all.'

Angela Hotchkiss leapt in to explain. 'We're all a bit uptight this morning, Ellis. You understand. . . .' Pringle nodded sympathetically.

After a long pause Haversham continued, although on a distinctly glum note.

'Well, that's about it. Except that I'm working up a routine to locate CIA blanks. Just before the Killtest show in Hong Kong, the known CIA agents in the area were down from their usual strength of twenty-eight to fifteen. I got Angela to ask Hong Kong to check. Some were on holiday, some recalled, some posted temporarily elsewhere. It may not mean a thing, but it seems a bit freakish, doesn't it?'

'It does indeed.' Pringle mused. He was deep in thought, evidenced by the charred cork tip in his mouth and the cigarette ash on his tie. 'Indeed it does. It's a very promising line of enquiry. You'll keep me posted on it, won't you, Ellis?'

To Kippy, Pringle seemed more intrigued by this oddity than by anything else Haversham had told them. Departmental one-upmanship, perhaps; it wasn't unknown when otherwise cool operators sensed an opportunity to nail a turncoat. It was instinctive among old hands. Pulling the rug on any renegade agent was top score, but a tall CIA poppy . . . ? That had to be top of the tops, front page, a bestseller, possibly *Her* tapping you on the shoulder. The only trouble was that diversions adulterated the main effort, and could be dangerously counter-productive. But these were early days. . . .

Concerned that he might have put Pringle to sleep, Haversham squeezed out a final offering. 'Then there are those Parker-Hale high velocity rifles.'

'Rifles?' questioned Pringle abruptly. The cigarette butt was stuck to his bottom lip.

'With Rank night-sights. Two crates were landed at Bilbao yesterday.'

'From where?'

'Port of origination was Cork.'

'Ireland!'

'A case of reverse traffic,' Sam observed. 'For the Basques, probably.'

'Perhaps,' Haversham said. 'But it's incongruities like this that interest me until there's an explanation. They have the perverse habit of linking up with other incongruities and apparent coincidences . . . and before you know it, it's all happening before your very eyes.'

Pringle stirred his bulk from the chair and peered into his empty cup, an established signal for Angela to make more tea. 'I wish it could be so,' he sighed. 'Only something tells me it isn't going to be that easy.'

During the next hour he outlined his reservations. There was no point embarking on fieldwork yet; the leads were too few and too slight. For the present the Unit would act as a nerve centre for the flood of information which would swamp it in the ensuing weeks, from alerted agencies and operatives spread all around the world and from Haversham's computer combing through it all for anything useful. From past experience, something was almost certain to turn up.

Waiting, Pringle impressed upon them all, had craft status in the intelligence business.

When the others had gone, Pringle rang to check on Shirley, then composed a telex to what, despite the massive organizational changes of the past few years, was still resolutely referred to as the Hong Kong Station. What remained of Ludovic Bernard's poor body was a mess, but someone would have to go over to examine it thoroughly, perhaps one of the Yard's forensic pathologists. It might reveal something. Meanwhile, he'd have it frozen, like so much Argentinian beef.

Even so, what Ludovic had achieved held the key to future action; it must be preserved and protected at all costs. The most urgent task was to lay a false trail, for God knows what Ludovic might have told under the effects of torture, drugs and shock. The false trail would have to be convincing. He'd work on it all night, if necessary. In a way it would be the very foundation of the project. If it failed more lives would certainly be lost, and he knew he could never bear that, not any more. Although Ludovic hadn't been his responsibility when he died, Pringle already had the blood of three agents on his hands, and on his conscience; three young careerists, just like Kippy and Sam. There was always a limit, and he'd reached it, he was convinced of that. The fiction he was about to create would have to be as bullet-proof as an armoured vest if the Unit's frontliners were to survive. Perhaps Humbert and Leering were lucky in a way, he mused, that he was the best-trained coward in the business.

Downstairs, Kippy Leering lingered by the rack of tourist brochures, and took one down: HONG KONG – PLAYLAND OF THE EAST! He flicked through the glossy pages . . . wildly colourful Chinese processions, seething streets and markets, opulent modern hotels, fairy lights on the harbour at night. He looked closely at the photograph, past the strings of bright lights, into the black, distant water. He hadn't known Ludovic Bernard, which made it a little easier, but the water frightened him, the dark water. It was so bloody final. He'd heard ex-servicemen recount that of all the things that scared the shit out of them what they feared most was being dumped in the drink at night. He felt a vague ache in his testicles, and closed the brochure, replacing it in the rack.

Then he went out through the plate-glass door into the Haymarket, into the London sunshine, among the people who felt safe.

7

Just two blocks away from SunFun Holidays, and two narrow flights of stairs up from the dark, seedy entrance off Leicester Square, was the office of the Universal Personal Improvement Institute. The name was spelled out in cream letters on the dark brown door. The approach discouraged visitors, which was just as well, for the Institute comprised only a single room, lit dimly from the grim no man's land of a light-well. The room was dominated by a large roll-top desk littered with papers, behind which sat a remarkably unlovely woman of about sixty, her dwarfish dumpiness emphasized by a shapeless navy-blue dress.

Winifred Brodie was tax-classified as an actors' agent; her specialty was supplying dancers and drag acts to clubs and parties. As a fifteen percenter on the bottom rung of the business she made barely enough to pay the rent, let alone pay income tax. On the other hand she spent four months of every year at a sumptuous villa and farm she owned near Malaga.

This contradiction could easily be explained by a brief examination of her undeclared activities, which stretched all the way back to her beginnings as a Mayfair prostitute in the war years. The black-out had helped, for while Winnie was far from pretty, any piece of well-hustled pussy could make money on a dark night. At the end of the war she graduated to management and established a small escort service, at first legitimate but ultimately a highly mobile brothel which she only abandoned after considerable harassment and several convictions.

Reporting on one of her trials a newspaper described her in a screaming headline as 'Miss Whiplash', and went on:

> The evil web woven by Winifred Brodie, the 38-year-old brunette known throughout London as Miss Whiplash, finally enmeshed the female spider herself.
>
> Men with strong tastes in the sexually bizarre became slaves to this woman, whose lair was behind the closed curtains of a back-street semi in West Kensington.
>
> One of the men is already under sentence for stealing sex-stimulating drugs from her.
>
> But one of her customers who also faced court charges last week described Miss Brodie as a 'goddess with the electric voluptuousness of Aphrodite, a woman consecrated to Venus, a lady of exquisite taste and refinement who rightly deserves the crown of Britain's supreme mistress'.

Recalling this now it was hard to believe that Winifred Brodie today and Miss Whiplash were one and the same woman. The woman who sat at the littered desk was fat and toadishly squat with a lined, sagging face, and with enormous brown pouches under heavily-lidded eyes. Age and experience had shrivelled her.

In the days when Winnie wielded the whip she'd met an itinerant American named Jay Simak, who at eighteen had been one of the original Flying Tigers, bombing and strafing the advancing Japanese from Kunming in Yunnan, and who for the duration of the war had grafted himself on to Chiang Kai-shek's payroll, subsequently bumming around the Orient until the mid 1950s when he landed in Britain.

Impressed by the amount of money lying idle in South East Asia, Simak conceived the idea of supplying English wives to rich Chinese, who seemed to regard them like bird's-nest soup. It wasn't a particularly brilliant or original idea, but the Simak variation certainly was, for it introduced re-cycling of the merchandise. After payment of the introductory fee the girl was found by Winnie and duly delivered, the remainder of the amount, usually £4000, being collected immediately after the marriage ceremony. A week later the bride simply walked out and disappeared, to repeat the venture in some other Chinese community. When a girl had done the rounds of Taiwan, Hong Kong, Singapore, Malaya, Borneo and Fiji she was retired with a bankroll sufficient for her to start a small business in England. The scheme made a fortune for Winnie and was only terminated when Simak was jailed for two years in the US on a malicious wounding charge after a nightclub brawl.

In 1975, when a much older and wiser Simak returned to Britain to set up a Killtest recruitment agency, he found a willing and trusted partner in Winifred Brodie, who'd suffered fifteen comparatively lean years. So Winnie's shabby Leicester Square office became the Killtest headquarters in the United Kingdom.

In the intervening years Simak had learned a lot about law avoidance. In place of his former punch-in-the-face, boot-in-the-crotch philosophy was a veteran's craftiness, a wary deviousness born from the scars of experience. His moves were apparently without logic until the final *dénouement*, so to the casual observer his acquisition of a small monthly tabloid, the *New World Times*, might have indicated nothing else than a hankering for respectability after a life of petty crime.

The *New World Times* was an underground newspaper providing a platform for the outpourings of *passé* hip poets, unpublished authors, Marxists and sundry individuals with real or imagined causes – the 'nut' brigade as Simak called them. It was edited and published from a small office in Islington; apart from writing cheques to cover the substantial monthly losses its owner played little part in the paper's production. He did, however, take great pains to build up the classified advertising section which to many readers was the sheet's most interesting feature – column after column of classified cries from the love-lorn, the lonely, the oppressed and the bewildered. It was among the small ads, and the large display advertisements placed by the Universal Personal Improvement Institute, that Simak cultivated the real purpose of the *New World Times*. From them he and his partner reaped a monthly crop of misfits from which might be winnowed suitable recruits for Killtest entertainments, some so desperate they would, according to Simak, 'eat shit for a shilling'.

The Universal Personal Improvement Institute itself was also a Simak–Brodie enterprise which existed solely to attract likely suppliants for Killtest sacrifices. If somebody ever walked in and demanded personal improvement lessons it would have been embarrassing, but the likelihood was remote. Everything was on a postal basis, and Winnie resolutely refused to see random callers. And in any case the entrance qualifications and the fees were so preposterous that few applicants ever got as far as wanting to sign up for a course; those who did, Winifred had endless ways to discourage them.

The half-page advertisements the Institute placed in the *New World Times* each month were designed to attract people at the end of their tether, broke and desperate, and in such an emotional flux they were blindly willing to go anywhere and do anything if it promised to solve their problems.

CHANGE YOUR LIFE – FOR THE BETTER! That was last month's headline. 'No matter what your personal problem is, no matter how painful your distress, no matter how deep you are in debt or how hopeless you might feel, YOU CAN CHANGE YOUR LIFE with the help of the U.P.I.I. – just like slipping out of your old skin and into a fresh, new successful YOU!' The ad was illustrated with anonymous agency photographs of UPII graduates, captioned with phoney testimonials: '. . . I was about to cut my throat,' says Mrs R. of Liverpool. 'Now I'm happily married, have lost weight and own a grocery store!' Under a photograph of a young man boarding an aircraft was printed: 'Just a year ago Mr T. M. of Bristol was bedridden, in debt, unemployed and suicidal. Now he travels the world as a highly-paid electronics sales representative.' Nearly 2000 words of copy glowingly testified to the success of the unique UPII techniques for overcoming emotional and financial hurdles, under which was the coupon: 'To the Principal – I wish to change my life from failure to success, from debt to riches, from illness to health, from losing to winning. Please send me full details of your unique course.'

'It's money for old rope,' commented Simak, who'd written the ad.

This particular advertisement had attracted ninety replies; each respondent had been sent a questionnaire to elicit further information, the first step in the Institute's screening. From the replies, Winifred had selected ten as potential Killtest material. To these she sent off a more detailed questionnaire designed to probe deeply into the applicant's personal background, and from their replies considered it safe to interview three. She was now dictating her notes on the interviews into a cassette recorder for Simak in New York:

'SUCH, Arthur Ronald, of Burney Street, Hartlepool, aged twenty-two, average physique, health good to very good, appears mentally disturbed and emotionally unstable. He's on probation after serving eleven months of a three-year sentence handed down at Newcastle-upon-Tyne Crown Court for manslaughter. A year ago, under the influence of drugs, Such was the driver of a car in which his girlfriend was killed; now, full of remorse, he feels he has nothing to live for. He also has the scars of a partly-successful operation for hare-lip, is out of work, without any qualifications of any kind and ***** desperate.' (Winnie clucked her tongue five times to indicate the candidate's rating on the scale known only to her and Simak.) 'On the questionnaire he listed amateur rugby as his active sport and is also interested in boxing and wrestling. In conversation he feels that money – like winning the Pools – is what he wants most, and says he'll do anything to get it, even crime if necessary. I'd consider him a 'D' class candidate because from the personality point of view he won't be much of a drawcard.'

Winnie paused and contemplated the questionnaire filled in by a young woman who'd visited her office the previous evening. It had been her second interview; at the first, instinctive alarm bells rang in Winnie's mind for there was something about the girl that suggested a policewoman. The interview had been wound up and the girl followed by a private detective retained by the Institute. But after several days' surveillance it appeared the girl was all she claimed to be.

Winnie resumed her dictation.

'GILLESPIE, Susan Mary, of Lancaster Road, Lambeth, London, aged twenty-six, blonde, excellent figure but – and

I have to be frank – a rather pretty face spoiled by an ugly nose. Susan is an unusual applicant, and I submit her only after careful consideration. Her problem is extreme shyness; she is terribly sensitive about her nose which was broken and badly set when she was a child. In fact she is positively neurotic about it, believes she is impossibly ugly and feels the only thing that will stop her from killing herself is an operation. She's had consultations, and the necessary cosmetic surgery, performed in Yugoslavia, I think, will cost something like £2000. She hasn't got the money and has no hope of getting it. In her present state it seems to me she's got a pronounced death-wish, and after a lot of probing I'm satisfied she'll react favourably to a K contract. Therefore I'm recommending her as a 'B' candidate with the additional bonus that she's a young woman of the kind you want, and **** desperate.'

The third and final interview had been conducted only that morning, and it had left with Winnie such feelings of elation that, even now, she smiled as she composed her report to Simak.

The subject of Winnie's satisfaction was a quite stunning, dark-haired woman of twenty-nine who on a superficial judgement might be thought to be a little mad. There were some complex neuroses gnawing away at June Harrison's mind, certainly; and she was surrounded by an almost tangible electrostatic field of hysteria. She was hostile and as unpredictable as a wild cat, and Winnie had spent two hours trying to determine why this was so.

June Harrison had a history of conflict with men. At nineteen she'd been raped by two youths but the charges were dismissed in court when the defence counsel, using an attractive model, demonstrated that any young woman wearing the mini-skirt June had worn that night could not have avoided displaying large, provocative areas of upper thigh, not to mention crotch.

At twenty marriage to a merchant seaman proved disastrous and after a year of drunken bashings she won a divorce on the grounds of cruelty. At twenty-two she won second place in a Bradford beauty contest and, as part of the prize, a minor role in a local pantomime. To June an acting career seemed assured and she promptly packed her bags for London. For the next five years she suffered the frustrations caused by an ambition that far outpaced her talent and intelligence, and the few parts she got did not even cover the rental of a telephone which never rang.

Then into her life came Mortimer Rank, one of London's most promising younger playwrights. What began as a casual weekend fling in Cannes during the 1975 Film Festival continued, solely through June's northerner persistence, as an on-off, knock-'em-down, drag-'em-out affair which soon became one of the West End's minor scandals. With the instincts of a leech June, not unmindful of her five destitute years as an actress, stuck to Mortimer Rank, whom she undoubtedly regarded as her meal ticket. But she'd reckoned without Rank's elegantly shrewish wife, an actress herself, seven years older than her husband and unexpectedly protective towards a marriage that was widely admired as one of the most successful show-business unions of the sixties. During a supper party at which all three were present she emptied a bottle of champagne over June's immaculately coiffured head and in her most contemptuous stage manner (she was currently playing *Medea*) commanded her bedraggled, gasping rival to 'piss off back to the provincial shitheap' she'd come from.

Tragic enough, but, badly advised by a lawyer, June then begged further disaster by sueing the playright for breach of promise, demanding £40 000 in damages. Predictably, she lost, and then proceeded to take it out on Rank by harrassing and embarrassing him at every public opportunity. After a succession of incidents – ramming Rank's car in the National Theatre car park, arranging his funeral, shouting during a performance of one of his plays, and calling a bedside press conference at an abortion clinic to name the playright as the cause of her visit there – June was finally silenced by a court action, placed on a good behaviour bond, and ordered to pay £6000 in damages. This public admonishment, the legal debts and the crushing blow to her pride put June into a nursing home with symptoms of classic paranoia.

All that was six months ago, and now June Harrison was abroad again, bristling with high-octane hostility. The morning's interview, still disturbingly fresh in Winnie's mind, both excited and troubled her. There was no doubt that for the magical sum of £40 000 the young woman would willingly kill, and for determining only that fact was why the Organization retained her. But . . . that hysterical edge to the woman's manner . . . might it not backfire in some way? Winnie recalled again the arresting brightness of June's perpetually wide-opened eyes, the diamond-hard, high-pitched voice, the body that seemed animated by hidden, snapping springs, the discomforting eagerness. The DADIN training arm of the Organization had a drug-based programme for correcting such aberrations in Killtest candidates, she knew, and from what she'd learned it had failed only once. But . . . well, she'd recommend Harrison, enthusiastically but with reservations to protect herself . . . and so she picked up the microphone to conclude her report to Simak.

'Harrison,' Winnie rasped into the mike. 'June Miriam, of Ealing, London. Aged twenty-nine, divorced, father dead, mother living in Bradford, no other immediate family or ties. Very attractive figure, physically fit and active. She has some acting experience which could be an asset. According to our screening guidelines, June is ***** desperate and without doubt an 'A' class applicant, the first I've recommended to you. The only reservations I have concern the woman's mental state. She appears to be a little unbalanced to me, but among people who want to risk their lives for money, who isn't? The thing is, I'd like to have your own views on Miss Harrison before I discuss a contract with her.'

It was a few minutes before nine o'clock. Winnie signed off, reversed the tape and placed the cassette in its plastic case. Tomorrow she would airmail to Simak *Bob McGee and his Big Band Sound for Dancing*, which was the music you'd hear if the cassette were played on a standard machine. On Simak's machine, though, the voice frequencies, separated on three razor-thin bands on the tape, would be combined again to reproduce Winnie's dictation.

Five per cent of the prize money for three candidates, win or lose! It would be a profitable week for her if Simak accepted them all.

Winnie Brodie sighed and tidied her desk, then picked up the mike again for the final task of the day. She must send a message on tape to her little pets in the house at Malaga.

8

Georges Mrabet, as usual, was early; it gave him the opportunity to tranquillize his mind before the others arrived. And today, particularly, he needed time to think.

The big room was stuffy; it hadn't been used for three weeks. Mrabet went to the control cabinet, switched on the air conditioning and activated the rows of detection and alarm devices. Then he returned to the big boardroom table, glancing briefly out through the windows at the end of the room. Far below, cabs and cars flowed down Park Avenue, all multicoloured streaks and blobs like a narrow strip from a Jackson Pollock painting.

He turned, and began to spread out dozens of press clippings on the polished table. You could never predict the strange workings of the media. For six months hardly a newspaper had printed a line of his press releases about the French Connection Committee, which was perfectly in accord with the Organization's intention. Now, suddenly, there was little news about, and editors were treating the proposed anniversary celebration as though Benjamin Franklin had risen from the dead. One newspaper had published an editorial urging Congress to vote a million dollars to Mrabet's mythical project. Requests for interviews and for more information poured daily into the small secretarial office on the floor below. Dozens of promoters wanted rights to manufacture souvenirs and to strike medals. They couldn't be fobbed off for ever or they'd smell a rat. Somehow, Mrabet worried, he'd have to find a way to cool interest in the French Connection Committee, which, instead of providing a low-profile cover for Killtest Inc., was in danger of becoming a topic of intense national concern.

'Jesus wept!' he announced to himself. 'When will something go right for a change?'

Moroccan born, Georges Mrabet was the product of a long line of grievances, real and imagined, which began when his rich family was dispossessed in 1956 with Morocco's independence. In a matter of months his lifestyle changed from that of a pampered youth with his own luxury penthouse to that of a poor student unable to afford the rent in a scruffy Latin Quarter back-street *pension*.

He'd arrived in Paris in the depths of a depression. On the eve of the family's departure from Morocco his mother's lover, after failing to dissuade her from leaving him, blew them both apart in a final, lethal embrace with four sticks of gelignite. All that remained were bloodied hips and legs. Every window in the house had been blown out. He remembered the nightmare of returning home from the Polytechnic in the afternoon to find pieces of his mother's flesh plastered to the courtyard wall; inside, under a sheet, two feet protruded, still wearing slippers. A fortnight later, in Marseilles, his father had committed suicide.

Mrabet had been unable to cope. After failing every examination he sat for, and finding few careers open to him, he tried crime as a shortcut to fortune. But even in this he was a failure, and when he'd served a year for theft emigrated in bitterness to Canada where he joined his uncle's small private security firm as a clerk. When his uncle died in 1967 he took over the business and rapidly expanded it by merging with a private investigation agency which had a number of lucrative accounts, including several banks.

From his youth Mrabet had been a keen boxing fan and claimed the former world heavyweight contender Georges Carpentier as a distant relative. With the profits from the security business he fulfilled a lifelong ambition to become a boxing promoter, and by 1970 was staging some of the most important bouts in Canada. Unfortunately Mrabet could not shake off a native aversion for paying taxes and in 1974 faced a long list of charges from tax evasion to fraud and conspiracy.

Contemplating certain ruin he grabbed a client's payroll in transit and the 60 000 dollar purse of a big bout he was promoting at the time, and disappeared south of the Canadian border accompanied by two colleagues.

One of these was Pat Galoot, who'd been a CIA plant in Montreal since the late 1950s. On Galoot's advice Mrabet took his bankroll to Washington and Henschel Oppenheimer, who was at the time a regional director of CIA covert action programming. An old friend of Oppenheimer, Galoot knew something of his chief's private ambitions, and both Mrabet and his money were to provide the catalysts for what later crystallized into the embryo Killtest Organization. The Frenchman became Oppenheimer's lieutenant, and with Galoot set up the *armée privée*, the Organization's private police and protection force, headquartered on a 900-acre estate near Atlanta and guarded by a 20 000 volt electric fence and twenty Dobermann pinschers.

All that had been two years ago, almost, and for a time Mrabet must have felt he'd at last got the monkey off his back. With Oppenheimer providing 22-carat information from inside the CIA there had been some rich pickings. On government security contracts, for instance, Oppenheimer always knew which department or official could be squeezed, and for how much. No work was ever involved; a brief meeting or two could net fifty thousand dollars. Then came the Mafia, and Killtest Inc., and suddenly the place was swamped with bigshots – arrogant, clever, dangerous criminals who were accustomed to giving orders and getting their own way. For Mrabet the cosy days were over; the friendly partnership had been replaced by a greasy pole, and Oppenheimer hardly ever met him socially any more. Bruised by the intense competition, threatened from all sides by iron-clad egos, he withdrew. A small, dark man, he shrank noticeably; and as he shrank the chip on his shoulder grew proportionally bigger. Only this morning he'd looked into a mirror on the wall of his Manhattan apartment; what scowled back was a younger but squatter version of the French wartime collaborator and traitor Pierre Laval. At that moment he made up his mind to escape the trap that yawned before him, to get out at the first opportunity and to start a new life with the private fortune he'd built up in Swiss bank accounts.

He hurriedly gathered up the press clippings as the door bleep began to sound *La Marseillaise*. The others dribbled in: first Dr Lethnal and General Ton Dinh Quan, then McSwiggan and Ginorini, and finally Taubes and Simak. It was to be a gathering of the full Ring. Oppenheimer, assured and elegantly tanned, came in last, exactly one minute late, as always. After pouring himself a glass of iced tea and indulging in the customary smiling politisms he walked to the head of the long table and called the meeting to order. They all promptly sat down.

'Well, gentlemen . . . success, success! Our efforts, you'll be delighted to learn, have earned us all a substantial bonus over forecast, to be paid according to the usual share-out percentages. I imagine Dr Lethnal will attend to this in the next few days.'

Oppenheimer turned slightly towards Lethnal, who was running an expert, over-manicured finger up and down a tiny calculator. Although he was well prepared for this cue, the doctor looked up as though interrupted.

'Yes,' he agreed. 'I think you'll all be agreeably surprised. The Macao balance sheet shows a gross of six and three-quarter million, and a net profit of two and a half million after allowing for contingencies and a million dollars for the establishment fund.'

After permitting his colleagues to congratulate themselves for a few seconds, Lethnal's face grew serious.

'But – ' he warned them, ' – I'm bound to say something about rising costs. If we don't soon do something about them we're never likely to repeat the profit performance of the Macao games.'

'You distress me, Carl,' Oppenheimer said easily. 'You know I have an obsessional fear of poverty.'

'It can't be so bad,' Tony Ginorini added. 'At least we've got something the Russians won't invent tomorrow and the Japs won't make cheaper next week – '

Lethnal rapped the table sharply with his calculator. 'I'm serious. I've stood by for months, watching costs rise out of all proportion to gross revenue. Security, in particular – '

Oppenheimer raised his hand to stop the Organization's financial wizard from continuing.

'Hold on, Carl. The security costs for the Macao operation were exceptional, but however high they were, they were justified. We couldn't afford to take any risks and we couldn't have made a better investment. Perhaps Frank will tell us why.'

Although elated by the successful outcome of the spy hunt, McSwiggan shuffled in his chair, cleared his throat and hung his head in false modesty.

'Well, yes, we got the mother, as you all know. Lao Man looked after him for a few days but, even so, we didn't learn much. One of the Limey Intelligence outfits, that's for sure, but why the punk was bugging us, I got no clue.'

'Ahh, then, perhaps I can enlighten the meeting on that point,' Oppenheimer intruded smoothly, taking over from his security aide. 'You're aware that I have to tread very carefully when it comes to information retrieval at Central Intelligence, but in this case it was a pushover. The wires ran hot. The man's name, not that it matters much, was Ludovic Bernard, formerly a British SIS agent but lately with MI6, based in London. He might just as well have told us and saved himself a few painful days with Lao Man. At any rate, Bernard won't worry us any more. Right now he's decorating a freezing cabinet in the Kowloon morgue. . . .'

'But what was the goddam angle?' Ginorini asked.

'The angle,' Oppenheimer continued, 'turned out to have nothing to do with Killtest. Bernard was interested in Gams – Ernest Gams – who you'll remember was our erstwhile chess expert at Paranagua. According to CIA input, Bernard had been assigned last year to instigate smears and threats directed at British cabinet ministers and politicians, allegedly masterminded by BOSS, South Africa's security set-up. There were some hoaxes and Scotland Yard cock-ups and obviously more nonsense floating around than facts, so the investigation went under cover.

'Now, before he was posted to Brazil, Gams was with the US embassy in Pretoria. And he also has a brother in South

Africa who works for BOSS, although in what category I don't know. But to get to the nitty-gritty, Gams was reprimanded late last year on a complaint from the British that he was passing highly confidential information to BOSS, most of it embarrassing personal sludge on British politicians. Gams was subsequently posted to Brazil, but it seems that Bernard suspected he might be part of some syndicate, operating within the US Consular Service and dealing in anti-British scandal for which BOSS might be expected to pay highly. My guess is that Bernard, by trying to photograph Gams at a Killtest show, was attempting some character assassination of his own. He failed at Paranagua, but apparently thought Gams might turn up again at Macao, which of course he didn't.'

'What worries me, though,' McSwiggan said at the end of all this, 'is that the British aren't likely to take this lying down. The fact that one of their men was knocked off will convince them they're on to something big.'

'That's true, Frank,' Oppenheimer replied easily. 'But I happen to know they're on the wrong trail. They think Gams, or whoever he's associated with, was responsible for the killing. Already they've assigned an agent to Brazil to shadow him – I learned that last week. And last night there was a request from London for background on Gams and his connections. Naturally I'll make sure they get what they want, and more, to keep them pointed in the wrong direction.'

'But what about Hong Kong?' Ginorini asked.

'What about Hong Kong? Ten to one the British will send a team there to nose around, but so what? We'll get Lao Man to make sure they get all the problems they can handle. Don't you follow? So long as we keep them preoccupied with Gams and the Hong Kong killing, it keeps the heat off us. Meantime, the trail's getting colder and colder, if they ever do find it, which in my opinion is unlikely. Frank?'

Most of this was new to McSwiggan, and he could only agree with Oppenheimer. But the disarming assurances of his chief worried him. Oppenheimer had been right about Macao; everything had turned out pretty much as he'd predicted. He was right about so many things, so many times. That didn't guarantee, though, that he was right this time. But already Oppenheimer had passed on to another subject.

'Now,' he was saying, 'we must finalize details of the next Killtest games. Unfortunately, mainly because of the security scare, we've decided to defer the Virgin Islands and Taiwan venues.' Oppenheimer looked at Mel Taubes. 'So it's definitely the Canary Islands, is it, Mel?'

'Yeah,' said the young promoter. 'It's being set up now. It was the safest location to proceed with, and I think we have to thank Carl here for that.'

Dr Lethnal took advantage of the questioning silence to explain his involvement in an area normally outside his jurisdiction.

'I've spoken to you about this before, Henschel,' he said. 'An old friend of mine, Henry Krausner, is opening a big new hotel on Gran Canaria, down towards Maspalomas. It's an opportunity too good to miss. We're still haggling about the price – I'm trying to get him down to a hundred and fifty thousand – but on the other hand there'll be seating for eight hundred.'

'Eight hundred! That's great, Carl!' But then, in his quiet voice, Oppenheimer queried, 'But you're happy with the security?'

'Well, naturally Frank has the final word, but Krausner is no stranger to the protection business,' Lethnal assured them. 'I knew him in Germany, before the war, when he was the assistant chief of Krupp's security force. He spent most of the war in Spain and stayed on, building and running big tourist hotels. Now he's started in the Canaries. He's in very big with the Spanish government, as you can guess.'

'So why should he risk his money and reputation by allowing a Killtest to be staged at one of his hotels?' McSwiggan asked suddenly. 'If news of it got out he'd lose everything.'

'Frank, I'm sure I mentioned that I knew him before the war, at Krupp's – you know, Krupp's, armaments, guns, bang-bangs?' He took obvious pleasure spelling it out for the Irishman. 'Certain information dropped in the right ears would be most embarrassing for old Henry. In other words, I leaned on him a little. Can I leave the rest to your imagination?'

Oppenheimer stopped the verbal sparring by returning to Taubes. 'Mel, you've looked the place over, of course?'

'Flew back yesterday. It's perfect. For a cover, Krausner will put on a big convention for travel agents. August the 31st is the date. And Carl's right – Krausner's so terrified you can be sure the security will be as tight as a fish's asshole. He's worried about his own skin more than anything else . . . in fact he threw a wobbly right there in his office while I was talking to him – '

'Heart attack?' Oppenheimer queried.

'Something like that, but he'll last the distance, don't worry. The point is that the cover idea – the tourist convention – should attract a big Stateside contingent. I can lay my hands on half a dozen jet charters, at a real knockdown price, too. Consequently, I'd like to suggest four thousand bucks a ticket, instead of the usual five. I want every damn seat to have a fanny on it.'

Oppenheimer pursed his lips thoughtfully. 'Well . . . maybe. We'll work something out. I don't see why we should charge four when they're happy to pay five. However . . . Frank better get over there fast to make an all-out security check – and without pushing Krausner's ticker over the top. And Georges, you've got the date now, so I want an all-out effort on closed circuit contracts. There are hundreds of guys with theatres and screens who're literally screaming for our equipment. Put a bomb under the suppliers – we're missing out on millions while they're sitting on their hands!'

'Check,' Mrabet said, although he knew it wasn't that easy. It would be another two months before they'd take delivery of the next batch of video scramblers from Japan. The last fifty units, received only a week ago, had to be used as replacements because earlier models, which incorporated some of the most advanced experimental circuitry in the world, were starting to pack up. He said, 'Check' again, however; he had no desire to pick an argument with Oppenheimer right now, not in front of the others.

McSwiggan and Ginorini, thinking the meeting had concluded, pushed their chairs back.

'Hang on!' Oppenheimer said testily. 'We haven't finished yet. In fact I'm just coming to the most important item of all. Security, venues, outlets, ticket prices – all of that's important, but what you have to remember is that Killtest Incorporated will only ever be as good as the entertainment it provides. And that's what I want to talk about now.'

The two men pulled their chairs back into line; at least they weren't going to be the targets. Instead, Oppenheimer fixed his gaze on Jay Simak.

'Jay, I think we were courting disaster at Macao. Apart from Whiplash, neither of the other two bouts had what I call real Killtest appeal. The sadistic element went over the top . . . too brutal, too gory. In fact I'm thinking of banning the use of explosive from now on – we're not here to create a new Golgotha, for fuck sake! What I want to see is a bit more tit and ass and a lot less piss and gizzard, and I'm sure the customers want it, too. Now, I'd like to hear what you've got in mind for the Canary games.'

Proposals for performances were never discussed in detail at Ring meetings, and Simak polished his head with a handkerchief. Oppenheimer had left nobody in doubt that he was making an example of him.

'I haven't finally decided,' he countered. 'But we're not short of options. I've got at least a dozen DADINS in the Bangkok bin – more than enough for a three-bout programme.'

'Well, then, let's have some of them.'

'There's Frisbees. . . .'

'Frisbees? Those toys?'

'Killer Frisbees. With edges sharp enough to shave the fuzz off a baby's bum – you know, the sort of thing Oddjob did with his bowler hat in *Goldfinger*.'

'I see.' The vision of razor-sharp discs flying through the air and neatly decapitating a man was more in keeping with Oppenheimer's Killtest philosophy, and he couldn't resist a smile. 'Go on,' he said.

'Then there's another game I'm having developed which has two men or two women, armed with tiny knives, in a big, sealed clear plastic globe, about ten feet in diameter. There's only enough air in it to last fifteen minutes, and the only way out is through a hermetically sealed trapdoor, which is locked with a key. Both the gladiators have keys, but they swallow them before the bout.'

Simak paused to let the ingenious implications sink in.

'So one of the gladiators has to kill the other one to get the key?' It was General Ton Dinh Quan, obviously no stranger to the art of disembowelling.

Simak continued. 'Then I've got a beast versus man stunt, which I bet will go down well. As you know I've got that liger in Bangkok. Well, now I've managed to buy a tigron from a zoo supplier in Singapore.' The two rare hybrids were the offspring of a lion and a tigress, and a tiger and a lioness respectively. 'What isn't generally known is that they will instinctively fight each other to the death. For a hundred thousand dollars I've got two idiots who're prepared to be strapped on the animals' backs, like buckjumpers.'

Simak was sure the diabolical originality of the examples he'd given would please Oppenheimer, and he laughed triumphantly as though he'd accomplished some tremendous feat.

But his chief's blank, disapproving look soon sobered him up. With great deliberation the chairman drew out a newspaper clipping from a folder in front of him.

'I quote from the latest issue of *Showbill*,' he said stiffly: ' "FEMMES BOFFO IN SNUFF EPICS. CUSTOMERS NEG BIZARRE COMBAT AS 'TOO CRUEL'. Sado fans are hardly swooning over the latest offerings from the video-snuff pedlars which have degenerated into bloody bouts of almost maniacal ferocity. Customers complain of being splattered with blood and sickened by the butchery.

' " 'I'm going back to skinflicks,' one disgruntled Chi patron was reported as saying. 'I can see this stuff for free any time in the stockyards.'

' "The distributors, not so long ago wallowing in illegal loot, are biting nails to the quick because of the bloody trend, and estimate capacity drop-off has been 30%.

' " 'What the trade has to realize,' one exhibitor lamented, 'is that it's the gals who draw the big audiences.' He said a single thirty-minute nudie male-femme bout with whips had pulled in over 100Gs in two weeks. 'It doesn't matter who wins,' he commented, 'it's the sex they want.' " '

Oppenheimer carefully replaced the cutting in the folder. 'And so on,' he said. 'It's mostly hearsay, I know, but *Showbill* didn't get where it is by being wrong. And I must say I agree. From now on we've got to have more female contestants. Christ! We've only had two woman-to-woman bouts so far!'

Simak protested. 'That's easier said than done! Jesus, I'm always in the market for spunky pussy, but you try to find it!'

'That's your job, not mine, Jay,' Oppenheimer reminded him sharply. 'And when I say, females I don't mean half-drugged slags and clapped-out whores, either. What we need, and what the patrons want, is good-looking, one hundred per cent WASP women, full of fight and spirit – '

'Like Patsy Kemper and Rusty Fender,' Mrabet put in. The two stars of Whiplash happened to be his discoveries.

'Right!' Oppenheimer agreed. 'Get some more gals like them, and get 'em before the Canary date, too. I want that show to have a line-up like the Rockettes, okay, Jay?'

Simak was on the verge of losing his temper at this impossible instruction when he remembered the latest tape from Winifred Brodie in London. She'd cornered three candidates, two of them women. But with the Canary Killtest just a month away he'd have to move fast to get them into performing shape. He looked up to find his chief still waiting for an answer.

'Okay, Hensch. Believe me, I'll do my best.'

Oppenheimer smiled and stood up and riffled his notes together, indicating the meeting was over.

'By the way,' he said to nobody in particular. 'Do the letters A-C-S-U ring a bell with anyone?'

No bells were rung, and the four letters were forgotten as they all filed from the room.

9

Jay Simak climbed the stairs to the Universal Personal Improvement Institute, cursing London's snarled-up August traffic. He was half an hour late, and June Harrison would already be there, waiting. He'd intended having a talk about her with Winnie, about this mental thing, but now it would be impossible. The office of the UPII did not include a waiting-room.

The two steep flights made him sweat, and outside Winnie's door he paused to blot his forehead. London's summer was getting as bad as New York's. But there were consolations; heat always made him think of flesh, female, the delights of; and he wondered if Winnie had procured a suitable young lady for his personal use during his two-day stopover.

Opening the door he found the women chatting on the battered chesterfield. Winnie grunted to a standing position and introduced him.

'This is Mr Vega,' she said to June Harrison. 'He's the producer of the film I was telling you about.'

Simak looked the young woman over with a shrewd eye, and was instantly pleased with what he saw. Miss Harrison sat ramrod straight and challengingly returned his gaze with startlingly large, black-accented eyes. Her pale face was lightly freckled and from a finely etched centre parting a shimmering mane of raven hair fell to several inches below her shoulders. And Simak could hardly help noticing the formidable bosom which strained every thread of her black-striped satin blouse. As a Killtest candidate the lady from Bradford scored ten out of ten for presentation.

'I've gone over the basic proposition,' Winnie said as Simak pulled a chair towards the chesterfield and sat down. 'That we're looking for an actress to play an important role in your new film. I've told Miss Harrison it involves a stunt which could be dangerous, but that by way of compensation we're offering an appropriately high fee. So far Miss Harrison seems to be most enthusiastic about the idea . . . aren't you, dear?'

The young woman abruptly leaned forward and placed a lean, well-manicured hand on Simak's knee.

'Mr Vega, I'll do anything, absolutely anything you want, providing the money's right.'

'Fine, fine,' Simak said. Then, remembering she'd been an actress, cautiously asked, 'Incidentally, do you have an agent?'

'Useless. I gave them away years ago. I never found one who understood my particular talents. No, Mr Vega, when you negotiate, you deal with yours truly.'

'Great! I admire independence.' He explored further. 'Would you call yourself a loner, June – if I may call you that –'

After a momentary flicker of indecision the young woman replied, 'I've had more than my share of masculine attention in my time, Mr Vega, let me make that quite, quite clear. Unfortunately, in the past, I've let my heart rule my head too often. I've given everything I've had to others, and a fat lot of good it's done me. If I can put it bluntly, I've been absolutely screwed, financially and in every way, screwed-up, made to look a fool, which I'm not – in fact right here in London there's one particular gentleman who –'

'It's really terrible,' Winnie quickly cut in. 'June's already told me how she's been victimized. But what's important is that this man has left her with a load of debts –'

'You can say that again,' June Harrison said with feeling.

Simak watched his candidate closely, for they were nearing the moment of truth: whether or not to offer the woman a Killtest contract. He wished he could have talked it out with Winifred before the interview, about the reservations she'd expressed about June Harrison's emotional state. So far he was more impressed than he'd expected to be. The woman almost crackled with body static, the kind of magnetism that, professionally tuned, would make her a wow in the arena.

But there was something about the tense, ambiguous mouth and the child-like eagerness that made him hesitate.

The woman must have noticed his hesitation, for she sprang forward again so that her intent face was only inches from Simak's.

'Mr Vega, I know what you're thinking – that here's a failed actress desperate for any job that's going. Well, not true. I'm only interested in something big, really big. I'm only in it for the money, big money – and if it's big enough, nothing's too dangerous or too dirty. If it's porno – if that's what the set-up is and you're too coy to come out with it – then try hitting me with a number. I can put a price on anything, literally anything!'

Simak was stunned by the outburst at such close quarters. He wanted to look away from her blazing eyes, but couldn't. The only escape was to make his mind up, in her favour.

'What then,' he asked her, laughing, 'would you do for fifty thousand dollars?'

'Pounds,' Winnie corrected.

'Fifty thousand?' June Harrison mused. 'For fifty thousand I'd cut my foot off and eat it. Want to try me on a hundred thousand?'

Simak abruptly stopped laughing. 'No, I'm serious. Fifty thousand is top whack. That's the fee we're offering for this particular role.'

'Where do I sign, then?'

'But aren't you at all curious as to what this assignment requires you to do?' Winnie asked her.

The woman was far too cool for Simak's comfort. 'Yes,' he added. 'For example, would you be prepared to die for the money?'

'If I thought I had a better than even chance to collect it, yes.'

'Because,' continued the Killtest chief, 'that's what it amounts to. I'd be dishonest if I didn't warn you that your assignment will be dangerous, with the chance of an accident. We'll take every precaution, naturally, but the possibility of injury is something we both have to take into consideration. That's why I want you to think about it very carefully – '

'I've thought about it,' the woman said, still unruffled, 'and the answer is yes. Show me the money and the answer is yes.'

Given the choice Simak preferred cool, cynical candidates to highly emotional ones; they were easier to handle when their moment came. But June Harrison fitted both categories. His instinct warned him – in fact it rang shrill bells – that introducing this female into the gladiatorial arena might be like carrying a ticking bomb right into the Waldorf Towers. But against this there was that curt order from Oppenheimer to recruit more female contestants for the next round of Kill-test games, and here was a woman with all the crowd-thrilling qualities he could wish for. Yes, his mind was made up. He rose from the chair and began to pace about the dark, squalid office.

'Okay, then, June, I'll give it to you straight. What we plan to do in this movie is unusual, but that's what the business is about these days. In some respects what we plan to do might be considered illegal. So I have to warn you that what passes between us now is highly confidential – got that? If you breathe a single word, you'll get nothing, and nothing but trouble, I can promise you that. And of course both Mrs Brodie and myself will deny everything. So you're on a hiding to fifty thousand pounds, it's your choice, one or the other.'

The young woman didn't flinch. 'You're talking to a thinking adult, Mr Vega,' she said, rather aggressively. 'If I make my bed, I'll lie in it. Just tell me what I'm supposed to do.'

'I can't give you all the details yet,' Simak told her, 'except that you'll be involved in a film stunt with another woman. We'd prefer to fake this particular scene, but we can't – '

'What are my chances, then?' the woman asked.

'Fifty-fifty, perhaps better. But what you have to remember is that if there was no risk involved we'd be paying you fifty pounds, not fifty thousand. And to prove we're on the level, that we're a reputable organization, we'll pay you the standard ten per cent advance.'

June Harrison did a lightning calculation. 'Five thousand pounds!' For the first time during the interview she briefly misplaced her composure.

'Yes, on the signing of the contract. The stunt will be

filmed at the end of this month, so in just over three weeks all your troubles will be past history.'

'And you're sure I'll be able to do what you want?'

'No doubt at all,' Simak reassured her, although this was hardly necessary. He had no intention of giving her the slightest clue of what he had in mind. Too dangerous. That would come later, when she was isolated, numbed by repeated brainwashing sessions supervised by Taubes, her reason distorted by drugs. By the end of the month, his experience told him, June Harrison would be ready to bite the balls off King Kong.

'What d'you think?' Winnie asked Simak when she'd gone.

Simak slapped his thigh. 'She'll be fine. She'll fight like a she-cat. I can just see her in the ring, standing up there, down to the skin, those whacking great tits – '

'I'm not so sure,' Winnie told him levelly. 'When the real risk sinks home to her she'll start shouting the house down. She'll think she's being victimized all over again – '

Simak's saffron forehead crinkled. 'You're getting soft, Winnie. You're also getting two and a half grand in commission on her contract, so start earning it. Get her in again while she's hot – like tomorrow – and sew up that contract. And give her the five grand. Money fixes everything, I've found. Now, where the hell is this goddam Gillespie broad?'

It was just eleven, and the clock of St Martin's near by had only just finished chiming when there was a hesistant knock on the door. The door opened and Susan Gillespie walked in.

From the neck down the girl had the kind of figure men used to whistle at. Simak's sharp eyes immediately focussed with approval on a pair of bra-less nipples which, probably from fear, protruded prominently from her green cotton sweater. The girl's face, however, was quite another matter. Attractive enough, and framed by bouncy blonde hair, it was dominated by a large nose which changed direction from a bump just below the bridge. Some clumsy doctor had bungled the operation.

Simak rose and introduced himself as Mr Rodriguez.

'Mr Rodriguez is the film producer I was telling you about,'

Winnie said to the girl. She was in her mid-twenties and very nervous. She lit a cigarette and looked expectantly at Simak.

'I'm not sure how much Mrs Brodie has told you about our problem,' he said. 'But we need somebody like you for a stunt we're going to film. It's a fight, with another woman.' Simak measured the girl carefully; you had to play each one differently. 'What will appear on the screen will look like a fight to the death, although neither you nor the other stunt lady will come to any serious harm.'

'What sort of fight?' Susan Gillespie asked.

'We're still planning it. A kind of wrestling match, something like that, with a crowd – '

'Oh, I couldn't appear in front of a crowd!'

'No worries,' Simak improvised. 'You'll wear a mask, so nobody will know who you are or what you look like. Okay?'

The girl hesitated, so he continued. 'The thing is – and I have to put it to you frankly, because we're shooting strictly to schedule – you'll have to make your mind up today. To help you, I can tell you that your fee will be twenty thousand pounds.'

'That'll buy a dozen operations, dear,' Winnie put in, gently placing a hand on the girl's arm. 'It's all strictly professional, so you don't have to worry about a thing. Twenty thousand pounds for twenty minutes in front of the cameras isn't to be sniffed at, you know – '

'Oh, no, I'm not! Please, I'm not!'

'I can name you half a dozen big-name actresses who'd snap up this part for a tenth of the money,' Winnie persisted.

'Think about it,' Simak added. 'In a couple of months you could be earning big money as a beautiful model. I'm sure you could help to get her established, couldn't you, Mrs Brodie?' He turned to Susan Gillespie. 'Mrs Brodie is a famous actors' agent, did you know that?'

'Yes, of course I'll help you get established!' Winnie chimed in, dangling the bait. 'You'll be able to afford the best nose-job in the world. We'll even find you the surgeons the film stars use.'

'It's a whole lot of money, though,' Simak continued. 'And

it has to be earned. That's reasonable, isn't it? You have to trust us and put yourself in our hands, do just as we say. It's as easy as that.'

'It could change your life,' Winnie went on, with unintentional irony.

'I guarantee it!' Simak added.

'You've been a very unhappy girl, haven't you?' Winnie said with a comforting arm about Susan. 'What you're buying is your future success and happiness.'

For half a minute the girl hesitated, and then a distinct change came over her. She stubbed out her cigarette and looked squarely at the two Killtest agents.

'It's not pornographic, or anything like that?' she asked. pointblank.

Simak looked aghast. Winnie took the question as a personal affront.

'Oh, Susan!' she cried in mock horror. 'Do you think for one moment I'd allow you to be approached for anything like that?'

'I already told you,' said Simak. 'It's with another woman. Because you've got such a beautiful body you'll be wearing very little, but there's nothing obscene about the stunt, I can assure you of that.'

'All right, then,' the girl said, brightening. 'I'll do it. Do I . . . when do I start?'

'As from tomorrow,' Winnie told her. 'I've already made up a contract and you can sign it now, if you like. Tomorrow we can go through the bits and pieces department . . . passport, tickets, how we pay you the money, things like that – '

'Passport? I thought you were making the film in England – '

'No, dear, but nothing to fret about. We pay all your travel and hotel bills.'

'I haven't a stitch to wear,' the girl said. 'I'm skint.'

'How much cash do you have in the safe, Mrs Brodie?' Simak asked.

'Two hundred or so.'

Pleased with the way things had gone, Simak turned genially to Susan Gillespie.

'How would you like a couple of hundred in advance? To buy some gear?'

'Oh, yes, thanks!'

'That'll give you some idea of the kind of people we are,' Simak lectured her. 'We trust you, you trust us.'

'Oh, I will!' the girl said. She appeared to be in a state of near-hypnosis.

'And remember,' he added. 'Making movies is a competitive business. Your job, and that twenty thousand pounds, depends on you keeping all this completely confidential. Not a word to anyone, understand, or you could be hurt!'

'No, I promise!' the girl protested.

'I mean it,' Simak said.

'I mean it, too,' Susan Gillespie told him with deep sincerity.

But it wasn't like that at all.

That same afternoon Susan Gillespie had the shopping spree of her life; down Regent Street, along Oxford Street, back along New Bond Street, feeling ten feet tall and more beautiful every time she slipped in and out of a fitting cubicle. Three salesladies told her she looked lovely. The face that smiled back at her from the shop mirrors grew progressively more assured, if not beautiful. An actress she'd be, like Elizabeth Taylor! And then a famous model, wearing new gear every day! Or not wearing it . . . that's what Mr Rodriguez had said. Twenty thousand pounds, just for a glimpse of her body! Laden with parcels and boxes, Susan hailed a cab and tipped the cabbie a pound when he dropped her outside her flat in Lambeth.

At six-thirty, Charlie Poyner arrived home.

Susan called to him from their tiny bedroom. 'Is that you, Charlie?' The bed was buried beneath a froth of new clothes.

Charlie was Susan's Jamaican boyfriend. They'd been living together for three months. He worked as an assistant storeman at a Hammersmith plastics factory. His eyes bulged when he walked into the bedroom.

'What's all this, then?'

Susan didn't answer. Instead, she slipped out of the dress she was trying on and stood there, radiant, in just her knickers. 'This is just the start, Charlie. I'm a film star!'

'How much did all this cost?' he asked, unimpressed. Sometimes, like this evening, Charlie stayed an extra half-hour in the pub on the way home. The extra time could usually be gauged by the increased degree of truculence.

'Two hundred pounds. Why?'

'Two hundred pounds? Two hundred! Like where the hell did you get that kind of money?'

'I just told you. I signed on to be in a film. A movie.'

'Movie, Crap! Who gave it to you – the money?'

'Charlie, listen! It's like a dream! A man signed me up today to act in a film. For twenty thousand pounds – it's true! He gave me two hundred pounds to buy some clothes, just like that.'

'You been hawking it again, haven't you?'

Susan took an involuntary step backward. 'What's that? Just let me hear you say that again, go on –'

'On the game. Like you're at it again, aren't you? Some old white creep, I suppose, that's all you could get with your screwed-up puss!'

Susan suddenly realized, with a justified stab of fear, that Charlie wasn't sharing her moment of glory. He began picking up the clothes and throwing them at her.

'Are you dumb, or somethin'?' he shouted. 'Nobody makin' a film would have you in it. Not with a face like yours – are you jokin'? Unless it was Dracula. What d'you take me for?'

Cowering under the avalanche of cloth the frightened girl tried to answer back. 'If you'd only listen, Charlie – I can take you to the lady . . . you can ask Mr Rodriguez – ' By now Charlie had hold of her wrists and flung her down on the bed, keeping her there with a barrage of swipes to the head. His words came out with hoarse breaths.

'You fuckin' tart,' he yelled. 'I always thought you was a tart. Deceivin' me, takin' money, feedin' me this load of crap –'

It wasn't their first fight. In the past, Charlie's tearful recriminations and tender loving afterwards seemed to Susan sufficient reason not to leave him. But at this moment, after the heady exhilaration of the most exciting day of her life, and knowing, for the first time, that the disfigurement which haunted her was merely temporary, she drew a deep breath and hit back.

'We're finished, you black git!' she shouted between slaps. 'You hear that – finished! You can go back to the trees where you came from, you greasy black git – '

Spinning around, Charlie brought the wardrobe crashing down on the bed. The mirror splintered over the room. He pounded holes in the thin veneer, then swept everything off the dressing table with a great crash and tore the bed-lamp from its socket and hurled it through the window. It landed between a group of pensioners sitting on the lawn five stories below. They thought it was an Irish bomb, and the police were called.

Half an hour later a crying, bleeding woman and a still violently struggling Jamaican were taken away in a patrol car.

IO

'Ak-soo!' Kippy Leering yelled as he entered the meeting room above the SunFun Holidays Ltd office in Haymarket. He accompanied the cry with a wild leap and a karate-style chop into thin air. 'Hell, it sounds like a Chinaman sneezing!'

'Hullo, Kippy.' Sam Humbert didn't look up; he was completing the *Times* crossword. He hadn't even bothered to take off his trenchcoat.

Kippy bowed in front of Angela Hotchkiss. 'Ak-soo! And how is our angel this fine morning?'

'I'm very well, thank you,' Angela said stiffly.

'And you Sox? All systems go?' Kippy could never resist the temptation to take the mickey out of these two members of the Anti Crypto-Sadism Unit. They'd all been working together now for almost a month, and a certain resistible camaraderie was developing among the team, mostly at Kippy's insistence.

Ellis Haversham was as perpetually engrossed in computers as Sam Humbert was temporarily absorbed in a crossword. His mind was an extension of the magnetized tapes which streamed through the electronic circuits at Megafile. When Sox died, Kippy joked, when he was called by the Great Computer in the sky, they'd wrap him in magnetic tape like a mummy, to puzzle some future civilization. None of this amused Haversham, who failed to see anything funny about computers.

'Since you ask, yes, I do happen to have some interesting information to impart when the time comes,' he said good-naturedly.

Disappointed by his failure to bait Haversham, Kippy turned to Angela.

'Mr Pringle asked me to ask you if you'd have his cup of tea ready for him.' Angela would never make tea for Kippy, and realized it was a ploy, but she switched the kettle on anyway. One day Mr Pringle might *really* ask him to ask her to have his tea ready for him.

Pringle arrived a few minutes later, carrying – despite the blazing sunshine outside – an umbrella.

'Arthritis playing up, Stan?' Kippy asked with studied innocence.

'No,' Pringle said, happy to get the daily joke over and done with. 'I lost it the other day and just collected it from the station lost property office.' He took several folders from his briefcase and sat down at his desk, momentarily surprised to find a cup of tea waiting for him.

'Ah, thank you, ahh. . . .'

Kippy beat Angela to the punch. 'Thought you might appreciate a cuppa, boss.'

Pringle merely grunted, telephoned Shirley and, satisfied that his wife was accounted for, coughed a couple of times to signal his team to settle themselves. The 9.30 meeting had become routine during the weeks of waiting.

'Well, now,' he began. 'Things are looking a bit brighter. You'll remember we decided to float a balloon on Ernest Gams, the American diplomat Ludovic reported at the Paranagua Killtest. Ludovic said he took some speculative pictures of Gams, thinking they might be useful to convince the Yanks just how serious this Killtest thing is and how it threatens to white-ant their Bureau of Security and Consular Affairs. At any rate the photos were apparently intercepted, alerting the Killtest people, and this led, I'm sure, to the tragedy of Ludovic's death.

'Now, if you'll excuse the metaphor, Gams was just a pawn at the Parangua Killtest. We know that, but we haven't let on. On the contrary, we've made it obvious that we're going after Gams. A request to the CIA produced a great shoal of information, much of it spurious, so someone there seems most anxious to help us. Or, rather, help us gallop off in the wrong direction. The Hong Kong station has been told that Gams had been there at the time of Ludovic's murder, but we damn well know he wasn't. So it seems our balloon is doing a good job for us.'

'We're still going through the motions of keeping Gams under surveillance, I take it?' Sam Humbert asked.

'Oh, quite. Our man in Brasilia is hamming away so hard it's a wonder the theatre critics haven't written him up.'

'How about some plumbing?' Kippy suggested. 'That ought to convince them we're serious about Gams.'

'Good idea. Nothing like a bungled burglary to arouse the passions. I'll fix it.' Pringle made a note and sipped his tea, his ponderous upper lip folding right over the lip of the cup. 'But let us move on to recent events. Ellis, I believe you have something to tell us.'

Haversham had been waiting like a sprinter on the blocks. He had a pile of print-outs on his lap, but this was just for show. He carried them about with him like a baby's security blanket.

'Yes,' he said enthusiastically. 'I did a three-avenue computer comb last night. Interpol's August 9 list of homicides included a German TV cameraman, murdered in Munich two days previously, so I set a comb for international TV production movements. According to the trip-out, a complete outside broadcast unit, with three cameras, editeç machines, fifteen technicians and crew plus two thousand metres of coaxial cable has been ordered for a job between August 28 and August 31. Gran Canaria.'

'Where?' Kippy asked.

'Gran Canaria. It's the biggest of the Canary Islands.'

'That's strange,' Angela Hotchkiss said. Also strange was the fact that Angela rarely spoke at these meetings. They all looked at her. 'Among a million other things, I've been monitoring the movements of those rifles that landed in Bilbao a month ago. Guess where they were shipped last night?'

'Canary Islands?' Pringle ventured safely.

'Yes. Las Palmas. Private jet charter, German-owned.'

'Ahh, ahh!' Pringle cut in triumphantly, throwing open a

folder. 'The lazy fox is about to jump over the quick brown dog, tappety-tap-tap! Now hear this! The night before last a young lady was taken to Brixton police station. She'd been bashed up by her boyfriend, but that doesn't concern us. I wish I could say that chance didn't play a part in what happened next, but for once Lady Luck was on our side. A call came into Central yesterday requesting information on an American named Rodriguez, who'd apparently offered this girl a part in a film he's making. We're copied in on all such requests and I look at a hundred of the things every day, at least. Phoney film producers working the old casting couch con are two a penny, and I was just about to pass it over when I noticed the fee he'd offered the girl – twenty thousand pounds! I jumped three feet in the air. So with Sam I went down to Brixton to interview the lady, prepared for disappointment of course . . . we've had so many let-downs. She'd been worked over rather badly, but from what she managed to tell us it has all the earmarks of a Killtest approach – the girl was hooked by a mail order ad, interviewed and offered a ridiculous amount of money for what this Rodriguez told her was a risky film stunt – note the 'risky' bit – subjected to a lot of pressure to take the job and threatened to keep the whole business quiet. Does that sound like the real thing or doesn't it?'

Nobody was remotely prepared to challenge Pringle.

'Furthermore,' he continued, 'the office where the interview took place is right here in London; just across the road in Leicester Square, in fact – right under our bloody noses, masquerading as the Universal Personal Improvement Institute! Needless to say I called in Fred Cordroy and his people who promised me that by this morning – meaning right now – the place would have more bugs in it than a Cairo brothel – ' Pringle paused. ' – sorry, Angela. What I mean is, it's being tapped and taped and if our luck holds we should learn some very interesting things very soon.'

At sixty cigarettes a day it didn't take a lot to make Pringle breathless. His eyes popped and he looked exhilarated.

'Christ!' Kippy said. 'At last we might actually *do* something instead of just talking!'

'What's the next step?' Angela asked.

'We sit on it,' Pringle told them all. 'It's too early for a plan of action yet. The last thing we want is a net full of small fry – it's the big boys we're after.'

The long faces this news produced didn't go unnoticed, so he added: 'Oh, come now! Before the pleasure of the kill there has to be the pain of waiting!'

Pringle's philosophy of patience soon bore fruit.

Forty-eight hours later it was all on several miles of audio tape and reams of transcript: June Harrison, advertisements in the *New World Times*, the contracts, Canary Islands, fake passports, the lot.

Pringle had Susan Gillespie admitted to the Oaks private hospital in Surrey and, after long sessions which were a blend of sympathy, appeals to the conscience and the guarantee of a free nose-job, the battered girl had agreed to see Winifred Brodie to sign the contract and receive instructions.

'You'll be an actress after all, my dear!' Pringle had told her.

While all this was going on, Angela Hotchkiss searched every section of the Department and even throughout the Foreign Office for someone who looked enough like Susan Gillespie to impersonate her. She found a suitable volunteer, eventually, in the DI6 Records Division.

Hilary Brooke was introduced to the AC-SU team at a special briefing meeting above the SunFun Holidays office on 15 August. Nicknamed 'Butch' Brooke on account of her severely cropped black hair, Hilary entered the room in a blonde wig, dark glasses and a patch of sticking plaster over her nose to disguise the fact that it was normal. She wore falsies under a white sweater. The likeness was stunning. Kippy, who'd only seen photographs of Susan Gillespie, was completely taken in.

'During the next few days,' Sam Humbert explained, 'we'll do a small implant operation on Hilary's nose. Even Susan's mother won't know the difference.'

'Crazy!' Kippy muttered.

'Not at all,' said Pringle guardedly, not wishing to undermine Hilary's confidence. 'And anyway, it's often the crazy ideas that succeed. I've given Miss Brooke some notion of the risks involved and it's a tribute to her courage that she accepts them all without reservation. Having said that, though, we'll naturally do everything in our power to minimize the dangers – for I want it clearly understood that wherever this assignment takes us it's imperative that the team remains intact at its conclusion.' Everybody except Hilary Brooke knew Pringle had neglected to mention the loss of Ludovic Bernard.

And the turkey buzzards, thought Kippy.

'Very well, then,' Pringle continued. 'I've worked out a two-pronged plan of attack. The sharpest prong will be directed right at the heart of the Killtest show in the Canary Islands. From the information we've already tapped from Winifred Brodie, Susan will fly from Gatwick with this June Harrison to Las Palmas in a week's time, on 22 August.

'Now, Susan Gillespie will be in no shape to see Brodie for three or four days. They're doing everything they can for her at the Oaks, but she's got some deep bruising and the last thing we want is to alarm Brodie that something's gone wrong or that she's not fit. So I'll have Susan telephone her this afternoon with a story that she's had a long-standing arrangement to go somewhere in the country for the next three days, and that if she doesn't go her friend might ask awkward questions. That should do it. I'll give her a good script, and she can make a firm appointment – Friday would be fine – to sign the contract, pick up her tickets and passport and that sort of thing.'

Pringle consulted his notes before continuing. 'We know from the tapes that Brodie won't be accompanying the women to the Canaries, but it seems she'll see them off at Gatwick. That's where we'll make the switch. Susan will walk into Immigration Control and Hilary – wearing the same clothes – will walk out to the aircraft – '

' – without even turning to wave goodbye,' Sam cut in.

'Exactly! We'll arrange a distraction for June Harrison, so she won't see the switch, and the only other risk will be with this Rodriguez character. He may very well be in the

Canary Islands for the Killtest, but as he only met the girl once the risk will be slight.'

Pringle turned to Hilary Brooke. 'In any case, Hilary, we have a deep cover man in Las Palmas, and he'll be briefed to keep an eye on you. We thought of grafting an implant bug on you to track your whereabouts, but knowing the Killtest people have a jolly smart electronic arsenal themselves it would be dangerous. However, once there, I want you to go along with everything they say . . . or better still, do exactly what you imagine Susan Gillespie might do in the circumstances. We'll give you an extensive backgrounder on the girl, and you can spend as much time with her as you want. Any questions?'

By this time Hilary had taken off her wig and removed her dark glasses. Made up as the girl she was to impersonate, she gave the impression she was nervous, even intimidated; a young woman out of her depth. But as Hilary Brooke she looked exactly the tough little nut required for a testing assignment like this.

'None now,' she said in a clipped, business-like voice. 'But I expect I may have some later.'

'Good, good!' Pringle beamed. He removed a forgotten cigarette end from his lip and turned to Kippy and Sam.

'The second prong of the attack will be a diversion. We've been leaking like mad that we think Ernest Gams is mixed up in some international blackmail syndicate centred on Hong Kong, and that Ludovic was on his tail. They must be wondering, though, why we haven't sent anyone to Hong Kong to try and find out what happened to him. Despite what the spy novels say, intelligence agents aren't murdered every day, or even month for that matter, and the Killtest crowd must know that as well as we do. They'll expect some sort of investigation – so that's exactly what we'll lay on.'

Pringle passed each of them a detailed three-page itinerary.

'Sam, you'll be trailing the cape, and Kippy will cover you. He'll arrive two days before, to dig in. I want you both to make lots of noise – you know, lots of smoke, lots of enquiries. If nothing happens after a couple of days, try treading on some Triad toes. The Hong Kong station will give you plenty of names. Or ask around after Lao Man. In his last despatch Ludovic said he was convinced that Lao Man is tied up with Killtest Inc. in some way, probably one of their protection people. But it's a real hot one, so be careful.'

'Thanks,' Sam said drily. 'But what if they're smart, and stay in their holes?'

'That isn't important in the final analysis. All that matters is that we make a presence, that they're made aware we're in Hong Kong on a wild goose chase.'

Sam was about to argue, but Pringle quickly intervened.

'Remember, both of you, that this exercise is a red herring tactic, not an avenging mission for Ludovic's murder. The revenge impulse must never be allowed to colour our judgement. As far as you're concerned, you're there simply as a decoy, to invite contact of some kind, probably hostile, with Kippy as your shadow for your protection.'

He swivelled his chair around to face Kippy.

'Now, Kipling, if it so happens there is no contact, if nothing happens, then you're to fly to Las Palmas to be there no later than August 28. We don't have an exact fix on the Killtest date but it's between August 29 and September 1. I can't give final instructions now; it's too early. You'll get them through our local man on your arrival.

The way Pringle put it, the way he always put it, made the operation seem as easy and as safe as walking into MacDonald's next door and ordering a hamburger. The reality was that three of them, including Hilary Brooke, would be in the field with their naked necks stretched out, half a world apart, while Pringle mowed his lawn in Esher.

'Angela,' he was saying. 'I want you to personally supervise all the ticketing and documentation. I want no silly slip-ups on this one.'

Kippy wondered, and tried not to think of the turkey buzzards.

11

From the upstairs lounge of Kai Tak airport Kippy watched the British Airways 747 taxi towards the terminal.

He wore check slacks, a red shirt with a drawstring tie, and a straw hat: the American tourist gambit. American tourists, especially the urban rubes from the Mid West, stood out in a crowd, but they were also an internationally recognized stereotype which nobody questioned, or indeed ever wanted to question. He ordered another Old Grandad on the rocks in a loud American voice and then sauntered to the big windows overlooking the tarmac to check Sam's arrival. Sam had a perfect Humphrey Bogart drawl; in fact Sam had so many things, all of them in one way or another endearing. Now his life was in Kippy's hands, and he surreptitiously felt for the 9 mm Walther nestling against his ribs and the new Immobilion-B ejector in his jacket pocket.

They were the first weapons he'd ever carried in his life, and neither had been fired at anything more threatening than paper targets. Pringle, he'd been told, wouldn't even know how to squeeze the trigger of a pistol, for all his years in the service; he'd even managed to dodge the regulation half-yearly practice sessions, and constantly deplored the wind of change which was sending more and more armed agents into the field. 'Dependence on firearms will simply make everybody mentally lazy,' he said once. The two instruments of death hidden on his person gave Kippy no feeling of security or dependence; nor did they lessen the crushing obligation thrust upon him. From the time Sam Humbert stepped off that jumbo he was Kippy's responsibility, along with his girlfriend, a new yacht, an icon collection, his raincoat maker and bartender, and the thought chilled him.

Downstairs, Kippy waited until Sam emerged from Customs, calculatingly disguised in sun-glasses and an air-crew steward's uniform two sizes two small for him. It was almost laughable as Sam attempted to shuffle his six-foot-four frame furtively across the arrivals lobby to the Ambassador Hotel's waiting mini-bus outside. After a minute, Kippy walked out, too, and climbed into the bus behind Sam with no exchange of recognition.

'Goddamned wife must have missed her connection,' he announced to the passengers. 'She'll fly in tomorrow, I guess.'

As instructed by Pringle he'd arrived in Hong Kong two days before to dig in. He'd arranged to occupy a room on the fourth floor of the Ambassador, directly across a light-well from the room booked by Sam. And from his own darkened room, through a crack in the curtained window, Kippy watched Sam settle in, not more than thirty feet away.

It was a ticklish game they were playing, particularly Sam, who was the living, walking bait, trailing a lure as ostentatious as a peacock's tail. In the hotel lobby he'd staged a beautifully clumsy meeting with a local intelligence operative and a Special Branch man for good measure, receiving behind a screen of potted palms a large white envelope which he carried, half-hidden under his trenchcoat, to his room. Clouseau couldn't have mismanaged it better. And his first telephone call was to London, to his girlfriend Sally, to tell her he 'was hunting the gang of political blackmailers who killed Ludovic Bernard', and that he 'expected to return home in a few days'. Having raised the guillotine with a single hair, Sam then sat under its blade.

Kippy had searched Sam's room, of course; a planted bomb would have resulted in useless sacrifice. He'd found a short-wave bug behind the panel of the light switch, which he left intact; it had a range of about 200 yards, so that although the enemy was invisible it was close. The other rooms around the light-well with visual access to Sam's window were all occupied but safe, according to Kippy's investigations. If there was to be a hit, he'd decided, it would come either through Sam's bedroom door or from outside the hotel.

He lit a cigarette and watched as his colleague unpacked, stiffening into alertness as a white-jacketed houseboy entered Sam's room with a jug of iced water. He stayed at the window unblinking, following every move as the houseboy turned back the bed cover and collected his tip. When he left, Sam emptied the iced water into the handbasin, threw on a dressing gown over his underclothes, spread out his false instructions on the writing table and made a phoney phone call to the local operative. You couldn't be more suicidal than that.

A light went on directly below Sam's window. A highly European impulse in the tropics is that of throwing off clothes at any convenient opportunity, and the impulse was being demonstrated now by the room's occupant, a nubile, sun-tanned American magazine reporter from Wisconsin named, according to the hotel register, Eugenie Cobb Butler. For several minutes she wandered about the room applying various lotions to her naked body before reclining on the bed to read a book. Kippy contemplated masturbating, the only kind of sexual indulgence possible while still keeping an eye on Sam, but by the time he'd run to the bathroom for the tube of handcream he kept for the purpose a light breeze had sprung up and the girl had drawn the curtains. Goodnight, Eugenie.

For some strange reason Kippy never seemed to make it with women the way other men of his age did. He'd been told enough times that he was devastatingly attractive and he believed he was at least passable to females; he didn't have bad breath, he felt horny a couple of times a day (except on missions – fear was a barrier that prevented blood racing to the groin), he was easy-going and generous, erudite and witty. But somehow he could never quite climb over the fence of commitment; he'd remain sitting there, baffled and undecided. He'd lived six months with Rosa but it had all been downhill after the euphoria of the first mad month, and eventually they'd drifted apart. But what had disturbed Kippy was not the parting but the cursed feeling of inevitability of it all. If he was such a good catch why was he always released back into the big, wide sea?

It was arranged that Kippy would take the first night

watch, between nine and three the next morning when Sam would take over until breakfast was served in his room at nine. In this way they slept six hours, and Kippy was fresh for his day-long vigil. They also each slept for an hour in the late afternoon before emerging from their rooms for dinner.

Predictably, nothing happened during the first three days, but by the end of the week it was difficult to resist the inclination to rush out into the street and demand to be shot at, simply to relieve the tension. The Killtest Organization, or the Triads or whoever they were up against, certainly knew a thing or two about psychology. Several times a day Sam would engineer ludicrously tempting opportunities for assassination – alone in alleyways (not an easy thing to accomplish in the overcrowded colony), wandering along deserted wharves and into dubious lavatories, riding a bicycle through the open fields of the New Territories and even taking late-night ferry trips across the harbour. In every way he presented the perfect target, for even in a crowd he stood a foot and a half taller than the rest of the population.

For ten hours out of each twenty-four Sam was a clay pigeon drifting slowly, invitingly slowly, through space, watching for a suspicious movement or signs of an ambush, waiting for the sudden crack of a sniper's rifle or the impact of a gun in the ribs. And as each day passed the tension mounted so that by the time he'd return to his room he was sick with nervous exhaustion. He was equipped with an auditory device which magnified sounds behind him, like footsteps and even breathing; and his sun-glasses concealed tiny rear-vision mirrors, but these offered no protection against a gunman on a rooftop or in a passing car. And Kippy, although never more than sixty yards away, was only human, with human reflexes that were no match against a bullet speeding on its way. Nevertheless the two men gamely tempted a lurking killer to squeeze the trigger.

But, no. Killtest Inc. held its enigmatic hand.

Then there was Hilary Brooke in the Canaries, masquerading as Susan Gillespie, the Killtest candidate. Kippy's time was already up. Pringle had sent a message that 30 August was the likely date for the Killtest show; and it was now the

28th, and Kippy had to travel half-way across the world to get there. They had a day at most to bring the Hong Kong exercise to a conclusion, for it was unthinkable that Hilary should remain unprotected any longer.

That evening Sam decided to exert some psychological pressure of his own. He 'discovered' the short-wave bug and excitedly telephoned the Special Branch contact without bothering to put the bug out of commission.

'I'm certain it's the Triad people,' he almost shouted into the mouthpiece. 'And I'm about to give them a big surprise. I've just had some information and if I can confirm it by looking at Ludovic Bernard's body tomorrow, I'll give you the names of his killers with all the evidence to convict them.'

The Special Branch man could hardly be blamed for failing to follow Sam's stratagem.

'Look, Mr Shortland,' he said. 'We've been over that body – '

Sam cut him short. 'No, this is something entirely new, just passed to me from London. All I need is a quick look at the body to make absolutely sure, and we've got them – Lao Man, the lot! How about tomorrow morning?'

'Okay, then,' said the puzzled Special Branch man. 'I'll meet you in the morgue. Would eleven o'clock suit you?'

'I'd rather be alone,' Sam told him curtly. 'For a number of good reasons. Alone – got it? After all, it's an Intelligence matter, isn't it – you know how it is with demarcation. Just leave the instructions. I'll be there at eleven.'

The following morning, at ten minutes to eleven, Sam left the hotel for the short walk to the Kowloon morgue, behind the new headquarters of the Royal Hong Kong Constabulary. Kippy, with an attaché case and in the light blue suit of a visiting businessman, followed warily at a judicious distance. God knows what Sam's heart was doing, but his was thumping away at an alarming rate, and every now and then he was forced to suck in huge gulps of steamy air. This could be IT.

It was so easy to be deluded in Hong Kong. In an average day a million people would pass you without taking a speck of notice, even if you had bright green hair. But it was just this – the impersonality of the place – that made it such a treacherous place to hunt potential assassins. Sam wasn't making it any easier, either, for he embarked on a sequence of obvious dodges designed to make it clear he didn't wish to be followed, first by diving through one of the big department stores, then riding in a rickshaw for three blocks and in a packed bus for two stops. Kippy arrived just in time to see Sam disappear into the six-storey operations block behind the administration building. For some reason they'd both arrived safely, and without incident.

After waiting a minute, Kippy climbed the steps and went through the entrance, showing his visiting card to a young Chinese policewoman. To avoid asking the way to the morgue he pretended to speak only Dutch, enabling him, while the policewoman searched for an interpreter, to study the plan of the building on the wall. By the time she'd returned he was at the entrance to the morgue in the basement, complete with stethoscope around his neck.

Through the glass doors he could see Sam at the far end of a long, bare white corridor, talking to a couple of attendants in white coats. Nobody else was about, so he waited. Sam and the two Chinese attendants eventually went into one of the dozen or so rooms which opened off the long corridor.

Kippy was disconcerted at the lack of cover so he walked boldly in and rapped a coin on the top of a little table with a SUPERINTENDENT sign on it. He pulled out a folder from his attaché case and was studying it when one of the Chinese peered from a doorway further up the corridor.

'Hullo, there!' Kippy cheerfully called to him. 'Is the Super about? I'm Doctor Greenglass.'

The attendant disappeared for a few moments and then came hurrying towards Kippy. 'You wait. I find him,' he said, without stopping, and almost ran through the swinging glass doors.

Alone again, Kippy wandered along the corridor, casually opening the doors and peering in. Most of the rooms were postmortem theatres or pathology laboratories. The place was deserted, the eerie emptiness emphasized by the acres of highly polished white floor tiles and bare walls. Then he heard a click and looked up to see the second attendant walking fast towards him along the corridor.

'Ahh, excuse me – ' Kippy said tentatively, waving his stethoscope for attention.

The Chinese attendant ignored him, almost ran past him, and quickly vanished through the morgue entrance. Kippy's already labouring heart began to pound furiously.

He ran to the door from which the two Chinese had emerged. It was locked, but after he'd hurled his body against it a couple of times the lock finally parted from the light metal frame. He switched on the light.

The large room was empty, but the banks of stainless steel drawers lining the walls left no doubt as to its function.

Frantically, Kippy went along pulling the heavy steel drawers out on their castors. Some were empty, but from others blotched green-grey faces stared back, mostly Oriental. The cold chill of death slid from the temporary coffins into the room, coiling around his legs like vaporized dry ice. He was nearly paralysed with the fear of what he might find next. One of the drawers contained just a few pieces of a body, each piece labelled with a white ticket. In another was a young woman, purple and black, horribly burned. By the time Kippy reached the end of the first bank of drawers the scene resembled the locker room of a team of monsters after some nightmarish game.

By now distraught, he began on the second bank, tugging at the heavy drawers in a frenzy. He pulled one out with such force that its occupant shot on to the floor like a frozen sheep's carcass. Then, with a shock that was as tangible as a punch in the face he found himself looking at a barely recognizable Ludovic Bernard, the figure and face roughly carved in rotten cheese which had been nibbled by some animal. Aghast, he rammed the drawer shut and sobbed, hardly stifling the impulse to run away and hide somewhere. Somewhere . . . Sam was somewhere – but where? He was too late. He had Sam's life on his conscience . . . how could he have allowed him out of his sight for so long? For several seconds the angry questions buzzed in his brain while he stood there numbly in the centre of the grotesque room. Only half a dozen drawers remained to be opened and, mechanically, without any hope, he walked towards them.

The first contained an elderly Chinese. In the second was a fully-clothed man, face down. It was Sam, and Kippy pulled him from the drawer to the floor. His face was dark red. With hands that trembled so much they would hardly work, Kippy cut through the tightly knotted tie with a scalpel he found on a trolley near the door. He nicked Sam's neck, but at least the blood still flowed. He pulled out the Walther and fired several shots into the ceiling, and then, bending down, breathed air into Sam's gaping mouth, expelling it again by pressing gently on his chest. He ripped the shirt open and rubbed his hand over Sam's heart, even thumping it with his fist as he'd seen doctors do on TV. The skin was cold, with the pallor of candle grease. He breathed into Sam again, pumping great gulps of the death-laden, life-giving air into his inert lungs. Good Christ! Tears of fear and guilt fell on to the unconscious man's face. From somewhere outside there was the sound of voices and running feet. Distracted momentarily, he stopped the resuscitation, and Sam coughed. Two white-coated Chinese and a uniformed constable burst into the room, alerted, no doubt, by the gunshots.

'Quick!' Kippy yelled at them, praying he wouldn't have to explain for five precious minutes. 'Oxygen! Man dying!' The two attendants ran off.

The constable, his shorts immaculately creased, his black leather belting polished to a mirror shine, bent and turned Sam over, face down.

'Stop him choking,' he explained. He poked a finger deep into Sam's mouth, making him retch. The constable then placed his knee in Sam's back, and pressed hard, causing a stream of bile to spill from his mouth.

'He be okay,' the policeman said.

Two minutes later a doctor ran into the room with a mask, followed by the attendants and a cylinder of oxygen on a trolley. Five minutes later Sam dragged his eyelids apart and looked about, uncomprehending, wincing with the pain from his neck. Kippy knelt down and put his face inches from Sam's.

'Hullo, Sam. Can you hear me?'

'What,' Sam demanded in a hoarse whisper, 'the fucking hell happened?'

The draft report that Kippy sent within hours to Pringle for circulation to the CIA and other interested intelligence agencies gave a version of what *didn't* happen:

HIGHLY CONFIDENTIAL/CIRCULAR 6AP–706631/SUB: GAMS REF: Previous Circular 6AP–706502.

The urgent cooperation of all agencies is now sought by this department in the investigation of GAMS, ERNEST FRANKLIN, and the suspected international political blackmail organisation of which he is thought to be a member.

It is strongly believed by this Department that the headquarters of the suspected syndicate, which has access to highly personal information on leading world political figures, is located in Hong Kong, and future investigation will be concentrated there.

Gams himself is under surveillance and is at present on US Consular duties in Brasilia, Brazil. By agreement with the US Bureau of Security and Consular Affairs he will hold his present post until the investigation is completed.

The urgency of this circular is dictated by the fact that two of this Department's officers have already been murdered in the course of their duties. The latest victim is HUMBERT, (alias Shortland), SAMUEL FREDERICK, 36, a senior field officer, who was killed in Hong Kong on 29 August by an unknown assailant. . . .

The truth, though, was that it was a terrifying narrow escape for Sam Humbert, who was within hours secretly transferred to a TB sanitorium on Victoria Peak to recover. Upon instructions from Pringle a convenient Caucasian cadaver was promptly substituted for Sam's body in the morgue.

After a week's convalescence Sam would go on to Bangkok as scheduled, to try and locate the suspected DADIN camp set up there by the Killtest organization.

Of the assignment itself, only a harsh judge would use the term 'fiasco'. Despite the near-disaster Pringle could reasonably hope that Killtest Inc. must now believe British Intelligence was irrevocably on the wrong track.

And he would be right. By the time Kippy was on his way to Las Palmas, a whole day late, an unauthorized copy of Pringle's circular had already landed on Oppenheimer's desk in New York. Delighted that Sam Humbert's death was confirmed, he called Lao Man to offer his congratulations.

'I'm surprised you thought it was possible we could fail,' was Lao Man's reaction.

Oppenheimer had no answer. 'You'd better send a message to the Canaries,' he suggested tartly. 'They ought to know the pressure's off.'

In the end, you had to hand it to Pringle. Within two hours of the attack he'd organized the monitoring of every cable sent from the colony for forty-eight hours. Among the nine thousand messages was Lao Man's, and before Kippy had even landed at Las Palmas, Pringle had prised open another tiny door, revealing yet another short passage in the complex maze. Together with Angela Hotchkiss and Sox Haversham he scanned miles of teletype throughout the day and night as the duplicate cables chattered into Telex Central in St James's. Although the cable was unsigned, Pringle spotted it immediately: THE CANARY CAN SING ADVISE MCS. It was addressed to Henry Krausner, Hotel Leopold, Gran Canaria.

'Well, Ellis,' Pringle sighed. 'That gives us the Killtest venue. Our man there wasn't sure. And this Krausner, too: another one for the net.'

'What about this 'MCS'?' Haversham reminded his chief.

'McShane?' Angela suggested.

'McSweeney?' said Haversham.

'McSharry, McShee, McSorley – it's dead simple, Ellis!' Pringle bellowed. 'We're not looking for a Jones or a Smith, for God's sake!'

12

The late summer sun was setting over the Canary archipelago as Kippy's jet began its descent to the Aeropuerto de Las Palmas.

The islands of everlasting Spring, the Canaries were called, the Fortunate Daughters of the Atlantic, the Gardens of the Hesperides, a place of peace and idyllic repose, solitary and melancholy. But to Kippy, volcanic Gran Canaria looked about as inviting as Death Row.

To his right he could just make out the capital, Las Palmas, barely visible under its almost permanent pall of cloud. He'd flown from Hong Kong in a series of long hops, via Los Angeles, Washington and Madrid, without even dozing; for the events of the previous twenty-four hours had left his nerves in neck-snapping tension. And his neck not only ached but itched, where the shirt label had been snipped from the collar.

Now it would be the Hong Kong exercise all over again, but with Hilary Brooke substituted for Sam Humbert. He was supposed to find her, shadow her and protect her, like some guardian knight, but without the armour.

As he filed into the Arrivals lobby he told his fogged mind he was John Bernard Papworth, an English travel agent on a world fact-finding tour. His baggage stuffed with tourist brochures proved it. And if further proof were needed he was spotted and welcomed by a courier and ushered through Customs with a minimum of delay; there was some kind of tourist convention on the island.

Once in the main concourse Kippy made his way to the cloakroom, and then to the public lockers. *Soixante-neuf* upside down: the old memory system, number 96. The door of the locker was jammed shut with a matchstick. Inside was a blue canvas hold-all. He carried it into the toilets and unzipped it in one of the cubicles. It contained a dozen or so bundles of holiday brochures; and hidden in one would be his instructions. He sat down on the lavatory bowl and examined them. A fat wad of rent-a-car leaflets was held together with a green rubber band; all the other bands were orange. He went through the pack carefully until, from one of the leaflets, a folded slip of paper fell out:

> Papworth booked Hotel Guanches, Playa de San Augustin. One week from Aug 28, Brooke at Leopold, Playa del Ingles, Manager Krausner. K connection confirmed. Will contact. Dolores.

Dolores was the code name for the local operative, whose name was Becker. Underneath the typewritten lines was a rough map, which showed the two hotels side by side, adjacent to the beach, and about half a mile from the Maspalomas lighthouse on the southernmost tip of the island.

It was nearly midnight when the cab dropped him at the ornate entrance of the Hotel Guanches. Two gardeners were hosing the profusion of shrubs and creepers which had been planted to soften the expanse of plastered concrete, stone and black wrought iron typical of the vast new holiday hotels which ran like a rash down the east side of Gran Canaria. Inside, a boy took his two bags and the clerk behind the desk in the lobby greeted him in German.

'Papworth,' Kippy announced belligerently. 'English. I was due yesterday.'

The Spanish clerk straightened up smartly and swivelled on his toes to study the card index system behind him. German management, Kippy concluded; their hotels ran like clockwork but it was difficult, sometimes, to erase completely the atmosphere of a concentration camp.

The clerk gave the bag boy a large key and Kippy signed Papworth in the register. The room was on the second floor, with a balcony overlooking paved gardens; at least it was a change from a light-well. One of the pockets in the blue hold-all had contained three hundred pounds in sterling and ten thousand pesetas, and from the hoard he gave a 50 peseta piece to the boy. Alone again, he chained the door and walked out on to the balcony, On the outer fringe of the garden below he could make out sand dunes and palm trees, and beyond the dunes he could hear the booming of Atlantic breakers. To the south a white beam knifed through the darkness every eight seconds, the Maspalomas lighthouse. A warm breeze, exhausted after its journey from the African mainland, barely fluttered the curtains. A few minutes later Kippy, no less exhausted, was asleep, fully clothed, on the reproduction Spanish medieval bed.

He was awakened next morning by the chambermaid rattling the door chain, trying to get in. It was ten-thirty; he'd forgotten to set his wrist-watch alarm.

Outside it was already hot, so he ordered *almuerzo*, a late breakfast, on the balcony. From there he surveyed the Hotel Leopold next door, a massive ten-storey block surrounded by gardens, swimming pools, tennis courts and a high stone wall. Two men, in adjoining courts, were inexplicably playing with Frisbees, aiming them towards targets at the opposite ends. German and Spanish flags flew from the top of the building.

Somewhere in that building was Hilary Brooke.

Not having binoculars was frustrating, for there was a good deal Kippy wanted to know about the Leopold before attempting to storm it. In many ways it was as secure as a castle, reflecting perhaps the Germanic passion for security. Who, after all, invented the Alsatian and the Dobermann? And on his way from the airport he'd pretended to be confused and asked the cab-driver to drive to the Leopold entrance; the place bristled with security guards and heavies, several of them wearing innocuous-looking lead-weighted sap gloves. The place seemed impregnable. But adjacent to the south wall a high sand dune overlooked most of the hotel's garden, and it offered a vantage point for a closer inspection. It wasn't as good as a Westland Wisp Spy-in-the-Sky, but it was better than guessing.

In the lobby, on his way to the beach, he was enthusiastically accosted by the chubby assistant manager. At least he could speak English.

'Aaahh, Mr Papworth! My apologies for not meeting you last night. Your room is satisfaction, I hope?'

'The room's fine,' Kippy said. 'I'm just about to do a spot of sunbathing.'

'You had a tiring flight . . . ?'

Could the man be fishing? You could never be sure. 'Yes. All the way from Los Angeles.'

'Aahh, a long way!'

'So I'm going to rest up for a few days.'

'Yes, certainly. The entire hotel is at your disposal. But . . . the travel convention at the Leopold – you're not attending?'

So that was the cover! A non-committal answer was called for.

'No . . . I'm not bothering. This is a holiday for me . . sun, sand and sea.'

Outside the sun blazed down from a turquoise sky, and the sea shimmered like mottled glass. Although it was not yet noon the sand was too hot for bare feet. From the conversations he'd over-heard, most of the guests were German, middle-class and middle-aged. Few wandered far from the ornamental garden, so he was alone on the sand dune. He spread his beach towel behind a low clump of dunegrass and flopped down, pretending to read a magazine.

One difference between the guests of the Guanches Hotel and those of the Leopold was starkly apparent; at the Leopold all but a few of the people swimming and sunning themselves were men. A dozen Spanish waiters were busy tending them with drinks at umbrella-shaded white tables scattered around a large swimming pool. Beyond the pool there was a roped-off section of paved terrace, on which was a solitary shaded table. Four women sat around it, two of them in white towelling robes. Kippy raised his sunglasses and squinted; he couldn't be absolutely sure, but one of the women looked like Hilary Brooke in her Susan Gillespie blonde wig. In any event it was obvious the Killtest performance hadn't begun; he noticed, in yet another roped-off section of the garden, several men wrestling. From what he'd read about Killtest, the combatants were thought to have a period of training and coaching before their bouts.

For half an hour Kippy reconnoitred the Leopold Hotel and its grounds from the sand dune, memorizing the lay-out, potential places of concealment, entrances and exits in the main building. Then two other peculiarities became apparent, and he swore at himself for not noticing them before.

Everyone within the hotel's walls wore a small lemon-yellow disc or badge, obviously a security measure; doubtless they also bore a number or the name of the wearer. The second observation had far more ominous implications. At least twenty of the men were guards, disguised as guests. Once Kippy identified their air of wariness and restlessness – for they seemed unable to sit in the same place for more than a few minutes – they stood out like sore thumbs. Two of them were together now, looking in his direction, so he flipped through a few pages of the magazine, then sat up and began to rub sun cream on his shoulders. With a sideways glance he could see they were walking towards him, now joined by a third guard. To leave now would arouse suspicion, but on the other hand the last thing he wanted was to be seen at close quarters by any of the guards. Fortunately, at that moment, a young woman in a black bikini was strolling from the Hotel Guanches towards the dune, and he called to her.

'Excuse me – do you have the time?' He hoped she spoke English.

'The time? About half-past twelve, I think.'

'Thank you. Have you been for a swim yet?'

'Swim?' The girl advanced a few paces up the dune. Kippy smiled and lowered his voice in an effort to entice her up further.

'I wondered if the water was cold,' he said conversationally. 'Have you been staying at the hotel long? You have a wonderful tan.'

He could see that the three guards were getting nearer, and desperately tried to think of other things to say.

'Would you like my magazine?' he asked the bemused girl. 'It's *Cosmopolitan.*' It wasn't at all, but the offer had the desired effect and the girl scrambled up through the loose dune sand to him. As soon as they saw her above the wall the guards hesitated, and Kippy continued his inane conversation with her until they dispersed, apparently satisfied. The girl, however, most emphatically wasn't, and threw the *New Statesman* back in his face.

A few minutes before three o'clock the following morning Kippy, waiting for the lighthouse beam to flash by, leapt up and slipped over the Leopold's garden wall near the high sand dune.

Crouching low, he scuttled from one shrub to another across the garden, always keeping in the shadows, and working up towards the hotel's service area which backed on to the kitchens and laundry. The complement of security men was now at its minimum; one guard patrolled the beach, another wandered around the swimming pool, and two sat by the terrace entrance to the hotel with a dog.

The dark green Leopold overalls helped in the darkness. During the afternoon he'd bought a pale blue turtle-neck sweater and a cheap, gold-plated chain bracelet from the Guanches shopping arcade, and sitting in his hired Fiat near the gate used by the Leopold Hotel employees had spent an hour waiting for the young men to come off shift. He'd often wondered to which of his physical characteristics he was obliged for the repeated and tiresome approaches of the Department's homosexual population back in London; now he earnestly wished he knew for sure. Should he flash his teeth and flutter his big blue eyes? Stuff a couple of handkerchiefs in his crotch? Bend down and pretend to fix a tyre . . . drape himself gracefully, shamelessly even, across the boot of the car? The questions, however, were never answered.

'Want two hundred American dollars?' wasn't difficult to memorize in Spanish, and the suggestive suggestion had worked on his third try. A young man with a gold earring glinting through his long black hair hesitated, then came over and sat in the car beside Kippy without a word. Kippy peeled off a hundred dollars and thrust the bills in the young man's hand, and drove back fast to the Guanches. In his room he passed over the remaining hundred dollars, and as the Spaniard stripped off his overalls, sewn to which was the vital lemon-yellow identity disc, Kippy shot him in the buttocks with an Immobilion-B needle calculated to knock him out for twenty-four hours. Now he was a very relaxed guest sleeping under a blanket on the sun-lounge on his benefactor's balcony.

The yard outside the Leopold's kitchen entrance was brightly lit and enclosed by another high wall. Kippy paused in its shadow and wiped his forehead. He remembered too late that he shouldn't rub his face, for it was dyed with quicktan; but on checking his hand he found it was not the tan coming adrift but the black combthru dye he'd used for his hair. It was now running down his face with the perspiration. He carefully mopped his face with some tissue while he waited. The early morning shift at the Guanches began at three, and he saw no reason why the Leopold should operate differently.

The calculation proved correct, and sharp at three all activity in the kitchen courtyard ceased. He took several paces backward and then leapt at the high wall, just managing to grip the top. He heaved himself over and, too late, could not stop himself falling on a row of garbage cans. One tipped over, its lid rolling and clattering almost to the kitchen entrance. He picked up a broom as an aproned man appeared in the doorway and shouted something in Spanish.

Then the man went inside. After half a minute, Kippy followed him, carrying his broom boldly through the huge kitchen and scullery to a corridor that led past the laundry to what, he hoped, was the area the cleaners used. From his brief, fractured conversation with the young man he'd kidnapped, he'd learned that his victim was one of the general servicing employees of the hotel.

By following some of the night shift workers he eventually discovered the service area in the basement. One elderly man nodded at him but the half-dozen others took no notice; he was just another new employee. The last person he wanted to meet was a foreman or superintendent, so he grabbed one of the cleaning trolleys, laden with buckets, brushes, brooms and dusters, and pushed it quickly into a waiting service elevator.

But which floor? Where the hell was Hilary? During the evening he'd gone over the problems that confronted him with the conclusion they were insoluble. The odds were so crushingly immense! The elevator stopped at the ground floor anyway, so he pushed his cart out into the lobby and began trundling it through the maze of green-carpeted corridors in a desperate search for a clue, any clue, which might lead him to Hilary Brooke.

The ground floor promised nothing, so he went to the first floor. As he emerged from the elevator two guards came towards him, so he busied himself by polishing the chrome indicator panel and attempting to hum. When they'd descended he walked with his trolley along the corridor opposite, wondering if it was a Spanish custom to hum, anyway. They sang, they danced, but did they hum? Perhaps those two guards were asking the same question.

The doors along the corridor had nameplates on them; these seemed to be the hotel's offices. At the far end of the corridor was a heavy, carved door, his first port of call; it bore the nameplate: H. F. KRAUSNER.

The door was unlocked. It led into a secretarial anteroom with desks, typewriters and accounting machines. Kippy pulled the trolley inside, locked himself in, and went over to the door of the inner office. For fifteen minutes he sweated over the lock before the pin tumblers yielded to a combination of pick and tension tool. He went in, drew the curtains closed, and switched on the desk lamp.

Spread out on the desk was a large diagram of the seating plans for the forthcoming Killtest show, and Kippy instinctively drew out his Velox-Scanic. The metal casing was hot from its hiding place in his underpants, where the tiny camera nestled next to his balls. He memorized the plan for five painfully long minutes, then copied it systematically in eight close-up sections before turning his attention to the rest of the room. Somewhere, he hoped, was a register of the room numbers occupied by the guests and combatants. Everything was in either German or Spanish, which didn't make it any easier. He searched all the filing cabinets without result, then the trays of correspondence and finally the drawers in Krausner's desk. Zero. The middle drawer was the only one locked and nothing Kippy tried would open it, so, stooping underneath, he opened his knife and cut an inch-wide strip out of the thin plywood bottom, through which he painstakingly jiggled its contents in much the same way as you'd rob a piggybank. One of the folders which fell out contained memos to staff, and in one was the information he wanted: 'Male contestants will be accommodated on the fifth floor, and the two female contestants on the sixth.' As he was replacing the documents a small, worn leather portfolio fell from the slit in the bottom of the drawer, and several folded letters and a photograph spilled from it. As they were in German, Kippy hurriedly shot them with the Scanic, the photograph included. It was a group shot of several men, two of them in the uniform of the Nazi SS.

Five minutes later Kippy was leaving the elevator at the sixth floor. He was closer, but not that close, for the rooms ran from 600 to 620. Twenty rooms! Which one was Hilary Brooke's?

Eight of the rooms had men's shoes outside the doors, waiting for the hotel's boots; that left twelve. From three others, by placing his ear to the doors, he heard the sounds of male voices, which reduced the possibilities to nine. Then down the corridor the door of 602 opened and two men staggered out, happily drunk; they sang their way to rooms 611 and 613 as Kippy polished the skirting board and pondered over the remaining six.

The floor went quiet until he heard the elevator door open behind him. It was one of the guards, who sauntered past him and up to the end of the corridor, where he paused and listened at two doors and tried the handles. Satisfied, he turned and came back, glancing casually at Kippy who was still on his knees with the polishing cloth. After taking a final look the guard pressed for the elevator and rode to the next floor up.

Kippy raced down the corridor to check the two rooms: 618 and 619. There was no visible sign that one might be Hilary's; he'd have to take a chance . . . 'You called, madam? Something wrong with the air conditioning? You didn't? But this *is* Room 619?' He pressed the buzzer of 618 several times, and waited. After an eternity a strip of light appeared at the bottom of the door, it opened a few inches, and there was Hilary Brooke.

'Kippy Leering,' he whispered. 'Kippy Leering!'

The girl's face showed surprise, confusion, then fear and panic, until he remembered his dyed hair.

'Ak-soo!' he whispered urgently. 'Quick, let me in, for Christ's sake!'

Hilary unhooked the door chain and, with a glance down the corridor, Kippy grabbed the cleaning trolly and pushed it into the room.

When the door closed, Kippy's relief expressed itself in speechlessness. She'd switched the bed-lamp on, and he could see it clearly through her nylon nightdress; not that he'd noticed the lamp in particular. Her body, from its silhouette, was formed like a ballet dancer's, lean and muscular. He raised his eyes to the tanned arms and shoulders, noting on the way the small, hard breasts with their surprisingly dark nipples, and then to her face. She'd taken off the blonde wig and was trying to tease out her black, cropped hair.

The relief that shone from her eyes matched his own.

'Shit!' he sighed, slumping into an armchair. 'I thought I'd never find you!'

'How did you?' she asked, still standing tantalizingly between him and the bed-lamp. 'They haven't let me out of their sight.'

'I saw you yesterday morning, I think,' Kippy said, getting his breath back. 'Sitting at a table on the terrace.'

'Oh, yes. With June Harrison. She's in the room next door. And two female gorillas – they're in 620 and 617, I think.'

Kippy motioned for silence. 'Jesus! I hope I didn't wake them.'

He rose and listened intently at the door for half a minute, but the silence seemed complete.

Hilary sat on the bed and he walked over to sit beside her. A plate with several uneaten *tortillas de langosta* was on the bedside table, probably laced with drugs. He checked his watch: 3.41. 'I can't stay long,' he said. 'It'll be dawn in about an hour.'

'Are you staying in the hotel?' she asked. There was a clear plea in her voice, and the strain of the past ten days showed only too plainly on her face. Her high cheekbones were practically bursting through the skin.

'No. At the Guanches, next door. I'm not far away.' To reassure her he added: 'Now I've found you, your worries are over.'

They sat silent for a while until she placed a hand on his arm and said, 'Well, I'm not too sure about that. How on earth are you going to take on all these Killtest people? There must be a hundred or more in this hotel alone!'

'I'm not sure,' Kippy said truthfully, his confidence ebbing a little. What was the point of being dishonest? Pringle had stressed to him that if Hilary wanted to pull out at the last moment, and for whatever reason, she was to be allowed to, regardless of the threat to the investigation. Her life was at stake, after all. If she wanted, they could both be out of the Leopold in minutes, and back in London in a matter of hours. There must be a hundred other ways to trap the Killtest moguls.

'To be absolutely frank,' he added, 'I have no idea. The fact that I've managed to get this far isn't much short of a miracle.'

At this admission Hilary abandoned any remaining pretence to a stiff upper lip, and lit a Gitanes with shaking hands. When the cigarette paper pulled on her lip it was the final straw, and she hastily wiped eyes that were swelling with tears. 'Oh, shit, I'm sorry,' she said in a muffled voice.

Kippy put his arm around her shoulders and kissed her on the hairline. She smelled good: Arpège. It would have been easy at this moment to roll over into the bed and to hell with Killtest, Krausner, the Harrison woman, Pringle, the lot. At this moment, certainly, the operation took on the perspective of a phantasmagoria, a mad illusion that had nothing to do with real life, and nothing to do with them. Hilary turned her face up to him, and he kissed away the tears, kissed her nose, kissed her wetly on the mouth, meeting her searching tongue with his and holding her tight. Perhaps, he thought, he *should* stay, and hide in her room until the Killtest show began; it would save breaking into the hotel a second time, with its attendant risks . . . but then he remembered the drugged Spaniard in his room. Reality like a corrosive acid began to eat into the brief, flowering fantasy, and with a reluctant final kiss to her temple he drew away.

'I have to go, Hilary, old love,' he said. 'Or we'll both be in the shit. When does all this frightful Killtest business begin?'

She stubbed her cigarette which had smouldered in the ash tray, unsmoked. She'd recovered her composure considerably.

'I know it sounds crazy, but early tomorrow morning – four o'clock, I think. God knows why!'

'It has to do with time differences around the world,' Kippy explained. 'Four in the morning here is probably early evening in New York.'

'I see. They've got it all worked out.'

'You can bet on that. Do you know what you have to do? I mean, your bout – '

'I've no idea. God knows what they've dreamed up. Something revolting, I'm sure.'

'Not even a hint?'

'Nothing. Apart from the two keepers and June, I haven't spoken to anyone, and nobody's spoken to me. A doctor has given me the once-over, that's all.'

'How is June Harrison, by the way?' Mention of her name was a harsh reminder to Kippy that he had two women to protect.

'Drugged to the eyeballs. All she cares about is getting the money. They've rammed it into her. The fact that she has to kill me to get the money doesn't seem to have registered.

And I can tell you this, Kippy – I have no intention of doing her in, under any circumstances. How do you get out of that one?'

Kippy had given the conundrum a good deal of thought. The scenario worked out at SunFun Holidays was that, somehow, he'd arrange for the bout to look convincing while avoiding harm to either contestant. Everything had seemed possible then, but now. . . .

'Hilary,' he said, avoiding her huge grey eyes. 'You can rest assured on that point. I'll be there. You'll just have to trust me. I realize it's asking a lot but that's all I can say right now. Just make it look good, whatever it is you have to do, that's all. It's absolutely vital.'

If Kippy avoided Hilary's eyes, she sought his, and looked deeply into them, seeking something to trust. Apparently, after several seconds, she found it, for she said: 'I'm in your hands, Kippy.' Then her voice trembled. 'Please don't let me down.'

He shook his head. 'I'm only human, love,' he said. 'I'll do my best. If you want to drop out – '

'No.'

' – I can get you out of the hotel now – '

'No!'

' – and nobody will ever blame you. Mr Pringle said – '

'No, Kippy. We've got this far. Let's stay the course.'

They were silent for a time, then Kippy stood and stretched himself. He parted the curtains slightly. There was a vague smear of pink on the horizon. He hesitated; it was hard to leave.

'Okay, then,' he said, letting the curtain drop back. 'I'd better vanish until tomorrow night. You probably won't see me, but I'll be there.'

He checked his face in the mirror, wiped some black dye stains from his forehead, and walked to the door. It was like pulling a nail from a magnet. He hesitated, took something from around his neck, and held it out to Hilary.

She rose from the bed; the silhouette again. 'What is it?' she asked, looking at the fine silver chain in his hand.

Attached to it was a tiny glass blue eye in a chased silver mount.

He placed it around her neck.

'It's Greek,' he said. 'It's the eye that watches over you and protects you from evil spirits.'

'Oh, thank you!' she whispered. She looked at the eye closely, then looked up at him with a smile. 'But I hope the British Government can do a little better than this.'

13

The high-frequency bleep from Kippy's wrist-watch alarm triggered off a scream and phased a dream into nightmare: a woman in a madly flapping white nightdress was running from pursuing dogs towards him across an area of paving stones. As she stepped on one it became the snout of an alligator and the girl, who was Rosa, overbalanced. He rushed to her but now the paving stones became pieces of cork and suddenly he was in the murky dark water with vile waterweeds entangling his legs. Then all the floating pieces of cork became alligators, with bits of stinking flesh still stuck to their teeth, all thrashing in the water, and the girl, who was now Hilary, screamed. . . .

It was nine o'clock and nearly dark. He sat up, suddenly, alerted by a slight movement on the balcony. The alarm had disturbed the drugged Spaniard, reminding Kippy he was overdue for another Immobilion-B shot. He groped for the tiny ejector from its pocket in the seam of his underpants, calculated a twelve-hour dose, walked out to the balcony and without ceremony shot a needle into the young man's arm. Then he sat down to wait for Becker.

Becker had called at eleven that morning, just as his breakfast had arrived; it was still there on the tray, untouched. The chambermaid had been and gone. He'd given the Scanic's tiny spool of microfilm to Becker to rush to London, with his interim report. The message he'd really wanted to send, though, was more to the point: HELP! And why not?

But now, after a good sleep, he felt contained in a membrane of numbness, a placenta through which was delivered all his bodily and mental nourishment. He had no more willpower than a foetus; his every move was, like breathing, instinctive. Perhaps the feared identity warp had got him at last; he was computerized. He tried to think for a moment, and could find not the slightest reason for fear. He would do whatever he had to do, and it would all work out.

He took up the individual-size packet of cornflakes from the breakfast tray, severed it through the middle with his knife and, as the manufacturer recommended, shook out the sun. The flakes fell into the bowl. They were all the same, only different, Kippy observed. Like a species, like humans: big ones, small ones, some as flat as fingernails, others curled up neurotically tight, some weirdos, but – he picked one up and powdered it between his fingers – all, ultimately, dust. Like people. Whether they disintegrated individually or were consumed in a mass, drowned in milk and sweetened with sugar, what did it matter? *La condition humaine* was cornflakes in a box; everything depended upon the inclination and appetite of the owner, the ultimate Guv'nor. What was so bloody sacrosanct about human life? Stand out in the open during a thunderstorm and find out, for you too could be in God's little acre receiving, on average, a mortal flash of lightning once per century; you'd have a 200 000 : 1 chance of being a smouldering statistic. Conclusion? The presence of an angry God?

But, anyway, death never worried humans unduly. The thought of standing up and speaking before a group of people exacted more fear than thoughts of death. So did thoughts of height, insects, financial problems, deep water, loneliness, dogs, driving a car, darkness, elevators and escalators . . . it was the ordinary things that made humans shit scared.

In fact humans were actually *confused* about the boundary between life and death; they still persisted in arguing over its definition, whether life ended when the brain ceased to function, or when the heart failed. It depended to some extent which country you lived in. If you were a foetus it most certainly did, for the constitutional, as apart from the moral, right to do with your body as you wish, even to destroy it, was far from universal.

So why all the furore about violence among the human

species? If it was instinctive, then breeding it out might result in extinction, like dinosaurs. If it was a trait acquired by learning, how could it be unlearned? No, humans would be better off accepting things as they found them instead of hypocritical posturing and nationalistic breast-beating. It ought not to be one country against another, or one ideology against another, but the entire world against the five per cent of the population with the fatal compulsion to fuck things up for the other ninety-five per cent.

Killtest Inc. could be doing the world a big favour by demonstrating that the sanctity of life was all hogwash. 'Now you see a live man, ladies and gentlemen . . . now you don't!' Why get uptight about the exploitation of death as an entertainment? Wasn't it the ultimate human freedom, so long denied? Kill the sanctity of life and there'd be no more wars – what would be the point? The most precious thing (so they say) one opposing side can sacrifice in an attempt to destroy the other is a human life. With the value of a life reduced to zero generals would have to trade beads or buttons. Wars could be fought on Monopoly boards. Or in Killtest arenas.

Perhaps. In Kippy's case, if it were some anonymous human and not Hilary Brooke he was expected to save, he might there and then have abandoned his task. As it was, spooning up the last of the sweet cornflakes from the bowl, Kippy never consciously paused for a moment in doubt, and thus never wondered why.

Becker arrived at nine-thirty, just as Kippy was swallowing the dregs of his cold coffee. The Canary operative didn't exactly inspire confidence; he was young, uncertain and shy, and he stammered badly. Nothing much ever happened in the Canaries, and all this was clearly a great shock to his quiet existence. The Canary Islands was no doubt a good nursery for the intelligence business, providing you didn't fall asleep with boredom.

'Sorry I'm late,' he apologized. 'But a message came through just as I was leaving. I've brought the ciphertext with me.' He took off his jacket and extracted a small folded sheet of thin paper from the shoulder lining. He really was trying hard to be a spy, Kippy thought, and took the message. Becker had typed it:

CONGRATS. KRAUSNER PHOTO IDENT KRUPPS WORK ESSEN C1938 OTHERS IN PHOTO BEING CHECKED. RE BOUT TONIGHT SUGGEST USE IMMOB AT APPROPRIATE TIME THEN EVACUATE BROOKE LEAVING HARRISON TO BECKER. EXPECT SEE YOU LONDON TOMORROW. GL ANTHEA.

'Good luck, Anthea. . . .' That was Pringle. Kippy screwed the message into a tiny ball, dunked it into what remained of his coffee and put it in his mouth. Becker was so impressed he *had* to swallow it.

'Okay, then,' he said. 'The Spaniard out there is knocked out until tomorrow morning, by which time we'll be far away. If we're not, then he'll be the least of our problems. I'm going to the Leopold now, the same way as I got in before – after that I'll play it by ear.'

'What can I do?' Becker asked, hopefully.

Kippy pondered, for there wasn't much he cared to hand over. 'I want you to take all my gear to the airport now and book it on the first plane out of here in the morning, to Madrid. I'll arrange a London connection from there.' He handed Becker a blue wallet containing tickets and passports. 'Mr and Mrs Papworth. Put it all in locker sixty-nine, as you did before.'

'Ninety-six,' Becker corrected.

'You're right. My depraved mind.'

'But won't they guess you'll try to fly out?' It was a reasonable objection.

'The way I hope to work it they won't be guessing anything. But just in case, we'll cruise around in the car I've hired until departure time. By then I want you at the airport to cover me, whatever happens. If things get really sticky, get the police in the act, somehow. You must know them enough by now to ask a favour or two. Okay?'

'Well . . . yes, okay. But what about Miss Harrison?'

'If everything goes off right she'll be very ill, perhaps unconscious. At six o'clock tomorrow morning get an emergency ambulance to the Leopold. With luck she'll be in room 619 – got that? Tell them on the 'phone you're a guest at the hotel and that she's had a heart attack, which won't be far from the truth. Tell them they might meet some obstruction but insist they get her to a hospital fast. Call them twice, three times even, as though it's a matter of life and death. Panic!' Becker wilted visibly under the weight of all these instructions. 'It shouldn't be too difficult,' Kippy concluded, pretending surprise.

Kippy could sense the atmosphere of some special occasion at the Leopold Hotel even in the basement cleaner's quarters; the building hummed with music, laughter and loud voices. Although it was just after one o'clock in the morning, the gardens and the pool were lit up like day, and at every second during his scamper from the outside wall to the kitchen he'd expected one of those Parker-Hale HV slugs up the backside. Even now he didn't have total command of his sphincter.

Most of the guests were either eating late or indulging in a second supper to fill in time, for the kitchen staff were in a frenzy. People were everywhere, and a large proportion of the guests were drunk, adding to the almost anarchic disorder. In all this confusion nobody had taken the slightest notice of the lone cleaner with the peculiar black patent leather hair.

At half past one Kippy grabbed a stepladder and rode the service elevator to the third floor, where he began changing lightbulbs. A few minutes later one of the guests stumbled from the main lift and, bouncing from wall to wall, attempted to negotiate the corridor to his room. He was about Kippy's build so he ran after the man to help.

'Which room is yours, sir?' he asked.

Without answering, the man handed him the key. In a few minutes he was slumped in his underclothes with his head over the toilet bowl, apparently the victim of alcohol but really senseless from a prodigious shot of Immobilion-B.

Kippy washed his dyed hair, dried it, and put on the man's dark blue shirt, striped blue trousers and navy reefer jacket, with its priceless lemon-yellow identity disc attached. He found a wallet in the inside jacket pocket, and opened it. The man's name was Earle W. Hopper, of San Antonio, Texas, and by the size of the billfold he wasn't exactly destitute. A yellow card fell out, marked G15 and initialled twice: the Killtest ticket, worth $5000. After stuffing his green overalls under the mattress of the bed Kippy checked the room carefully and went to the door, taking a last look at the inert and graceless figure spreadeagled over the toilet floor.

'Well, Earle,' he said. 'Won't this be something to tell the folks back home?'

The Canary Killtest took over the vast banquet room on the first floor of the Leopold.

Kippy arrived there half an hour before the start with a bunch of other guests, all volubly drunk and carrying their drinks with them. He'd filled in the previous two hours wandering over the huge hotel, memorizing possible avenues of escape. Once he'd been caught on the fire stairs by a guard but, feigning drunkenness, had been gently headed back to the bar for another belt instead of being smashed over the head with one of the plastic-coated iron bars most of the heavies carried. A drunk, he'd learned, can get away with almost anything.

The walls of the banquet room were stacked with the paraphernalia of a TV studio: five cameras were mounted on towers of scaffolding, connected by clusters of cables to an adjoining control room. Technicians were testing and adjusting rows of stage lamps, and spotlights hung among the glittering chandeliers. High up at each corner of the immense room were smaller remote cameras which, Kippy guessed, were there to shoot not the performers, but the guests; what they would make of his simple disguise of dark glasses he had no way of knowing. He hoped Earle didn't have too many friends.

If the perimeter of the banquet room was in disorder, the centre was as composed as a shrine. Fifty spotlights gave the white stage an incandescent, crystalline quality. It was half the size of a tennis court and separated by ropes of red silk from the tiers of seats which surrounded it. With pulleys suspended from the ceiling half a dozen men were raising a net of fine nylon mesh around it. At one end of the stage, standing on the floor, was the ominous shape of a gallows, stoutly built of timber, with five steps leading up to a small platform with two trapdoors, all painted black. The two hanging ropes dangled still and slack, awaiting their victims. At the other end of the stage was a large copper tank, into which flowed four thick insulated hoses. Another team of men were moving it off the stage and on to the floor, leaving the stage clear. To what diabolical use the stage and the equipment would be put, Kippy could only wonder.

Looking about, he also wondered at the size and skill of the organization that could make all this possible, and the thought that he was pitched alone into this hell-hole, one man against all this, made him tremble so much he spilled his tumbler of sangria. He felt like a black at a Ku Klux Klan picnic. Hilary had been right with her estimate; there must be at least a hundred people here all directly involved in the staging of Killtest.

By now the aisles were filling with drunk and partly drunk patrons filtering in from the betting rooms, queuing up to take their seats. Kippy waited in a corner, casually smoking, intending to take his seat at the last moment to avoid conversation and, he hoped, recognition. While he waited he watched he watched the half-dozen usherettes who were guiding the guests to their seats; they were all young women, naked under near-transparent green pyjamas.

At two minutes to four the audience lights dimmed and Kippy, swaying convincingly and wearing what he intended to be a grinning dumbfounded face, presented his ticket and was led by one of the girls to his seat, seven rows back and dead in line with two of the audience monitor cameras.

A bell rang and the audience lights were doused. The stage, picked out by the powerful lights, glistened like a block of rock salt. Across it, like a solitary penguin, strode the master of ceremonies in a dinner jacket. As he reached the centre of the stage a microphone descended and, alongside it, an ornate, gilded birdcage. The birdcage was stuffed with dollar bills.

The man held up his hand for silence.

'Good evening, folks, and welcome once again to another great gladiatorial spectacle – a spectacle of the kind that hasn't been witnessed in the world for two thousand years!' His voice came over distorted, accompanied by feedback shrieks, and he glared at a technician huddled over some audio equipment by the stage.

'I'm Buck Lines,' he resumed, 'and it's my great pleasure to tell you that tonight you'll thrill to three bouts of the quality that have made Killtest events justly famous throughout the sporting world . . . three daring tests of human endurance and courage for which there are only two rewards – riches or death!'

At this dramatic announcement there was a roar of approval from the audience which the announcer did his best to extend.

'That's it! Let the gladiators hear you! Cheer the gladiators!'

Kippy wondered what Hilary, wherever she was, would make of this deafening demonstration of human blood-lust. He stole a glimpse of the men sitting beside him; one was a tubby American voluptuary in a yellow sweatshirt, already displaying large damp areas, while the other appeared to be European, possibly German. Apparently neither of them knew Earle W. Hopper.

'Tonight, folks,' Lines was saying, 'there will be no intermissions between bouts because of limited satellite time. Our gladiators can take it – but can YOU!' The question was greeted with another howl of approval from the crowd. 'Oka-aay, then! Let's meet our first two gladiators of the evening! From Montana, United States – Henry Schneider – a big hand, please!'

From the stage apron sprang a young man in a green towelling dressing gown. He stepped into a green-painted circle on the far corner of the stage and raised a gloved hand in acknowledgement. Under his other arm he carried a stack of metal discs the size of large plates, and Kippy realized he was one of the men he'd seen throwing Frisbees on the tennis court two days before.

When the din subsided, Lines introduced the other contestant.

'And now your appreciation again . . . from Montreal, Canada – Jacques Leclerc!' Like his opponent the red-gowned Canadian leapt from the shadows on to the stage, and stood in a painted red circle.

Lines revolved on his soles so that he addressed all the audience. 'Killtest fans, this bout is a fight to the death and is for one hundred thousand United States dollars. Now, about fifty years ago in America, there was a bakery which made wonderful apple and blueberry pies, called the Mother Frisbee Baking Company. One day, two of Mother Frisbee's customers had an argument, and started to throw pie dishes at each other . . . well, you know what happened. Tonight though, folks, you are going to see a different kind of Frisbee fight, because the Frisbees our gladiators have under their arms have edges sharp enough to give you the closest shave you're ever likely to have . . . sharp enough to slice through a baseball bat and sharp enough to take your head off!'

The announcer started to retreat to the edge of the stage and two assistants took the dressing gowns from the combatants. Apart from their black leather gloves they were naked.

'However, folks,' Lines concluded, 'you won't be in any danger of losing *your* heads, so don't wet yourselves if a Frisbee comes whizzing in your direction. You're protected by this super-tough nylon netting. Oka-aay, then! On with the show! Tonight's Killtest begins!'

Lines jumped down from the stage and first Schneider, and then Leclerc, gave the ancient gladiatorial salute to the gilded cage of cash hanging above them: *Ave Imperator, morituri te salutant*! Then a bell sounded and both men crouched low, like tennis players about to receive service.

Suddenly a flashing disc spun towards Leclerc but it began to glide and he easily stepped out of its path. The Canadian was deeply tanned except for a white V at the top of his thighs; the genitals were as clearly marked as a target. No doubt, thought Kippy, everybody present was thinking the same thing: what happens if one of them gets his cock cut off? Would that be counted as a kill?

The pace speeded up and the two men pranced about the stage, weaving between the flying Frisbees, dodging serious laceration by inches. Schneider, the heavier man with a chest matted with dense black hair, unleashed a salvo of the lethal discs, the last of which caught the Canadian on the thigh, slicing through an inch of flesh. Blood spurted out and Leclerc was obviously lamed. It was a critical handicap, for survival depended above all on mobility. But he forced himself to move and dodge, ignoring the blood that quickly enamelled his leg a gleaming red.

Sensing a kill, Schneider threw another fast salvo, but so recklessly that most of them missed their target and soared harmlessly into the net. This was what Leclerc was waiting for. Schneider had only one Frisbee left, after which he'd be forced to retrieve fallen ammunition from the floor of the stage. The Canadian, though, still held perhaps half a dozen, and the men circled warily until Schneider threw his remaining disc and then bent down to gather up several more. He had only just straightened when Leclerc aimed one at his feet, putting him off balance, following with three more in quick succession. The third disc sliced deeply into Schneider's shielding arm, so deeply that it hung there for several seconds before clattering to the floor. So did the other Frisbees Schneider was holding, leaving him unarmed.

The effect of this on the crowd was adrenal. The scream of 'Kill!' went up, swelling from a small section of the audience until the entire room rang with the blood-curdling chant: 'Kill! Kill! Kill!'

On the stage it was match point, and Schneider knew it. Should he dare risk bending down to pick up a disc with only one hand? His cut arm was troubling him, apart from being useless. As if to demonstrate his superior position Leclerc, dragging his right leg, picked up several Frisbees without fear of being attacked by Schneider.

For a minute or more the Canadian stalked his opponent, catching his breath before launching an attack. Schneider successfully evaded four of the flying discs but a fifth, which glided up from low down so that he didn't see it, sliced into his chest. It was like walking into a circular saw, and the murderous blade only stopped spinning when it hit bone. Schneider screamed with the pain. He realized he had only a few seconds to fight for his survival and any thought of caution was forgotten.

Scrambling among the fallen discs he hurled them, almost blindly, at Leclerc who, in trying to dodge the barrage, slipped in a pool of his own blood. Schneider was shouting now, with banzai cries, but the prone target was difficult to hit; most of the discs spun harmlessly over Leclerc and veered away into the net. For more than a minute Schneider picked up and threw, picked up and threw, until there were no more Frisbees on the stage. He was empty handed. The chant rose again and flowed like hot lava down the tiers of sweating spectators to the bloodied stage. 'Kill! Kill!' They'd been cheated once; now the bloodlust was overpowering, like a gale.

From his position on the floor, Leclerc rose painfully. Exhausted, in excruciating pain, Schneider searched the stage for a stray fallen Frisbee. 'Kill! Kill!' The racket was deafening. Leclerc was standing now, and held three discs in his gloved hand. One of them *had* to have Schneider's name on it. Schneider turned to face him, nursing his injured arm, his eyes wide, waiting for the shock of that razor-sharp steel against raw nerve. Leclerc crouched and with a sharp flick spun a Frisbee towards his opponent. The disc seemed to float, travelling so slowly it almost hung stationary in the air, and Schneider could easily have stepped out of its path. Instead he simply stood there. Perhaps he lost sight of it in the glaring light. Kippy certainly did, for there seemed no visible reason why Schneider's neck should have erupted in a fountain of blood, or that his head should have fallen to his shoulder so awkwardly. The whole business of Schneider's death seemed to be in slow motion, like a sports replay on television. For seconds he stood there, with the severed head on his shoulder, anchored to his gaping stump of a neck by a few lengths of cartilage, the eyes open and the mouth still moving but voiceless; then his legs buckled and, like a great tree, his body fell forward on to the stage.

In contrast to the roaring before, the audience was now

strangely hushed. Some averted their eyes from the sprawled body but most were still transfixed, in a kind of cataleptic state, perhaps reliving Schneider's final moments. The American beside Kippy let out a breath he must have been holding almost since the bout began: 'Jeeee-zuzz!' His other neighbour was unblinking, frozen, refusing to take his eyes off the stage even while the white-coated attendants were removing the body and scouring off all the blood.

Within minutes Jacques Leclerc had limped off the stage with his purse, and the well-drilled team of stage hands had restored the spotlit centre-piece to its wedding cake whiteness, raised the protective curtain and erected the gallows.

Kippy had decided not to take photographs during the bouts, but now he changed his mind. Photography by patrons was strictly forbidden; the remote cameras constantly revolved and the guards constantly patrolled to ensure that this direction was faithfully observed. Yet he felt the darkness that enshrouded the audience during the contests was sufficiently protective. Photographic evidence would be valuable, if not vital, evidence in any future prosecution. He'd hidden the Velox-Scanic in a packet of cigarettes, and he produced the packet quite openly, hoping the cameras were watching, offering cigarettes to his two neighbours. Both refused, so he lit one himself, continuing to hold the packet in an absent-minded way.

The second bout, codenamed GALLOWS, was a diabolically ingenious exercise in which three wrestlers, all naked, were set the task of hanging two of their number. None of the trio had ever met before, so there had been no collusion prior to the bout; but once on the stage they had to decide who would be the first victim. When one had been despatched the survivors would set upon each other, in free unarmed combat, with the sole aim of hanging his opponent. The purse for this stupendous diversion was two hundred thousand dollars.

For the first ten minutes the men wrestled each other in random fashion, trying to isolate the weakest among them. This proved to be a middle-aged Egyptian ex-pro who'd spent most of his life in and out of the ring on the American West Coast circuit. The fact that he was the weakest did not mean he was intended to be the first victim, however; he would be reserved for the final two-hander against the strongest survivor. Consequently, by mute understanding, the Egyptian and a Scottish veteran named the Red Laird turned on the remaining member of the trio and after a monumental struggle dragged his eighteen-stone body up the stairs of the scaffold and hung him.

Seconds after the trap had been sprung the Egyptian stunned the Scot by suddenly slamming his head viciously against one of the heavy uprights. The Red Laird, disadvantaged by years of professional wrestling that was ninety-nine per cent show and sham, was not only incapacitated but shocked, and never quite recovered his wits for the duration of the bout. By then, of course, it was too late. Even by Killtest standards it was a far from entertaining match; the Egyptian toiled for half an hour to drag the Scot to the gallows, while all the time the body of the first wrestler hung disturbingly from the gibbet, his contorted face turning black in the process. The crowd was quite sobered by the horrifying spectacle, and many vacated their seats, some for good, despite the much ballyhooed all-female bout to follow.

By the time the main event was about to commence, most of the spectators had regained their high spirits, treating the final match like strawberries and cream after a particularly nauseating main course.

So far, Kippy's own state of mind had not been too far removed from that of the paying customers, but now his nerves tingled like struck slivers of glass wire. During the second bout he'd begun to worry about the distance separating him from the stage, for at twenty yards the accuracy of the Immobilion-B ejector left a lot to be desired. Below him, however, there was a vacant seat in the second row, and in the short interval between Buck Lines's introduction and the dimming of the lights he scuttled down to it.

'Another bloody pervert!' one of his new neighbours said goodnaturedly. 'Want a closer look, huh?'

The big copper tank had been lifted to the centre of the stage and the insulated hoses which snaked into it now hissed and pulsed with steam – superheated steam, as Buck Lines had explained. The tank itself, some six feet high, was covered with a circular platform about eight feet in diameter. Lines had explained that the platform was made of a special plastic which, heated by the steam underneath, was calculated to melt in twenty minutes.

Above the tank was lowered a thin cotton rope, on the end of which was a handle, dangling about six feet above the platform, and as Lines elucidated on the apparatus its repellent purpose gradually became clear. After twenty minutes the platform would melt and give way, and anybody standing on it would be deposited into the steam tank where death would follow in a matter of seconds. The only escape was by holding on to the suspended rope, but this would bear the weight of only one person; if two were hanging from it, both would drop into the tank. One of the contestants had to kill or disable the other to remain alive, with a twenty-minute time limit. By the time the two women had been led to the stage, Kippy's head was pounding with the depraved enormity of it all.

Two female escorts assisted the plainly frightened women up the steps and took their robes. For several seconds the naked figures on the platform appeared to be marble statues, gleaming white in the pool of powerful light. Then, needled by the whistling and cheering from the eager crowd they moved around the tiny space in an embarrassed shuffle.

Both women seemed high on drugs; they acted like insects in syrup, with vague swimming movements. Kippy wondered how on earth they were expected to engage each other in combat while so obviously stunned, until he saw the two female attendants stab what appeared to be tiny glass capsules into the back of each woman's hand. The effect was almost immediate. Hilary first, then June Harrison, appeared to grow taller. They began to strut about their tiny stage, arrogantly almost, acknowledging the brutal cheers and shouts of the audience by waving their arms. Kippy found himself momentarily lost in the weirdness of it all, quite numb. All around him the patrons wailed and screamed in a babel of languages, provoked by the sight of the two female gladiators, the shrieking, blaring quadrophonic rock music that was being expertly bled into the background, and the fierce heat from the great canopy of spotlights.

June Harrison, particularly, looked magnificent, with her alert, erect stance and large, out-thrust breasts. In contrast, Hilary looked a lithe goddess. An announcement came over the PA system with the news that June was the betting favourite by five to two. 'You'll eat her alive, June baby!' one man shouted. 'I got a bundle on you!' A gale of laughs followed. Kippy froze at another shout: 'She'll trip on her tits! I've got my money on the two-tone job!' His heart jumped and he hoped that in the excitement few would question the contradiction of Hilary's blonde hair and jet-black pubes – and, for that matter, her diminutive breasts. It was an inglorious, bestial spectacle, and only with great difficulty did Kippy restrain himself from spraying the bawling, clamouring, sweating men about him with a salvo of Immobilion-B needles. As it was, the tiny ejector was clenched in the palm of his hand and his finger itched with the urge to put both women out of their misery as soon as possible.

He'd been warned repeatedly at training sessions about moments like these: the fleeting, dangerous triumph of emotion over intellect. 'It's not called intelligence work for nothing, you know,' one of the lecturers was fond of saying. But Hilary up there, drugged and vulnerable, the puppet of a monster, exposed to the baying lust of eight hundred men! He dragged his eyes away in an attempt to cool his rage, away from Hilary and June Harrison, away from the audience. While the clamour continued he watched the deadly steam hiss from joints in the hoses, the TV cameramen, the usherettes clustered around the entrance to the banquet room, the two men standing with them. One of the men, entirely bald and deeply tanned, walked quickly down to the front of the stage and stood there for a time, looking up at the two women. There was something about him that suggested authority; perhaps he was one of the Killtest organizers. The chaotic conditions were perfect, so he raised his cigarette packet and snapped the bald man several times.

Then something caught his eye. A large object was being lowered from the ceiling. He hadn't noticed it before, a large, open-ended plastic cylinder, ten feet high and wide enough to fit snugly over the platform. Its purpose was obvious – to enclose the two women gladiators and to prevent them from jumping off the platform.

In a flash Kippy realized how complete the trap really was. Once the cylinder was lowered his Immobilion-B needles would be useless as dressmakers' pins against steel armour. He hadn't intended using the ejector until after the bout had actually begun, but now there was no alternative. The cylinder was already descending past the women's heads. He'd set the ejector for two-hour doses but there was no time to change it now. There was no time to think, even.

With the ejector enclosed by his hand he raised it, as if to scratch his ear but really to steady his aim, for he was shaking uncontrollably. The big cylinder was down to their shoulders as he squeezed the release. He couldn't afford to miss and there was no way of knowing if he hit the targets or not. He aimed at Hilary and then at June Harrison. It was a case of overkill or nothing. As the plastic cylinder dropped down he continued firing, hoping the delicate mechanism would stand the pace. Now he was aiming at their exposed thighs, and then below the knees. As the transparent cage finally plopped into position on the platform he'd managed to eject a dozen or more needles, and prayed that at least two of them had found their mark.

The bell sounded and the sadistic appetite of the crowd expressed itself in a crescendo of demoniac roaring. Inside their plastic prison the two women faced each other uncertainly. Then June lurched forward and grabbed Hilary's arm, trying to pull her down on to the platform. Hilary fell prone, and lay still. Moments later June staggered and tumbled on top of her.

Neither moved. The spectators were stunned. The deafening howl that had filled the room almost non-stop for an hour and a half suddenly diminished to a subdued mumbling, and finally to a hush, like the dying notes of a concerto.

'Are they dead or somethin'?' one of the men near Kippy asked.

'They've been gassed!' another man shouted.

Kippy seized the opportunity. 'We're bein' taken for suckers!' he drawled to the men near him. 'It's all a big con. What, five thousand bucks for this crap!'

The reminder of value for money cracked the dam of pent-up emotions, Within seconds there was an explosion of red-faced, roaring fury. Before he'd even managed to reach the aisle the stage was stormed by shouting, gesticulating people. The big cylinder was raised and the bald-headed man ran up the steps to inspect the unconscious women. Most of the spotlights were doused and Buck Lines came on stage, calling for the microphone to be lowered.

While all this was going on the spectators, feeling cheated, started to slow-clap and stamp their feet in protest. The bald man came down the steps again and spoke to Lines. Two men in white coats clambered up to the platform to examine the two fallen gladiators. Lines finally got his microphone and was trying to make an announcement. He could barely be heard above the tremendous din, and his appeals for silence went unheeded. To Kippy it was glorious chaos.

'Folks!' Buck Lines shouted. 'Folks – please! It seems that both our lady gladiators have suffered some kind of collapse or shock or something. Our doctors are looking at them now and a full report will be circulated to your rooms in the morning. The bar will stay open indefinitely and all bets will be returned. So please – please! – I appeal to you all to leave the auditorium. . . .'

While the announcer was pleading with the disgruntled fans Kippy walked with a group of Americans to the exit. He remembered that hanging in one of the basement lockers was a white coat. The white coat was a passport to almost anywhere in the hotel right now. The most difficult part of the nightmare operation was over. The rest, he convinced himself on the way downstairs, had to be a push-over.

14

That night Oppenheimer's scrambler alert ran hot for an hour. By midnight the entire Ring, with the exception of Simak, had assembled at the Waldorf Towers.

Oppenheimer tersely sketched a picture of the disaster before training his verbal armament on McSwiggan.

'What completely baffles me, Frank,' he said, addressing the ceiling, 'is why you felt your security was so goddam brilliant you could afford to leave everything to Simak and Taubes!'

'What the hell does it have to do with security?' the Irishman yelled back. 'You – all of you – went over the security plans with me and you all agreed everything was buttoned down tight. So don't drop the shit in my lap!'

Lethnal attempted to lower the temperature. 'To be fair, Henschel, we're not entirely sure what exactly happened. According to what Simak told you, everything seemed to be going smoothly until those two women – '

'That's just it!' Oppenheimer exploded. Nobody in the room had ever seen him so agitated. 'Two women don't simultaneously pass out for no reason! Someone got to them – someone slipped them a mickey. Our medic never got a chance to examine the younger one, but he did spend an hour with the other woman before she was taken away and he's certain she was pumped full of some drug – and it wasn't one of ours.'

'Where are they now?' Mrabet asked.

'I was coming to that!' Oppenheimer shot back testily. 'Someone called the hospital at Las Palmas and the police and an ambulance came to investigate. There was nothing

Simak or Taubes could do without raising suspicion – they were sitting on the edge of a goddam volcano! But at least we know where this June Harrison is. What we don't know is what happened to the other girl – she just vanished!'

'I don't believe it!' Mrabet said, glancing at McSwiggan.

'You'd better believe it, all of you!' Oppenheimer continued. 'She sure didn't get up and walk away all by herself! And if this little episode has nothing to do with security, Frank, then I'm a monkey!'

'Might I be permitted to make an observation?' General Ton asked suddenly. Because he so rarely spoke, the diminutive Vietnamese commanded instant attention.

'Go for your life!' Oppenheimer told him. General Ton turned his smiling face towards McSwiggan.

'Frank – I hesitate to tell you your business, but possibly your security posture is a little too defensive?'

McSwiggan's response began on his face – its features swelled as if about to explode – then traversed his entire body, which stiffened as though expecting some physical attack, to finish in his hands, which crumpled a memo pad on the table in front of him.

Oppenheimer took all this in, and spoke with deliberate firmness. 'Just listen, Frank. After all, Dino doesn't often hand out free advice.'

General Ton paused for a moment, and then continued. 'We have an old saying,' he said reflectively. 'A man who secures his house by closing the window shutters is blind to the dangers outside.' He waited for a few seconds to allow this to sink in. 'Perhaps there is wisdom in that saying. I hasten to add that our internal security is beyond criticism, for which we have to thank you, Frank. But outside . . .?'

'I'm not a one-man CIA!' the security boss growled. 'My outfit is stretched to the limit as it is – '

'Then this might be the right moment to get some help, Frank,' the general went on. 'Lao Man, for instance – '

Oppenheimer leaned forward. 'Yes, Frank, exactly! I'm damned if I know what you've got against Lao Man, but he's there in Hong Kong with half the Chinese population at his elbow – the Triad, I mean. He'd sell his ancestors' graves for the chance to help us!'

'Don't think I haven't given it some thought,' McSwiggan parried. 'But once you let that horde in the doors they'll swamp us. They're not called the Yellow Peril for nothin'!'

'I'm reminded of how they handled the Macao Killtest,' Mrabet mused. 'As clean as a church picnic – *and* they collared that British agent as well.'

'All right, Frank,' Oppenheimer summed up. 'This is an order. Call Lao Man immediately and tell him we want his Triad boys hooked into our own security network – as from tonight. I want that girl traced. I want to know how she gave us the slip, and who helped her.'

McSwiggan doodled on his crumpled pad, and said nothing.

'Tonight, Frank!' Oppenheimer emphasized. 'Tonight!'

The nurse gave Pringle two aspirins to take with his cup of tea as Kippy's Mini crunched to a stop in the gravelled driveway. He tossed them down and walked out to meet his young colleague.

'How is she?' Kippy asked, squinting in the September morning sun. The golf course surrounding the Oaks was a sea of glistening green. A golfer near the thirteenth watched them. Adamson, of Surveillance.

'The prognosis isn't good, I'm afraid,' Pringle said, draining his tea. 'She's still knocked out, poor girl.'

'Christ! It's history repeating itself!' Only two months before, Kippy had been in the same hospital for the same reason. He remembered the dizziness, the numb hands and feet, the acrid stink he exuded.

'You put six shots into her. She's saturated with the stuff.'

'Bloody hell!' He moved towards the hospital steps but Pringle stopped him.

'There's no point in seeing her now, Kipling, believe me.' He patted the young man on the shoulder. 'Don't blame yourself, son. What else could you do? You saved her life – '

'It seems we should have reservations about that – '

'I'd have done exactly the same in the circumstances,

Pringle assured him, as though anything Pringle did had the blessing of the Deity. 'And I don't think there's the slightest doubt about her pulling through; Hilary's a tough little number, remember that, otherwise we'd never have let her go.' There he was, using 'we' again. Although sending Hilary had been his idea and decision he was now using 'we'; there *was* some doubt.

'What about June Harrison?' Kippy asked. Under orders he'd been out of contact with the Unit for the three days since his return from the Çanaries.

'A much better picture there, I'm happy to say,' Pringle said, absently scratching at some birdshit on the windscreen of the car. 'Becker arrived with an ambulance and police escort and although there was a hell of a fuss they managed to get her away safely. She's in hospital in Las Palmas, being treated according to our instructions.'

'How many?' Kippy asked.

'You were obviously gunning for Hilary,' Pringle observed, still scratching. 'Only three needles. What was the range?'

'About twenty, twenty-five feet.'

'You're a passable marksman, then.'

'Perhaps too good,' Kipp said sullenly. 'But what about those bloody gangsters? Aren't they after her – June Harrison?'

'Well, yes. It's a prickly situation. We have Becker and another man to stop the Killtest crowd from getting at her, and they have two men watching to make sure she doesn't talk or disappear.'

'In other words, it's a bloody mess!'

'I wouldn't say that. Stalemate, perhaps, but all under control. She won't come to any harm.' For a while they stood there, mulling over the thousand possibilities.

Pringle placed his empty cup on the steps. 'We've got a Unit meeting set for eleven, so why don't we drive back together?'

With some reluctance Kippy climbed back into the Mini. The quiet warmth of the Surrey countryside had begun to envelop him with a feeling of guiltless peace, and he had to drag himself from its seductive caress. He started the engine and they drove back along the half-mile of private road to join the A23 for London.

'Before I fill you in,' Pringle said after a long silence, 'how did you spirit Hilary out of the Leopold Hotel? You didn't include that in your report.'

'I waved my magic wand and became a doctor,' Kippy said. Then he became serious. 'After the bout was stopped she was taken to her room. There was a genuine doctor there, American I think, but when he went downstairs I nipped in, kidded the guard, and took Hilary down to the basement in the service lift. Luckily the confusion was unbelievable. I took off her wig, dressed her in some overalls and frog-marched her through the kitchens and staff rooms to the service entrance, propping her against the wall while I got the car. Would you believe she passed for one of the Spanish houseboys?'

'One advantage of looking butch, I suppose,' Pringle commented.

'Well, I got the car and bundled her in and drove like hell for the airport, incidentally passing Becker's ambulance on the way. The plane left at 7.30 and we were first on it. Put the fear of hell into the crew, too. I changed Hilary into a dress, stuffed a cushion up it and told them she was due to have a baby any minute and had an appointment that morning with her gynaecologist in London.'

'Good work, Kipling,' Pringle acknowledged, as though this sort of thing happened every day.

'I wouldn't like to chance my luck again, though,' Kippy said with feeling, unable to escape from visions of the girl, unconscious in a hospital bed.

'Any loose ends?' Pringle asked. 'Loose ends that you haven't told me about?'

Kippy thought hard. The tangled threads of those three deranged days were bound to include some loose ends. 'Well, Hilary's disappearance, for a start – '

'We've covered that. We had Becker telephone Simak to tell him he was Hilary's boyfriend, and if they tried anything funny he'd carve them up and go to the police. He asked for the twenty-thousand-pound fee, too. I thought that bit of cheekiness would convince them.'

'Who's this Simak?'

'He's the bald-headed gentleman you photographed at the Leopold, Winifred Brodie's contact, as it happens, the one who passed himself off as Rodriguez. Jay Simak, American. We're getting his number right now. So far all we know is that he was in the Chicago slammer for malicious wounding in 1957.' Kippy loved the way Pringle's clipped and proper Esher dialect lapsed into slang when he talked about the criminal world.

'But what else?' his chief was asking.

Kippy wheeled the Mini into the slow lane and concentrated. He remembered Earle W. Hopper.

'I knocked out one of the American guests, but he was stinking drunk and neither he nor anybody else will know any different. But he'll wake up with one daddy of a hangover!' He forgot about the overalls he'd hidden under the mattress.

'And – ?' Pringle prompted.

'The Spanish houseboy I kidnapped. The last I saw of him he was sound asleep on my hotel balcony. Seeing he came up to my room for the sort of immoral purpose that's frowned upon by the Spanish authorities, I don't think he'll make much of a fuss. And in any case he got two hundred dollars out of it.'

'Nothing else?'

'No, nothing.' The slate seemed clean, and it gave him a comfortable feeling.

'Very well, then,' Pringle said, finally satisfied. 'I'll bring you up to date. Sam, I think I told you, is fine. We replaced him with another corpse in the Hong Kong morgue, so officially Sam isn't with us. Unofficially, he arrived back here last night, via Bangkok. By sheer good luck he saw Lao Man boarding a Cathay Pacific plane for Bangkok so on the spur of the moment he switched his ticket and flew there too. He thinks he's got a fix on the DADIN training camp, something we can follow up, anyway. After Hong Kong that took a lot of nerve, I must say.'

'I agree,' Kippy said. 'He's got cojones.' He turned and noticed Pringle's puzzeld face. 'Balls,' he added.

'We're breathing down their necks, Kipling. We're getting awful close to the top. Simak, for instance – he's one of the tall poppies, for sure.'

'What about Krausner, the boss of the Leopold Hotel?'

'Small fry. He was just being used. But the photograph you copied is a different matter altogether. It was taken in Essen, at the Krupp works just before the war. Krausner was deputy chief security officer there until he was posted to Madrid in 1942. The others in the photograph, if I can remember, were a couple of minor Nazi officials, Burchardt and Hindemith, both dead, and a character named Franz Luebke, who we're still trying to trace. He seems to have disappeared just before the end of the war, possibly to Switzerland. Although he had something to do with German armament production, his file doesn't rule out the possibility that he also played an important part in a massive Nazi counterfeiting operation, forging British banknotes to finance their foreign espionage during the war. An old SIS memo named Luebke as one of the top Nazi economic advisers, so he was close to the bunker crowd. That was in 1944, just before he disappeared or defected, and after that he seems to have gone into smoke . . . wisely, I should think.'

'What,' Kippy asked, 'makes you think this Luebke has any connection with the Killtest crowd?'

'We're simply investigating every lead that presents itself,' Pringle said. 'And any friend of Krausner's is no friend of ours. As far as I'm concerned anyone in that photograph who's still alive is hot until proved innocent.'

He was silent while Kippy negotiated a complicated interchange.

'Then,' Pringle continued, 'there's McSwiggan. Frank McSwiggan.'

'Another biggie?'

'Big enough for Lao Man to mention in a telegram, at least by his initials. Anyway, in yet another stupendous computer coup, Haversham identified him. Not too difficult, really . . . record as long as your arm, half a dozen convictions for theft and violence back in the sixties and a Special Branch report on his activities as an IRA supplier and mercenary recruiter as late as last year.'

'Things are really moving, then!' Kippy said. 'How many more?'

'That's it. But with our finger on three key Killtest people I think the time's ripe to try something really big.'

'How big?'

'All the way to the top, Kipling. All the way to the top.'

The others were waiting above the SunFun Holidays office in the Haymarket when they arrived back from the Oaks. Pringle dealt immediately with the questioning faces.

'Hilary's not out of the woods yet,' he told them. 'She's still on the critical list, but improving. And incidentally I've sent a memo to the Ministry requesting some urgent research into antidotes for Immobilion-B.'

'We sure need it,' Sam Humbert agreed. 'We seem to have shot up more of our own people than anybody else.'

Pringle sighed, sat down behind his desk and automatically opened his top drawer for the aspirin bottle. Just as automatically Angela Hotchkiss fetched a tumbler of water from the sink in the corner.

'What,' Pringle suddenly bawled, 'in God's name is this?' He held up two yellow pages of ciphertext from Telex Central, marked with the familiar codestamp of CIA Records, Washington.

'It's a reply to our request for information on McSwiggan and Luebke,' Angela told him.

In seconds Pringle was livid. 'What request?' he shouted. 'I distinctly remember giving instructions that no – repeat NO – contact of any kind was to be made with the CIA anywhere. Who's responsible?'

Sam Humbert crossed and uncrossed his long legs and then spoke up. 'It was an oversight, Stan. As you instructed, Angela sends every agent working on this project a daily report. The Hong Kong station is on the list, you know that, and when they read that we were scratching our heads over McSwiggan and Luebke someone there sent a routine retrieval request to both the FBI and the CIA in Washington. Hong Kong, you may remember, was copied in after everyone else, and we forgot to tell them about the no-no *vis-à-vis* the CIA.'

Pringle clamped his eyes shut and shook his head in dismay.

'That's champion, that is! Bloody champion!' From the bottle he added another aspirin to the two already in his hand. 'What a cock-up!'

'I agree about the cock-up,' Sam said soothingly. 'But it isn't quite in the disaster class. Anyway . . . why don't you read what they say?'

Pringle gulped the tablets and scanned the ciphertext. Then he read it aloud to the room:

'YOUR REQUEST LUEBKE FRANZ REFER OSS FILE LUEBKE D273/4077/N (1944) OTHERWISE NEGATIVE. NO REFERENCE MCSWIGGAN BUT PREVIOUSLY INVESTIGATED (1975) AND CLEAN. COGNAC.'

Cognac was the codename for the section of the CIA Records Division which kept files on foreign nationals.

'The OSS file they refer to,' Sam explained, 'is also in our own records as a copy. All it says is that Luebke disappeared. Presumed dead. Useless!'

'Yes, it isn't very helpful of them,' Pringle agreed. 'And they offer nothing on McSwiggan, either?'

'The CIA might say he's clean, but the FBI has no such illusions. See the other telex. They've already authorized a stake-out. He's not in New York at the moment, incidentally. He's got a dozen different visas, so he could be anywhere – temporarily, we hope. But you might be interested to know that he flew out of Kennedy for London via Hong Kong on July 12. There's no record of him arriving here, but he certainly landed at Hong Kong and departed on the 17th under an assumed name.'

'July twelve and seventeen,' Pringle mused, calming down considerably.

'Just before and after the Killtest show there,' Angela reminded him in her crisp, oddly-pitched voice.

'Well, all this is dandy, as far as it goes. We seem to have blundered into some sort of confirmation that somebody in the CIA is deliberately trying to steer us away from Luebke and McSwiggan, and we've made a bit more progress on the Irishman. But that's not enough. If we're supposed to be gunning for Gams what the hell are we doing asking rude questions about Luebke and McSwiggan, who have nothing to do with Gams? We've punctured our own balloon! And now our friends will be on the alert because of this stupid, unauthorized request. I do wish I'd been consulted!'

Pringle was now buzzing again like an angry wasp while the others tried to rationalize what advantages might result from the mistake.

'It could be argued,' Sam said in an exploratory way, 'that our balloon on Gams has served its purpose.' Pringle said nothing for half a minute or so, when he nodded towards the computer expert.

'Perhaps you should put your oar in at this point, Ellis,' he said to Haversham. Sox, who'd been daydreaming, stood up abruptly and a stack of computer print-outs slid from his lap to the floor. He stooped to pick them up.

'Leave them, Ellis, leave them!' Pringle said irritably. 'Tell us about this . . . combing you've been doing.'

'Well, yes, I did one on Luebke yesterday, or rather on German economists and financiers, every one I could find on our files.'

'And . . . ?' Pringle prompted.

'Nothing. No analogues, no correlations, nothing. But Angela, who was punching the cards from the files – which usually include mugshots – noticed a similarity between Luebke and a Swiss financier named Dietrich.' Haversham stopped, and motioned to Angela, standing by the episcope. 'Angela?'

She switched the instrument on and they all turned to look at the dazzling white rectangle on the wall. Kippy drew the curtains. Two photographs of faces, side by side for comparison, were projected four feet high on the wall.

'The one on the left is Luebke,' Haversham explained. 'Enlarged from the group snap Kippy copied in Krausner's office. The one on the right is Joachim Dietrich, taken by a Zurich newspaper is 1966 to illustrate a story about a bank takeover. Although one was taken twenty-five years after the other, the resemblance is quite positive, don't you think?'

Pringle's own face was lit momentarily by the flare of his lighter. 'What does everyone think?' he asked the room. 'There's a resemblance, but isn't it dangerous to jump to the conclusion they're the same man?'

Kippy detected rehearsal.

'Of course!' Haversham agreed. 'But there's more. I got our New York people to check the *Wall Street Journal* photo files for Dietrich and any other Swiss or German financial bigshots. He sent back forty photos on the fax link about an hour ago, and one of them – ' He cued Angela to project the photograph alongside the others ' – is our man!'

Despite the poor reproduction, the faces looked identical.

'Dietrich!' Pringle exclaimed.

Haversham corrected him. 'No. Dr Carl Lethnal. He's a Manhattan stockbroker, emigrated to the US late in 1973.'

'I see.' Pringle pretended to be cautious. 'I accept that Lethnal is undoubtedly Dietrich, but is Lethnal the man standing by Krausner in that Nazi family photograph in 1938?'

'It's either a reasonable assumption,' Sam said, 'or a way-out coincidence.'

Angela broke in. 'I should like to add that, as Dietrich, he flew out of Switzerland under a cloud of suspicion. Nothing was ever proved, but he was to have been called as a witness in a Bank of England enquiry in 1974 into the disappearance of international funds running into millions.'

'It does seem to add up,' Sam urged.

Pringle was satisfied; his conclusion had been verified by Sam before he'd totally committed himself. He tipped his chair back, put his feet on the desk, and pondered while Kippy opened the curtains and Angela made tea.

'There's one way to test our theory,' he said, after a long pause. 'And that's with a full-frontal challenge!' Then, enigmatically, 'If you eat a toadstool and don't die, you've found a mushroom.'

The others looked at him intently.

'So far,' he said, 'we've been sitting here like sponges, just soaking up information and making intelligent guesses.'

'You could have fooled me,' Sam mumbled.

'And me,' Kippy added, louder. 'And Hilary – '

Although a flicker of his eyes betrayed his discomfort at the *faux pas*, Pringle ignored them.

'As I see it, we have two alternatives. The Unit can continue as it is, penetrating into this Killtest Organization a little bit each day, advancing its investigation inch by inch, working its way slowly but surely to the top – and warning everybody in advance. But, as Sam and Kipling rightly point out, this method isn't without its risks; we've lost one man already, almost lost another, plus one on the danger list – so any other reasonable option ought to be examined. One option is that we simply challenge them outright. Anyway, I've come to the conclusion that at this point in time this course is the right one to follow.'

'I hadn't thought we'd got to that stage yet,' Haversham said unexpectedly, for he never contradicted Pringle. Perhaps he was shocked by visions of premature retirement from the Unit; his computers would be redundant in a hand-to-hand clash.

'Come, now, Ellis!' Pringle said diplomatically. 'It's you who've made it largely possible – and we're by no means out of the woods yet. Only I think we must force the issue now that we have sufficient ammunition to do it. The question is, how?'

Aware that Pringle intended answering his own question, the others remained respectfully silent.

'You all know of Sir Finlay Watkins, I take it?' he asked them.

'Sir Showbiz!' Kippy announced. 'The man who brought TV entertainment down to the level it is today!'

'He's running about in a Rolls and you aren't,' Pringle shot back acidly. 'Anyway, he's a member of my club and we were chatting about the problem last night over dinner. And I think he came up with the answer.'

It never ceased to amaze Kippy that despite the extraordinary secrecy surrounding their activities, the millions of pounds spent on security devices, the continuous checking of every operative and all the other measures designed to seal up the department as tight as a can of beans, Pringle thought nothing of discussing their investigations at his club; indeed he would have been most affronted if it were suggested this had the remotest semblance to a security leak. It was an echo, perhaps, of the intelligence service's past – élitist, eccentric, public school, Pall Mall Club.

'It's all very simple,' Pringle was saying. 'Here's the scenario. A certain infamous person who is well known internationally, and who for the present I'll refer to as X, actually challenges Killtest Inc. by threatening to set up a similar, but larger, organization. This X already knows enough about Killtest Inc. to convince them he means business and he'll be able to prove he has the financial backing and the necessary connections. Sir Finlay's view – and he's had no end of experience on this point – is that Killtest will react exactly like any other entertainment conglomerate would react to a competitive threat of this kind – they'd want to negotiate for a merger!'

Pringle paused to let this sink in, replacing the dead cigarette between his lips with another. Then he glanced up, hardly disappointed that everyone in the room looked sceptical.

'As boardroom theory it sounds fine,' Sam said finally. 'But I'd hate to have my life staked on it.'

'Yes,' Kippy agreed. 'It doesn't sound all that convincing to me. But who's this "Mr X"?'

'That, Kipling, is the real pearl in the abstract oyster. Now, when we identified Luebke in Krausner's photograph I had a hunch there had to be an ex-Nazi connection somewhere. Krausner is a highly respected man in Spain and the Canaries – I've checked. He's a millionaire, a great success. He's practically on sleeping terms with the Spanish cabinet. In other words Krausner had nothing to gain and everything to lose by allowing the Killtest crowd into his posh new hotel. There had to be some very heavy pressure, like exposure and blackmail. The Spanish government no doubt knows something about his Nazi past, but that's nothing new and there are hundreds of ex-Nazis running around in Spain. So perhaps there's something in Krausner's past they *don't* know. So I tackled Sir Finlay, who's a Zionist – I knew he had some pull with Mossad, the Israeli secret police and as a result I discovered that Krausner was a member of the Waffen SS from 1940 to 1942.'

'Wow!' Kippy breathed.

'Which makes him slightly vulnerable to blackmail,' Sam said. 'I take it you won't tell the Israelis where he is until after our show is over?' Pringle certainly hadn't been sitting on his arse.

'I'm not sure whether he's important to them or not,' Pringle said coolly. 'But I'm quite prepared to trade him. But to continue: whatever it is in Krausner's past it must be top secret material or it would have been discovered long ago. So whoever is leaning on Krausner must have been well up in the Nazi hierarchy – and thus would also have known Mr X. But since my theorizing with Sir Finlay last night, events have raced ahead, and tend to prove my hypothesis. The ex-Nazi applying the pressure on Krausner could very well be Lethnal, who we think was Luebke when Krausner knew him. And there is little doubt that Luebke would have known Mr X.'

'Okay,' Kippy said cheerfully. 'I'll be the bunny. Who is Mr X?'

'Martin Bormann.'

Kippy mentally unscrambled what he knew of the former Nazi leader. 'Bormann? Bormann's ghost? He died in 1945!'

'Nothing has ever been proved,' Pringle said. 'I know, because I directed a hunt five years ago when he was reported to be working as a farm labourer in the East Anglian fens.'

'He's also been reported in Buenos Aires, Mexico City, the Congo – '

'Exactly! So long as people have imagination, Bormann is alive and well and could be anywhere. It's a wonder some newspaper didn't report him on the moon! But to get back to the point, although there's medical evidence suggesting his death in Germany in 1945, it's far from conclusive. The East Anglia report turned out to be a wild goose chase; someone met a septuagenarian farm worker with a Kraut accent and thought he recognized the face. At one stage Bormann was thought to have fled from Germany in a U-boat, transferred to a freighter and landed with false papers on the Norfolk coast, so the report had to be taken seriously. But it was just folklore; the man turned out to be a harmless old labourer with smoker's cough in a Norwich scrapyard. I was kept on the case for another couple of weeks, even going to Germany to interview his surviving relatives. In the end I couldn't say for sure whether he was alive or dead.'

Sam could not disguise his incredulity.

'But do you mean to tell us that Martin Bormann – or his ghost – will simply pick up the phone and call this Lethnal in New York?'

'Hello, dere!' Kippy spoke nasally into his cupped hand. 'Is dat you, Carl? Howdy! Now listen, Carl old Buddy, I got dis dandy idea – '

'Yes. Why not?' Pringle said calmly. 'The bold lie is the next best thing to the truth.'

The preposterous proposal stunned them all. Was Pringle going around the twist at last? There was a long silence.

'You know,' Sam said. 'It's so bloody silly it might just work.'

Pringle continued to gaze searchingly at the others.

'Yes, it's a pretty cool idea,' Kippy ventured. 'It'd be totally unexpected; full marks for that.'

Pringle agreed. 'I think it will throw them completely, and diminish their suspicions, too.'

'They'll be as intrigued as hell.'

'That's part of the intention,' Pringle purred. 'We can surmise from that old SIS memo – which stated that Luebke was one of the Nazi Germany's top economic advisers about 1944 – that Luebke – that's Lethnal – was almost certainly a close associate of Martin Bormann. There's the tiniest risk that he wasn't, but it's one we'll have to accept. But if we do accept it, then Lethnal *has* to be dead keen to meet his old Nazi chum after all these years.'

'But what if Lethnal knows more than we do?' Sam objected. 'I mean Lethnal may know for certain that Bormann is dead. Perhaps he might have actually seen him die – in which case it'll rebound on us.'

Pringle was firm on this. 'No chance. No documentation

exists and I doubt if any did exist. And remember that Lethnal was out of Germany before 1945, with the Nazis hunting him. He wouldn't be privy to any information about Bormann's alleged death.'

'But as a top brass deserter during wartime,' Sam prodded, 'mightn't Lethnal avoid any contact with Bormann – who was still with the German High Command at the time?'

'On the contrary. They were, in the end, birds of a feather. They both defected. And think for a moment about the loneliness of a Nazi on the run . . . there are hundreds of them still at large, even now. They're still human, though – I know some will disagree with that – and the opportunity for a safe renewal of contact with one of their former colleagues must be irresistible. The way they'll see it is as two old comrades swapping fond memories of a time when they shared tremendous power, memories of the most triumphant years of their lives. In my view Lethnal will fall for it, hook, line and sinker!'

Sam hadn't given up yet. 'Until he recognizes that our Martin Bormann isn't his old chum at all.'

'Don't worry on that score. They last saw each other thirty-five years ago. We have access to dozens of photographs and all Bormann's documentation until 1945. The rest we can invent.'

'So we're looking for a seventy-seven-year-old man with a Kraut accent,' suggested Kippy, with just a trace of malice.

'And a first class make-up job,' added Sam.

'How is it boss – ' Kippy asked Pringle, 'that you dreamt this one up, and I didn't?'

'Perhaps that's why you're not running this outfit,' Pringle told him smugly, 'and I am.'

15

Mrabet was fond of philosophizing from the windows of the Waldorf Towers suite. Today he was even more expansive than usual. A few hours before, he'd given lunch in the suite to a dozen government dignitaries after which, over cognac and cigars, he'd dilated for half an hour or more on the importance of Franco-American relations. Just after a State governor, two mayors, a congressman and three senators had listened to him in respectful silence, Mrabet doubtless found it both irritating and puzzling when Lethnal, General Ton Dinh Quan and McSwiggan, who'd just entered, ignored him completely and began to conduct a private conversation at the other end of the big room.

Depressed, Mrabet looked down again at mid-afternoon Manhattan, neutralized to a dun colour by the low cloud, and could not resist uttering his thoughts aloud.

'Look at it. The shitty city – *merde!* A city of dead and dying dreams, a city of ten million windows looking out on another ten million windows. Bankrupt! Sinking under the weight of its own absurdities, a funeral parlour of American ingenuity descending by the gutter to its grave.' Sirens sounded far below as two prowl cars sped along Fifty-first Street towards Madison.

The buzzer sounded, its successive changes of pitch and tone indicating the correct key combination. Jay Simak came in and threw his wet mac on to a settee. It had just begun to rain.

He walked to the bar and poured himself a large bourbon. 'Oppenheimer's downstairs,' he said to the others. 'Having a haircut. He'll be up a few minutes, I guess.' He lit a cigar and slumped into an armchair.

It was to be the first full Ring meeting for over a month, called by Oppenheimer to 'overhaul the machinery' as he'd put it. Once regular weekly affairs, full meetings were now quite rare, and the suspicion was growing among some of them that this was Oppenheimer's strategy to deny them knowledge of those aspects of the enterprise outside their own specialized spheres. Somebody once called it 'divide and rule'.

'He needs a haircut?' Mrabet said, turning eventually from the windows. 'Apart from half a milligram of fuzz, he's as bald as you, Jay.'

'Uneasy lies the head that wears the fuzz,' Lethnal observed archly, although his own skull was a testimonial to transplants.

They all smiled. It wasn't often anyone spoke out against Henschel Oppenheimer, nor was it easy to score off him, for he kept an arctic distance between himself and his colleagues.

In the eight months of their association, most of the men present felt they knew no more about him than they did at their first meeting. None had ever been invited to his apartment. None had met his friends – if indeed he had any. None knew more than the sketchiest details of his past life, and what he actually did in the CIA was, despite their professed knowledge, a complete mystery.

Yet, frustratingly, he seemed to know everything about *them*. Once a week, using his wheedling voice with the finesse of a surgeon's probe, he'd grill them privately about their activities and opinions without imparting a single fact or attitude of his own. And there was very little they could do about it. They were more than hazily aware that with a technique not far removed from thought control, Oppenheimer could manoeuvre them like pawns and assassinate with a slice of patronizing smile. Dr Lethnal, the others reflected, had once called Oppenheimer 'Mr Smile-in-the-back'.

A few minutes later the man himself walked into the room and, smiling at each of them in turn, sat down at the head of the conference table. He waved away the offer of a drink from Simak.

'We have a full agenda, gentlemen,' he said brusquely. 'So I'll be most grateful for your attention.' The hint shafted home and the others sat down immediately.

Oppenheimer opened his attaché case and drew out several folders. 'Lao Man offers his apologies,' he told them. 'He has more than he can handle at the moment in Bangkok, and can't be here. We lost a DADIN last night.'

'We what!' McSwiggan asked in disbelief.

'I tried to get you on the telephone early this morning, Frank, to tell you.'

'I was at home,' McSwiggan protested, puzzled. 'All last night and all this morning.'

'I'm sure you were. But your phone is bugged, and I discontinued the call.'

They all turned to look at the unfortunate security chief. If he'd had his trousers stolen from him in Fifth Avenue in broad daylight it couldn't have been worse.

'What d'you mean, bugged? There's no way – '

'Bugged, Frank. All the giveaway signs. An infinity transmitter, I'd guess. Call your number now if you don't believe me, and connect the analyser. You'll get feedback howl – '

'I believe you!' McSwiggan said hastily.

'Good. I want to know by whom in the next twenty-four hours. I know your phone's on our scrambler circuit and none of us uses it for anything confidential, so whoever it is won't learn anything. But they're on to you and I want to know why.'

McSwiggan was stunned. 'Who the hell is it?'

'That's why you're here, Frank,' Oppenheimer said with deadly enunciation. 'I told you weeks ago that a request came through to Central from British Intelligence for a backgrounder on you – '

'It was routine!' McSwiggan complained with feeling. 'I had it followed up – you know that, for Christ's sake! That fuckin' Gams! I met his brother once in Beirut; I was supplyin' a couple of thousand lousy Armalites to the

Rhodesians, that's all. He must have written about it to his brother – '

'I know all that, Frank,' Oppenheimer interrupted in an icy voice, 'but I would have thought it would have put you doubly on your guard. Now I happen to know that Central isn't doing any surveillance on you, so who is?'

Oppenheimer hadn't voiced his doubts about the reasons for the British request, nor had he ever mentioned that a request had also been submitted for information about Dr Lethnal – as Luebke. And he didn't intend to. Although this was far more potentially explosive, he had the Organization's morale to consider, and also a private undertaking with Lethnal never to reveal his origins. For the time being his doubts and suspicions would remain his own.

'Wouldn't it be a good idea for Frank to temporarily retire?' Mrabet asked the others. 'I mean, how effective can he be while he's being watched?'

Oppenheimer welcomed Mrabet's thrust but chose to deflect it from McSwiggan.

'That, Georges, will prove to be quite unnecessary, I hope. Please remember that what we're dealing with now is probably the end result of our sideplay in Hong Kong. We disposed of two of their men, so I'm not surprised the British should want to pursue their investigation further. They plod along light years behind, but they don't give up easily. The point is, though, they're hopelessly on the wrong track so far as Killtest Incorporated is concerned. Anyway, I'm sure Frank can take care of it . . . right, Frank?'

McSwiggan, still shattered by the bugging revelation, probably hadn't digested a word, but nodded in agreement.

'But,' continued Oppenheimer, 'getting back to the Bangkok calamity, our DADIN reserves there were raided by persons unknown who succeeded in spiriting away Huw Gwent.'

It was Simak's turn to be shocked.

'Huw Gwent!' Gwent was the Welsh gladiator who'd survived two Killtest bouts and, as the Organization's biggest crowd-pleaser and betting favourite, was being primed for a third. 'He must have been kidnapped,' he said angrily. 'He knows damn well his next purse will be a quarter of a million bucks, the biggest ever. He'd never leave us willingly.'

'I agree,' Oppenheimer said. 'Therefore we must assume he was abducted by force. Or blackmail. Or even money.'

'This is your territory, General,' Mrabet appealed to Ton, who'd sat through this catalogue of catastrophes without the slightest twitch of a facial muscle. 'You know who's behind it?'

Before the Vietnamese could stir himself to answer, Oppenheimer interposed.

'I'm coming to that, Georges.' He reached into his attaché case and withdrew a folded copy of *Showbill*, opening the paper at a marked page. 'It's an advance copy, and I quote:

' "MEX ORG THREATENS KILLPIX MONOPOLY.

' "A Mexican challenge announced today aims to siphon off a quota of the rich pickings from the prohib but profit-rich killpix industry.

' "Despite its vaporous existence an organization known as Killtest Inc. holds the lucrative million dollar gladiatorial business in an iron grip, and a fight looms if the Mexican challengers attempt to prise it open. Killtest Inc. peels off an estimated ten million dollars per event from live performances, closed circuit screenings and video repeats in several continents.

' "The latest event, which included three 'fights to the death' bouts, was staged in the Canary Islands last month, and Killtest Inc. is expected to announce its fall program next week.

' "The new challenge comes from a multinational org calling itself DEATH BLOW which claims financial backing of $30m and an initial 200 closed circuit outlets, mainly in Europe. It shares the view that the sado boom is just beginning and that profits promised by the genre will make porno sexploitation look like chickenfeed.

' "So far there is no reaction from the Killtest camp but when it does come is likely to be less than friendly. With Killtest Inc.'s known Mafia connection in the US and Triad pacting in Asia, the battle between the two illicit corporate gladiators could be mortal.

' "Perhaps human greed will achieve in the next few months what the FBI and government agencies have been unable to accomplish in a year." '

Oppenheimer threw the paper on the table and looked up. 'You all get the gist of it, I'm sure.'

'Pure speculation,' Mrabet said. 'They're fishing.'

'Not at all,' Oppenheimer said levelly. 'Perhaps you'd like to tell everyone about the call you had this morning, Carl.'

Dr Lethnal coughed, and studied his well-manicured hands. 'The story's correct. We *are* being challenged. I received a personally delivered letter this morning at my apartment and, half an hour later, a telephone call from Acapulco, from the person behind this new operation. And I can tell you, without any doubt at all, these people mean business. They're to be taken seriously.'

'Why's that?' asked Mrabet.

'Because,' said Lethnal with heavy deliberation, 'it was from a person I knew many years ago and know to be extremely gifted and also supremely ruthless. To come to the point, Killtest Inc. is being challenged by Martin Bormann.'

'Bormann!' McSwiggan betrayed his scepticism with a braying laugh. 'Wha-aat! The Nazi? He was maggot meat thirty years ago.'

'I told you I spoke to him this morning.'

'How do you know it was him?' McSwiggan demanded.

'Look, Frank, I'm suspicious by nature, the same as you. I believe nothing until I can feel it and see it and understand it. But I knew Bormann well, and I have an excellent memory. We talked . . . for perhaps ten, fifteen minutes. Nothing confidential, just personal recollections, about things only the two of us would know, private jokes, things like that. It was vital to him, of course, that he had to convince me he *was* Martin Bormann, otherwise I'd have treated his letter and proposition as a joke. He rambled on about what he'd been doing these past thirty years or so, and what happened to mutual friends . . . you can imagine the shock I've had, his coming back from the dead, so to speak. But . . . he *has* to be Bormann!'

Oppenheimer stopped him. 'I think the situation is this – that we should have reservations, but for the present we have to take this man seriously.'

He opened a folder and picked up the letter, showing it to the others. It bore a prominent letterhead consisting of the words DEATH BLOW in red, separated by a skull in a centurion's helmet. Bormann's scrawled signature was at the bottom. There were several silver-grey blotches on the sheet. 'I've had it dusted for fingerprints. They've been photographed and I've got a Pentagon contact checking on them now. We have to move fast.'

'What's the letter say?' Simak asked.

'It's in German, but Carl's given me the gist of it. It's a feeler, that's all. Bormann, or whoever he is, claims to have set up an organization similar to ours, although nowhere near as extensive, but with enough financial backing to mount a monthly series of gladiatorial shows. They have equipment on order from Germany and Japan for transmitting, receiving and closed circuit screening, and are about to start recruiting.'

'It could be a load of crap,' Simak said. 'Pure bluff.'

'I'm not denying that. But Bormann seems to know a hell of a lot about our set-up,' Oppenheimer went on. 'He's also intelligent enough to realize that without some proof to back his claims, we'd throw his proposition into the trash can. That's why he had Huw Gwent kidnapped from right under our noses.'

'So it was this Bormann outfit!' McSwiggan exclaimed.

'So it would seem. But here's the real crunch. Bormann says he'd prefer some kind of partnership or amalgamation with us rather than outright competition. He's prepared for either, he says, but wants a meeting to discuss it.'

'I still think it's a heap of horseshit,' Simak said.

'Or even a fuckin' trap.' McSwiggan swivelled around in his chair to confront Lethnal. 'But what I want to know, Carl, is how this Bormann got on to you. I mean someone just walked up to your apartment and shoved the letter under your door, just like that?'

'I can't answer that,' Lethnal said defensively. 'As far as I know, my personal security has been a damn sight more watertight than yours, judging from what we heard just now.

What it does demonstrate, however, is that Bormann knows rather too much about us for comfort.'

'Well, you're fingered yourself,' McSwiggan said aggressively, stung by Lethnal's reference to his bugged telephone, 'so how do you know you weren't followed here this afternoon?'

'Please don't take me for an idiot, Frank. I took the usual manoeuvres, and then some. But come to that, how do we know we aren't *all* being watched? Isn't it your job to prevent this kind of thing?'

Oppenheimer leapt in to cool the situation. 'Back to your corners, gentlemen! We won't get anywhere like this.'

He left his chair and began to pace around the room, circling the table.

'Let me see if I can sum up the position. Then we can all present our views and perhaps make a decision – agreed? Fine! Okay, let's deal first with Bormann, the man who's returned from the dead. I ask myself – is he real? My response to that is why would anybody impersonate a supposedly dead Nazi for the purpose of horning into our organization? Isn't that doing it the hard way? Of course we get our quota of nut-cases wanting in, but if a solid proposition came to us, even from a stranger, providing he had the muscle to hurt us and was able to prove it, and had the money and all the rest, wouldn't we be equally convinced? I must say I entertained the thought that it might be some government intelligence trick but I just can't bring myself to believe any government agency anywhere would have the flair or originality to dream up a wooden horse in the skin of Martin Bormann. Then we have Carl's belief, based on actually knowing the man, that this character definitely is Bormann. Adding all this up, I'm inclined to think we'd be crazy not to accept that it is Bormann who's making the bid, at least until it is positively proved to be otherwise, okay?'

Oppenheimer paused to pour himself a glass of iced water from the crystal jug on the long table.

'The next question is whether Bormann is bluffing or not, or whether he's just a front for somebody else wanting in. That's more difficult to answer. He certainly isn't a lone wolf, because to find out so much about us he has to have some kind of an organization. We've all been very careful and despite this morning's lapse Frank's security screen isn't easily penetrated. That agent Bernard was only scratching the veneer, and British Intelligence, for all their resources, has been sent on a wild goose chase. But Bormann is another matter. He's tracked down Carl, sniffed out our DADIN hide-out in Bangkok, and knocked off our superstar, just for starters. Whether Gwent was bribed or taken by force we don't know, but it strengthens Bormann's bargaining position no end. So, as I see it, Bormann appears to have some leverage, but it remains to be seen how much. Do you all agree with my reasoning so far?'

He stopped pacing and faced the others. They each nodded in agreement.

'Okay. Now let's look at how we might handle Bormann's proposition. The first step, I think, is to meet the man. Not you Carl, nor any of us, but a neutral messenger with a back-up team of Frank's boys – '

'What I can't understand,' McSwiggan broke in, 'is why we simply don't waste him. I'll soon sort him out – '

'You're being naïve, Frank,' said Oppenheimer, irritated by the interruption. 'If Bormann has survived this long you should assume he intends to go on surviving. You wouldn't get within IBM range of him – '

'Then why the hell don't we hand him over to the Israelis? A thousand Israelis would give their right arms to get at him – they've been hunting bastards like him since the end of the war!'

'I've thought of that, too, and in the end we may well hand him over. But you're making the mistake of assuming Bormann is alone. Removing Bormann won't necessarily remove his organization, or its threat to us.'

'Yes, I agree,' Dr Lethnal broke in. 'Let's not underestimate Bormann. Martin's a master organizer. He's cunning. He's set this challenge up very carefully, I can guarantee that. What I can't guarantee, though, is that it's not a trap – '

'Aha!' Oppenheimer resumed his pacing. 'I was coming to

that. Whatever Bormann's intentions are, I think we'd be smart to treat his entire proposition as an ambush. Speaking for myself, I've not the slightest inclination to hand over Killtest Inc. or any part of it to anybody else. We've all risked a lot to get where we are, and now we're about to get our rewards we'd be crazy to toss it all away. We've overcome no end of difficulties, we've bulldozed our way through all kinds of threats, we've originated something new that's taking the world by storm and we control a private fighting force that's second to none – so I'm sure we can sort out Herr Bormann. So what I propose we do is this – we agree to see him, through a messenger. The meeting can be videotaped and brought back here, and we'll also ask for iron-clad proof that Bormann is who he claims he is, and that he does have the wherewithal to bargain with. The messenger will be shadowed by Frank's people who'll find out as much as they can about Bormann's outfit as a preliminary to busting it for good. Well, what do you think – let's have it!'

Oppenheimer leaned on the high back of Lethnal's chair. 'How about you, Carl?'

'I agree with everything you say,' Lethnal said. 'Although he's an old friend, he's cast himself in the role of an enemy now – I can't emphasize that enough. I think our interests would be best served by eliminating him as soon as possible.' He thumped his fist on the table. 'Eliminate him without delay!'

Oppenheimer smiled and moved on to Mrabet's chair. 'Georges?'

Mrabet had lit a cigar, and he pulled on it thoughtfully. 'I'm not so sure. I think we should kid him along for a while, you know, pretend to take him into our confidence. We might find he's got something we can use. We haven't learned everything in this game yet, you know.'

'So you're for going ahead with some negotiation?'

'Why not? What have we got to lose? And the man interests me . . . to come to us with a deal like this. That's spunk for you! Let's talk him into a trap of our own. When he's softened up he'll be that much easier to hit.'

'Frank?' Oppenheimer was looking down at the top of McSwiggan's head.

'Stamp him into the ground like rat shit,' McSwiggan said with some force. 'I'd like to see to it personally that Bormann disappears for good – and that also goes for his tin-pot organization!'

Oppenheimer walked to the other side of the long table and stood behind Jay Simak. His saffron-hued dome shone in the light of the late afternoon sun.

'I agree with Frank and Carl. I think it's just a fuckin' bluff and we're not likely to learn anything useful by stringin' him along. We'll just be wastin' time.'

The Ring chief was about to move on, but paused. 'It worries me when I hear people say things like that, Jay. I would have thought that you of all people had a little to learn. The Canary Killtest, for example, was an utter shambles.' His voice rose. 'I ask you to get two women, two raunchy ball-breakers, and you turn up with a skinny broad with no tits!'

Simak turned to face Oppenheimer. 'She had tits when I vetted her,' he protested.

'I asked you to inject some sex into the event, and what happens? They both have heart attacks, for Christ's sake! You probably overdosed them with drugs! Then one disappears and the other one's a goddam security risk – a real time-bomb!'

'That's not my department,' Simak shot back. 'And, anyway, you rushed me. It takes time to set these things up properly.'

'Okay, then. But perhaps Bormann *has* found a way to set them up quickly – and properly. Perhaps he's got a dozen young ladies already recruited. We don't know, do we? So what's wrong with finding out?'

Oppenheimer moved along to stand behind General Ton Dinh Quan's chair. 'And you, General? Let's hear some of that famous eastern wisdom!'

Ton smiled, and his sunglasses caught a reflection of the Olympic Tower across on Fifth Avenue. He'd had the benefit of hearing the others and had also followed Oppenheimer's reasoning that something useful might result from a double-cross.

'If Mr Bormann insists on putting the hook in his mouth,' Ton said through his smile, 'what alternative do we have but to play him along like a fish?'

'That echoes my own thoughts perfectly,' Oppenheimer beamed.

16

The meeting between Martin Bormann's ghost and the Kill-test Inc. emissary took place on 19 October.

The messenger, a New York private detective and old friend of Oppenheimer's named Ed McShure, flew into Mexico City the day before with a group of five American tourists, all staying at the opulent uptown Hotel El Presidente. Two of the tourists hammed away as hard as they could, acting out the roles of bumbling security men trying to pose as tourists, but the AC-SU contingent was hardly taken in by the decoys – even allowing them to do a blackbag job on Bormann's room at the Continental Hilton to collect evidence they were intended to collect. The two hams were left with an audience of none while the other three were constantly shadowed during the two days and nights they were in Mexico City.

The meeting itself was held in the downtown offices used seven years before by British soccer officials in Mexico for the 1970 World Cup Finals. The lease had been acquired by an MI6 proprietary and held ever since. Sir Finlay Watkins had supervised the installation of video recording equipment and even the casting of the veteran actor to impersonate Bormann. Pringle had initiated a crash research programme to provide the actor not only with every background detail known about Bormann's life, but also a persuasive fictional biography covering the Nazi leader's later years.

According to the AC-SU fictioneers, what happened to Martin Bormann after 1945 was this: in the confusion of Germany's collapse he commandeered a U-boat from one of the remaining pens near Bremerhaven and headed for Sweden. The submarine was treacherously scuttled a mile off the coast near Gothenburg while Bormann and a couple of officers made their escape; the rest of the crew perished.

In Sweden the three men, now in the uniforms and carrying the identification papers of three of the dead sailors, allowed themselves to be captured and were repratriated to Germany some months later.

For the next ten years, under the alias of Kirchmer, Bormann worked at a variety of occupations before emigrating to Brazil. He married, and founded a building business which expanded spectacularly; he won contracts for building several government offices in Brasilia, the new capital, worth millions.

Soon after this, Israeli agents began to close in, for Borman was high on their list. He'd always been prepared for this and slipped off to Mexico in a cargo plane loaded with silver and gold bullion to retire to Acapulco. And from this luxury hideaway (rented by the British Embassy through an intermediary to provide the cover) he operated a rapidly expanding chain of cockpits, bullfight rings and sports stadia throughout Mexico.

That is only an outline; the full biography was as long as a novel. Following representations to the Ministry, Pringle was given full access to the Department's facilities and personnel, but just the same it had taken almost three weeks to put the jigsaw together. Everything had been covered; if Killtest Inc. were to check any statement of Bormann's (which they subsequently did) they would find nothing to arouse their suspicions (they found nothing).

The incarnation of Bormann was an impressive achievement, and no detail had been overlooked. The aged appearance of the Nazi, thirty years on, was a triumph of cosmetic art. The actor* even wore microscopically thin latex 'gloves' on which had been reconstructed the whorls and arches of Bormann's fingerprints from US Army files. The artificial scar on his neck, evidence of throat cancer surgery, explained the husky voice. Several German guards and retainers, all actors in their sixties, fluttered about the ageing Nazi.

*Who later refused an OBE, preferring to remain anonymous.

The meeting lasted exactly one hour, at the end of which Bormann imperiously raised a hand signalling the close of the interview. In a hotel room a block away Kippy watched the proceedings on a monitor, secretly beamed from Bormann's temporary office. Most of Bormann's message was directed at 'my old comrade Franz', and shrewdly sprinkled with enough personal reminiscences to convince Lethnal that he was indeed the hated and hunted war criminal thought by most to be dead.

'You know Franz,' he appealed in German, 'it is the dearest wish of my life to become your comrade again in an enterprise which together we can forge into a world giant. I have all the means to oppose you but neither of us would want it to come to that, I'm sure. My plans are well advanced for our first gladiatorial exhibition in a month's time, but I will hold my hand while you and your colleagues consider the advantages of a merger. I beg you to ask your friends to seriously examine my proposal. If they still have doubts about the strength of my organization, they'll have further proof of it by the time you view this tape. I trust you, Carl – I trust you implicitly – but I hope you will not be offended when I tell you that my own colleagues do not share this trust, to the extent that they have arranged for your top ten men to be eliminated at the first sign of insincerity.'

The 'proof' Bormann referred to was the capture of three of McSwiggan's undercover men – not the hams – at the airport just as they were about to board their executive jet for Fort Worth, from where they intended to fly on to New York.

'Well, Carl?'

Lethnal had played and replayed the videotape for over two hours in the Waldorf Towers suite. Because of the incriminating references to his past Oppenheimer had not invited the others.

'It's Martin. No doubt about it.'

'None at all? Not even a slight reservation?'

'I only wish I could say there was. I'd feel a whole lot better about it. But . . . nothing.'

'I didn't tell you before,' Oppenheimer said, 'because I wanted you to view the tape with a completely open mind, but his fingerprints checked out.'

'That proves it, then! It's remarkable, unbelievable! Fancy old Martin rising from the dead like this – the old fox!'

Lethnal looked at Oppenheimer. He couldn't fail to note the man's persistent scepticism. 'But you're not convinced, Henschel is that it?'

'Gut feeling, Carl, that's all. There's something weird in the air . . . an albatross feather. . . .'

'Yes, I agree. Witnessing a man coming back from the dead is about as weird as you can get!'

'I don't mean that. I'm talking about tangible things – like Bormann's file at the Pentagon. My contact tells me it hadn't been opened for a year and a half – until 4 October last.'

'Two weeks ago!'

'Check. An FBI request. I'm trying to find out why.'

'Perhaps it was Bormann himself,' Lethnal suggested. 'Nothing's impossible with that vulture. If you were in his shoes wouldn't you want to know how close the hounds were before embarking on a proposition like this?'

'Maybe,' mused Oppenheimer, deep in strategic calculations.

'He's certainly got the connections to do it. Look how he snatched three of our men – three of McSwiggan's best operators!'

'That isn't saying much, Carl. Incidentally, I got a message from Washington an hour ago; they were held overnight and they're on their way back now.'

Both men were silent for several minutes while Oppenheimer took the video cassette over to the magnetic field generator and wiped it clean.

'So what do you think we should do?' Lethnal asked eventually. 'All I can say is that my eyes and ears tell me it *is* Bormann, whatever tricks he's up to. I must say I'd sleep more soundly if he was put away – I particularly didn't like that threat of his about doing ten of us in. For our own peace of mind we should get in first – '

'Probably bluff, Carl. But just the same you'd better use your other apartment – '

'I'm switching tonight. But as I was saying, Bormann's the one behind it all, he's the brains. Get rid of him and his organization will run about like a headless fowl. I say hand him over to McSwiggan.'

'No, Carl, that's just what we won't do,' Oppenheimer said firmly. 'For one thing that's just the move he'll expect, and judging from his performance so far he's more than ready for a hit attempt. There'd be reprisals. None of us would be safe. I don't go around admitting this to everybody, but I'm far from satisfied with Frank's safety precautions.'

'I'm pleased to hear you share my view at last!'

'No . . . I think we have to go along with Bormann for the moment. And, in any case, I'd like to meet the man. I've never shaken hands with a ghost before.'

'What about his proposition?'

'Ingenious, to say the least,' Oppenheimer mused, standing by the window and looking down at mid-town Manhattan. It was raining hard and the pavements thirty-nine storeys below were almost hidden by the moving black dots of umbrellas. 'He wants us to combine forces in a Killtest spectacular – a four-bout programme on a fifty-fifty profit sharing basis. He wants to supply two of the acts – including Huw Gwent, the cheeky sonofabitch! Plus a secure location, security and all the TV transmission hardware. We, it seems, are to supply the outlets.'

'And you'll go along with it?'

'Yes, of course we'll go along with it. It's the only sure way of putting him to the test. And think of this – financially the combined venture could be mind-blowing!'

'I would have thought,' observed Dr Lethnal, 'that at this particular time financial considerations would be furthest from our minds.'

'That's strange, coming from our financial genius!' Oppenheimer replied, smiling. 'But on the contrary – the way we'll plan things, Herr Bormann and his organization will never survive to collect!'

Half an hour later Oppenheimer was left alone in the Killtest Inc. suite to reflect upon the responsibilities of leadership. There was, he knew, a frightening element of chance in the cool judgement he'd just delivered to Dr Lethnal. The Bormann challenge was as weird as anything he'd encountered in all his adventurous life.

Then there was Lao Man's perplexing piece of news, conveyed directly to him and not via McSwiggan. The Triad chapter in London had shadowed the missing Killtest girl from the time she'd landed at Heathrow Airport; she'd spent several days at a Harley Street clinic, several more at a London Hospital for Tropical Medicine, and was now at some obscure nursing home in the country. The threatening telephone call from her supposed boyfriend and the big black cars that were used to rush the girl from place to place simply didn't add up. Nor did the fact that Susan Gillespie had changed her appearance in a quite remarkable way. Who was behind it all? Bormann? Whatever the answer he resolved to order Lao Man to arrange for the prompt disposal of the two women; for while alive they could only threaten Killtest activities.

Kippy parked the Mini on the roadside outside the entrance to the Oaks, and waited in the afternoon sunshine.

Two hundred yards away, up on the gentle slope near the thirteenth hole, Adamson took a wild swing and then clapped a hand to his head in annoyance. The ball bounced to a stop in the uncut grass a few yards away from Kippy's car.

After watching the security guard poke about in the grass for a minute or two, Kippy sauntered over to help him look for the ball. Adamson was wearing a striped yellow and orange shirt, and puffed from the exertion.

'Nobody told me you were coming today,' he said.

'It's okay,' Kippy lied. 'But unofficial.'

'Won't wash, squire,' Adamson said, still pretending to look for the ball. 'Pringle gives the orders, not me. No visits, he said – least of all from you.'

'I know all that. But the doctors can do only so much for her – and she's pretty low at the moment. A bit of hand-holding might work wonders . . . you don't write a paper for this sort of thing, for Christ's sake!'

Kippy suddenly spotted the ball and squashed it into the soft earth with his shoe. He glanced at the security man for any signs that he might relent. Everybody in the AC-SU team had been given strict instructions to stay away from Hilary Brooke – especially Kippy. He'd followed the instructions to the letter with mounting impatience, for six weeks. But what Angela Hotchkiss had told him this morning had constricted his stomach with a sudden unaccountable fear. There had been complications, even for the complex effect of Immobilion-B poisoning, and he hadn't been informed. Two weeks ago Hilary had lapsed into a deep coma from which she only intermittently emerged. Pringle's instructions, Angela had told him, were issued purely out of consideration for his feelings; he'd shot the girl, after all. Or perhaps it was Pringle's obsessive caution about emotional entanglements developing among the staff. Anyway – to hell with all that; he was here, and he meant to see Hilary, and Adamson would have his work cut out to stop him!

As though cued by Kippy's thoughts, Adamson spoke from one side of his mouth. 'Give me a reasonable alibi and I'll give you ten minutes.'

'How about this, then – I called you on the phone from London, imitating Pringle's voice, giving me emergency clearance . . . ?'

'That'll do. So get your foot off my ball, see the bird and piss off as fast as you can. Understood?'

It was the same room he'd occupied months before. The same white everywhere, the same bars, the same little observation window in the door, the same peculiar odour. Even the nurse was the same, the one he'd socked in the jaw. Kippy glanced out of the barred window; Adamson was back at his post on the thirteenth.

He walked over to the bed and sat on the white metal chair. Hilary was unconscious or sleeping; around her, hung on a kind of scaffolding, were flasks and tubes for intravenous feeding. He peered closer; she still wore on her neck the tiny blue and black evil eye he'd given her on Gran Canaria. He thought of the slim, pocket-edition heroine in that hotel room just before the Canary Killtest, aware of the God-awful risk she was taking, the greater for sensing the human frailty of the man supposed to protect her. She'd placed her life in his care, and all he'd managed to say was, 'I'll do my best' . . . no wonder her big grey eyes had brimmed with tears. That bloody Immobilion-B! Why in God's name did they use it when so little was known about it?

That hour they'd spent in the hotel room seemed light-years away. He leaned over and kissed the waif-like face on the cheek. Her short-cropped hair was spiky with perspiration and her forehead was cold and white. He picked up a towel and gently wiped her face, and found himself looking into wide open eyes. The pupils were enormously dilated.

'Hullo, kid,' he mumbled. 'You're going to be okay, you know that?' He reached under the white bed-cover and withdrew her hand, squeezing the damp, finely-formed fingers.

She continued to look at him for a long while before speaking.

'You say it, they all say it,' she whispered with difficulty, 'but my body says different. I ache all over.'

'I know the feeling.' He felt his hand being ever so slightly squeezed. 'But look at me now – no guy's going to kick sand in my face!'

She forced a smile. 'I wish I could stop passing out. How long has it been?'

'Couple of weeks,' Kippy lied. 'You've hit bottom, and now you're on the mend.'

They were silent for a minute or more. 'Would you do something for me, please?' she asked eventually.

'Of course.'

'Emma, my little girl – '

'Don't worry. Your sister's looking after her – '

'I'd love to see her.'

'I'll do what I can. I'm sure it can be arranged. In any case, I intended paying her a visit myself, this afternoon. With a big bag of sweets. We get on fine, incidentally.'

'That's lovely.'

'She wants me to take her to see a circus.'

'Yes, she adores clowns.'

'Perhaps that's why she likes me. I only hope her mother feels the same way. . . .'

Hilary turned very slightly to look searchingly into his face.

'We'll have lots of good times when you're up and about,' he went on. 'I promise.'

She smiled again and closed her eyes. Her grasp weakened and then her fingers slipped from his. He replaced her arm under the covers as a nurse hurried in, signalled by instruments wired to Hilary's pulse. The nurse looked urgently at Kippy.

'I'm afraid there's little point in staying,' she said crisply. 'She'll sleep now for hours, perhaps days. . . .'

Outside again, Kippy leaned against the car to smoke a cigarette. There had been something knowing in Hilary's eyes when she'd looked intently at him . . . something like a look of deliverance, like the one he'd experienced in that hotel room. Perhaps . . . love was like that, at some unexpected moment you placed all your trust, all your being, your whole future in the hands of another. His hands were shaking, and he felt a warm choking sensation swell up inside. The grass on the hillside in front of him glowed bright lemon-green in the late afternoon sun. Yes, he'd return to the flat, garage the car, call the office and visit Hilary's little daughter at her aunt's in Chelsea. And then, as a cloud shadow crawled towards him he ground the cigarette beneath his shoe, climbed into the car, and drove off fast towards London.

Too fast, perhaps, to notice the white laundry van near the hospital's service entrance. Inside the van, behind the piled-up bags of soiled linen, squatted two Chinese with a radio transmitter. A third came out of the entrance, wheeling a trolley loaded with laundry. He watched as the Mini disappeared around a bend on the road, then opened the door of the van, and nodded.

Kippy arrived back at his Marble Arch flat just before ten o'clock.

He felt good. Emma was a real little dolly, a three-year old smasher. He realized, as he threw his jacket on the settee and kicked off his shoes, that he knew nothing about Hilary's life, and whether she'd been married or single when Emma was conceived. But who fathered the child didn't matter in the least; this evening, *he'd* been her father. With Hilary he'd have a ready-made family! He switched on the stereo, still day-dreaming. The three of them . . . in a quiet country village somewhere, with an old, rambling house. You could buy those country houses quite cheaply, he'd been told. A few more years in the Service, and with extras and bonuses he'd get out, right out, with quite a bundle! He sat down on the settee and picked up the little pile of sweepstake tickets from the coffee table. Or if he was lucky – to hell with waiting! He riffed through the tickets. He'd bought them from one of the Telex Central secretaries who sold them as a side-line, and only then because the number of the first ticket in the book had coincided with his initials and year of birth: KL00001945. It *had* to be an omen. Anyway, he'd bought the remaining tickets in the book, six of them. There had to be something magical about a coincidence like that, and he looked again at the number.

Strange . . . the KL00001945 ticket had been on top, he was certain of that. Now it was at the bottom. The tickets were all in reverse order. His scalp tightened. He stood up and paced about the room, his mind in turmoil. Steady, steady. . . .

After a minute or so he went to the tall bureau in the bed-room and, standing on his toes, examined the half-dozen books there. He hadn't touched them for months and Mrs Belcher never dusted there, either – a long bone of contention. But now there was a polished area in front of the books, to-wards the edge of the bureau. Someone had disturbed them.

His pulse slowing a little, Kippy continued to prowl around the flat, all his senses alert for signs of a recent foreign presence. Someone had been here; he could *feel* it. Finally, as though he'd just finished playing some mystery game and wanted to know whether he'd won or not, he went to the walnut side-table near the window of the living room. Carefully avoiding the area in front of the table, he moved it aside, and then peeled back the carpet, revealing a quarto-sized sheet of black paper. When he stripped off the sensitive carbon flimsy, the white sheet underneath bore the unmistakeable impression of a man's shoe.

Immediately he went to the grey telephone, activated the day's code, and dialled Sam Humbert's number.

'Meet me at Duck Egg Blue, Rendezvous Two, as soon as you can, Sam,' he said huskily. 'I've been blown.'

Sam slipped into the upstairs bar at the Portman Hotel twenty minutes later, caught the all-clear sign from Kippy, and joined him in one of the plush red-leather booths. A waiter came up.

'Two double Glengarries,' Kippy told him, automatically. Then he filled Sam in with the details.

'Well, chum, they've done you over good and proper, by the sound of it. Good job they didn't find your safe place, though.'

'Fuck!' was all Kippy could manage to say.

'Have you called Pringle?'

Kippy moved closer to Sam. 'No. That's why I called you. If I tell Pringle I'm washed up with the Unit.'

Sam peered over his glass at Kippy. 'You mean you don't intend to report the break-in?'

'Look, Sam – we're almost there. Another week or so and we'll be wrapping up the Killtest file in pink ribbon. So how the hell do you think I feel? How would *you* feel?'

'Very unhappy, I would think. But that's hardly the point. You've been blown, that's all there is to it. And you know the rules as well as I do – they're not only for our personal protection, but also to secure the investigation – '

'Christ! I'm aware of all that, Sam. But now we've been alerted, we're actually in a strong position. If I'm moved off the Killtest case, they'll know – whoever they are – that the break-in has been discovered, and then *they'll* be on the alert!

They'll drop me and poke into some other crack, perhaps eventually blowing you, Pringle and the whole Unit. By doing nothing to indicate we're on to them they'll concentrate on me. And the great advantage here is that I can trail a cape – '

'Why don't you put that argument to Pringle, then?' Sam asked, draining his Scotch.

'Come off it! You know as well as I do that Pringers will play it by the book. That's how the man's made. The Unit will lose me, the plumbers will know they're on the right track, and we'll lose the best chance we'll ever have of laying a trap before the big showdown. That's why I'm asking you to let me start up a second front. If it comes unstuck, then you don't have to know anything about it.'

Sam signalled the waiter for another round of Glengarry, then lapsed into thoughtful silence. 'You've no idea how they sniffed you out?' he asked eventually.

'No, but I'm going to sleep on it.'

'You haven't done anything we don't know about?' Sam persisted. 'Something trivial, perhaps . . . ?'

Kippy reflected for some seconds. 'Well, yes. I went down to see Hilary Brooke this afternoon.'

Sam raised his eyebrows, but checked himself from speaking.

'The reasons aren't important,' Kippy continued, 'but I felt I just had to see her – '

'I understand,' Sam said, sympathetically, 'although millions wouldn't. Including Pringle.'

'So you'll say nothing?'

'I think I'm going to hate myself, but, yes, I'll say nothing.'

'Thanks. Okay, then – I might start by carding the hospital personnel. Hilary could have been induced to talk while unconscious.'

'Yes, it has been known to happen. And furthermore it's significant that the break-in occurred a few hours after you'd visited the Oaks.'

The drinks arrived and the two men sipped in silence for several minutes. Finally, Kippy spoke.

'What I really wanted to ask you, Sam, is – will you help me?'

Sam had been waiting for it. 'I'm afraid I'll have to think about that, chum. There are rather too many ponderables floating about for a quick answer.'

'I'll accept your decision, one way or the other, and no hard feelings.'

'That's good to hear, Kippy. I'll give you a sign tomorrow morning.'

17

At ten the next morning, while hanging up his trenchcoat, Sam gave Kippy the nod, as Kippy assumed he would.

Kippy had already opened up his second front in a modest way: sweeping the street below his flat at intervals for signs of surveillance, and using Sam's reflector sunglasses on his way to the office to watch for following spooks. So far he'd spotted nothing out of the ordinary, but these were early days. Or were they? He pondered over how he might precipitate some move from the dogs on his tail; some kind of trap, perhaps, baited with whatever it was the spooks might want. But who were they, and *what* did they want?

'Where's our glorious chieftain, this morning, Angela?' Sam asked. 'Did he miss his train?'

Angela Hotchkiss looked at Sam disapprovingly from over her spectacles.

'No, not at all. He's having breakfast at his club with Sir Finlay Watkins.'

'That fat old fart!' Sam let out a long, theatrical sigh. 'I suppose we're in for yet another lecture . . . The Great Death Blow Show!'

The spirited exchange was interrupted by the urgent bleep of the electric eye downstairs in the SunFun Holidays office. They all looked at the monitor to see Pringle holding the door open for Sir Finlay Watkins – wide open, for Watkins had a figure designed for double doors. And someone should have told him long ago that the wide stripes on his suit looked like the staves of a barrel.

A few moment later, flushed from the effect of several cups

of after-breakfast Irish coffee, the two men entered the meeting room.

'Sorry to keep you all,' Pringle apologized with his usual correctness, then gestured to Watkins. 'Ahh, Finlay – you know everybody – why don't you take the chair over there . . . we've got a few prelims to attend to first.'

He stood formally behind his desk and cleared his throat. 'First of all, congratulations, Kipling, for your excellent job in Mexico City. Everything worked out perfectly.'

Pringle's right hand wandered into the top drawer of his desk; he was a grand master at unscrewing the aspirin bottle with one hand. 'For everybody's benefit, we treated those Killtest thugs with Cylert as they were coming around from their Immobilion-B shots, with some highly interesting results.' He rose and walked to the sink in the corner of the room for a glass of water. 'In case you aren't aware of it, Cylert is a new memory-boosting drug. In the event, two of them sang, confirming McSwiggan as their boss. Other names mentioned were Dupré, Ginsberg, Marabay, and Simak – although we already know about him.' Pringle turned his back to the others and with a quick movement threw the aspirin into his mouth and washed them down. 'Oh – and a very odd fact emerged. One of the men claimed to be an ex-CIA employee, attached at some time to the Inter-Community Balance Module, as a clerk or messenger, I would think. It was one of a cluster of think-tank groups under the control of the CIA's Global Strategy Department.'

'That *is* interesting,' Sam interrupted. 'Inter-Community Balance Module. It acronyms to ICBM.'

'It does indeed,' Pringle agreed good-humouredly. 'But what is even more interesting is that the man – the Cylert gave him verbal diarrhoea – named his former CIA boss, somebody called Oppenheimer. Went on and on about him . . . what a great guy he was, that he was his bodyguard once in Africa, how he used to procure black ladies for him . . . on and on and on. Nothing incriminating really, but we're doing a card on him as best we can without alerting Washington.'

Pringle settled down behind his desk again. 'Well! It seems

that everything is now ready for the big showdown, and that's why Sir Finlay's been good enough to come here this morning.'

'I take it we've got the okay from the Killtest crowd?' Kippy asked. He'd been out of touch for several days.

'This morning. Lethnal sent our Mr Bormann the code wire, as we instructed. And tonight Bormann will despatch a formal proposition from Acapulco – which we've just finished drafting – with detailed submissions on how we should set up a joint working committee to organize the combined Killtest.'

This was to be the first fruit of their month of labour, but it still seemed too good to be true.

'There's nothing outrageously unusual about this,' Sir Finlay Watkins broke in. 'Just think of it as the BBC and America's NBC combining forces to make a TV spectacular – it's as simple as that.'

'Precisely,' Pringle concurred. 'Perhaps, Finlay, you'd be good enough to outline the proposition we're putting to Killtest Inc.'

'Death Blow's proposal to Killtest Inc.!' Sir Finlay corrected. He sat forward, so that his vast stomach almost hid his knees, and entered into the spirit of conspiracy with the enthusiasm of a schoolboy.

'Now, first of all, we're proposing a profit split right down the middle, which we'll allow them to trim down to sixty-forty, our loss – that'll make 'em feel better about the deal, get it? Next, we're proposing a four-bout show, with us contributing two bouts. I've already got two of my top programming boys working on it and I'll make damn sure we come up with something really stupendous. Next, we've got this fellow Huw Gwent, who I understand is a Killtest veteran. I've met him and he'll do anything for fifty thousand pounds, which is exactly what I've offered him – although we'll tell the Killtest people we're putting up a purse of half a million.' He paused. 'Ahh, where is Gwent, by the way – ?'

Pringle glanced at Sam Humbert.

'He's tucked away in a little farm cottage in Wales,' Sam said. 'And I must say that telling him we'd buy him the farmhouse he was born in was a stroke of genius. Sweating it out in Bangkok made him quite homesick, and getting him to come over to us was a piece of cake.'

'He's safe . . . quite safe?' Sir Finlay queried in his no-nonsense manner.

'It took me half a day to find the place myself, even with instructions!' Sam assured him.

'Good, good!' Watkins resumed. 'Now, the location of this stunt. I've thought long and hard about this, and my best suggestion is to hold the show on one of those mothballed oil tankers anchored off the Scottish coast, right up north. There are fifty or more to pick from. Some of 'em have never been used, and one of the big tanks could easily be converted into a TV arena.'

'Fantastic idea!' Pringle enthused. 'I'm sure our people can organize a suitable tanker – and a floating ship will be ideal! Staging a convincing Killtest-style show will be only half the operation – the real purpose is to entice the whole top brass of the Killtest outfit into the trap. The bait, of course, will be good old Martin Bormann, plus around two million pounds in ticket money – and once we have the blighters on that ship we'll have them for good. That's just sketching it in, I know, but are there any questions at this stage?'

He looked around, and Kippy eventually spoke.

'It seems to me we're taking quite a lot for granted. Having had some contact with the Killtest organization I think they'll suspect a trap – '

'Of course, dear boy, of course!' Pringle intoned cheerfully. 'You don't think that I believe for a moment they'll fall for this malarky, do you? Of course not! My scenario is that they're bound to want to meet Bormann – even if they're not totally convinced he *is* Bormann – and they'll also want to see with their own eyes exactly what he's up to. The idea of staging the showdown on a ship will give them a sense of false security, and I doubt very much that they'll be able to resist the temptation to grab the ticket money. But the real reason they'll come is to sink Mr Bormann good and proper – don't you agree, Finlay?'

'Absolutely,' the fat knight beamed. 'It's sound psychology.'

'It may be sound psychology,' Sam Humbert said. 'But it's still psychology, a very inexact science, incidentally. In other words, guesswork. There are a hell of a lot of untidy ends – '

'We'll work on those,' Pringle promised. 'But if you don't like it, then give me a plan that's more likely to attract practically the entire Killtest heirarchy to a single location and which allows them to incriminate themselves in British territory so we won't get tangled up in international law? Well?'

Sam shrugged. 'You've got me there, pardner,' he admitted.

Pringle turned to Kippy. 'And you, Kipling? Any suggestions?'

'No,' Kippy said, with more than a trace of resignation in his voice. 'We're only the idiots who have to try to make it work.'

That same afternoon, Kippy's secret second front widened to a considerable degree.

Pringle came into the meeting room at about four with a sheaf of daily reports and began to read them at his desk. Suddenly he threw the papers down and thumped the desk.

'Hullo, hullo! It appears there are some chinks in our armour!'

The others looked at him.

'Listen to this – from DI5 Local Surveillance: "18.33 hours, Leicester Square. Followed Mrs Winifred Brodie to Gerrard Street where she had a meal with two Chinese males, identity unknown, at the Eternal Felicity Restaurant. Left at 19.40 with one of the men and entered the Pao Chung News Agency from where she departed at 2.10 to walk to Shaftesbury Avenue to hire a cab to take her home, which is her usual custom. The Pao Chung News Agency is a suspected meeting-place for the London chapter of the Triad movement." ' Pringle placed the report on his desk. 'The Chinese dragon has woken up, I see!'

'What does it mean?' Angela Hotchkiss asked, on behalf of them all.

'It could mean many things or nothing at all, my dear,' Pringle mused, tipping back his chair. 'We already suspect a Triad link with Killtest Inc., so it could mean they're trying to unravel the Canary foul-up. It could mean they're trying to trace Susan Gillespie or Hilary Brooke, or both. It could mean they're warning Winnie she's being watched. Any thoughts, Sam?'

'I'm thinking back to our red herring operation in Hong Kong,' Sam said, his forehead crinkling. 'All Triad orders come from there. Perhaps we tripped a wire without knowing it. . . .'

Pringle looked at Kippy, who appeared about to say something. 'Yes . . . ?'

'No . . . nothing,' Kippy said.

'Well, obviously we must all put our thinking caps on. And naturally I'll ask for extra manpower to cover Gerrard Street. It would be disastrous at this time if our Death Blow showdown was nipped in the bud, wouldn't it?'

The rest of the afternoon was torture for Kippy, and it wasn't until nearly seven o'clock before the others left the office, leaving him alone with Sam. He went behind Pringle's desk and switched on the white noise generator.

'Sam – listen to this! You know I went out for an hour about lunchtime – down to Whitehall, actually. Well, all the way there and back I'm looking out for spooks, you know, the usual routine, feeling I was being followed but not able to put my finger on anything. Not until Pringle read out that Triad report, that is! Then the penny dropped – I remembered seeing rather more Chinese gentlemen behind me than I'd normally expect!'

'And now you're thinking what I'm thinking?' Sam said.

'That they're the spooks who did over my flat yesterday?'

'Very likely, wouldn't you think?'

Kippy walked over to Sam and sat on his desk. 'How about it, Sam? You're in big with the Far East Section . . . they'll help you on the side. Why don't we try to trigger something off?'

'It's entirely possible.'

'Just between us?'

'This little private duet of yours makes me nervous, but, yes, I think we can cobble something together.'

'I've been thinking overtime ever since Pringers mentioned the Triad. If they're working for Killtest then they're in the market for information – on Bormann, for instance. So why don't we offer to shop him? That should bring the worms out of the woodwork!'

'You really want those four bunches of cherries on your first pull, don't you?' Sam smiled, and smacked Kippy hard on the knee with the flat of his hand. 'And why not? It's about time we had a change of luck.'

Henschel Oppenheimer took the 5 a.m. call with bad grace. During the Bormann negotiations he hadn't scored more than four hours' sleep a night for a week.

It was Lao Man on the scrambler from Hong Kong. 'I'm calling you direct as you instructed, Mr Oppenheimer.'

'Yes, yes – what the hell is it?'

'I've just heard from London. A person there claims to know some things about our German friend that we should know.'

'Bormann? What things?'

'I do not know, Mr Oppenheimer. An Englishman, an addict. He is a little known to my people there. He claims he has the information, and wants to trade it for H.'

'Heroin. I see – '

'Yes. Ten thousand pounds' worth. It is a safe risk to proceed, I am assured, and he is safely disposable. We have nothing to lose by the transaction, and perhaps much to gain.'

'If you say so, then get on with it!'

'Very well, Mr Oppenheimer. I'll send them a message.'

'Fine, fine. Get the information to me as soon as you can.'

'It will be done, of course.'

'Ahhh – Lao Man . . . ?'

'Yes?'

'The girl – Gillespie. Have you fixed that?'

'We have it under control.'

'Under control? What sort of Chinese double-talk is that! Why the delay, for Christ's sake? I thought I ordered – '

'It will be done, Mr Oppenheimer, be assured. But my

people inform me that at present she is more useful alive. Things are developing in London. . . .'

The sleeping pill was still exercising its powerful effect, and the Killtest chief was yawning uncontrollably.

'Okay, Lao Man. Play it your way. But I'll have your little yellow balls if you bugger it up – understood?'

'I understand thoroughly, Mr Oppenheimer,' Lao Man replied. 'Totally and completely.'

Sam Humbert's old cronies in the Far East Section were a zealous bunch of intriguers, and he had little difficulty persuading them to help him. Within a few days they'd come up with a suitable heroin addict to act as a dummy; for a month's supply over and above his prescription he was prepared to do anything. 'Slightly unethical,' Sam observed drily, 'but all in a good cause.'

As a dummy, the addict was embarrassingly successful, for within twenty-four hours of receiving his brief he'd not only made contact with the Triad but had also received the go-ahead for a pass. This didn't fit in with Kippy's and Sam's plans at all, for they wanted to delay the transaction until the last possible moment before the Death Blow showdown, six days away. But with their hands forced, as it were, they worked all through two nights to produce the kind of dossier calculated to lure the Triad and lull Killtest Inc.

The dossier itself, manufactured largely from the extensive material in Bormann's fictional file, contained sufficient verifiable information to convince the most redoubtable of doubters. Most of the documents were Xerox copies of counterfeit telegrams, letters and notes which were supposed to have passed between Bormann's Acapulco and London contacts. But among these items – which contained only information which Killtest Inc. knew about, anyway – Kippy and Sam salted several red herrings, including a long report describing how Bormann's organization had successfully escaped the attentions of Britain's various security and police agencies. The dossier gave the clear impression that Bormann had an extensive organization in England, that he had unlimited financial backing, and that, with a few sensible reservations, he trusted Killtest Inc. implicitly.

Once the dossier was ready for delivery, the second front manoeuvre was completed within a few hours. It was delivered by the addict on the night of 15 November – forty-eight hours before Operation Death Blow was primed to erupt. He was dropped by an agent-driven cab at a lane off West India Dock Road, near Charlie Brown's pub, as arranged. At a few minutes past nine o'clock a cream Mercedes loomed out of the river fog and pulled into the lane, disgorging four Chinese. The sight of the advancing quartet quickly convinced the addict he'd pulled a tiger by the tail and he dropped the papers and ran for his life. At the same time whistles blew and ten Special Branch officers materialized in the dark lane from doorways, windows and even rooftops. In the pandemonium that followed three of the four Chinese were caught; the fourth escaped in the Mercedes with the parcel of papers, exactly according to plan. And less than an hour later the morning papers were slipping in a rush story describing a dockland drug raid, following a tip-off.

All that remained was to inform Pringle.

To put it mildly, Pringle was not amused at having a 'snide operation', as he called it, conducted behind his back. It was a four-aspirin situation, and it wasn't yet 10 a.m.

'You know, I've been foolish enough to deceive myself that I was running an operational unit! *Unit* – are either of you aware what the word means? How bloody-well dare you! My God, if you're accepting Her Majesty's money in your pay packets you might at least have the common decency to follow Her Majesty's Government's orders! I'm speechless!'

'But Stan, you must agree – '

Pringle cut Sam short by thumping his desk with such a wallop his cup of tea jumped a clear two inches.

'I don't agree with anything!' he shouted. He bent down and turned up the white noise generator to full strength. 'I know what you're going to say – that because your little game was successful – and we're by no means sure about that, by the way – that because it went off without anybody actually being killed, then everything in the garden is roses. Well it isn't! Here we are, only a few hours away from one of the most colossal showdowns in the history of espionage, brought safely to this point by months of devoted work by dozens, no – hundreds – of loyal, disciplined people, and – I'm speechless, absolutely speechless!'

The factor contributing primarily to Pringle's speechlessness was, of course, the tug of war with his own professional conscience. According to the rules both Kippy and Sam should have been summarily dismissed for their misconduct. On the other hand, at this delicate stage, Pringle knew he simply couldn't afford to be without them.

'Quite bluntly,' he went on, 'you're both guilty of nothing less than sabotage. It's a serious allegation and it's one I hope I'll be in a position to pursue when all this is over. For the moment, however, my duty is clear, and that is to complete preparations for tomorrow night. Both of you are due to fly to Scotland in two hours' time, and I want you on that tanker by early this afternoon. And once you're on it – STAY ON IT!'

Pringle sneezed several times. He'd been complaining about flu symptoms for a couple of days and this business wasn't helping. Exhausted and distressed, he lapsed into an extended, morose silence which ended only when he answered an insistent telephone.

After a short conversation mainly of grunts he replaced the receiver and glared at his two lieutenants with a look of utter disgust.

'That was Adamson, gentlemen,' he informed them, 'making, I would guess, his final report, as far as this unit is concerned. Just in case you've been congratulating yourselves over your little tussle with the Triad, I ought to tell you that Miss Brooke was abducted from the Oaks early this morning.'

Kippy's face received the news like a smash to the jaw.

'Hilary? Oh, no –'

'Oh, yes. And she's being held as a hostage to guarantee our good behaviour at tomorrow night's show.'

18

The *Gudrun Atlas* sat squatly in a sea as flat as hammered lead at the mouth of Loch Eriboll, twenty miles from the northernmost tip of Scotland. A few miles up the coast huddled the tiny crofting and fishing villages of Balnakeil and Durness; Thurso, the largest town on that wild and desolate north coast, lay a good forty miles to the east. It was the ideal spot in which to lay up the carcass of a supertanker, and the perfect spot for a floating illicit gladiatorium.

The *Gudrun Atlas* belonged to the generation of supertankers built on the eve of the oil crisis of 1973, one of five hundred similar craft mothballed because of the calamitous drop in oil consumption. Although capable of carrying nearly 200 000 tons of crude in her bowels, it had never held a single drop, but sailed directly from the shipyard to its lonely berth off the Scottish coast. And there, like a giant marooned whale, it had remained for over a year, its white upper structure mercilessly fleshed by the winter gales, its black hull battered by the Atlantic waves. But tonight it rode under a full moon, as still and steady as a floating ballroom.

After weeks of hectic activity the supership now seemed strangely quiet, like a darkened theatre deserted of players and patrons. Apart from three helicopter platforms erected on the vast deck there was little above to show for all the activity. Below, an extraordinary transformation had taken place, for one of the ship's immense compartments was fitted out as a television studio, with a centre stage and tiered seating for five hundred spectators. Within hours it would be the scene of a blood-curdling celebration reminiscent of some barbarous Viking ritual of a thousand years before.

Kippy checked his watch and walked with Sam along the deck towards the bows; they were at least a quarter of a mile from the bridge, which itself soared a hundred and fifty feet above the lapping grey-green water. Ships of this size needed three miles to come to a stop, even at moderate speed, and a sea-space the size of Greater London in which to make a turn. They could, and sometimes did, run down and sink a fishing trawler without anyone on board being aware of the collision. Perhaps, thought Kippy with some awe, tethered off the coast of Scotland was the best place for them.

It was 15 November, and already the icy, drifting breezes from the north were making themselves keenly felt. The four small patrol boats, lit up with festooned fairy lights to look like chartered ferries, bobbed and rocked near by in the evening swell. Sam turned up the collar of his trenchcoat and Kippy huddled deeper inside his fur-lined parka to escape the cold.

The Triad business aside, it had been a momentous month; only a week before had the AC-SU unit known for certain that Killtest Inc. would come to the expensive party.

The brinkmanship had played terribly on everybody's nerves, Pringle's particularly; and now he was confined to his bed with exhaustion and influenza.

At first cooperative, the Killtest representatives on the joint committee organized by Sir Finlay Watkins had proved frustratingly elusive when it came to making the actual arrangements. They had wanted proof of everything, and the business of forging letters and documents – for chartering the ship, hiring equipment, catering, printing tickets, contacting patrons – had occupied a specialist team for weeks.

Relaying Watkins's instructions through half a dozen German- and Spanish-speaking agents recruited to make up the working committee also proved to be chancy, for one false move, a single comment out of place, would have blown the whole scheme sky-high.

Then there was the carefully rehearsed protracted argument over the financial split; Watkins – through the actor playing Bormann – finally agreeing to 70:30. Bormann was instructed to turn on a tantrum over the screwing, which he did so convincingly that an incensed Oppenheimer suddenly pulled the rug on the joint enterprise. Bormann then had to apologize before Killtest Inc. could be dragged back to the conference table. A valuable week had been lost, but the performance finally convinced Oppenheimer that Martin Bormann was real and that his considerable organization meant business.

Throughout the negotiations, Killtest Inc. had given very little away, despite Pringle's most strenuous efforts to penetrate into its network. Nothing was learned about Killtest's satellite receiving set-up, nor the principle of its computer scrambling system, nor even the location of more than a few of its closed circuit outlets. The Killtest representatives on the joint working committee were all middle-level people who had no direct contact whatsoever with the Ring. If Oppenheimer had not, twenty-four hours ago, agreed to meet Bormann on the *Gudrun Atlas*, hardly a point would have been won after months of work and the spending of at least half a million pounds.

While all this was going on, massive preparations were being made aboard the supertanker, doubly difficult because of the strict security imposed. Winifred Brodie's dingy office off Leicester Square had become headquarters for a team of McSwiggan's agents detailed to keep an eye on the *Gudrun Atlas* to make sure Bormann was keeping his word. Every day Fred Cordroy expected one of his bugs to be discovered, especially when Jay Simak flew in for two days and ordered Winnie to hire a delousing expert to go over the place. Tipped off in advance, Cordroy managed to ensure she hired one of his own men, who not unnaturally pronounced her grubby office clean. Pringle's most exacting task was to allow the Killtest agents to see what he wanted them to see, but to avoid giving away the fact that the dozens of workmen, technicians, transport drivers and launch operators involved in the preparations were Army and Navy personnel in civilian clothes.

It hadn't been difficult to devise two Killtest-style bouts, to find actors willing and able to impersonate the contestants, and to equip and staff the TV recording and transmitting complex, but finding five hundred spectators who could be trusted not to talk was a baffling problem. The eventual solution had been to arrange a boxing tournament between two Royal Navy ships, inviting five hundred ratings aboard the *Gudrun Atlas* to watch.

The two warships involved had been kept at sea for a month as a security precaution. Now the sailors were below, having their evening meal and happily drinking the unlimited free booze, all in civilian clothes and augmented by Wrens and a sprinkling of older men from various intelligence sections to add verisimilitude to what was hoped would look like a typical Killtest audience. Only half an hour before the first bout would the sailors be informed about the switch in the programme, and why.

There was a time when nobody in the meeting room above SunFun Holidays Ltd thought the project would ever arrive at a conclusion, let alone a successful one. One crisis had followed another; as soon as one difficulty or objection had been overcome, another seemingly insurmountable hurdle would be bolted in its place. But now, its navigation lights twinkling, the transmitting mast silhouetted starkly against the full moon, the giant floating trap was sprung and waiting for its victims.

'How do you feel?' Sam asked as they reached the ship's bow.

'Like a lump of shit – how do you think?' Kippy muttered.

'Come on, chum! We haven't lost the war yet.'

Kippy creased his eyes against the wind and gazed across the dark water, hands deep in his pockets. Sam leaned on the railing and turned to him.

'They've still got four or five hours to find her. The entire Branch is out.'

'Yes – thanks to me.'

'Crap! It's a game of chess, Kippy. We didn't make a wrong move – it's just that they made a better one. And forget the valiant-hero-riding-to-the-maiden's-rescue bit, too – there's nothing you can do except to do your job here. Hilary is only part of the reason why we can't afford to bomb out tonight!'

After a while Kippy mumbled: 'I'll be okay, Sam. Don't worry.'

Suddenly the huge deck lit up like day. The landing lights made circles of white fire at each of the three helicopter pads.

'That's to help them find the target,' Sam said drily. 'Shit! I never felt so bloody naked in all my life!'

The two men turned and walked back along the deck towards the towering bridge, which looked like a distant skyscraper. The Death Blow symbol was everywhere. The grim skull in its centurion's helmet grinned perversely from a giant sign painted on the deck, from posters stuck up here and there, and even from the flag fluttering from the radar mast.

'I know how you feel,' Kippy admitted. 'I can't believe we'll get out of this lightly. They've got a bloody big surprise dreamed up for us, I'm sure.'

'Right! The only certainty in this business is the inevitability of a surprise.'

'I wonder how many of the Killtest mob will come?'

'Well, they asked for three 'copter pads . . . I'd imagine between twenty and forty. Coming by sea is out of the question.'

'So it's not a labour-intensive operation. I mean they won't overrun us.'

'I know what you're getting at. The indications are that they'll have some fancy high-powered armament.'

Kippy reached into his parka and pulled out his Immobilion-B ejector. He tested the release and kissed the warm casing. 'Sorry, old chum,' he said to the tiny instrument. 'The usual odds, as always – a few bazookas, the odd airborne tank – '

'Listen!' Sam's arm shot out to stop Kippy. They turned and tilted their ears to the wind. After a tense few seconds Sam relaxed. 'Thought it might have been one of the 'copters arriving early to catch us unawares.'

They continued their walk back along the deck in silence. Gradually Sam increased the pace.

'Souvenir from Bangkok,' he said. 'I think I've got a touch of the tropical tummy.'

'I feel the same,' Kippy sympathized. 'Only in my case the tropics have got nothing to do with it.'

Below the towering bridge they met Sir Finlay Watkins, wearing a false grey beard trimmed short, and the uniform of a ship's captain. He was standing in for Pringle and clearly relished the role, even though he had no authority. The operation was being conducted by a committee, on which Sam was now the AC-SU unit's senior representative.

The PA system crackled, calling for Edna and Evelyn to report immediately to the communications control centre. Sam and Kippy left Watkins in mid sentence and bounded up the maze of stairways to the radio room.

One of the operators waved to them.

'Just had a message from the mainland. Busload of Japanese tourists have just embarked at Thurso on a ferry. Expected at shipside in two hours – and they've got VIP clearance.'

Sam gaped at the operator. 'What d'you mean – Jap tourists? And what's this nonsense about clearance?'

'Came through in code from your auxiliary operations people. It's genuine, otherwise obviously I wouldn't have accepted it. And they particularly stressed the VIP clearance.'

Sam took the message sheet and turned to look blankly at Kippy. Several seconds passed before the light dawned.

'Japs be buggered!' he breathed. 'They're a bunch of bloody Fu Manchus!'

'Triad!'

'Right. And there's nothing we can do, otherwise . . . Hilary –'

'They've got us by the short and curlies, the bastards!'

For several minutes they looked gloomily out from the windows of the radio room, each deep in thought. Eventually Sam said, 'Well, let's get on with it. We're doing no good just standing here.'

For the next couple of hours they traversed the giant ship, checking every detail. Kippy's observations at the Canary Killtest had been invaluable, and most of the arrangements on the *Gudrun Atlas* followed closely the Organization's standard procedure. Down below the arena itself had been built in the largest of the crude tanks, a steelplate chamber the size of a bowling green and forty feet from floor to ceiling. Five TV cameras were mounted on scaffolds, while dummy remotes were positioned high at each corner. Fifty spotlights hung from a grid mounted on the ceiling, aimed at the centre stage around which were erected the steep tiers of seats. The usherettes were incessantly whistled-at WRENS in red baby-doll nighties. The sailors could hardly believe their luck. And near the main entrance to this improbable theatre-cum-arena were displayed the four purses for all to see: bundles of stage money sandwiched between genuine notes, and totalling a million pounds, stacked neatly into four ornately-carved wooden treasure chests.

Just before midnight, an hour before the Killtest contingent was due, the audience of sailors filed into the improvised arena to take their seats. At the same time a large diesel launch pulled alongside the ship's boarding platform and, under powerful searchlights, some two dozen Chinese, all dressed in dark suits, clambered aboard and made their way up to the lower deck. Sam and Kippy watched while a group of DI5 men, dressed as stewards, led them to a cabin which had been hastily converted to a reception room.

'Now I know what it felt like to be invaded by Genghis Khan,' Sam said with feeling.

The Chinese seemed to be well under the weather, either from drink or sea-sickness. Several were singing while others lurched about, and one had to be carried aboard by two of his companions.

'I'll ask the stewards to get them pissed as quickly as possible,' Kippy suggested.

Sam stopped him. 'Don't be fooled, chum. It's a put-on. They were sober enough on the launch, just before they boarded us.'

Kippy pounded the deck rail with his fist. 'What a cock-up! Half the Triad population of London land in our laps and we can't touch a hair of their heads!'

At that moment half a dozen tough-looking Navy Police in civilian clothes passed them on the gangway, frog-marching three men held in arm-locks. These were three known Killtest agents who in order to maintain the cover until the very last minute had been allowed to buy tickets. A launch had fetched them from Thurso in the company of Special Branch officers disguised as patrons up from London. The ruse had worked, for just before they'd left their hotel one of them had phoned Kirkwell in the Orkney Islands with a coded message, presumably to advise that everything was proceeding according to plan. It also tended to prove Pringle's hunch that Killtest Inc. intended to charter helicopters owned by some foreign-based oil exploration company active in the Orkneys. The three intruders had been quietly disarmed and were now on their way to a secure cabin.

Satisfied that everything had been done to counterfeit the trappings of a Killtest spectacle, Kippy and Sam climbed up to the bridge of the ship which was to be the nerve-centre of the whole exercise.

'Does it strike you,' Sam said as they climbed, 'that all this might be some crazy, surrealistic dream?'

Kippy paused and glanced at Sam. The appearance of their faces had been subtly altered by the Unit's new make-up expert and this added force to Sam's comment. Visually, they were strangers to each other. They stopped on a landing and shook hands.

'Hullo. I'm K. Leering.'

'Jolly pleased to meet you, old boy. My name's Humbert.'

On the bridge they nodded to two security guards, both wearing a prominent Death Blow badge struck for the occasion, and entered the captain's cabin. Martin Bormann sat in an armchair, adjusting his bullet-proof vest. His two henchmen snapped to attention and extended a Nazi salute. They all laughed.

'Everything okay?' Sam asked.

A frown clouded Bormann's face. 'I'm a little worried I mightn't recognize Lethnal immediately,' he said. 'Those photos you gave me aren't very good.'

'He'll probably have trouble recognizing you, too,' Sam said reassuringly. 'You haven't seen each other for over thirty years, remember?'

'Then I'll play it as it comes. It'll be right on the night, as we say.'

'That's all you can do, Martin. Act a little shortsighted, confused, excited – and above all, arrogant.'

Sam and Kippy left the cabin and closed the door behind them.

'What about this Oppenheimer?' Kippy asked. 'I wonder if he'll come?'

'He's the king pin,' Sam said, looking out into the moonlit darkness. 'Or at least we think he is. But whether he's Father of Killtest or not, he's an amazing character and as slippery and as dangerous as an electric eel.'

Down in the water below one of the fairy-lit patrol boats hove in sight to starboard, with its concealed complement of paratroopers and divers huddled below the deck.

Kippy walked up close to his colleague. 'Look, Sam, I'd like to ask a great favour.'

'Fire away.'

'I'd like to swap marks.' Eight field men, including Kippy and Sam, had each been instructed to mark individual Killtest bosses to reduce confusion. 'You've got Oppenheimer – '

' – and you've got Lethnal. What do you want, a medal?'

'No, just Oppenheimer. Come on, Sam – please!'

'Hell, Kippy – we're up to our tits in trouble already, ignoring Pringle's orders and all that. And what if you missed him?'

'I don't intend to miss.'

'But why – ? Not Hilary, for Christ's sake?'

Kippy remained silent, and looked away. Sam thought for a moment and then gave him a playful punch in the ribs.

'Okay, you silly shit, what the hell. I can miss him just as easily as you – '

Some way along the bridge a cabin door opened and a young man ran towards them. He shouted as he passed.

'They're on radar! Three aircraft approaching from the north-east at a hundred and ten knots!'

'Right!' Sam said, buttoning up his trenchcoat. 'We're the greeting party. Let's get down on deck and smile.'

19

With its blades juttering, a helicopter circled for several minutes in the darkness above the ship before descending to land on the brightly lit pad nearest the bridge.

While the rotor continued to revolve, eight men in white overalls filed smartly from the hatch and ran in pairs in different directions to the sides of the tanker. Trailing cables to the helicopter, each pair of men carried a heavy object which they dropped over the side.

'Bloody great limpet mines!' Sam breathed to Kippy, standing by a deck entrance to the bridge. 'Hope the patrols have spotted them.'

Their explosive cargo deployed, the eight men returned to the helicopter and formed a ring around it. Then three more alighted, one carrying a heavy metal case. They walked towards the bridge, obviously the advance party.

The leading man, in a fawn overcoat and grey homburg, came up to Sam and extended his hand. Sam shook it heartily, and addressed the visitor in German. When it was obvious he didn't understand Sam reverted to heavily-accented English.

'Welcome aboard the Death Blow Special!' he said, smiling his head off. 'Come – Mr Bormann is waiting.'

With Sam in front and Kippy at the rear they guided the visitors up the stairs to the bridge and then into Bormann's cabin. The actor greeted the trio with effusive embraces.

'Welcome, welcome! This is the greatest day of my life, gentlemen!' He was carrying it off perfectly. 'Please sit down. Make yourselves comfortable. A drink, perhaps?'

The man in the homburg shook his head. 'No time. Just

show us the arrangements, that's all.' He was unsmiling, dour, and had pockmarks on one cheek.

'Yes, of course, of course!' Bormann said, unruffled. 'I suppose I shouldn't blame you for being suspicious. But where is my old friend? Franz – Dr Lethnal . . . ?'

'If everything checks out, Mr Bormann, you'll see him. But I want you to know that if we find any irregularities, this tub will be blown to pieces. We've mined it – '

'Ahh, so unnecessary!' Bormann interrupted, aghast at the idea he should not be trusted.

' – I'm only doing what I'm told. As I said, if something doesn't check out . . . up she goes. There're eight men around that 'copter with a couple of thousand rounds, so no tricks there, either.'

'You make your point beautifully,' Bormann murmured, appropriately subdued.

'The same goes with us,' the man continued. He indicated the younger man carrying the heavy case. It's sending out a signal. If he let's go the handle the signal stops. Boom! Get the message?'

'You're obviously very brave and loyal men,' Bormann said, not without genuine admiration. 'But everything is in order, I assure you.' He snapped his fingers in the direction of Kippy and Sam. 'Show the gentlemen around. I'm sure they'll be quite pleased with what they see.'

The party left the cabin and clattered down the stairs again, right down to the ship's tanks and along the series of specially constructed catwalks which led to the arena. Walking behind, Kippy was hypnotized by the metal case which could blow up the ship and the six hundred people on it. What if the man dropped it by accident? Or it slipped out of his hand? If the man didn't have sweaty palms he wasn't human.

Signalled in advance, the sailor stooges were putting on a deceptively enthusiastic show, calling for the bouts to start, whistling at the usherettes and shouting for drinks. Technicians were running about, absorbed in their spurious duties.

One of the Killtest trio snapped a sequence of Polaroids of the scene, and then went over to the chests of money, guarded by two armed security men. He was plainly impressed.

'Would you like to meet tonight's gladiators?' Sam asked their leader.

The man turned, and called the others. 'No. We've seen enough. I have to go back to report.'

Kippy led the tortuous way up to the deck.

'You stay here,' the pock-faced man instructed him firmly. 'And remember what I said.' With the other two he walked briskly towards the waiting helicopter, its blades still in motion.

They also walked towards the moment of truth, and both Kippy and Sam realized they had been outmanoeuvred. What if the men had seen something suspicious during their tour? They could not be stopped. They could simply board the helicopter and take off, then detonate the charges.

The two agents watched as one by one the three men climbed into the craft. After the warmth below the night breeze chilled the perspiration on their faces. Above them they could just make out the winking red and green lights of the other two hovering helicopters.

'What now?' Kippy asked, for something to say.

'I would think Scarface is sending a radio message to the others,' Sam said, intently watching the cluster of white uniformed men standing around the pad with their automatic weapons at the ready.

'I wonder what the hell he's telling them?'

'That's a somewhat academic question, but we'll know soon enough.'

A minute dragged by. Both men thought about the sailors below, half-boozed and happy, hardly conscious of the danger they were in. Explosives had been half-expected and no doubt the Navy divers were already at work down there defusing the four mines. But it was an incredibly difficult procedure and they'd need an hour, at least. And although the sailors all had life preservers under their seats, many of them would certainly be trapped and drowned if the ship broke up and sank.

'We should have stalled the buggers,' Sam said, angry at himself for allowing the oversight.

They waited several more minutes. The wet salt-laden wind began to sting their unblinking eyes. Snatches of music and chanting drifted up from below, to be suddenly drowned by the clattering of feet behind them; the Triad contingent were being led down the stairs to the arena.

'What do we do about *them*?' Sam glared out into the darkness for inspiration. 'The Navy Police on board could sort them out easily enough if it wasn't for bloody Hilary – '

Kippy turned violently. 'Christ! It wasn't her fault – '

'I'm sorry. I didn't mean it that way.'

'Nothing's come through, I suppose?'

'No. But we'll know the moment they find her.'

'But what if . . . ?'

'She's already dead? Yes, that's already occurred to me. She was under intensive care at the Oaks and without that we have to face the fact she might only survive . . . well, perhaps only for a few hours, in her condition.'

'If only we *knew* . . . !'

Suddenly, Sam cocked an ear to the wind. 'Hang on!' he whispered. 'I think we're about to advance one square.'

From behind them, from behind the enormous red funnel, one of the other helicopters swooped down like a great whirring bat to land on the centre pad. Sam stepped back into some shadows and raised a small pair of binoculars to his eyes.

'Security heavies and Killtest performers, I think. About ten of them, climbing out now. Scarface has gone back to talk to them.'

More minutes passed as Sam watched.

'What the hell are they doing now?' Kippy asked urgently. The third helicopter had descended to a few hundred feet, but was still circling.

'They're looking at those Polaroid shots. Christ! They're really giving us a right going over! Hold on – Scarface is coming back.'

They watched as the man in the grey homburg walked to the first helicopter and climbed into the cabin. Then, less than a minute later, the third craft descended to settle on the furthest pad.

'That'll be the big boys,' Sam said. He handed the binoculars to Kippy. 'Here – give me a commentary.'

Through the glasses Kippy watched as five men stepped out through the cabin hatch of the third helicopter, followed by another whose tunic and white peaked cap identified him as the pilot. The last landing pad was near the ship's bows, and so far away he couldn't identify any of the others. But he kept looking through the binoculars as they approached.

'Anyone we know?' Sam asked, as the group joined the others by the second helicopter.

'McSwiggan, I think – yes, and Simak, I'd know him anywhere. And one in dark glasses . . . an Oriental –'

'Lao Man?'

'No, much shorter, and smaller. Ahh – and Lethnal! Might be a good idea to get on the intercom and warn Bormann that Lethnal's the one in the black overcoat and fur cap.'

While Sam was calling the operations room on the bridge above, Kippy continued to observe the advancing party. Walking between the short Oriental and the uniformed pilot was a dark, squat man he couldn't identify. But there was no sign of Oppenheimer, nobody remotely resembling the set of mugshots sent to them by the FBI.

Sam returned and Kippy handed him the glasses. 'See if you can spot Oppenheimer,' he said urgently. The party had passed the first landing pad and were getting closer.

Sam scanned the Killtest contingent for the face whose features they'd memorized for ten days. 'He's not there. The bastard hasn't come!'

There was no time for further discussion. Sam parked the binoculars in a porthole recess. 'It's party time,' he whispered to Kippy.

They walked out of the shadows to meet the Killtest men. With Oppenheimer there it would have been as momentous an occasion as Stanley's meeting with Livingstone; instead they felt cheated and disappointed. The supreme prize, the white leopard, had eluded their snare.

Apart from a slight bow from Lethnal and a nod from Simak, Kippy and Sam were ignored. Scarface, with McSwiggan by his side, took over and led the party up the stairs to the bridge. He opened the door of Bormann's cabin without knocking, and motioned McSwiggan and the five Killtest VIPs inside. The others, including the pilot, remained on the bridge.

Immediately he clapped eyes on Lethnal, the veteran actor jumped up and embraced him fondly.

'Franz! Franz! After all these years!'

'It's Carl – Carl!' Lethnal reminded him in an audible whisper.

Bormann stood back, laughing, to look at Lethnal. 'Of course, Carl! But you look wonderful, magnificent! I can't express to you how happy I am! Carl – feel me, pinch me – tell me I'm a dead man! What a joke on the world, what a joke!'

Lethnal pulled off his fur cap, which had been knocked over his eyes during the wild greeting.

'It's good to see you too, Martin. I see you've done well, very well.'

Bormann looked at the others and snapped his fingers at Kippy and Sam.

'Take their coats and hats! And drinks – we must drink to our mutual success. We still have fifteen minutes before the start.'

Lethnal introduced Bormann to the others while Kippy and Sam helped with the coats and poured drinks. So far everything was going according to their expectations – except the non-arrival of Oppenheimer. But how could they find out why he hadn't come, when they weren't supposed to know about the CIA man's connection with Killtest Inc.? It was too early yet; that conundrum would have to wait.

One by one the visitors sat down in the ring of leather armchairs, and relaxed. A few of the others outside now came into the cabin to help themselves to drinks, and for a while the room could have been mistaken for a friendly gathering at some exclusive London club.

'I'm greatly honoured,' Bormann said, 'that you should all come here as my guests.' With that prompting he waited, perhaps hoping that someone would apologize for Oppenheimer's absence, but there was no reaction. Perhaps, after all, Oppenheimer didn't exist outside their imaginations.

McSwiggan stood up. 'Before we start, Mr Bormann, I'd like to explain our security measures, which might have alarmed you. You'll understand that being the kind of organization we are, we live or die by the effectiveness of our security. This ship is mined with high explosive, as you're aware – we studied the plans of this tanker so as to be sure that the bombs were placed where they'll do most damage. But if everything's clean, you and your buddies can relax – '

'But I don't understand!' Bormann interrupted, upset by this outrageous absence of trust. 'Of course everything is clean, as you put it. What kind of man do you think I am?'

'It's a standard precaution, that's all,' McSwiggan said. 'Our policy is to shoot first and ask the questions after. We can't afford to do it any other way.'

'Yes, I see. But . . . those bombs? If – hypothetically, you understand – if you decided all this might be some sort of a trap, and the possibility of you thinking this did cross my mind, what then? If the bombs go off, wouldn't all of you perish also? What would be the point of that?'

McSwiggan swaggered over to the onyx cocktail bar and helped himself to more Scotch. He examined the label on the bottle.

'That's a risk we have to take,' he said easily. 'Although I don't believe it concerns us much. For example, your entire organization is aboard this ship. You have hundreds of people here, but I personally doubt many of them are going to do anything that might endanger their lives.'

Suddenly McSwiggan turned. He pulled an automatic from under his coat, pointed it at a very surprised Bormann, and lifted the safety catch. The range was three yards.

'If you want to put my theory to the test, old man,' he said, 'I'll shoot you right here and now. Then I'll walk back to the helicopters with the others and nobody will lift a hand to stop us. If they did they'd risk certain death either by the bombs or by drowning. You follow?'

For a moment Kippy thought the aged actor might keel over with a heart attack, and was relieved when McSwiggan replaced the automatic with a laugh.

'And another thing, old man,' he went on. 'As I said, you've got all your Death Blow eggs in this one floating basket, including yourself, number one. We haven't. Whatever happens to us here tonight, Killtest Incorporated will survive. And it'll keep on surviving providing we're always one step ahead of the competition, which we are in this case. You're out of touch, Mr Bormann. You're dealing with professionals, not a bunch of cream puffs.'

With a masterful effort Bormann recovered his composure, and even managed a serene smile. Watching closely from near the door, Kippy was filled with admiration for professional actors, and marvelled at this dangerous and ironic contest of bluff between the two men.

'Well, Mr McSwiggan,' Borman croaked in his husky voice. 'That remains to be seen. I also have survived, as you can see, and despite what you say I also will continue to survive. You will see tonight that I have achieved in a very few months what has taken your organization over a year. And as for your threat a few moments ago – ' The actor unbuttoned his jacket and lifted his shirt to reveal the bullet-proof vest ' – you will observe that I was even prepared for that. We are not cream cakes as you unkindly suggest, Mr McSwiggan, and any time you want proof I shall be delighted to arrange it.'

It was now McSwiggan's turn to be surprised; taunted by Bormann's mocking smile, he turned and busied himself at the cocktail bar, even though his glass was still full.

A bell sounded below and a voice came through the PA: 'Performance due to begin in three minutes, Mr Bormann.'

The actor stood up. 'Ahh – yes, we must be going down to the arena. A pity, because I wanted to show you our transmitting set-up.'

The others rose and, led by Bormann, filed out of the room, on to the bridge, and then down the stairs to the arena below.

Sam and Kippy remained behind, their nerves still screwed-up from the confrontation, pondering hindsights. So Oppenheimer had deliberately stayed away! Why hadn't they considered that obvious possibility? And the drinks – why hadn't they been drugged – laced with Immobilion-B, for instance? A fantastic opportunity missed. With the entire party knocked out the lights around the helicopter pads could have been dimmed and several of them could have walked back disguised as the Killtest party; overpowering the man with his finger on the button wouldn't have been too difficult. More to the point, Kippy wondered what progress the divers were making on those fuses.

Even so, nothing had gone wrong – yet. The plans for staging the mock bouts had been elaborately prepared. Death Blow was to contribute the first match, in which the kill would be convincingly simulated, even to the extent of having a doctor to pronounce death. The second and third bouts were to be Killtest affairs, but there would be nothing faked about those – except that the third bout would not take place. Nor would the final Death Blow bout, which called for the champion Huw Gwent, Bormann's drawcard, to challenge four naked Amazons.

At least that was the plan – the swoop would be launched just before the third bout, providing a signal was received that the four mines had been defused.

The one aspect of the operation which had nagged at their consciences for weeks was that one cold-blooded killing could not be avoided. It was considered necessary, in order to bring the ghastly progress of the Killtest machine to a stop, that unarguable proof was required in the shape of a corpse. This would be provided by the result of the second bout, which called for two Killtest gladiators to fight to the death in one of the most nightmarish and bizarre contests ever to be ejected from the human imagination. From the dressing-rooms below a man was to be deliberately led to the sacrificial altar of the gladiatorial arts, the final victim of the Killtest cult, an unsuspecting martyr to humanity.

When the three-minute bell rang, Kippy and Sam left the cabin and closed the door. Outside, the VIP pilot was talking to a group of Killtest guards; he turned and nodded a vague greeting as the two men passed.

'I've seen that chap before, somewhere,' Kippy brooded, as they walked along the corridor towards the stairways.

'Who?'

'The pilot. The face rings a bell, somehow, a distant bell.'

They were passing the cabin used to entertain the uninvited Chinese guests. Sam stopped, opened the door, and peered in.

'Just checking for strays,' he explained. 'You can't watch those buggers too closely.' He was about to close the door when Kippy stopped him.

'Hold it, Sam!' He walked into the cabin and wandered about, his face creased in concentration.

'What's the matter?' Sam asked. 'You feeling okay?'

Kippy remained silent for several seconds, taking deep breaths. 'That smell – '

Sam sniffed. 'What smell?'

'Here . . . in this cabin. Once you know it you never forget it. Yes – it's here, all right!'

'*What* bloody smell?'

'It's the smell you give off from Immobilion-B poisoning. No doubt about it . . . like crushed ants. I reeked of it for weeks when I had my dose. And Hilary smelled of it, too, when I saw her at the Oaks – '

Kippy looked at Sam as they arrived at the same conclusion.

'So they've brought her with them, the bastards!' Sam said.

'Remember when the Chinese came aboard . . . and one had to be carried, dressed like them . . . we thought they were drunk, and he'd passed out?'

The one-minute bell sounded and the two men ran from the cabin and along the corridor towards the bridge where they almost collided with Bormann and the Killtest party on their way to the gladiatorial arena below.

Falling in behind, they followed the others, down the flights of stairs and along the catwalks suspended in the empty belly of the *Gudrun Atlas* towards the theatre of death. Lit by festoons of red-tinted lamps the place looked hellish, and sounded like it, for the yelling and stamping of the five hundred well-drilled spectators thrummed and echoed back and forth through the abyss-like chambers of the tanker.

The main doorway to the area came into sight, a harsh white rectangle in the sanguine gloom; and beyond it, certain death for one, possible annihilation for all.

20

All Sir Finlay Watkins's years of showmanship were reflected in the Death Blow gladiatorial programme, and to Kippy it looked more real than real.

In the centre of the vast steel cavern, surrounded by the steep tiers of seats, was the familiar garish pool of glittering white light. The announcer, a young presenter from a Midlands television station who'd been coached by Kippy, was winding up his introduction. He wore a bright yellow tee-shirt on which was emblazoned the Death Blow logo in red.

'. . . and now, my friends,' he yelled into the microphone, 'prepare yourself for a feast of gladiatorial combat . . . not three, but four life-and-death contests of a standard never witnessed before . . . exhibitions of human courage and endurance that will reach new Olympian heights never before thought possible!

'My friends, Death Blow presents the first contest of the evening – SAWMALE – for a purse of two hundred thousand pounds sterling . . . come on, now . . . let's hear it for the gladiators!'

A rumbling roar went up, to Kippy hardly discernible from the chilling ululations he'd heard on Gran Canaria. What was the source of this hideous howl for blood and death, this hateful, searing cry from contorted larynges that unified men into a hungry wolf pack? Was it the missing link between animal and man, ignored by scientists afraid of its implications? But then he himself was engaged on bloody business; could he ever really justify it? 'It is often necessary for one to kill on behalf of the many,' he'd been taught in the department's instructional groups, but who was to be the judge?

Not Pringle, surely, who often couldn't even make his mind up whether to take the 6.12 or the 6.42 to Esher. Nor did their business take into account the emotions. Why, half an hour ago, had he asked for Oppenheimer's scalp – was he a computer killer or a romantic avenger? That Oppenheimer had escaped him wasn't the point; he'd been ready to kill the man to avenge Ludovic Bernard . . . and Hilary; and that was little different in spirit or intention from the lust of men who gathered together to witness murder being done in the name of entertainment, and whether it was man or animal didn't matter much. He resolved, at that moment, to get out as soon as this was over, right out; for the moment he protected himself from the abominable screaming with warm thoughts of Hilary Brooke.

He'd spotted her without difficulty within seconds of entering the cavernous steel chamber: a tiny, black-suited figure in the middle of the Triad party, three rows down from the topmost tier of seats to the right of the centre stage. Obviously still unconscious, her short-cropped head lolled on the shoulder of the man next to her. Every fibre of his body ached with the frustration of being so helpless; every cell in his brain strained to find some way to whisk her away safely from her captors.

A bell sounded above the racket.

Below him, on the stage, two men clad from head to toe in silver suits advanced upon each other, carrying motorized chain saws. Unknown to Killtest this would be a mock fight; the lamé suits were lined with high tensile metal foil and packed, at certain points, with plastic sacs of stage blood. When the saws were switched on the hundred knife points attached to the chains tore at the air at several hundred revolutions a minute. What they would do to a human body would not be left to the imagination for very much longer.

Kippy scanned the makeshift arena for the Killtest delegates. Most had front row seats but there were enough of them wandering about the aisles or at the rear of the seating to be worrying. When he was satisfied that all were accounted for and all marked by departmental agents he walked behind the tiers to Sam, who'd just returned from the bridge.

'I've just been up to Control to organize the Navy Police,' Sam told him quietly. 'They'll gradually filter in and position themselves to cover those Triad creeps.'

'Hilary's in K22,' Kippy said. 'And for Christ's sake make sure they all know – '

'They'll know, all right. I'll get as many men as I can in the seats above and behind to cover her.'

'I'll get up there myself – '

'No, Kippy. You're too bloody trigger-happy just now. I'll go up there. You've missed out on Oppenheimer, so why don't you take my mark instead – Lethnal. Is that a deal?'

Kippy found himself unable to argue with Sam's cool judgement. 'It'll be a pleasure.'

A Killtest guard sauntered by, looking questioningly at them.

'We'll all be on the same payroll after the show!' Sam called out cheerfully. The guard frowned, and walked past. The vast chamber echoed with the whine and shriek of the chain saws.

'What's happening down below – with the mines?' Kippy asked Sam.

'They're reporting every few minutes. It'll take about an hour and a quarter to defuse them all, they reckon.'

'Bloody hell! Bang goes our schedule!'

'I know. But they've got two divers working on each mine. They're doing their best, but it's ticklish, obviously. If we don't get the all-clear from the divers we can delay the interval until we do.'

The barracking around the tiers suddenly stopped, and the two agents ran to an aisle to see. One of the gladiators on stage had made a hit; his opponent was down with a gash in the lower abdomen and his loins were drenched with blood. It looked so much like the real thing it made Kippy shudder. Then a cheer went up as the wounded man wobbled to his feet and lunged at his opponent with his saw. They had been rehearsing the moves for weeks. For several minutes they sparred with the deadly tools until the wounded gladiator, as though weak from loss of blood, appeared to stagger and fall. The saw shrieked and bit deeply into the wooden stage, sending up a shower of chips. But he recovered in time to meet his opponent, first with a slash to the thigh and then across the buttocks. Blood was everywhere, even splattering some of the patrons in ringside seats. The audience yelled itself hoarse for a kill. Then it was over; the first man to be wounded lunged forward and missed, allowing the other to bring his saw up against his chest, felling him in a spray of blood. Many of the spectators were so dismayed by this convincing exhibition that the applause was patchy and subdued. A red mist of vaporized blood hung over the stage. Looking around, Kippy noted that the Killtest contingent seemed well satisfied, and were talking excitedly among themselves.

The second bout was introduced without an intermission, while a net about the height of a tennis net, was strung across the middle of the stage. Then a clear plastic curtain was raised to enclose the entire stage. From inside, speaking into the microphone, the announcer was explaining that the bout had been codenamed ACID PIE, for reasons, he said, which would soon become apparent.

Then, from the dressing-rooms and along the aisle, trooped four men dressed like old-time vaudeville comedians, with baggy trousers, great floppy boots and bowler hats. They each carried a box and a breadknife and raised a roar of laughter as they climbed on to the stage.

In this especially obnoxious bout devised by Killtest Inc. the men formed two teams either side of the net. The boxes each contained half a dozen custard pies which they would throw at one another like they did in the old slapstick silents – but the cruel catch was that one pie in each box, although it looked exactly the same as the others, had a lethal filling: jellified concentrated nitric acid. Any contestant receiving one of these in the face would be blinded instantly as his skin and flesh was eaten away to the accompaniment of the most excruciating pain. To put him out of his misery the scoring team was to leap the net and despatch the wretched man with their breadknives. The winners took all; the surviving loser was rewarded with his life.

As the bell went, Kippy left the horrifying scene to wander back along the catwalk and up to the deck for some air.

Up on deck it was clear and cold, almost brittle. The air cut Kippy's throat like an icy knife and his exhaled breath hung like a cloud of cigarette smoke. The white deck, its flatness broken only at intervals by tank hatches, rolled away to infinity in the darkness. The three helicopters were still on their illuminated pads, guarded by the white uniformed sentries. The rotors of the furthermost machine were still revolving slowly. Two of the pilots were standing by the middle chopper, chatting and smoking; their fellow pilot, down below, would no doubt tell them what exotic sights they'd missed.

Kippy sensed a movement behind him, and from out of the door walked McSwiggan.

'We've decided to stay on board for the night,' he said, lighting a cigar. 'I'm just going to tell the boys.' He walked off and had only gone ten yards when his mark appeared in the doorway, a young agent named Davidson.

'I'm watching him, don't worry,' Kippy said. 'You go up to the ops room and see if there's been any message from the patrols.' He looked at his watch; just over an hour had elapsed since that first helicopter had landed on the *Gudrun Atlas*. What was happening! Without that vital all-clear from the divers, he was helpless, for on no account, bluff or no bluff, could he risk the lives of all those Navy men below. Or Hilary's.

He continued to watch closely as McSwiggan swung himself into the cabin of the first helicopter. Almost at the same time a roar boomed and echoed its way up from the bowels of the giant ship; one of the gladiator clowns must have collected an acid pie. Mercifully, it would soon be over.

During the intermission Bormann was to take the Killtest VIPs to his cabin for a snack and drinks, the idea being that if there was a delay of some kind the interval could be surreptitiously stretched. The cabin would by then be surrounded by armed men, ready to swoop. Half a dozen armed agents, each shadowing their mark, were to be in the cabin too, all waiting for the sound of Sam's compressed air shrieker, the signal for action. Another armed team would take care of the helicopters and their guards. Pringle had worn out a dozen ballpoints going over and over the plan; good old Pringle. Except he'd reckoned without the Triad.

Kippy tensed as he heard a second rumble from below, a dull, rolling boom, which he took to be applause. The bout had ended five minutes earlier than anticipated. He looked towards the bows, and saw McSwiggan returning. He waited until the large man was near before stepping out of the shadows.

'Everything fixed, then?' he asked cheerfully.

McSwiggan, who'd been preoccupied with some thought, looked up in surprise. 'Yeah, no problems.' He removed his cigar and blew out a fog. 'I'll just go down and tell the others everything's fine. We'll stay the night.'

'They'll all be coming up in a minute or two. Why don't you wait for them here – save your legs?' Kippy had to stall him as Davidson had not yet returned from the ops room; clearly there had been no signal. 'What do you think of it so far?'

'Bit goddam bloody for me, but smooth enough, I guess.'

'You have to remember it's our first show. You have to make allowances. We'll improve.'

'I guess so.' McSwiggan fell silent, and shuffled restlessly in little circles around the deck. 'It's fuckin' cool out here. I'm goin' inside.'

Fortunately at that moment Bormann's head appeared at the top of the stairs from below deck, followed by the others. As there were at least six agents, including Sam, shepherding the party of VIPs, Kippy let McSwiggan go. He'd wait for Davidson to return.

More dull rumbling floated up from below as five hundred ratings moved from the arena to the bars set up in an adjacent tank. If only they could be discharged from the ship, like oil, to safety!

He moved back into the shadows to watch the distant helicopters; a few well-placed shots from the snipers on the patrol boats could quickly put them out of action – and with their escape cut off McSwiggan and the others might not feel so aggressive. He spotted the binoculars Sam had left in a porthole recess, and raised them to his eyes. There were four guards by the first chopper, and two each by the others. Two of the pilots were still standing there, smoking; they must be immune from the cold, he thought. Just then the remaining pilot climbed from the last machine and, with his hands in his pockets, walked towards the others. No doubt they'd prefer to fly off in the morning, for night flying in this region of sudden gales was notoriously dangerous.

But . . . the third pilot!

The third pilot? The pilot from the third helicopter to land had come up to the bridge with the VIP party. He'd sat down in a front seat to watch the bouts, and now he was upstairs on the bridge, in Bormann's cabin – Kippy had seen him, watched him pass by, less than a minute ago.

Perhaps with such important cargo there had been a co-pilot. Or . . . perhaps the pilot upstairs wasn't a pilot at all. Why had he been the only one of the three to leave the machines?

A hand touched his arm, and he jumped. It was Davidson, a little breathless.

'Have we got the all-clear from the divers?' Kippy demanded.

'No. Two defused and two to go . . . they say another ten, fifteen minutes.'

'That's a great help! Anything else?'

'The Chinese are staying put in their seats – and Sam asked me to tell you he's got them covered like a coat of paint.' Kippy smiled at the reassurance. 'Oh – and Communications Control has just intercepted a message relayed from the Orkneys.'

'Message? From the Orkneys?'

'To the call-sign of one of the helicopters out there.'

'What message? What did it say?'

'No satellite reception.'

'Jesus!' Kippy shoved the binoculars back into the port-hole. 'Jesus!' The worst had happened, a possibility the Unit had discussed many times, but unable to arrive at a workable solution had, in the end, dropped the matter. No satellite transmission had been sent out from the *Gudrun Atlas*; it was complicated and it hadn't been considered necessary. The

Killtest Inc. engineers had delivered an Infinicron digital scrambler and specifications for a video–audio link from the tanker to a mobile transmitter set up on Ward Hill, the highest peak on the Orkney islands. From there it was to be relayed to a pirated satellite and bounced to the ultimate receiving centre in Nevada, and thence to the hundreds of closed circuit outlets. The question that had worried the AC-SU team was what would happen when the receiving centre in Nevada failed to receive the transmission.

Now Kippy knew; the Killtest engineers, who had put up with a lot of stalling about test transmissions, finally sent a message of complaint to the Orkney link station and they, in turn, had radioed one of the helicopters. McSwiggan doubtless carried a bleep which had signalled him to return to the chopper to take the message. Now he must know something very unfunny was going on.

For several seconds Kippy was frozen in indecision. Then, along the deck, near the first helicopter, he noticed that one of the white-uniformed Killtest guards was at the ship's rail, calling to one of his companions. And then he, himself, was racing up the stairs to the bridge with the enigma of the third pilot sharpening into focus at every step. Of course – it *had* to be!

He almost flung himself into Bormann's cabin, only to find it empty. He ran back along the bridge to the operations room. Sir Finlay Watkins was there with a couple of others.

'They've defused three of the bastards,' Watkins said excitedly as soon as one of the security men had closed the cabin door. 'And they expect to knock out the other one in a few minutes. Three divers are working on it now.'

'Where the hell are Bormann and the others?' Kippy asked, his chest heaving from exertion and near-panic.

'They've all gone on a guided tour,' one of the men in the room said. 'I went out for a leak just now, and saw them.'

'Where – where?'

'Over to the port side, I think. To look at the accommodation. Don't tell me those buggers are going to stay the night?'

Kippy paused at the door. 'I hardly think so!' he shouted back.

Port was left, wasn't it? He ran through the dim-lit maze of narrow corridors, stopping every few seconds to listen for voices or footsteps, only to be mocked by echoes of his own running and harsh breathing. What a fuck-up! He propelled himself along each passageway, then into the next, and the next, but they were all deserted. Finally, satisfied he'd covered the entire upper structure of the tanker, he worked his way back to the bridge.

There, looking out through the plateglass over the foredeck, was Bormann, with Simak, Mrabet and General Ton and the agents marking them. Kippy walked quickly to them and also looked out. Halfway between the bridge and the first helicopter strolled Lethnal, McSwiggan and the VIP pilot, with Sam and two departmental agents about twenty yards behind them.

'Our friends have decided to stay on board for the night,' Bormann said to Kippy. 'The others have just gone to fetch their things.' General Ton turned in surprise; for the first time in the whole masquerade the old actor had lapsed into his everyday speech.

Kippy leapt down the stairs to the deck. The Killtest guards had obviously spotted the underwater lights of the Navy divers working below, and had bleeped McSwiggan for the second time. Something warned Kippy that the Killtest bosses might be baling out, cynically leaving Simak, Mrabet and General Ton behind. But there was no time to sift through possibilities; Sam had to be warned, and they'd have to risk the chance of the remaining bomb detonating.

He shot out of the bridge companionway on to the deck like a bullet from a gun, and crashed straight into two burly Killtest guards standing by the open door, sending them sprawling. Their loud cursing signalled the start of a fearful uproar. As Kippy scrambled to his feet on the slippery deck, one of the uniformed men by the helicopter started firing bursts into the water below. A searchlight spat white light from the bridge and at the same time McSwiggan and the others began to run towards the bow of the tanker. The other helicopter guards started shooting and Kippy saw Sam and one of the agents fall, their contorted bodies silhouetted against the lights around the landing pads. He kept running, trying to keep in the sparse shadows on the vast expanse of bare, grey deck. He'd almost reached Sam when the lights were extinguished.

He dived to the deck and skidded the remaining few yards into Sam's body.

'You okay, Sam?'

Sam's face was squeezed tight with pain, but as least he was alive. 'Bloody leg, that's all. What's going on?'

'That pilot – that's Oppenheimer!' He heard a curse nearby; it was the other wounded agent, with his hands to his face. 'It's Oppenheimer!' he repeated. Raising his head he could see white uniformed figures scrambling aboard the first chopper, covered by the guard walking back from the ship's rail who was firing indiscriminately in the darkness towards them. Bullets bounced and ricochetted, whining across the steel deck in a deadly spray.

The rotors of the first helicopter were beginning to turn as the last man heaved himself into the cabin hatch.

Kippy placed his dry mouth against Sam's ear. 'What about Hilary?' he yelled. 'You promised me you'd stay with her!'

Sam pulled his left knee up to his chin, and winced. 'Get your priorities right, man!' he said through clenched teeth. 'If you don't stop those bastards there'll be no Hilary, no anybody – they can still trigger off the remaining limpet!'

Kippy leapt up and, crouching low, ran along the deck. Most of the firepower was now locked inside the leading machine although one automatic weapon still spat bullets from an open hatch. Beyond it he could see the three figures of McSwiggan, Lethnal and the phoney pilot run towards the second helicopter and climb in.

Shots were now coming from the patrol boats ringing the tanker but they were hardly effective because the towering sides of the *Gudrun Atlas* sheltered the deck. Kippy threw himself down behind a pump housing as a flare erupted overhead, and in its glaring green light he saw McSwiggan haul himself into the helicopter and slam the hatch closed.

The night was lacerated with cracks and whines and the whirring, juttering of chopper rotors gathering speed. Behind him, the first machine had lifted from its pad, still trailing the detonator cables to the mines and appearing to be chained by an arc of tracers to one of the patrol boats. Then suddenly, just as it reached the protective ring of darkness, it blew apart with an ear-splitting roar and a tremendous blue and orange flash. Flaming debris sprayed skywards like some gigantic firework display, and then rained down on the tanker.

The shooting on the deck stopped now but the rotors of the second helicopter were spinning fast; within ten seconds it would be ready for take-off. From his refuge behind the pump housing Kippy estimated the distance that separated them: perhaps sixty yards. It was clear the remaining Kill-test VIPs were being abandoned, but even with them in the bag all the effort would have been wasted if the three most powerful men in the organization escaped. He glanced back towards the bridge. Several men were running along the deck but they'd never reach the helicopter in time – he was the only one able to attempt anything at all.

Without any plan in mind he leapt up and ran full belt to the machine, against the buffeting wind from its whirling rotors, trying to loosen his Walther from its holster and clawing air into his lungs which seemed paralysed with fear. He could see faces inside the plastic bubble, illuminated by the instrument panel, and they could certainly see him. He managed to free his gun and doubled up low as he ran under the rotor blades, firing two quick shots into the bubble. The shots ricochetted off harmlessly and the chopper began to lift, at first only a few inches and then, as the pilot gunned the engine hard and increased the pitch of the rotors, by several feet. By then he'd run right under the landing skids and instinctively reached up to grab one in a hopeless effort to pull it down, firing three more shots into the fuselage.

Seconds later he looked down to find himself suspended fifty feet in the air, with the great hulk of the tanker receding below. The helicopter banked sharply, enabling him to swing a leg over the skid. His arms ached and he'd lost all sense of direction; all he could see through the red film on his eyes was the expanse of pale grey undercarriage. A single shot was all he had, but one shot into a fuel tank, or through the thin metal skin to where the pilot sat was all it needed. With the sea several hundred feet below there was now little point indulging in a personal survival exercise. With hands that were shaking uncontrollably Kippy placed the Walther against the fuselage and, imagining the pilot's bum just eighteen inches above, fired. Almost immediately the hatch opened just by his head and a hand emerged, holding an automatic. Its owner was guessing too, and blindly fired six shots, expecting one to find its mark, but all went wild. When the hand withdrew Kippy wrestled his body against the wind to a more secure position on the skid, so that by standing on the bottom bar and holding on to the front leg he might just be able to reach into the open hatch. That hand would come out again and spray some more bullets around so, impossible as the odds were, he had to take the initiative.

He threw the pistol away and groped in his pocket for the Immobilion-B ejector, barely able to hold it because of the numbing cold. The helicopter was at full speed now and the wind threatened to tear him from his tenuous perch. It was now or never, and he stood up as far as he dared, raising his hand level with the floor of the hatch, squeezing the ejector release and aiming an arc of needle into the cabin, firing without pause just as he'd shot Hilary Brooke and June Harrison, pressing the tiny button until the chamber was empty of its deadly drug.

The ejector dropped away into the whirring darkness and with both hands free now he hugged the skid support and closed his numb lips and wind-seared eyes to wait. He felt dead, as though every drop of blood had drained from him, and he wanted nothing else but to abandon his body and mind to space, like a free-fall parachutist, to enfold himself in its vast blanket. . . .

Suddenly the helicopter banked and seemed to stall, its black rotating arms trying to scratch the black air for something to grip. Some of the Immobilion-B needles must have found their mark. The engines revved and screamed and the angle increased and a body slid out of the hatch and shot past Kippy into the void below. The machine was now losing height, dropping at an increasing rate until the engines abruptly died, their howl replaced by the eerie whistling of the wind. Then, slowly at first, like a fairground roundabout gathering speed, the fuselage itself started to revolve around the almost stationary rotors, gyrating faster and faster, spinning out of control, spiralling down through the rushing air until, a few seconds after Kippy was hurled off by the force of the spin, the rotors broke away and the pale grey coffin plummeted into the wild black water.

Postscripts

KIPLING ANTHONY LEERING's body was never recovered, nor was the helicopter and its passengers, although its last position was pinpointed by the *Gudrun*'s radar as seven miles due east of the Cape Wrath lighthouse. Officially pronounced *missing, presumed dead*, Leering's contribution to the success of the AC-SU operation received no other public acknowledgement, although Pringle nominated him as a posthumous member of the Special Forces Club.

SAMUEL TERENCE HUMBERT recovered from a leg wound. He resigned from the Service in December 1977 to accept a senior lecturer's post at a Canadian University, specializing in biofeedback technology.

STANLEY BERESFORD PRINGLE was awarded the OBE in recognition of his services, and also received a special citation from US President Carter. He helped supervise the preparation of evidence for the dozens of Killtest trials conducted during the months that followed Operation Death Blow, and stayed with the Service as a senior tactical advisor. His triumph was somewhat marred by his divorce from his wife Shirley, on the grounds of adultery with her tennis instructor.

HILARY MARGARET BROOKE died early on 16 November, a few hours after Operation Death Blow, from respiratory failure as the result of the Immobilion-B overdose. She never regained consciousness. Her tragic case led directly to the setting up of a £400 000 study into the drug's physiological effects on body metabolism.

Hilary's captors were speedily rounded up. Twenty-one members of the London chapter of the Triad on the *Gudrun Atlas* were disarmed and arrested, and two were shot dead. As a result, the Triad's growth in Europe was halted although Lao Man, one of the movement's leaders, has never been found.

SIR FINLAY WATKINS was further honoured for his part in the Killtest coup, and utilized the experience (to his considerable profit) as the basis of a highly successful ITV series, *The De Sade File*, and also in the making of a TV documentary feature, *Come In Martin Bormann, Are You There?*

JUNE HARRISON was flown back to England from the Canary Islands after the coup. After three months of hospitalization she not only made a full recovery from the effects of the Immobilion-B poisoning but with intensive psychiatric care overcame her neurotic condition as well. She received a modest grant from the British Government, and from the proceeds of the sale of her story to an international magazine bought a small boutique in Manchester, where she now lives.

HUW GWENT, like Miss Harrison, received a special grant from public funds with which he purchased a sheep farm in Montgomeryshire, Wales.

With the capture of Mrabet, Simak and General Ton Dinh Quan, and the deaths of Oppenheimer, Lethnal and McSwiggan, Killtest Inc. as an organization fell apart. Equipment worth millions was impounded and Killtest funds totalling £13 million were retrieved and paid into US government revenue. In a series of FBI raids in the US, over 300 individuals in the employ of the Organization were rounded up and charged with an impressive variety of offences.

Mrabet, for example, pleaded guilty to 21 of 117 separate charges brought against him, and after a hearing lasting 56 days was sentenced to a total of 120 years imprisonment. Jay Simak got life while General Ton got 20 years.

The only Killtest prosecutions in Britain were of the

Triad gangsters and Mrs Winifred Brodie, who was charged with 'conspiring with others to use criminal means to commit an illegal act' and sentenced to six years' imprisonment. As the result of a successful extradition application by the FBI she faces further serious charges in the US at some future date.

In a further round up in America, 642 owners, lessees and exhibitors of the Organization's closed circuit theatres and outlets were charged with State violations, resulting in hundreds of prosecutions, mostly successful.

Of greater significance was the wave of public revulsion in the US at the disclosures made as a result of the Killtest trials which, in the words of a *Showbill* report, exposed gladitorial combat for what it was – 'commercialized sadism . . . which for the good of humanity has put the gladiatorial clock back another two millennia'.

But the most scathing public approbation was reserved for the Central Intelligence Agency when it was revealed that a 'most senior official' of its Special Projects Division was the head of Killtest Inc. The Agency had clearly declined in both expertise and public respect since the days when Allen Dulles was its director; and the new Democratic administration's first move was to withdraw the vote for its 'non-accountable funds' and to order a complete reorganization. Similar crack-downs were ordered by Congress on Mafia activities, and by the British Colonial Office on Triad expansion in Hong Kong.

Other countries which had played unsuspecting hosts to Killtest events – Canada, Spain, Mexico and Brazil – also initiated investigations to probe the extent an illegal organization seemed able to insinuate itself into the top echelons of government, resulting in many charges of conspiracy and corruption. Such investigations and trials will extend through 1978 and beyond.

An interesting sidelight was the world-wide manhunt for Henry Krausner, the ex-Nazi with millions held in property in Spain and the Canary Islands. He committed suicide in South Africa.

Another was the ill-fated French Connection Committee. By an embarrassing irony the French Ambassador to the US chose the very day Mrabet was arrested on the *Gudrun Atlas* to announce at a press conference his country's wholehearted support of the mythical celebrations, fifteen million francs having been voted by the French Assembly as France's contribution to further cement a French–US alliance. Plans were also announced for a large contingent of the French Navy to sail to New Orleans for the occasion. An American newspaper columnist wrote that it should qualify for the 1978 edition of the *Guinness Book of Records* as 'the most spectacular non-event of all time'.

Although President Kim Il Sung of the Democratic People's Republic of Korea failed to score over his capitalist rival President Park of South Korea, he apparently didn't feel his investment had been wasted.

'The decline and decay which brought about the fall of the Roman Empire,' he stated in a speech (5 December 1977), 'has its parallel in contemporary capitalist ideology, which as all the socialist peoples have seen demonstrated is nothing more than evil feudal exploitation; for only in imperialist countries is it possible for the capitalist rich to hire the poor and the oppressed to do their dying for them.'

'The Killtest example,' he concluded, in his 6000-word speech, 'exposes the extent to which the imperialist order is decayed, and how close it is to total collapse.'

Bibliography

The Killtest phenomenon and the circumstances which nurtured it from fantasy to reality became the subjects for dozens of academic studies sponsored by universities and social science institutions in the US and Britain, of which the following are representative:

BEKAY, ELLERY, and ZANDER, VICTOR, *The Psychology of Killtest Dadins*, New York: Luce, Oswald, 1978

JESSEL, SAMUEL, *The Psychiatric Origin of the Killtest Urge*, New York: University Studies Institute, 1978

KRENEV, W. L., and GAD, S. G., 'Psychic trauma of sadistic confrontation', London, BJAP, vol. 19, no. 3

LEVY, WOLFGANG, *Tests on the Urine of Killtest Survivors*, Chicago: Horder & Armitage, 1978

MURRAY, THORNTON J., *Alcoholism among Killtest spectators*, New York: Placebo Political Press, 1978

PLATZ, IRVING, and KLINE, GROVER C., *Psychiatric Explorations into Killtest Attitudes*, New York: Science Today Press, 1978

ROVINSKY, NICHOLAS J., *The Therapeutic Argument for Gladiatorial Impulse*, London: International Psych-Medical Press, 1977

SELMAN, P. M., *Addictive Sadism: The Genetic Shadow*, Toronto: Syndrome, 1978

SPITZ, ERWIN, *Cybernetics of Annihilation*, New York: Academic Studies Press, 1978

TIETZE, MARGARET, 'Killtest and the sanctity of life – an overview,' *Pacific and Universal Studies*, vol. 8, 1978

ZWEMMER, RAPHAEL, *The Financial Structure of Killtest Inc.*, Tel Aviv: *World Economic and Financial Abstracts*, vol. 2, 1978

The characters and events portrayed in this book exist only in the world of my imagination.